JANIE'S LAW

CARROLL LACHNIT

BERKLEY PRIME CRIME, NEW YORK

JANIE'S LAW

A Berkley Prime Crime Book / published by arrangement with the author

PRINTING HISTORY
Berkley Prime Crime edition / October 1999

All rights reserved.
Copyright © 1999 by Carroll Lachnit.
This book may not be reproduced in whole or in part, by mimeograph or any other means, without permission.
For information address: The Berkley Publishing Group, a division of Penguin Putnam Inc., 375 Hudson Street, New York, New York 10014.

The Penguin Putnam Inc. World Wide Web site address is http://www.penguinputnam.com

ISBN: 0-425-17150-7

Berkley Prime Crime Books are published by The Berkley Publishing Group, a division of Penguin Putnam Inc., 375 Hudson Street, New York, New York 10014. The name BERKLEY PRIME CRIME and the BERKLEY PRIME CRIME design are trademarks belonging to Penguin Putnam Inc.

PRINTED IN THE UNITED STATES OF AMERICA

10 9 8 7 6 5 4 3 2 1

For the Prince of Cats

Acknowledgments

Thanks to the National Center for Missing and Exploited Children and Officer Michael W. Streed, a forensic artist for the City of Orange Police Department, for information on the art and science of age-progressing photographs. Thanks also to Long Beach Police Detective J. Craig Newland for acquainting me with Megan's Law and California's CD-ROM directory of sex offenders. Tracy Weber, a terrific reporter and good friend, shared her knowledge of the Orange County child protective services system. I appreciate the cooperation of defense attorney Julian Bailey and bail bondsman Josh Herman, who explained aspects of the criminal-justice system to me. Thanks to the staff of the Burn Center at Torrance Memorial Medical Center. All these people were generous with their expertise, and any errors in the story are mine alone.

I also thank—as always—my agent, Susan Ginsburg, for her keen story sense and good guidance, and my editor, Hillary Cige, for her thoughtful reflections on this novel. The Mavericks, a terrific group of writers, once again gave me honest and insightful feedback for which I am incredibly grateful. Alec helped me back to the light when my research led me to some dark places. His love and support mean more to me than I can ever say.

1

Henry Charles parked the Ford Econoline van on a street bordering a weedy park. He checked his watch: eleven-fifteen. It was a quiet, cool night in late April with a full, glinting silver moon.

He'd been cruising this part of Santa Ana for a week, and he knew its rhythms now. The people fled here from Mexico, Honduras, and El Salvador. They settled down, hustled work, lived hand-to-mouth. Their children played in this park while the mothers tended fair-haired children in Las Almas, a few miles away. The dads were picking strawberries, fixing cars, mowing yards, doing whatever work they could find. The grandmothers, aunts, older daughters, and sour-faced teenage sons were the child-minders. They had their orders: watch them, for the love of God.

But no one was perfect. They slipped inside sometimes, for just a minute of their *telenovelas*, to answer the phone, to get a snack. It was the minute for which Charles patiently waited, hook baited, line cast. The hunger was almost unbearable at that moment. He knew he would catch something, but he didn't know when.

He needed to make an early start in the morning. He felt famished, almost to the point of rage. He had accepted the hunger a long time ago. No one questioned the need to eat, to drink, to crap, to sleep. Charles no longer fought the engine that flamed in his heart, head, and cock. It was fate, nothing less. There was an adage that he liked. It acknowledged his assumption of responsibility: Give a man a fish, and you feed him for a day. Teach a man to fish, and you feed him for life. Charles didn't take handouts—not much, anyway. He was a fisher.

The need was roiling in him, hot and nearly unbearable. He tried to calm himself, imagining the feast that he'd have tomorrow. No later than the day after tomorrow. He had to sleep, had to be alert and ready in the morning. He knew he could safely stay overnight here without fear of being rousted. The vehicle looked like something a gardener would use—the cops wouldn't bother with it.

Henry Herbert Charles, known at one time as Hank to friends—when he had friends—knew how he would read on paper: fifty-six, balding, last gainfully employed during the Reagan administration, vagrant, ex-con. But that wasn't how he saw himself. What he did took skill, planning, long hours, and concentration. It wasn't sport, although some people treated it like one. This was sustenance. This was the staff of his inner life. He hadn't decided whether it was best to continue feeding himself here in the *barrio*. The parents might work long hours, but they were fanatically devoted to their offspring. If any of them spotted him scooting a dazed, half-naked child out the van's back door, they'd pound him into a pile of *masa*. But the richness of his meals kept him here. They were beyond compare.

Charles could be fast, when he had to be. He could hook his catch, quell the growl and pain, and hit the road in under an hour. If he took pictures—and at times, he absolutely had to have a picture to keep—that meant the tripod and the timer, so it took longer. Still, he hadn't been caught, not in a long time. He'd learned from his mistakes: no more diversions with catch he already knew. Fresh schools were better. As a consequence of that, his style had changed, too. Subtlety was less important. The moment when his real aim revealed itself came more quickly, more brutally. He allowed himself to enjoy the baring of his real face. And he liked their sudden fear, instead of the slow, uneasy realization. Fear sweetened the meat.

For his kind of life, Charles needed mobility. He had lived in the van for more than six years and as a silent protest, stopped registering with the cops. Drop out, Timothy Leary said. Charles followed the good doctor's advice. He had grudgingly bartered his way into the Econoline van, though it wasn't his first choice. He wanted a Winnebago and saved for one, only to be cheated out of the money by one of his lawyer's conniving clients—an "investment counselor" who promised a 40-percent return on his money and promptly lost it all, babbling something about a rogue tsunami swamping Kyrgyzstan's gold mines. Charles thought he'd been scammed. He knew it for sure when he discovered that the country lacked any sort of coastline for a tsunami to ravage. He had started plotting his revenge.

In the meantime, he'd found the Econoline and swapped a former cellmate's brother a comprehensive collection of his best shots for it.

"They're young, right?" The guy had scowled at Charles after scrutinizing the shots. They were Charles's favorites. He never tired of looking at them, although he didn't remember their names. Never knew their names, sometimes. But he still could hear the keening music of their little voices, which sometimes grew sharp as cut glass until he slapped a hand over their mouths or hit them hard enough to quiet them. Charles never hurt them badly. He wasn't a monster, after all.

The children whose pictures he cherished were grown, he assumed. But he never visualized how they were now. They'd served their purpose. They had fed him. He had the pictures, which ignited vivid memories. And Orange County, thick with parks and trails and shopping malls, still teemed with fresh, sweet flesh.

"Not one was over seven," Charles told the van's owner. What did the guy think—that he'd pared down some teenage hookers and dressed them in pinafores? Some people were just idiots.

"Looks like you hadn't missed dinner in a while." The guy laughed and waved one of the pictures at him. Charles's face couldn't be seen, of course, but essential portions of anatomy were required to make the pictures worthwhile. Charles didn't like people making fun of his body. And no one understood that he *had* to do this, or die. This was his sacred journey in life.

"If you don't like the pictures, give them back," he snapped.

The guy shut up. The deal was done, and Charles had a new home. He made a few modifications to the van, which already had smoked windows and a built-in bunk. He threw in a mattress, a cooler, his clothes, and his cameras.

Then Charles got back at the man who'd stolen his Winnebago money. He offered him a choice: his life, or a little time with the sweet child. He'd done it in this very van, to remind the creep that he'd cost Charles a far nicer home. The creep nearly wept at the sight of the child violated, and how delightful that was. An extra helping of enjoyment.

Now Charles turned his attention to the morning's work, beginning with his tackle box. He used the standard lures: candy, ice cream, Nintendo, and toys. Occasionally he added a puppy or kitten to his kit. Live bait worked best, but the animals were such a pain in the ass. He got rid of them after a couple weeks. He had lately wondered if a puppet might not work just as well. He would have to try one.

What was the word for puppet? He looked in the dictionary and then slotted the word into the phrase he'd learned from a Spanish textbook he'd found at the swap meet.

"¿Quieres ver mi títere?" He said it twice, making sure he had the accent right. He got into his bunk and said it again. He already knew the Spanish for the most important phrases. Get in. Don't move. Shut up. Don't tell. I'll kill you.

He'd had plenty of practice.

Ten minutes to midnight. The moon drifted on cloud waves, white and gray, and then disappeared behind them. In the park's shifting darkness, a bum turned in his nubby yellow Catholic Charities blanket and awoke. He was sobering up, damn it. He closed his eyes and tried to ignore the wormy restlessness in his legs.

Weeks later, when the police caught up with him, he told them he hadn't seen anything. And that was almost entirely true. But he didn't tell them what he smelled and heard.

He was on his side, blanket up around his face, trying to go back to sleep, when he got a whiff of gasoline. It was strong, as though it was right under his nose. Then it was gone. He opened his eyes. A smelly hallucination, he thought. That was a new one.

He readjusted himself on the picnic table and closed his eyes again. He heard it then, a whispered voice. A shrill laugh. Silence. He covered his eyes. He didn't want to see what was laughing at him. He'd been in that bad dream before.

A minute later, he heard glass break. Then a scream. He

peered over the blanket. The white van on the other side of the park looked like a cracked egg. A fiery yolk spilled out of it. The bum cackled at the sight of the flames that lapped the windows and roof. He could hear more screaming inside. He hoped it was the paunchy, pale-skinned pervert he'd seen eyeing children on the playground the day before. This sure as hell would serve him right.

"Burn in hell, you goddamned filthy molester!" he screamed. Then he packed up his blanket and set off for one of the bus shelters on Grand Avenue. Maybe he could get some sleep there.

2

The man was waiting for Hannah Barlow and her law partner, Bobby Terry, when they got back to the office from a late lunch. He jumped from his chair when he heard the door open and jammed the Terry and Barlow business card on which he'd been nibbling into the pocket of his jacket.

Hannah liked to take a long look at potential clients, if she could get away with it. She could with this one. His eyes were trained on Bobby.

Fine brown hair fringed the visitor's face, which was pale except for two flames of color on his cheeks. His bangs nearly brushed his eyelashes. His small mouth was pinched in an anxious expression. The jacket—Façonable, seafoam green—seemed too small for him, as did the starchy madras-plaid sport shirt underneath. His khakis had a perfect crease. Hannah wondered if he gave ironing lessons in his spare time.

The jacket fell open as he extended his hand to Bobby. The would-be client had big, pendulous breasts. Sweat stains circled his armpits.

"Freddy Roche. The legal assistance clinic at Douglas said you might be able to see me." His diction was clipped, precise. "They want me dead. Nothing less than that." He still was addressing himself to Bobby, barely making contact with Hannah's eyes until they shook hands.

Hannah did a quick summation of Freddy Roche. He was saddled with a name fit for a vaudevillian. He'd gained weight recently, but hadn't accepted it as a permanent condition. He was low on cash, hence the need for pro-bono lawyers. He harbored at least one paranoid idea. And he disliked women. Maybe, charitably, he only mistrusted them.

Hannah glanced at the secretary, Vera, who raised her eyebrows as if to say she didn't know what Roche was talking about. Her fingers clattered on the keyboard.

"Let's talk in my office, Mr. Roche," Bobby said.

"I'll be right there," Hannah said.

An e-mail message waited on Hannah's computer. Vera preferred written communication whenever possible. It was a quirk, but not an insurmountable one. It made for a quiet office.

He's been waiting for more than twenty minutes, twitching like a raw nerve the whole time, Vera had written. *The third-year who called from Douglas wouldn't say what his problem was. Something civil, maybe. Just what you want on a Monday, I'm sure.*

Hannah typed a quick acknowledgment. She and Bobby were alumni of the William O. Douglas School of Law. They offered their services to indigent clients from time to time, if it was something the third-year students who ran the legal-aid clinic couldn't handle. She picked up a notepad and went to Bobby's office.

Roche was in mid-rant, his lips trembling in anger. "I paid and paid. For three years and every day since. Why won't they just leave me alone?"

Blackmail? Hannah thought. The IRS, maybe? Tax season had ended two weeks before.

Bobby scribbled notes. "Hannah, Mr. Roche was just saying that he is the target of some harassment."

Hannah nodded. "What's been happening, Mr. Roche?"

"It has to stop," he said. He was changing colors like an octopus, his cheeks going from red to purple. "At Douglas, they said you have helped people get restraining orders. I need one. And I want the police to enforce the whole damn law. It's supposed to protect me, too. There's a fine up to twenty-five thousand dollars for denying me my rights to housing and work."

Hannah wondered what law he was talking about. Apparently she wasn't as up on housing and employment-discrimination law as the potential client was.

"We have helped people get restraining orders, usually in

domestic violence cases," she said. "You don't have a domestic violence situation, I take it."

He shook his head. "I live alone."

"But someone is bothering you?"

"To say the least. Phone calls in the middle of the night. They smeared feces on my car. Punctured the tires. And someone almost succeeded in setting my house on fire last night. That was it. My landlord terminated my lease today. I think that's illegal, isn't it?"

"I would have to look at the lease, but it sounds like he's putting the blame in the wrong place," Hannah said. She stole a look at Bobby. He had said very little since she arrived. "Do you know who's doing this?"

"It's probably one of the fascist assholes that have been marching in front of my house every day for the last week," Roche said.

"Why are they . . ." Hannah stopped. Now she knew who Roche was. She hadn't read the paper much lately, but she had seen a story in the *Orange County Register* about a neighborhood protest in Las Almas. Roche was what the state called a "serious offender"—a somewhat sanitized term for someone who had gone to prison for molesting a child. In this case, a twelve-year-old boy, the story said. She felt a chill begin at her feet and course up her spine, like a pipe freezing in a bitter wind.

That's why Bobby had been so quiet. He had guessed how Hannah might react once she understood. She imagined, in vague, shadowy images, what Roche did to the boy. Even those half-formed pictures turned her stomach. She saw Janie Meister in them.

"These protestors are your neighbors?" she asked.

Roche locked eyes with Hannah before he answered. He'd heard the coolness in her voice. But instead of shame, she saw defiance in him. "Yes. I've been there two years. These are people who borrowed my lawn mower. I fed their cats when they went on vacation."

"And this started with the Megan's Law CD-ROM?" Hannah asked.

"Technology strikes again," Roche said. He laughed harshly.

He was right about that, Hannah thought. She'd followed the state's efforts to tell communities about sexual offenders in

their midst. The issue had come to California a few years
earlier, when the legislature had instituted its version of New
Jersey's community notification measure known as Megan's
Law.

The first statute was named after Megan Kanka, a child who
was sexually assaulted and killed by a neighbor who was a
paroled child molester—a fact not revealed to any of the
families living near him. After the first Megan's Law, other
states followed suit, reversing the laws that barred police from
telling residents about the paroled child molesters and rapists
who lived in their neighborhoods. In California, the law
encouraged police to let the residents know where the worst
offenders lived. And the high-tech state gave the law a
high-tech twist.

It required police departments in large cities to give residents
access to a Megan's Law CD-ROM, containing the state's
database of registered sex offenders—some sixty-four thousand names. Adults who wanted to look through the database
could do so. Concerned citizens merely had to fill out forms,
state that they weren't sex offenders, and attest that they
understood it was illegal to use the information for harassment
or discrimination. Then, they presented drivers' licenses (which
the police would run through a statewide computer to ensure
that they weren't sex offenders), and sign a viewer's log.

After punching in a last name, county name, or a ZIP code,
the reader could get molester names, descriptions, sex-crime-
related criminal histories, and photographs—nearly everything
but their actual addresses. Roche said that's what happened to
him—someone went trolling for molesters and caught him.

"It's an automated harassment device," he said. "One day,
I'm a good neighbor. Then someone looks me up in the Boogie
Man Index and I'm Frankenstein's monster."

"A lot of people would rather have Frankenstein's monster
next door," Hannah said.

His expression said he knew she was one of them. "Do you
have children?"

She could have said, "Not anymore." Except Matthew
Drummond wasn't really hers. She and her lover, Guillermo
Agustin, aided by a nanny, had cared for the toddler for six
months after the killings that had deprived him of his parents.
Hannah always knew her home was only a temporary haven for

Matthew, so she resisted the threads she felt lacing them closer. Love, but don't bond: that was her mantra. She couldn't say that repeating those words had done any good. She still ached in the middle of the sleepless nights, as she had since the day after Matthew and his nanny, Connie Westerland, had left for Vancouver, where Matthew's uncle and aunt lived. That had been four months ago.

As if losing Matthew hadn't been bad enough, Guillermo was gone, too. She hadn't had any time to prepare for that. Some days it felt as if she had lead weights in her chest. It hurt to breathe.

Roche was staring at her, waiting for her to answer.

"No, I don't have children," she said. "But I understand why your neighbors are fearful."

"I did my time in prison," he said. "I got treatment. I still get treatment. I don't bother anyone. And there are lots of people like me: three thousand paroled offenders in Orange County alone. We have to live somewhere." He paused, as though considering what his next argument might be. Then he said, quietly, "Your brother understood that."

For a moment, Hannah thought she'd misheard him. But then she knew how there could be a connection: the confessional. It was logical, given Roche's crime and his proclamations of change.

"You were a parishioner of Michael's? Or did you know him through Sanctus?" She hated saying the name of the cult that had ruined Michael's life.

Roche shook his head. "I'm not Catholic at all. We met when he gave a talk up at San Luis Obispo CMC. I'm sorry he's gone."

Hannah nodded. CMC was short for the California Men's Colony, a more discreet term for a prison. When Michael had been a vicar of religious education for his diocese, he'd made occasional pastoral visits to such places.

"We talked afterwards," Roche said. "And when I got out, I started visiting him. He was helping me."

"Helping you do what?"

"Deal with my . . . impulses." He was silent for a moment, and then gave Hannah a long look, taking in the red hair and blue-green eyes. "I can see the resemblance now. He talked about you, you know."

"Oh?"

"He said you were another Joan of Arc."

Hannah wondered when that conversation had taken place. For years, Michael had hated her, although they'd had moments of reconciliation before he died. Hannah was grateful for those times. They showed her that there was goodness in Michael, beneath the layers of lies and hypocrisy that had buried his soul for so long. But maybe this talk had been before that, back when Michael still thought Hannah was a heretic. "Did he say something about burning me at the stake?"

Roche smiled. Almost against her will, Hannah saw what Michael might have seen: a glimpse of a human being. "No. Michael said you were a hell of a fighter. And he said you knew how to see into a person's heart."

If I were that perceptive, Michael might be alive today, Hannah thought. It was possible that Roche was bullshitting about knowing her brother, but the words did sound like Michael's. The idea of him praising her made her eyes sting. She countered the feeling with a challenge.

"Why didn't you say right away that you knew my brother?"

Roche shrugged. "I didn't know if saying I knew him would help. He didn't tell me anything specific, but I got the idea that you two had problems. Stuff in the past."

True enough, Hannah thought.

"But once I saw how you reacted to me, I thought, what the hell? Take a shot," Roche said. "I thought that if Michael believed in me, maybe you, you know . . ."

He let the words trail off, but Hannah knew what he was going to say: he thought Hannah would help him, for Michael's sake. But Michael was dead, unavailable for a character reference. For all she knew, Michael might have thought this guy was unsalvageable scum.

"How do you want us to help you?" Bobby said to Roche. Hannah's silence had gone on too long.

"For starters, you could sue the people who are trying to ruin what's left of my life," he said.

"Have you gone to the police?" Hannah asked.

Roche rolled his eyes. "Of course. They were less than sympathetic, as you might imagine. Their brilliant solution? Move. They didn't think the pickets were harassment. Freedom of expression, they said."

"Do you have any idea who made the phone calls?" Hannah asked. "Or who damaged your car?"

"I have a very good idea. The ringleaders are the ex-cop and his wife who live across the street. Self-righteous jerks."

"Did you see them do any of these things? Get their phone calls on tape?"

Roche shook his head. "It's all happened at night. The police told me they could try to trace the calls, but they always hang up right away."

Bobby caught Hannah's eye. "Will you excuse us for a minute, Mr. Roche?"

He nodded. "Take this with you."

He held out an envelope, its corners softened by the rub of his jacket pocket. Hannah took it. It was addressed to Roche. The return address was the rectory at which Michael had once lived.

Bobby shut the door to Hannah's office behind him and glanced at the letter. "What is that?"

Hannah knew the handwriting in the two-page letter. She recognized the phrasing, the quotes from scripture—heavy on the gospel of John. There was none of the Sanctus cant that Michael sometimes employed. It seemed that Roche had just been released from prison, and he was afraid of life outside: the temptations and the label he wore as a pedophile. Michael urged Roche to acknowledge his weaknesses and repent his sins. He offered Roche the hope of healing. He offered him the strength of God and the power of grace.

You've shown God your willingness to change, Michael wrote. *Now let him help you do that. Continue to pray for His guidance. And if you feel yourself slipping into trouble, you can always turn to me for help In prayer. Go to Hannah, as we discussed, if there's a problem with the disclosure law we talked about. All of us, your brothers and sisters in Christ, are here for you. We will not let you down.*

"Roche is telling the truth. Michael did know him," she said to Bobby when she was finished reading. "He seemed to think Roche was trying to be a different person."

"So what do you want to do?"

Hannah shook her head. "Without some better evidence of who's doing the harassment, I wouldn't know who to sue."

"We could try to get a restraining order to limit the protests."

She nodded. "We could. But he won't be living there long enough for that to be worthwhile."

Bobby nodded. "We could try to stop the eviction."

"Maybe."

He'd heard the hesitancy in her voice. "You don't want to?"

She folded her arms and tried to think clearly. Surely Michael's promise didn't commit her to anything. Michael hadn't bothered to ask if she was willing to help Roche out. She hadn't volunteered to be his sister in Christ. Even if she wanted to pick up a strand of Michael's good works, a rare, shimmering thread in the dross of his difficult life, it couldn't change how she reacted to Roche.

He didn't look or act like Janie Meister's molester. But he awoke in Hannah the same feelings of revulsion and anger. It was as though Roche was another head of the same monster. No, she told herself. That wasn't quite true. Roche supposedly was trying to change. Janie Meister's live-in monster never did that.

"Hannah?" Bobby said. "What do you want to do?"

"He repulses me, but . . ."

"If he was trying to do the right thing, maybe it's different?"

"Maybe."

Bobby cleared his throat. "Well, just for the sake of argument, doesn't he have the right to be left alone?"

She nodded. "Probably." She certainly wanted to leave him alone. She wanted to forget that people like Freddy Roche and Janie Meister's monster existed.

"We could probably take care of this pretty quickly," Bobby said. "At least get the cops to step up to the plate, help this guy out."

She felt a tic of annoyance. "You're pushing me, Bobby."

He ruffled at her tone. "What I mean is, if we tell this guy to get lost, what are we doing in this practice? If we wanted to stay above the ugly human fray, we could be over at Gibson, Dunn and Crutcher or O'Melveny and Myers, doing the corporate-money mambo. We're supposed to be working for real people, and real people aren't perfect. If they were, they wouldn't need lawyers."

He'd ignited her anger now. "Tell me again, Atticus Finch. What did you do before law school?"

"You know what I did."

"Right. You worked in two or three restaurants. You went to the Culinary Institute. You decided that making a career out of cooking would ruin the joy of eating, so you picked law school instead. In short, you never had to deal with anyone like Freddy Roche, unless you were filling his order for an endive salad."

"Christ, Hannah. Give me a break."

"Sorry," she said. "But you're acting like I'm shirking my sacred duty. You never saw what people like Roche do to children. I did."

"Like that little girl you tried to help."

Hannah interrupted before he could recite any more of Janie Meister's story. "Yes. When I look at Freddy Roche, I see what happened to her."

He nodded. "Okay. I'm sorry. I just thought it might be different, if Michael had been working with him."

"I know," Hannah said. "Maybe it should be different. But I have a hard enough time trying to keep the pictures of Janie out of my mind as it is. I don't think I could do that if we had Mr. Roche around."

"Okay," Bobby said. "I'll go tell him."

Hannah shook her head. "No. I'll do it."

When she had finished her explanation, Roche glared at her. "Michael was wrong about you. You're blind."

The jibe was meant to hurt her, and it did. But not enough to make her change her mind. "Michael might have been a more compassionate person than I am. That's why he was a priest. I was a police officer. I've put people like you in prison. I'm not accustomed to representing them."

"I'm not asking you to beat a rap for me. I'm asking you to preserve my civil rights."

"Lawyers have rights, too," Hannah said. "One of them is that I don't have to take every case that's put in front of me."

Roche stood up. His face burned red. He blinked fast, fighting angry tears. He looked like a big, soft child himself. "Goddamn it, I've changed."

"So you've said. But in my experience, that rarely happens."

"Even Michael saw how I'd changed. He said so in that letter."

"I'm sorry."

"Look, I take responsibility for what I did. I don't pretend that nobody got hurt."

"I'm glad to hear you say that," Hannah said.

He didn't seem to hear her. "I haven't gone to a park or a beach in four years. I don't go to movies—any movies—that have little boys in them." He was shaking now. "I'm on this drug, you know?"

Hannah shook her head. She didn't know. Thorazine? Some other tranquilizer? If so, it wasn't working.

"Once a week, I get a five-hundred-milligram injection of Depo-Provera. This is my choice, not something parole made me do. And you know what? It makes me fat. It gave me tits. My pubic hair fell out, and my balls are no bigger than marbles. I haven't had an erection in a year. I've been chemically castrated, Ms. Barlow. If that's not changed, I don't know what is."

He pushed past her and she heard the outer door slam. She sat down at Bobby's desk and put her hand to her face, feeling the burn in her cheeks. She'd told Roche the truth—nothing compelled her to take his case. So why did she feel so ashamed?

That night she stumbled through a series of hazy dreams, all featuring Michael. He scowled. He stared. He pleaded with his eyes. She understood his silent dream language, and remembered it, word perfect, when she awoke: I reached out to Roche because he was in need. I sent him to you for the same reason. If you can't do it for him, do it for me.

In the morning, Hannah got to the office early. She found Roche's number in Bobby's interview notes and dialed it. The phone had been disconnected.

3

Roche's new house was tiny: only one bedroom, instead of the two he really needed. Mother was storing the stuff that wouldn't fit: some clothes, a couple of dozen books, a desk, and his snow domes. There were two hundred of them, and there was no place to show them off here.

He put down his last box — a set of Fiestaware that his boss, Caesar, in an uncharacteristic fit of generosity, had let him buy at cost. The living room carpet was an awful shade of dried apricot. A conga line of ants danced on the kitchen counter, despite the traps he'd put out. The bathroom smelled like someone had just taken a dump, although he had scrubbed the toilet with bleach every morning since moving in, the first Monday of May, three days before.

Still, he thought, he was lucky to have a place at all. For a week, he'd searched on his own. If he told landlords the truth about his background, they found some reason not to rent to him. But he couldn't risk hiding the fact. That would be worse. He'd just be evicted once the neighbors found out and started a campaign of terror. Roche had resigned himself to one thing: with the goddamn CD-ROM around, someone would always find out. So he decided to rat himself out before anyone else did.

The strategy failed miserably. He was staying at Mother's house, and she wanted him to move back permanently, but after the shit and flames at his house, he knew he couldn't do that to her. She still was a warrior queen, but she was nearing eighty.

Lying on the bed in his childhood room, he wondered why

he bothered with any of it—the Depo-Provera, the behavior-mod program, the constant self-monitoring, the prayers that felt so foreign on his lips. If the world thought the worst of him anyway, why was he trying so hard to be good? For a while, he considered skipping his next shot.

Then Lisette called to tell him that she'd found a house for him. It was a granny flat, a little place behind a home in a run-down, semi-industrial part of Las Almas. It belonged to Ralph, a man who had worked with Lisette in the prison ministry. He was a widower, about ten years older than Roche, and worked in a tool shop nearby. When they met, Ralph made it clear that they weren't going to hang around together. That was okay with Roche. He didn't think they had much in common. The guy smelled like 3-In-One oil.

After he paid Ralph first and last month's rent, Roche hugged Lisette, smooched her cheek, and thanked her until she blushed and told him to stop. Roche still couldn't say he understood why she cared about him, but he didn't know what he would have done without her.

She had started visiting him while he was still in prison. Lisette was the one who had driven Mother four and a half hours to San Luis Obispo, waited during her visit, checked her into a motel, and then took her home again the next day. On the first visit, Lisette had brought Roche brownies—and a Bible, of course. He thanked her for both, even if he wasn't that excited about yet another copy of the Good Book. People were always pushing it into his hands. He did not find anything in it that directly addressed his situation.

Nevertheless, Lisette meant well. She had introduced him to Father Michael. She'd listened when things were bothering him—things that he couldn't talk to Mother about, like the Depo-Provera and its side effects. The urges he'd had before the drug really kicked in. The boy. He had seen Lisette less lately. He'd had to break a dinner date with her when it was time for inventory at the store. But she'd been right there when he called in desperation, nearly homeless. And thanks to her, he now had a place to live.

Before he even unpacked, Roche registered with the police. It was a relief not to worry about how some new agency would treat him. He knew what the Las Almas cops would do if he was harassed again: nothing. But he didn't think they'd go out of their way to roust him, either.

He finished putting away the dishes. He was exhausted, suddenly. He flopped on the bed for a minute and closed his eyes. Without prompting, the memory of the boy drifted into his mind.

Midsummer day. The boy took off his T-shirt. Sweat gleamed on his shoulders. He was older than Freddy remembered him. He was taller, but still slim and beautiful. He dove onto the court, snatching the basketball away from Roche with a laugh. He drove toward the basket. One bound took him up. He hovered there, suspended in weightless perfection, ball poised over the hoop. Roche waited below him.

Roche awoke and realized someone was knocking at the door. He sat up and peered out the window. Lisette stood on the doorstep, holding a plate crowned with a huge, heavily frosted coconut cake that looked like one of Mother's Easter hats. Lisette was dressed more casually than during her prison visits, wearing baggy jeans, a floral blouse, and sandals. Her hair, black shot with gray, was pulled back in a ponytail.

Roche had asked her to come, thinking he shouldn't be alone for what was going to happen later. But now he'd changed his mind. He would have to convince her to leave. The dream had given him an idea.

4

Hannah went to bed late, turned sleeplessly, dozed off, and woke in time to hear the Sunday newspaper hit the ground. She lay in bed and stretched her arm to the empty space beside her. The sheets felt cold. Without the soft sounds of another sleeper's dreaming sighs, the room felt oppressively quiet. She dressed and went downstairs, into more silence.

A few months ago, when four people lived in Hannah's oversized Victorian house, quiet times were rare. Weekend nights, when everyone was home, were particularly raucous. Matthew thumped and clanged the pots he liberated from the kitchen cabinets, squealing gleefully when Connie chattered to him in her Texas drawl. Guillermo, in ripped jeans and a white shirt with the cuffs rolled, softly sang while he graded tests at the kitchen table, pausing every few minutes to check on Hannah's dinner experiments, including several variations of chicken *con salsa mole*. Hannah, who had always thought of herself as a solitary person, found she liked the company of voices that didn't come from a television or CD player.

But that time passed quickly. Matthew and Connie left on a rainy December morning. He was more than a year and a half old, a talkative, outgoing boy who had overcome his restless nights and had started calling Hannah "Mama." It delighted Guillermo. It made Hannah's heart ache.

Hannah managed not to cry as Connie's car pulled away from the house. The boy turned in his seat to wave goodbye. Guillermo sniffled and wiped his eyes. Hannah thought him particularly handsome at times like this, when his tenderness surfaced and the stern face he presented to the world softened. He caught her look and shrugged defensively.

"Well, I'm going to miss him," he said.

Hannah nodded. "He's a great little kid."

He frowned at her composure. "You're taking this awfully well."

"Give me time," Hannah said.

The collapse began the next morning. When she awoke, her first thought was of Matthew and what she should make him for breakfast. Her second thought was the realization that he wasn't there to be fed. She found herself crying unexpectedly. She could stand seeing babies on television, or in the supermarket, but in the middle of dinner, balancing the checkbook or getting ready for bed, she fell apart. Guillermo rocked her and told her she should let it all out, cry the pain away.

Two weeks passed like that. Then, on a Saturday morning, Hannah realized that she hadn't yet cried that day. And she hadn't the day before, either. Soon, she thought, I'll be able to go a whole week without losing it. She went into the bathroom and put on some mascara, which she had stopped doing four smeary days after Matthew's departure.

Later, when she went back upstairs to put away laundry in the bedroom, she found one of Matthew's toys, a daffy-looking stuffed squeaky doll called a Whoozit. It had been one of his favorites when he'd first come to live with Hannah. And now, he doesn't even care that it's gone, she thought. He's forgotten about it. The world and the people of the old house in Las Almas might not even be a ripple in his memory by now.

She pressed the toy's face and it honked at her. She sat down with it and fought the tears. Just let me go two days, she thought. She heard the front door open—Guillermo, returning from the grocery store.

He came upstairs calling her name and stopped when he saw her teary eyes. He no longer asked why, but she held up the toy as an explanation anyway.

Guillermo sat on the bed and wrapped his arms around her. "Do you want to call up there, see how he's doing?"

She shook her head. "Next week. They need to bond as a family now."

She felt him nod. His embrace tightened. "And what about you and your family?"

She pulled away and looked at him. There was a trace of weekend stubble on his cheeks. His hair, glossy black and straight as a ruler, brushed his collar.

"My family? Dad and Theresa?"

"No," he said. "The family we should have, before it's too late."

She felt jarred by the suggestion. Did he think he could replace Matthew? That he could make her forget him? She shook her head. "I don't want to talk about that right now."

"No, hear me out. It doesn't have to be a big production. We could have a quiet little wedding. A year from now, we could have a family of our own."

The proposal, she noticed, was tucked between Guillermo's procreative imperatives. She knew family was vital to him. And she had to admit that the six months of caring for Matthew had gone well. But Matthew wasn't theirs. They had done long-term baby-sitting, which wasn't the same as parenthood. They needed to stabilize as a married couple before a child could come into their lives. At least, that's how she thought about it.

Marriage scared her. She'd made sure Guillermo knew that from the start. She explained her parents' union: a bitter mess that would have ended in divorce if her mother hadn't died first, falling against the edge of a glass table in a drunken stupor. That had happened when Hannah was seventeen. She and the other two Barlow children bore the scars of those days. Guillermo, raised in a large, seemingly angst-free family, didn't always understand how deep those cuts went.

She looked up at him and tried a smile. "Guillermo, I don't want to rush into anything so soon after giving up Matthew. Can't we just wait a while before we tackle this? There's no hurry, is there?"

He scowled at her and dropped his arms from her shoulders. "I don't call two years a hurry. I think I've been very patient, Hannah. I haven't been with anyone else in that time. You, on the other hand, had your hot night with the fireman. If it was one night. So for you it would be, what, maybe seven, eight months that you've been faithful to me? Maybe this is about the fact that you're getting itchy again."

She clutched Matthew's toy so tightly that it squealed again. She had only herself to blame for this. She'd tortured herself over whether to tell Guillermo what had happened when he left her during their last fight about marriage and commitment. She thought then that their relationship might be over. She acted impulsively with Mike Feuer and regretted it almost immediately. But when Guillermo came back to her, she decided to level with him. She was determined to leave nothing that could loom up later to haunt either one of them. And now he'd turned her honesty on her.

"It was once, as I've told you," she said, trying to sound contained but wanting to scream the words. "I asked you to forgive me. You said you had. You said that was the past. But I guess it's not."

"I only bring it up because it's relevant to what I hear from you now."

"You bring it up to remind me who's the better human being. Okay, Guillermo. You're the paragon." She left the bedroom before he could answer.

She strode to the park, half a mile away, circled it, and started back, trying to decide what she could say to him. He had proposed marriage, but the words had hardly been romantic. Why had he chosen that moment to push her? He had waited until she was grieving the loss of Matthew. He waited until she was miserable, weakened by tears. Then he stretched his hand down to her, offering the solace of a husband and children. And she was supposed to grab onto that hand, covering it with kisses of gratitude. His attitude irritated her. But she reminded herself that he probably didn't mean it that way. He loved her. He wanted a family. She would be forty in a few years. She knew they didn't have forever. But she wasn't ready to marry him now. A few months, she thought. Maybe six months to live a normal life, and then they could talk about marriage. A reasonable compromise.

He was in the living room watching the news when she came back. She sat next to him and reached for his hand. Instead of letting her take it, he snatched the remote control and clicked off the television. He gave her his cool, appraising look. It was fine when he was evaluating a piece of art pottery. She hated it when he turned it on her.

"I need to think about this," she said. "I love you, but I need time."

He stared at her. Something flickered and dimmed in his

eyes. "You can have all the time you want. But I'm finished with putting my life on hold for you."

He left that night. By the middle of the next week, everything of his was gone from the house. He told her he'd have a new number, and she could find it by calling 411. She hadn't heard from him since.

In the kitchen, the clock read six-fifteen. A long, quiet day loomed ahead of her. She made coffee and thought about what she'd done by refusing Guillermo's offer. She couldn't claim temporary insanity or demonic possession. She had chosen to consider marriage and motherhood carefully and not just to pounce on them like a life raft.

She glanced at Guillermo's new number. A magnetized Roy Lichtenstein drawing of a happy housewife held it in place on the refrigerator door. She knew he would expect an apology from her and an acknowledgment that she'd been foolish and selfish. She wasn't sure either of those things were true. And she didn't want to grovel.

Another part of her decided to weigh in: the traitor, the Guillermo-lover. Well, isn't that great, she whispered. You've preserved your pride and independence. For whatever good they do you on these ungodly quiet, depressing mornings. Then the traitor went into a sulk. Stiff-necked, solitary Hannah went outside to get the Sunday paper.

As usual, it lay in the middle of the wet lawn. Hannah slid on a pair of rubber garden clogs that she kept on the porch, and tramped through the grass. If she hadn't looked up to judge the weather, she would have missed seeing the skinny kid leaning against the camphor tree across the street. The teenager wore a crocheted beret in Rastafarian shades of green, yellow, and red over long, stringy, light-brown hair. Boy or girl? The beret was pulled so low and the clothes were so monumentally baggy that Hannah couldn't be sure.

The kid leaned out from the trunk and watched as Hannah picked up the paper. He ducked behind it when Hannah raised her hand in greeting. The kid didn't look like any of the neighborhood kids she knew, but children changed so fast as they grew. Still, the local teenagers seldom emerged before noon on a Sunday.

She paused on the porch and looked across at the house the

kid seemed to be watching. The family there had twin teenage girls, juniors in high school. Their second-floor bedroom overlooked the front yard. Maybe the kid was this week's Romeo, waiting for light from yonder window. She went inside, opened the paper, and scanned the local news briefs.

The lead item told of a transient whose van had burst into flames at a Santa Ana park on April twenty-fifth. He still was clinging to life, two weeks after suffering third-degree burns on more than half of his body. The police finally had an identification, a history, and some speculation on what had happened: Henry Charles was a paroled child molester who had left his permanent address in Anaheim several years before and hadn't bothered registering as a sex offender since. It appeared that someone had firebombed the van. The story said police found the remains of a large beer bottle in the rubble, along with evidence of a gasoline-soaked wick. They theorized that Charles had gotten into a turf hassle with the meth and crack dealers who claimed the park after dark. Witnesses were being sought. Oh sure, Hannah thought. Those crackheads will be lining up to tell the police what happened.

Charles's past as a molester made her think about Roche. It had been about two weeks since he came to Terry and Barlow's offices. In the morning, she would check with the Las Almas police to see if he had registered at a new address.

She went for more coffee and checked to see if the Juliets had made an appearance. Their drapes were still closed. And Romeo was gone. So much for romantic devotion.

5

Roche was nearly asleep when he felt it: something crawling across his upper lip. He slapped himself, sat up, turned on the light, and beheld the smashed ant body in his fingers. He knew there had to be more of them. Ants seldom came singly. But did he have enough spray left? He hoped so. The clock said SUN 11:30 P.M. He didn't think he should go out this late.

It wasn't that his behavior mod required him to stay in. There were pervs who absolutely had to maintain a curfew. If they used to cruise at night for kids, staying in after dark kept temptation to a minimum. But night trolling had never been Roche's approach. He was about light and sunshine, sports, and trust. Sleazy, violent encounters in the bushes at night repelled Roche. It turned his stomach to think about forcing boys, scaring them. He loved boys.

He got out of bed right away and shut off the fantasy before it assumed a more definite shape. He *said* he loved boys. But what he really loved was getting off. It was all bad, whether it started with bushes or basketball. It all ended the same way—with prison. And what became of the boys? He thought about David. God, he thought, I am so sorry about David.

The mental exercise worked, steering his thoughts away from desire and back to somber reality. But that didn't solve his problem. Did he have to go out? He thought about the night the neighborhood Blackshirts had tried to burn him out. He could still smell the singed shingles. If he'd stayed outside for long that night, someone would have killed him.

But he had nothing to fear here, he reminded himself. There

were no neighbors, except Ralph, his landlord. His was the only other house on the short block, which otherwise consisted of the tool factory, some garages, and a little sweatshop. At six, everyone went home. Roche hadn't seen any kids at all, day or night.

So it was safe on both counts. No temptation, no torturers. But Roche decided he should wait until morning anyway. He fell back on the bed and saw an ant insouciantly stroll across his pillow. He crushed it between his fingers and sighed. If they had infiltrated the bedroom, what on earth had they done in the kitchen?

He hesitated for a moment before he turned on the light there. Then he flicked the switch. The counters were thick with ants. They swarmed over the sink and made for the cupboards. Roche shuddered. He grabbed the can of Raid and shook it hard. The nozzle emitted a little fart and a pitiful bubble of insecticide. Roche imagined ant laughter and ant jeers, the sound of the crowd outside his house that night, sniggering as he tried to douse burning shingles with a garden hose.

"Goddamn it." He threw the can away, wet a sponge, and wiped the counters. But the ants kept coming, and he found their route. They were slipping in under the front door, bivouacking in the hall, then pushing on into the kitchen, and victory. And now he spotted a second wave, moving up through a gap in the caulking around the kitchen sink. Even in this new house, they came after him. But he could do something about this horde.

Roche got dressed and threw on his birthday jacket. He opened the door and reassured himself before he stepped outside. The all-night Sav-on was only about a mile away. By midnight, there would be nothing left but the tiny, writhing corpses and a faint smell of formic acid and insecticide. He drove off, relishing thoughts of carnage.

When Ralph went to work at seven on Monday morning, he saw an ant trail snaking its way up Roche's front steps and into the house. He knew it wouldn't be long before they forked left and infiltrated his place, too. He would have to buy some Raid during his lunch hour.

6

Since Hannah hadn't been able to sleep past five in the morning for weeks, she started going to the office early. She could work uninterrupted and bill a solid two hours before Bobby and Vera showed up.

So at six-thirty on Monday, the day after she decided she wasn't ready to beg for Guillermo's love, she was already in the office making coffee when the phone rang. That early, it was probably a wrong number. Or it was someone calling collect from jail, using the Yellow Pages to find a defense attorney.

But there was another possibility. Bobby was working on a case with a Miami lawyer they had started calling Mr. Spacy. If Bobby told Mr. Spacy to call at three, he would chirp, "Your time?" Yes, Bobby would say, my time. Mr. Spacy would then call at three *his* time, while Bobby was at lunch. Hannah wondered how someone could get through law school and not grasp the notion of a three-hour time difference. She picked up the call before it rolled over to voice mail.

"Oh. I expected a recording." The voice was not Mr. Spacy's. But it wasn't a collect call from Orange County Men's Jail, either.

"No. I'm really here," Hannah said. "Can I help you?"

"Is this Ms. Barlow?"

"Yes."

"It's one of your clients, ma'am. I know it's early, but do you think you could swing by?"

"Who is this?"

"Sorry. Sergeant McCabe, watch commander, Las Almas P.D. I wanted to handle this before I went off shift."

She knew the name and had a vague memory of a guy with a waxed moustache and a fondness for dove hunting. "Jerry McCabe?"

"Yeah." He hesitated. Hannah imagined him trying to place her. A born-slimy criminal-defense attorney? Some former DA, now gone over to the dark side? A cop-suing harpy he hadn't been warned about? "Do I know you?"

"I'm Jimmy Barlow's daughter."

"Is that right?" Now that she'd identified herself as a member of the Las Almas P.D.'s extended family, his relief was audible. "How's Jimmy, anyway?"

Hannah didn't really know. She hadn't seen her father, a retired Las Almas cop, in several weeks, not since Estelle, his wife and Hannah's stepmother, had called to congratulate her for dumping "that uppity Messican." That was her pronunciation and her notion of a compliment.

Hannah had blown up. How dare she comment on Hannah's personal life? How dare she try to include Hannah in her racism? She hung up while Estelle sputtered. Hannah decided to be out of town for the Fourth of July, Thanksgiving, Christmas, and St. Swithin's Day, for that matter. She'd had it with Estelle. But she missed Jimmy.

"Jimmy and his wife are up at Tom's Place this week," Hannah told McCabe.

"Lucky folks," McCabe sighed. "All those glorious trout to catch."

"So, Sergeant, which of my clients do you have locked up?"

"Not locked up, I'm afraid. He's in the county morgue."

Hannah sat down and picked up a pen. She prayed that this was a mistake, that McCabe would give her a name other than the one she had in mind. "Who is it?"

"The wallet was gone. But the victim was lying next to a car registered to a Freddy Roche. The victim also had your business card in his jacket pocket."

Not a burned-down house, then. And not a mob beating. Not even a suicide, which is what she supposed Roche's former neighbors had been praying for. "It was a robbery?"

"It looks like one. We got the call about one this morning.

They found him in a Sav-on parking lot. Two shots, head and chest."

"Is your victim medium height, clean-shaven, brown and brown, long bangs?"

"Yes."

"A fat man?"

McCabe clicked his tongue. "That sounds like our guy."

"I think so, too." Hannah remembered Roche as he had been in the office that day, trying to maintain the crisp look of a good citizen, but feeling sweat-soaked and frightened. The taunts and threats that rattled him then were nothing compared to what he must have felt in that parking lot, staring at a gun while someone hissed or screamed a command to give up his wallet. What did he feel when he realized that the wallet, no matter how much was in it, wasn't going to buy him his life?

"Hannah, do you have any idea about next of kin for Mr. Roche?"

"I'll see what I can find. I'd like to do an I.D. first, if that's okay."

"I'll let them know you're coming."

Hannah consulted Bobby's notes again, and saw a scrawled line that she'd missed before: *Marian Roche—F.R.'s mom,* and a number with a Las Almas exchange. She left Bobby a message, explaining where she was. She wanted to see the body before the police called Roche's mother. Maybe it was a mistake. But as she drove to the morgue, she heard Roche's shaky voice: "They want me dead."

Hannah was back at the office by eight. Bobby met her at the door.

"Was it Freddy Roche?"

She nodded, took off her coat, and sat down. Bobby poured coffee. "Someone shot him in the head and chest," she said. "Took his wallet, but left his car. The police will go over to his mother's place in a little while to tell her."

"Do you think it's a coincidence that Roche tells us someone is going to kill him, and two weeks later, someone does?"

Hannah had stopped herself from thinking about that on the way back from the morgue. She had a headache. Her hands were freezing, and she knew that the morgue's smell would linger in her nostrils for the rest of the morning. "I told the detective what happened to Roche in his old neighborhood. He said they'd check that aspect out. But the store is in a crappy area. It's been robbed twice in the last year."

Bobby nodded uncertainly. "Still . . ."

Hannah froze him with a stare. She was having a hard enough time stifling her own recriminations. She didn't want to hear any from Bobby.

"I wasn't going to blame you," Bobby said.

"Good. There was nothing we could have done about this."

"Right." He nearly sounded as if he meant it.

"What should we have done?" Hannah said. "Followed him around like the Secret Service?"

Bobby threw up his hands. "I'm not going to argue with you, Hannah."

He went into his office and shut the door. Hannah decided she needed a walk.

Terry and Barlow had offices in the Orange Empire Building, an artifact from the thirties that managed to retain its dignity despite the benign neglect of the management company. The suites had frosted-glass doors and a lobby paneled in maple and oak. Bits of gilt clung to the skin of the plaster orange that sat in a niche, like a guardian totem, over the building's front door. The Orange Empire was the queen of downtown Las Almas, towering over the smaller, plainer brick-and-plaster buildings. There was talk of declaring it a historical district, and Hannah supported that wholeheartedly. The city's best structures were in constant danger of being ripped down to make way for some hideous Snak Mart or other.

She headed for the Plaza, the small circular park that was the hub of the old downtown district, stopping at the Cuban restaurant that fed Bobby's weekly need for *arroz con pollo*. It was open early for *cafe con leche* and pastries, but Hannah passed on the sweets—the dripping fillings turned her stomach. With a large black coffee in hand, she walked another block and deliberately selected one of the Plaza benches that faced north. She managed to distract herself for a while, first by thinking of a way to apologize to Bobby and then by wondering who had decapitated several of the city's parking meters. Finally, she couldn't force the other thoughts away anymore. She turned and looked south, making the journey in

her mind: three blocks down, make a right turn. Two blocks
more, and a left. And then you were at Janie Meister's house.

She didn't need to close her eyes to see it: a modern remodel
with faux Colonial touches. The house was clad in white
clapboards. Bright marine-blue shutters hung at the windows.
A carob tree shaded a suede-smooth Marathon lawn. A plastic
swing hung from the tree's thickest branch.

A mother, father, and daughter had lived there once. Janie
was in kindergarten. Small for her age, with fine, chestnut hair.
She won a prize for growing the most luscious tomatoes in the
class garden. Like some nursery-rhyme character, she was
accompanied by a beloved animal—a stuffed one, in her
case—wherever she went. A bright little girl, who seemed to
live in a sunshiny world.

Except that Janie's father molested her. He went into her
room on Saturday mornings, as Bugs frolicked on the television and Janie's mother slept off Friday night's martinis. He
rewarded Janie's compliance and silence with trips to Toys "R"
Us, where Barbie's wardrobe grew dramatically. One day, Janie
hauled the doll's collection to a friend's house. The girl
admired the clothes and wished that her dad were as generous.
Janie fell apart at that, telling her friend, and then her friend's
mother, what the cost of Barbie's couture had been.

A phone call later, Janie haltingly told her story to Hannah,
a sex-crimes investigator for the Las Almas Police Department.
It was one of the few Orange County agencies that still had its
own officers do such interviews, and Hannah was good at
them.

Despite what had happened, Janie wanted to go home. She
pulled her stuffed toy close. She wanted her mother. Hannah
told her she couldn't go to her, not just yet. But Hannah
promised she would be safe. Janie would have been, except for
a series of decisions that cascaded down on the girl, turning
into the flood that finally drowned her.

Orangewood, the county's home for abused and neglected
children, had once again exceeded its capacity. The word was
out: kids weren't removed from their homes unless they were
in imminent danger.

The callow, cocky social worker had been bowled over by
the fact that the Meisters bathed regularly, owned property, and

shopped at Nordstrom. They were a switch from his usual caseload of grubby, druggy, inarticulate wretches.

Cases crammed the maw of dependency court. The county lawyers tried to break the logjam with informal diversion of the weakest cases. And that's what Janie's case was.

Meister wasn't stupid. He denied everything. A colposcopy was negative—Meister had never penetrated his daughter. It all came down to Janie's word. She told Hannah how her father ejaculated in her mouth every Saturday morning. Hannah related that to the social worker.

He came up with what he called a workable solution for a wobbly case: an informal agreement to return Janie to her mother, on her promise that Meister would stay out of the home pending a hearing, counseling, and a plan for family reunification. The Meisters had agreed, for the sake of their daughter, the social worker said.

Hannah didn't think it would work. She thought Bill Meister was a weasel and a liar. In her interview with him, he'd given her a business card, identifying his employer as CARNECO. It was a company name so vague it could have been anything from a meat-packing plant to a builder of roller coasters. She knew the Newport Beach address: his business was in a neighborhood rife with investment-scam boiler rooms. She'd glanced at Meister's title: "Growth Specialist."

"What do you do, exactly?" Hannah had asked him.

"I maximize opportunities for gain in a high-risk environment."

"Stock market?"

"Chump change." He gave her a glittering smile. Hannah had a glimpse of how he could make people believe in him, whether it was the mark looking to get rich quick, the harried social worker trying to lighten a caseload, or the trusting wife desperate to keep her family together. "When this all settles down, I could . . ."

"No thanks," she said curtly. His smile withered like a cut weed.

In her interview, Claire Meister made no such sophisticated plays. She just stammered nonsense. Janie made the story up. She must have seen the sexual act on cable—television was just outrageous these days. When Hannah asked why Janie would do such a thing, Claire said that she was mad at her father for refusing to get her a kitten. Hannah had heard songs of self-deception before, but Claire's perfervid denials were nearly operatic. Her disgust waned for a moment when she thought she saw a shadow of a bruise under the woman's eye. But Claire caught the glance and denied that Meister ever hit her. Ever. Loving father, perfect husband. Hannah couldn't stomach any more.

She knew Meister would find a way to move back home before a month was out. But when she protested the plan to return Janie to her parents, Hannah's boss told her that her opinions were no longer needed. The workers at Children's Services knew what they were doing. Time for her to back off.

She drove to the Meisters' house anyway, on a Friday night, skipping a friend's party to do her surveillance. She watched from the darkness as Bill Meister carried suitcases to a rental truck. Then an exercise bike. Some files. She felt the tension in her neck ease slightly—maybe she'd been wrong about him. But then she saw the next load: a dollhouse. A Barbie case. A stuffed animal. She was back on the phone—to her boss, to the young social worker, to the social worker's boss. The loop closed when her lieutenant told her to butt out or find herself working traffic.

This was the point at which Hannah wanted to stop the story. Because she could have done the right thing. She could have told her boss—all the bosses—to fuck off. She could have driven back to the Meisters' house, taken Janie home with her, and refused to let her go until someone ensured her safety. It could have cost her her job. But that would have been worth it, if it had saved Janie.

But that wasn't what Hannah had done. She hated thinking of that younger Hannah, selfish and ambitious. She had worked for more than ten years to be where she was on the day she met Janie Meister. She wanted to move up. She wanted to work homicide, to run the squad some day. So when they slapped her down, she stayed down. She lulled her fears that weekend with three bottles of red wine and a half-dozen phone calls to the watch commander. With increasing irritation, he told her that if he heard of any kidnappings, he would certainly let her know.

Two days later, she learned that the Meisters had disappeared. Tough break, her lieutenant said. Let the county's kiddie-minders find them. It's their fuckup. You did what you could. He said he would make sure people knew she'd tried.

Hannah took little consolation in that. She'd made calls up and down the state. Colleagues in other departments agreed to help, informally. The only thing the Meisters had done was blow off a diversion program. It was not the kind of offense that would put the world on red alert.

Four weeks after the Meisters disappeared, one of Hannah's informal contacts called. The decomposing body of a child had been found in the surf near a beach town in Oregon. The girl was probably four or five, slightly built, with brown hair. A drowning victim. There was no confirmed identification, no match to missing children from that area, either. Hannah pressed the local cops in Oregon for whatever information they could share. They didn't offer much. Hannah had few evidentiary fragments that would rule out Janie as the victim. Janie hadn't been fingerprinted—it wasn't part of the county's child-protective protocol. She had no dental records that Hannah could find.

She finally flew north, went to the county morgue, and saw the body. Made herself examine it minutely. Was it Janie Meister? She couldn't see her in that bloated, bleached skin, fish-bitten and rock-scraped. She stared into the night on the plane ride home and knew that her uncertainty only was wishful thinking. A month later, she resigned from the department. She served summonses for an attorney friend of Devlin Eddy, her former partner, to support herself. She ran up her credit card in searches for the child. But the sanest part of her knew that that was futile. Janie was dead, and the only way to reclaim her own life was to accept that. When she began law school a few months later, the crush of work kept her from thinking about Janie. It was a relief.

Hannah looked away from Janie's street. Several teenagers, lingering on their way to school, had occupied one of the other benches. They chattered as noisily as a flock of parrots as they opened cartons of orange juice and pulled out packs of cigarettes. They looked like a short history of recent American fashion to Hannah. A lanky boy had chosen a chartreuse-striped orange sweater to pair with purple-checked bell-bottoms, while one of the girls opted for pegged denim pants and a yellow-checked blouse that showed her bare midriff. Her hair was pulled into a severe ponytail, and her lipstick was sports-car red. She languidly blew smoke from that voluptuous mouth. The hillbilly diva, Hannah thought. She understood, having tried wildly different styles in her time, putting on clothes in an effort to see if one could clarify the muddled girl inside.

As she was turning her attention back to her coffee, a kid in baggy jeans, a navy sweatshirt, and a burlap backpack skate boarded into the fashion parade, nearly colliding with a tall, closely shorn blond boy whose plain, white T-shirt and khakis made him a crow among the fashion swans. Hannah recognized the skater, even though he'd dumped the Rasta beret. It was the Sunday-morning Romeo.

"Hannah?" She looked over her shoulder. Bobby was standing a few feet away, out of striking range. "I'm sorry."

She shook her head. "No, my fault. I was being defensive."

He sat down next to her. "You coming back to the office? We have a conference call with Mr. Spacy at ten. Our ten. I think he's catching on."

"Shit. I forgot." She took a last sip of coffee and carried the cup to the trash next to the teenagers' bench. Romeo flicked her a glance, then turned away to cadge a Marlboro from a girl in pink-suede platform shoes. Now that Hannah was closer, she could see she'd been wrong about Romeo. The kid was a girl, younger than Hannah had guessed. Not sixteen. Thirteen, tops.

Hannah looked over her shoulder as she and Bobby walked back to the office. The child pack was on the move, sauntering toward school. Romeo-girl was at the back, carrying the skateboard under her arm. The boy in the white T-shirt fell back, grabbed her just-lit cigarette, and tossed it into the gutter. Good for him, Hannah thought.

The kids walked for a block before the girl turned to watch the lawyer and her dumpy friend as they went back to their office. She assumed, from the way they'd acted at the bench, that they were sleeping together when they weren't fighting. Yuck, she thought. He was as fat as that harmonica-playing guy she'd seen while watching MTV on the many screens at Circuit City.

She glanced up at Jared's back, noting the way he tensed and released his shoulders as though the previous day's workout had left him sore. She was pissed that Jared had taken her morning cigarette away from her. It was true that she'd promised him she would quit. But she liked smoking. It gave her a buzz while managing to keep her calm. He'd told her more than once to take up meditation if it was inner peace she needed. Mantras weren't carcinogenic, he'd said. She'd stuck her tongue out at him.

In the cigarette's absence, she turned to Bert. He was her peace-bringer, too. There wasn't much left of him, but enough. She reached into her pocket and ran her finger over a patch of soft plush of his cheek.

She had to be careful with the lawyer. She had gotten a little too close. She knew better than to let herself be stared at. She knew, from experience, that people who looked too long began to ask questions. How old are you? Where do you live? Questions she didn't want to answer. And yet, she needed to be seen—but just enough. Then she had to retreat a little. Cat and mouse. Flirt and fall guy. That's how Jared put it.

Jared looked back and waved her forward. "Hey, Maisey-Daisy—did you finish your homework?"

"Don't call me that."

"Touchy, aren't we? Did you do the lesson or not?"

She scowled at him. "I did it."

"Let's see."

She swung her backpack around and pulled out the workbook pages. Spanish was sort of fun, once you got into it. But she wasn't going to tell Jared that. Bossy, cigarette-snatching jerk. She was afraid she loved him.

"Muy bien, Maesita!" He plucked at the sleeve of her shirt. It was as close to touching her as he ever got. He was nearly six feet tall, with blue-green eyes. His stubble of hair shone in the sun. She wished he liked her more. Liked her in that special way. She was pretty sure she was the problem. She knew her shortcomings. His dread of touching her just proved she was right.

"Cut it out!" She slapped at his hand, feeling the electricity that came from his near-touch. Her heart jumped at it. He laughed until he saw that she was angry.

"Sorry." He shrugged and smiled. The girl flicked her hair and sulkily faded back into the middle of the crowd. The group slid forward like an amoeba, its edges pushing up and lapping back, making a slow progress toward the side-by-side campuses of Las Almas High School and Rattigan Middle School. The cell turned left, rolling toward the school gates as the bell rang. Jared and the girl turned right.

7

The Oriental Dream Card Club's electric marquee exploded in green, pink, and white, burning the words into Cotter Davis's vision: MEMORIAL DAY SPECIAL!!! 24–HOUR PAI GOW POKER & KARAOKE JACKPOTS!!! The words' ghosts hovered there, even when he closed his eyes. A win would be nice. Even a few bucks could lift him out of the pit his life had become.

The freeway dots bumped under the wheels of the car, telling Davis he had drifted into the lane to his left. He overcorrected, nearly winding up on the shoulder to his right. A sharp left on the wheel brought him back where he'd started, but by then the car behind him had sped up. It nearly clipped his rear bumper as he swerved back into his lane. The tailgater fell back, chastened. Goddamn idiot, Davis thought: that's what he gets for driving so close.

Davis sped up, left the Harbor Freeway and made for the casino, which was three blocks away. His fingers clenched the steering wheel so hard that the joints ached. He tried to relax. He'd nearly let his roommate's car get hit. Mike Seward had pretty much said he'd kill Davis if hc so much as scratched it.

Seward drove a tough bargain for the loan of the car. Davis initially offered to cook a dinner and do a week's worth of their laundry in return for two nights' use of the car. He could see Seward enjoying his power as he weighed the deal. He knew how desperate Davis was. Two dinners and two weeks of laundry, Seward countered, and you get the car for one night. Davis reluctantly agreed.

Seward tossed Davis the keys. "And park it away from the other cars. I hate getting the doors all dinged up."

He was talking about a ten-year-old piece-of-shit Corolla, not a Lamborghini Diablo. But Cotter wasn't in a position to argue. After his last layoff—drinking and photographing little kids at Sears didn't mix—he'd had to sell his Dodge. That left him with a bicycle and Orange County's buses. Neither would whisk him away to a card club in Gardena.

Cards were the only pleasure life still afforded him now that he no longer drank. He'd been miserably dry for six months, as required by his nearly ex-wife. She wouldn't take him back until he was sober for a year. He would have settled for a girlfriend to pass the time, but at fifty-one, he didn't have much to offer: he rented a room in Mike Seward's tumbledown Las Almas house. He had a crappy job as a stock boy at a Sav-on in Orange. He was carless. Funless.

Thank God for poker, a game of infinite joy and variety. And legal to play in some cities, thanks to loopholes in California law. He hadn't played in months. He tried to get friendly games going with the nightside crew at the store, but they were busy shooting hoops in the alley. When he first moved in with Seward a year ago, he asked him if he and his friends were up for a game. He was even willing to tolerate that pudgy, stuck-up Roche guy that Seward seemed to like. But Seward gave him a weird look and said they were not really interested in cards.

That left the local casinos. They were illegal in Las Almas and elsewhere in Orange County. The Indian gaming clubs were too far away to be practical. But up the freeway in Los Angeles County there were several to choose from: Hollywood Park, Normandie Casino, The Bicycle Club. But Davis picked this new one: Oriental Dream Card Club. It had all the weird Asian card games, which he had no idea how to play, but there were poker tables, too. Seven-card Stud. Hold 'Em. Lowball. In keeping with the casino's theme, cute Asian girls in dresses cut up to their sweet little butts brought dim sum right to the tables. Dishes serving dumplings while he played cards. Davis liked that idea.

As he drove, Davis considered what he'd play while he nibbled on the various Chinese delicacies. He settled on California Lowball, in which the worst poker hand won. Life was dealing him bad cards lately—maybe that brand of luck would carry over to the game.

It was nearly two in the morning when he pulled into the parking lot. Working the night shift left his body clock all screwed up, so it felt like early evening to him. There weren't many cars in the lot, but Davis parked by the back fence so Seward's precious Corolla couldn't possibly be scratched. Little things set Seward off, and Davis wasn't taking any chances. He knew Seward had done time. He said it wasn't anything violent, and he wasn't a thief. Davis had nothing to fear from him. He sometimes wondered if that was true.

He locked the car and shook out his limbs, still shaky from the near-accident on the freeway. He saw the round headlights of a car pull in two rows over. Davis thought for a minute it might have been the tailgater, but he couldn't be sure. Not a good idea to hang around and find out, he decided.

Quickly he opened the trunk and took out Seward's mustard-and-black houndstooth check jacket. At the last minute— impulsively, almost like a shoplifter—he'd taken it from the downstairs closet where it had been stored unused for months. It fit Davis pretty well, and it looked good with the black jeans he wore. Seward would still be asleep by the time Davis got home. He wouldn't even miss it.

Davis shrugged it on and instantly felt lucky. He was going to look good for the dim sum ladies. He was going to win a few hands of Lowball. His luck was going to change.

8

The phone was ringing, but Marian Roche ignored it. She knew it couldn't be Freddy, and he was the only person she wanted to talk to. She tried to conjure the sound of his voice in her head: Freddy asking if she needed something at the store. Freddy sweetly asking her to dinner at Revere House, which he knew she loved. But he was fading. Her son was gone less than two weeks, and she was already losing her memories of him. She would have to play his answering-machine tape again, bring out the photo album, smell the clothes he left behind.

She pulled two pillows over her head. The ringing went on. Only Caesar would so stubbornly stay on the line, knowing that the jangle of a phone annoyed her. He had done the same thing yesterday. Then he showed up at the house, shouting through the mail slot that he would have the police break down the door if she didn't let him in. She threw on the pale lavender cashmere robe from Neiman Marcus, opened the pink castle's wide front door, and let him see that she was alive, albeit barefoot, with hair awry like some grief-mad Greek queen. Then she told him to leave her alone.

Alone she was. Freddy was really gone, not just locked up this time, but dead. The young police detective who brought her the news said he died in a robbery, but Marian didn't believe it. She said so: What about the phone threats and the attack on his house? She told the detective that Freddy had tried to get the police and those lawyers to help him, to no avail. He'd moved to get away. But his tormentors had found him and killed him. The detective nodded and scribbled in his little notebook, but Marian could see he was humoring her. Five years earlier, when Freddy had been arrested, she had come to hate police for how they had persecuted him. They were still persecuting him, this time by refusing to really investigate who had killed him. They had a convenient explanation in the robbery. That's all they wanted.

Marian took the pillows away from her ears. The ringing had stopped. The bedside day-date clock said it was Monday, two in the afternoon. Memorial Day, she remembered. How appropriate. Memories of her son were all she had now. She did wonder how it got to be Monday, when Saturday was the last evening she could clearly recall. Caesar, abetted by that little turncoat Lisette, had taken away her Seconal, so she rummaged the marbled-topped French sideboard for a liquid sleeping aid. That turned out to be Drambuie. She remembered taking out the bottle sometime around midnight on what she thought was Saturday. Apparently, it had worked better than she'd expected. Her head hurt. She put on her robe, which reeked of scotch and honey. She must have spilled the liqueur, but she didn't remember when.

In the white-tiled bathroom, she washed her face. Other women her age were a mess of wrinkles and age spots, or had faces pulled as tight as cellophane by some laser-wielding playboy surgeon in Newport Beach. But Marian was still smooth and blotch-free. She had worn hats all her life, for shopping, gardening, and church, when she still went to church. She hadn't been in months, because of the unpleasantness with that boy's mother. Marian's face still colored at the thought of the things that woman had said about Freddy in front of everyone who'd gathered for coffee after the service.

Such minor humiliations had begun to age her. The tragedy of Freddy's death would surely accelerate the decline. But she knew she still looked a good fifteen years younger than her eighty years. Next to her skin, she liked her eyes best: they were free of the rheumy clouds of old age, still the black-brown color of rich earth.

As she lifted her face, she saw that the race to the coffin had begun. She was winding-sheet pale, eyes as sunken as the grave. She turned away and ran her fingers through her hair as she walked down the stairs, holding the wrought-iron railing to counter her dizziness. One of Freddy's snow domes was lying on the steps. She must have brought it upstairs with her when she went to bed. Marian sat down on the step and picked it up. It had been one of his favorites: Peter Pan flying over London. But the dome was cracked, and the water had drained away. Silver glitter stuck to her fingers. She found herself crying at the sight of it.

She was huddled there, blotting up the water with the hem of her robe, when the doorbell rang. Caesar. She'd slept with him once, twelve years before, and he somehow thought that meant he owned her.

"Go away, Caesar," she yelled. "I'm all right."

"Mrs. Roche? Las Almas Police."

Oh, good God, she thought, Caesar had actually followed through on his threat this time. She came down the stairs, pulled open the little brass viewing door, and peered out. But it wasn't a uniformed officer. It was the young detective again. She wondered if he'd come to his senses and finally started a real investigation. She asked him to wait a minute. She put the Drambuie back in the sideboard, made sure Baby was penned up in her run, and let him in.

He turned down her offer of coffee. He took a Xerox of a driver's license out of his jacket pocket and showed it to her. Marian was trying to remember the detective's name. Jim? That sounded right. "Did you ever see this man with your son?"

Marian looked closely at it. Freddy was a private person, a man who loved books and long walks and the Sunday morning swap meets, which he attended alone, looking for additions to his dome collection. He didn't have many friends.

The license belonged to Cotter Davis, fifty-one years old. He was short: five feet, five inches, and thin: 110 pounds. He had a face like a dead rose, withered and dry. He looked used up by life. She handed back the paper. "Freddy didn't know him."

"You mean you never met him," Jim said. "Or Freddy never mentioned him to you."

"No, I mean Freddy didn't know him. He told me about everyone in his life."

"Casual acquaintances? People he saw at the supermarket?"

"Everyone." She knew what he was thinking, what he was dying to ask: Did that mean Freddy had told her about David Alvarez? And of course Freddy had. He was Freddy's young friend, until he told the horrible lies that ruined him. To Marian,

David Alvarez had revealed himself then and there as a sneaking, ungrateful wetback. With a bitch for a mother.

Jim held out another picture. "How about this guy?"

It was a color photograph, a man holding a slate at shoulder level. A mug shot. Marian was sorry she knew what one looked like. The name on the slate said MICHAEL ALLEN SEWARD. He was in his forties, with long, black hair and a beard-stubbled face. He was staring expressionlessly at the camera with eyes like smooth, green stones.

Marian recoiled at the memory of him. He sat in this room, sipping iced tea and heaping smarmy praise on her taste in decorating as Freddy unpacked the box they'd brought her. Marian took the pieces to Caesar, who whistled under his breath at the vintage Rolex, the diamond-studded platinum art deco bracelet, and the sterling-silver pieces by Spratling and Georg Jensen. He asked Marian where they came from. A relative of a friend of Freddy's, Marian lied. An old woman, dead of liver failure. Somehow, making up details of the imaginary woman's illness quelled her nervousness. She hadn't fenced jewelry in years.

But now she pushed Seward's picture away. "Never saw him before."

"He didn't know Freddy, either?"

"I said no. Who are these men?"

Jim put the pictures back in his pocket. "Thanks for your help, Mrs. Roche."

"Did they have something to do with Freddy's death?"

"Maybe. I'm not sure."

"Were they shot in a robbery, like Freddy?"

Jim started to get up. "Thanks again."

She put her hand on his wrist. It was thick and tanned, circled in a bracelet with heavy links. She saw the pity he felt for her. He sat down. "Seward's got a record."

Marian knew that the first time she met him. But that wasn't what the detective meant. He was saying that Seward was someone like they imagined Freddy to be: a child molester.

"He was on that state computer disc, then."

Jim nodded, and Marian felt a flicker of satisfaction. First there was the child molester who had been burned in his van. Then Freddy, who had tried to protect himself, but who had been sabotaged by that heartless lawyer. And now there was Seward.

"Seward was shot, like Freddy was?"

"No, no. He's alive. Cotter Davis is the one who's dead. He and Seward shared a house a few miles from here."

Marian frowned. "Was Davis on the disc?"

"No."

Marian wanted to scream with frustration. "For God's sake, what's going on?"

He looked away from her. She could see he was deciding whether he should say more. "On Saturday, Davis went to a casino in Gardena," he said. "It was early—two or three in the morning. Someone shot him to death in the parking lot."

Marian covered her mouth. "So it has happened again."

He took her hand. The grip was strong, and Marian felt as though her fingers were brittle twigs. "No, Mrs. Roche. See, that's why I didn't want to get into all this. It wasn't like what happened to your son."

"But you said . . ."

"That somebody shot Davis in the parking lot. That's the only thing the incidents have in common. We have a suspect, a motive, and everything but the weapon in the Davis case. We wanted to see if your son knew these two. Just to make sure some surface similarities aren't more than that."

"This suspect of yours—how do you know he didn't kill my son, too?"

"Because what happened between Davis and Seward was a personal thing, Mrs. Roche. If your son didn't know these guys, then it closes off the possibility that it was a personal thing that got him killed, too. With your son, it was very likely a robbery, as we've told you before. I'm sorry I interrupted your afternoon."

She tried to keep him from leaving, but she couldn't explain now that she and Freddy had known Seward. If she did, she would have to tell him about the jewelry she took to Caesar. Caesar would tell the police her phony story about the dead owner. Before long, the theft would come out. She couldn't risk that. As she tried to think of a way around the lies, he slipped out of her grasp and let himself out. Marian Roche thought for a few minutes, then picked up the newspaper and the phone.

9

"Did you see the paper today?" Bobby tossed a copy of Tuesday's *Register* onto Hannah's desk.

Hannah shook her head. "I'm swearing off. Too much bad news."

"You have no idea," he said. "Take a look."

She read the headline: "Death Stalks Molesters, Victim's Mother Says." "What the hell is this?"

"It's Marian Roche," Bobby said. "She thinks someone is stalking child molesters."

Hannah looked up, perplexed for a moment. "A molester besides Roche?" Then she answered her own question. "Henry Charles. What's their connection?"

"I don't think there is one. But there's more than two dead guys now. A man was shot in Gardena Saturday. That seems to be what set Roche's mom off."

Bobby perched on the edge of Hannah's desk as she read the story. In the beginning, it was well-written, full of suspenseful and menacing scene-setting. But once the reporter got past the mystery-novel color, the factual fabric was as thin as gauze. Marian Roche was the sole proponent of the molester-stalker theory, which seemed to have started when a Las Almas police detective visited her with a picture of the man shot in Gardena. The detective declined to be interviewed for the story.

The link, according to Marian, was the Megan's Law CD-ROM. Freddy had been terrified of it, she said. He'd told her it was "automated harassment." He described how his attempt to protect himself from "computer-assisted vigilantism" was "ruined by an unfeeling, incompetent lawyer who refused to take his case."

"At least she didn't mention me by name," Hannah said, turning the page.

"I'm sure she did," Bobby said. "The paper's lawyer probably took it out. Defamatory."

Hannah read a little further. "So Marian really thinks the CD-ROM is how this alleged stalker found his victims?"

Bobby nodded. "There are a few problems with that theory, I think."

The reporter pointed those out in one succinct paragraph. Henry Charles, burned in his van but still stubbornly alive after more than a month, had failed to register as a sex offender and was listed as "whereabouts unknown" on the CD-ROM. The man killed in Gardena, Cotter Davis, had one D.U.I. conviction but no sex-crimes record, so he was absent from the disc. But Marian, undaunted by the facts, theorized that Davis was probably an undiscovered molester.

"Great," Hannah said. "First you're dead, and then you're accused of molestation."

"It's the safest way to libel someone—wait till they're in the ground," Bobby said.

Marian Roche recounted what the detective told her: The man suspected of Davis's killing was Michael Seward, his roommate. And he *was* a convicted molester. But when the reporter asked the Las Almas police spokesman to confirm that Seward was on the molester CD-ROM, he wouldn't, citing an ongoing investigation. Further, the CD-ROM was "unavailable" for the reporter's review, because of the Memorial Day holiday.

"It sounds like Seward is on the CD-ROM, and they don't want to say so," Hannah said.

"So what?" Bobby said. "Seward's not dead. So far, Freddy is the only victim who could have been tracked down through the disc. But that fact doesn't stop Marian." He gestured for Hannah to keep reading.

The *Register* reporter couldn't find any next of kin for Davis or Charles, so the story only had background on Roche, as seen through the filter of his mother. It briefly reported his conviction: one count of molesting a twelve-year-old boy, whom he'd met through a church-affiliated basketball league. It recapped

the protests at Roche's house and sought comment on his
murder from his former neighbors. Most wouldn't talk, but a
man named Dick Barker was happy to speak on the record:
"Our neighborhoods should be kept free from this kind of
slime. If somebody is killing off molesters, he ought to get a
medal."

Barker admitted that he was the one who'd checked the
Megan's Law disc for potential neighborhood monsters. It
wasn't that he was worried for his own children: they were in
college, at Cal State Fullerton. But he told the reporter—
indignantly, Hannah thought—that he still had a perfect right
to keep his block safe. He wouldn't say if anything in particular
about his neighbors had prompted him to check the CD-ROM
in the first place.

Hannah read Barker's quotes to Bobby. "Is this the guy
Freddy told us about? The neighborhood ringleader?"

Bobby nodded. "The former cop."

"I wonder if the police ever got around to talking to him
about Freddy's death?"

Bobby shrugged. "It's hard to tell. The police aren't talking."

The story concluded with the three investigating police
departments saying the same thing about Marian Roche's
theory: "No comment."

"It leaves the impression that Marian might be onto something," Bobby said. "Why didn't they just say her theory is
baloney?"

"Maybe that's not what they think," Hannah said.

At home that night, Hannah flipped on the local news and got
her first glimpse of Marian Roche. There was no resemblance
to Freddy. Marian was a tall, bony, broad-shouldered woman
with feathery peach-tone hair done up in a topknot. She
reminded Hannah of a character from a Toulouse-Lautrec
poster, the flame-haired, sharp-featured dancer they called La
Goulue. Marian didn't look eighty, but the story made sure
viewers knew she was. She clutched a picture of Freddy at the
age of twelve and demanded that the police admit the truth: a
sick maniac was responsible for the murderous spree. She
actually used the word "spree," and Hannah was sure she had
rehearsed her speech.

The segment was followed by a live story, in which the

station's investigative reporter, a rotund man whose toupee resembled a captive ferret, sought comment from something called the Golden State BoyLove Congress. He hammered away at an unmarked door in a scummy Hollywood office building, calling for someone to come out and talk about their fear of the molester-killer.

Finally, the racket brought out a girl from a neighboring office. She said the boy-lovers had moved out a long time ago. The reporter tried to get her outraged reaction to the killings, until it became clear she was ignorant, underage, and involved in some kind of dubious massage service. As she tried to give the service's phone number, the camera abruptly cut away. Such were the vagaries of live TV news, Hannah thought.

When Hannah entered the office early the next morning, Bobby was sprawled on the reception area's couch, reading a copy of the *Register*'s competitor. "The story's spreading," he said.

Hannah glanced at the lead, in which the *Times of Orange County* quoted unnamed police sources who tut-tutted Marian's comments, calling them "several facts short of a theory." Of course there was no serial killer of molesters on the loose. The attacks were coincidence and nothing more. Summoning up something like compassion, one of the sources said that Mrs. Roche's upset was understandable—even though Roche was a child molester, he was nevertheless her son. In her grief, the source continued, "she saw a pattern where none existed."

Hannah shook her head. "That last part? It's code for 'she's loony.'" She walked to her office.

"You don't want to read the rest?" Bobby called after her.

"Not now. I've got a headache."

Bobby's brow furrowed with concern. He sat up. "No sleep last night?"

"A couple hours. A few ibuprofen and I'll be okay."

Bobby followed her into her office and perched on the edge of her desk. Hannah leaned back in her chair, closed her eyes, and opened them again. "If you're so anxious that I know what's in there, why don't you summarize it for me?"

"I will, but first there's something else."

"What?"

"Marian Roche called this morning. For you."

Hannah groaned. "What does she want?"

"She wouldn't tell me. She just wants to talk to you."

Hannah shook her head, but that only increased the pounding. "What if I don't call her back?"

"Your decision."

"She's just going to chew me out, Bobby. I don't need that."

"Okay. No pressure from me."

"Tell me what the paper says."

He shook it out and skimmed through the story. "The cop sources say that the attack on Charles was a turf hassle with the local crackheads. Roche's murder was part of a robbery."

"Nothing new there. What about the other guy, Davis?"

"Well, that's the interesting part. It sounds like they think Mrs. Roche might have been right about him."

"He *was* a child molester?"

"Maybe. After his body was found, an informant called police and said Davis and Seward—that's the roommate—were trafficking in kiddie porn. They'd had a falling out over who owned some pictures, so Seward killed Davis, the informant said. He made it look like a robbery."

"It doesn't dovetail with Marian's theory, though. Unless Seward is both a molester and a stalker of molesters."

"I know. The *Times* interviewed Seward in jail. He says there wasn't any kiddie-porn ring and swears he didn't kill his roommate. But he doesn't have an alibi for where he was when Davis was killed, either. He claims he was home asleep."

"What does he think happened to Davis?"

"His guess is that someone saw Davis counting up his poker-stake money in the card club's parking lot and shot him for the cash."

"What do the unnamed cop sources think of the theory?"

"They think Seward is lying. They say the Las Almas P.D. seized a computer from the house, and they're trying to get past the security passwords now. They also found some burned Polaroids in Seward's garage. Might have been kids' pictures. So something was going on."

"They confirmed Seward has a record, right?"

Bobby nodded.

"Is he on the CD-ROM?"

"Of course."

"So two people involved with molester murders are on that disc."

"Three, counting Charles. But again . . ."

"I know. The only dead man who could have been tracked with the CD-ROM is Roche. But it seems too weird to be a coincidence, doesn't it? Maybe Mrs. Roche is right."

"The cops think there's nothing there. Here's a quote: 'Scum kills scum. That's what Cotter Davis's murder is about. Nothing more than that.' "

"Did the *Times* get a maternal reaction?"

"Oh, yes. She replies that the police are 'obdurately fatuous.' "

"She knows how to sculpt a phrase," Hannah said.

"Here's where she blows it, though," Bobby said. "Listen: 'It's clear to me that the police have no interest in solving this crime. They hated my son. The Las Almas Police were the zealots who railroaded him into prison. Freddy was not a molester. He was merely the victim of police, prosecutors, and the lies spread by an ungrateful boy he tried to help.' "

"That's it," Hannah said. "Game over for Mrs. Roche."

Bobby nodded. "She comes off as deluded. Spinning herself a conspiracy theory, just like she talked herself into thinking Freddy wasn't a child molester."

"Unless there's another killing, there's nothing left to write about," Hannah said.

There was nothing in either paper the next day, or the day after. The story's life span, Hannah thought, was approximately that of a vinegar fly.

And Hannah gave it no further thought, until a few days after the *Times* story. She found herself awake in the middle of the night, startled out of a dream. In it, a gun had gone off at close range, loud as a thunderclap. She had watched the victim fall, but couldn't quite see who it was. Roche? Davis? Or Michael? The images were blurred, scenes rendered in smudged gray chalk.

Lying there, heart beating hard, the dream not quite forgotten, she found herself going over the accounts of the Roche and Davis killings: late nights, dark parking lots, the victims apparently followed, death by gunshot. The police hadn't talked about ballistics—had the same weapon been used in both shootings? If not, why hadn't the police said so? It would have been more proof of mere coincidence. The phone tip about Davis and Seward dealing in kiddie porn also seemed conveniently timed to divert attention from the similarity of the killings.

By then she was fully awake. Counting criminal coincidences was no way to get back to sleep, she decided. She got up, put on a robe, and went downstairs. In a few minutes, a NEXIS search of several newspaper databases yielded the first account of Davis's death, a City News Service story that hadn't run in the Orange County papers.

It told Hannah something that Marian Roche hadn't mentioned—something she might not have known, but the police certainly did: Davis drove to the casino in Seward's car. Hannah wondered if someone mistook Davis for Seward. If Seward had been the real target, then there were three attacks on paroled child molesters in fewer than six weeks. A hell of a coincidence.

She wondered if Charles and Seward had been threatened and harassed before the actual attacks, as Roche had been. She considered whether fire-setting was a connection between Charles and Roche. Fire worked on Charles, the first victim. Maybe the attacker thought it would work on Roche, too. But a house was harder to ignite than a van. When it didn't kill Roche, the attacker switched methods: gunshots for Roche, and when that proved so much tidier, the same for Davis, whom he'd mistaken for Seward.

She ran a search for all their names, but only came up with hits for Roche and Charles. Seward must not be notorious enough, she thought. She printed out the stories and began reading.

Roche had befriended a twelve-year-old boy—unnamed in the story because of his age and the crime—during a basketball game and wormed his way into the trust of the boy's single mother. Reading between the lines, Hannah imagined her: hardworking, loving, but overwhelmed by too many responsibilities and too little money. Freddy must have looked like a godsend. Roche bought the boy clothes and sports equipment. He took the boy along on youth-group camp-outs and on an excursion to a Lakers-Bulls game in Chicago—a special treat. They spent nearly every weekend together. Contrary to what Marian had said, the boy hadn't turned Roche in. Another child had.

During a camp-out, the boy's eleven-year-old tentmate realized that he was gone. It was the middle of the night, and he imagined that a bear got him. The friend went outside to look for him, heard strange noises coming from Roche's tent, and saw the boy leaving it a few minutes later. He was unsure what to do, but finally told the youth minister what he'd seen. From there, the matter went to the police. The victim finally, reluctantly, said Roche had been fondling him. Police found pictures of him in Roche's house. Roche pled no contest. Marian had neglected to mention that point, too.

Hannah turned to the stories on Henry Charles, nicknamed "Hank," which were a dozen years old. His victim was a five-year-old girl. Charles's wife, unnamed in the story, baby-sat her after school. Occasionally Hank would watch her when his wife went to the store. That was fine with the girl's family. Everyone liked Hank. Their quotes could have come from the story about Roche. He seemed to love children. He was good with children.

On some of those afternoons, though, Hank took the girl to his garage and used her sexually. It may have happened once or twice or a dozen times—there was no way to know with certainty. At first, the girl did not talk about what happened to her. But she spoke in other ways: bed-wetting and fits of rage in which she smashed dolls and tore flowers from her mother's garden. She had to be removed from school. She wouldn't go to her baby-sitter's house, and she refused to discuss the reasons. One day she saw Hank in the supermarket. She shrieked and fled into the parking lot, where she was clipped by a car. In the hospital, she haltingly mimed some of what Hank Charles did to her. Eventually she talked about it to the police.

Charles was arrested, entered a plea, and earned himself seven years in prison. It didn't seem long enough to Hannah. But the story hinted at the family's unwillingness to put their child through a trial. Hannah understood that, but wondered if something else had softened Charles's sentence. She put the stories in a file folder, went upstairs, and tried—with minimal success—to go back to sleep.

She got to the office early Friday morning and was rereading the story about the Davis shooting when she heard the rare sound of Vera's voice. It was high-pitched and anxious, vainly commanding someone to stop. Hannah watched as her door banged open, as though hit by a gale-force wind.

Marian Roche barreled into the office and planted a pair of bony hands on Hannah's desk. Her face was heavily made up, the eyebrows thickened with orange pencil. Her peach hair was freshly dyed and now was as vivid as a flame. She was wheezing with exertion. Hannah caught a whiff of scotch and wintergreen mints as the woman leaned into her face.

"You won't call me back," she said.

"Mrs. Roche, I was just—"

She shook a finger at Hannah. "You could have kept my boy from dying. You didn't, and I think you're a vicious harpy. You have an obligation to make this right. For Freddy."

Maybe not for Freddy, Hannah thought. But for Michael, in his memory? Perhaps. There was no need to tell Marian Roche about her dead brother, who apparently believed Freddy was worth saving. No need to talk about how she'd fallen short of Michael's St. Joan image of her, fierce in the service of the downtrodden and possessed of the power to see humanity in a pariah like Freddy. Instead, she just nodded at the old woman's demand. "I've been thinking that myself."

10

Vera appeared at the door then, her face poppy-scarlet. She seemed ready to drag the old woman out of Hannah's office, if so ordered. Hannah shook her head, and Vera, scowling, retreated. She hated it when people made her talk, let alone shout.

"Please sit down, Mrs. Roche." Hannah indicated her office's most comfortable chair. "Would you like some water? Coffee?"

"No." She lowered herself to the edge of the seat and glanced up at Hannah. She seemed disappointed that she wasn't going to get a fight. Her breathing was more measured now, and she slid off the black suede jacket she was wearing. Underneath, she had on a purple cashmere sweater and black trousers. The outfit clashed with her hair, but it indicated a youthful attitude that Hannah hoped she would have at eighty.

"You've read the papers?" Marian Roche asked.

Hannah nodded. "But they seem to have lost interest in your son's story."

"Vultures. All they want is a flashy headline a day. They don't care about Freddy. They won't even return my calls now."

"This is a matter for the police, anyway, not the press," Hannah said.

"The police will do nothing. You saw that yourself," she said. "I don't particularly care about the other two men who died. They might have deserved it, for all I know. But Freddy didn't."

"I'm sorry for your loss, Mrs. Roche." A phrase from Hannah's cop past, extending sympathy to the bereaved without actually mourning the dead.

She hooted at that. "Balderdash. If you really cared, you would have done something to stop it."

The old woman used verbiage that sounded as if it had been lifted from a Victorian melodrama. But maybe the stagy lines masked real hurt. Hannah decided not to defend herself.

"What do you want me to do?" Was she after a wrongful-death claim, naming the neighbors or the police? It would never succeed, Hannah thought.

But Mrs. Roche surprised her. "I want you to find out what the police really believe. Do they honestly think these are separate crimes? If they do, they're idiots. They'll never find out who did this if they think that way. I think what they've told the newspapers is just a smoke screen."

"Mrs. Roche, I'm not a private investigator. I could refer you to someone who—"

"No." She slammed a calcified hand on the desk. "You owe me this, Miss Barlow. You've admitted that you do. You can't subcontract your penance. Besides, I know your history. You're just the person to do this."

"My history?"

"You were a police officer. That's what you told Freddy. You know people. They'll talk to you—particularly knowing how you hate child molesters."

"That's it? Interview my old friends and see if they're doing a competent job?"

"I also want you to look into Freddy's death yourself. The police have done a poor job of it. That man in the paper who said the killer should get a medal? You should start with him."

"Dick Barker?"

She nodded. "He's in this, no matter what he says. He and his harridan wife drove Freddy out of his house. And have the police ever had a chat with him? I doubt it, because he's one of them. I intend to pay you, of course. Freddy was going to."

Hannah wasn't sure she could do Mrs. Roche's formidable bidding. The woman would demand nothing less than a serial killer—preferably Dick Barker—served up on a platter with mint leaves and an apple. Hannah didn't think she'd be happy if the truth turned out to be something other than what she had in mind.

But was Marian really in charge here? She was beginning to think not. It was Michael who had sent Freddy Roche to her. She'd shirked the responsibility once, and as a result, Freddy's life was no longer in her hands. But now his death seemed to be. Michael had saddled her with a soul debt. Marian had just been sent to collect on it.

Marian Roche squinted maliciously at her when she didn't respond right away. "Freddy might not haunt you, but I'm not long for this world, and I will. Count on it. And I won't be nearly as polite or quiet as my son."

Hannah suppressed a smile. It wasn't hard to imagine Marian as a nagging shade. "Let me talk this over with my partner. He'll be back Monday."

"I would expect regular reports from you, well before I get your bills, which I am sure will be well-padded."

Before Hannah could respond to that insult, the old woman hoisted herself out of the chair. "You should get rid of that secretary," she said. "She's shrill and impertinent. I know a very good girl who needs a job. I'll have her call you."

Turning on her heel, she was gone.

11

The first old friend Hannah called was a Las Almas homicide detective, Ivan Churnin. Over the course of several years, she had helped Churnin on cases, building assets in their goodwill and reciprocity account. On Sunday night, as she parked in the lot of a Lakewood sushi restaurant and saw Churnin's Volvo station wagon, she took a deep breath. Unlike an actual bank, this goodwill transaction was not a sure thing. Their personal history complicated it.

A year before, when Churnin's marriage was ending, he'd taken on the desperate attitude of an inept trapeze performer. He'd lost his grasp on a relationship, and in free fall, he was clawing for a woman to grab onto. It was Hannah who'd swung into his path. But she'd already made one mistake, with Mike Feuer, and she was determined not to let herself be compromised again. She pulled back from Churnin's reach. She liked him, but not enough to pluck him out of midair.

Apparently another woman appeared to soften the fall. In the courthouse—a stewpot of gossip for lawyers, cops, and judges—Hannah had heard that Ivan Churnin had quit binging on bourbon. He was entering ten-kilometer runs and turning in decent times for a relatively sedentary man in his late forties. He was dating a thirtyish bookkeeper who liked her men bald and armed. Churnin fit her bill. And, mirabile dictu, she had convinced him to moderate his strict vegan diet.

Hearing that Churnin was coupled again, Hannah thought she could risk a withdrawal. She caught him at his postdivorce apartment, and although he was panting from his evening run, he sounded pleasant enough when she asked if they could meet to talk a little business.

"You want to give me a sneak preview?"

"Freddy Roche," she said.

"Freddie's dead." He sang it as Curtis Mayfield's lyric. Churnin had seen *Superfly* at least seven times.

"I know," Hannah said. "Freddy's mama is not happy about it."

He wouldn't meet her at his office, her office, or anywhere in Orange County. Instead, he told Hannah he'd see her Sunday night at Tokyo Hibachi. "My girlfriend digs the place."

"Get your lingo right. Your chick digs it," Hannah said. Churnin chuckled and hung up.

As Hannah passed his car, she saw a suit bag hanging in the back, doubtless containing his Monday work clothes. She figured it would be no more than two months before Churnin and the bookkeeper were working out of the same medicine chest. She went inside and saw him at the sushi bar, sipping an Asahi.

Churnin's bald head seemed to glow, a beacon of his new vitality. He was thinner, more relaxed in his body. He wore Ralph Lauren jeans and a knit sport shirt that showed off his runner's tan. He waved her over and rose. She leaned in for a kiss on the cheek, which is what he would have given her the year before. He deftly intercepted with a handshake, and Hannah wondered if that meant trouble.

She settled onto a tall stool and asked for a sake. "You're not mad that this isn't a purely social outing?"

"Hell, Hannah, if it wasn't for death and mayhem, you wouldn't call me at all." He smiled. Christ, she thought, he's had his teeth whitened. "But, since I'm getting a great lay elsewhere, I won't hold that against you."

She laughed. "A great lay? What a romantic you are."

He put on a somber voice. "The great lay is practically a sacrament to me, and you shouldn't mock it. I hear I'm not the only one who could use some sexual healing."

She didn't rise to his bait. She wondered who had been spilling the details of her private life to Churnin. It probably came from the same courthouse tureen that had served her gossip about him.

"You've heard of sexual healing, haven't you?" He wasn't giving up.

"Sure. I have a Marvin Gaye album."

"Right, Hannah. Go ahead and mask your deprivation with quips."

The lack of sex, along with the absence of every other kind of touch, was indeed beginning to make her feel empty and needy. But the last thing she wanted to do was talk about that with Churnin. Her silence worked.

"Sorry," he said. "I didn't mean to make light of it. Guillermo, I mean. . . ."

Quips she could handle. Pity was something else. She interrupted him as smoothly as she could by greeting the sushi chef. "How about some tuna sashimi and a Long Beach roll?"

Churnin belched contentedly and smiled. He poured her a beer. "Here's to Freddy Roche. R.I.P."

"What about Cotter Davis? And Henry Charles?"

Churnin sipped his beer. "Oh, I get it. This is Marian Roche's trinity theory. Say, do you like *uni*?"

"Sea urchin? Never had it." It was graduate-level sushi and probably the price of getting Churnin to talk about the cases. "But I'll try it."

"Good." He called for two orders. Hannah wondered if he'd refuse to tell her anything if she couldn't choke the stuff down.

The sushi chef presented her with a two-piece serving: rice on the bottom, sidewalls of crisp seaweed wrapper, and layers of brilliant orange sea-urchin roe. They had the shape and spongy texture of a cat's tongue. Hannah bit into her first piece. It had a sweet, nutty taste.

"Tastes good," she said.

"It's the little critter's sex organs, you know." Churnin gave her a satyric grin.

"Now I like it even better."

Churnin patted her on the back. "That's the Hannah I love. So you're working for Mrs. Roche now."

Hannah nodded. "She doesn't think you're taking Freddy's murder seriously. Not you personally, but Las Almas P.D."

"What do you think?"

Hannah shrugged. "Well, the Deep Throat cops were pretty quick to tell the *Times* that there was no connection between Freddy Roche and the other two attacks. What do you think?"

Churnin turned coy. "I'm not on the case."

"I didn't think so. We wouldn't be sitting here if you were."

"True enough." He caught the chef's attention. "Do you have *mirugai* tonight?"

Hannah knew what that was: giant clam. Unsliced, it looked like a king-sized phallus.

"You have sex on the brain," Hannah said.

"That's not the only place I'm having it. Want to try this?" He held out a piece of *mirugai*. Hannah bit into it. It was crunchy, with the fresh taste of salt and ocean.

"Excellent."

"Two for two. Now what do you want to know about Freddy?"

"I just want an idea of whether the departments are looking at three unrelated attacks or three pieces of the same puzzle. If Mrs. Roche knew the investigators were putting out the no-connection story so they could quietly work the cases as one, she would settle down."

"Ha. She'd blab like hell."

"I could get her to be quiet, for the investigation's sake. She's a little addled right now, but I think she sincerely feels that Freddy's getting short shrift."

"You can't tell anyone we talked about this."

"Fine. So is this three investigations, or one?"

"It's . . . God knows what it is. First off, there's the jurisdictional problem: three crimes, three different cities. Santa Ana, Gardena, Las Almas."

"Who's taking the lead?"

"Las Almas. Two of the victims lived there. So did the suspect they've got in custody. Problem number two: the victims are demonstrable scum. These are not grannies, preachers, and valedictorians."

"That's not supposed to make a difference."

Churnin shook his head, disappointed at her display of uncharacteristic naivete. "Hannah, please. You've got dozens of cases. You prioritize. Druggie kills high-school teacher? Top of the pile. Druggie kills druggie? Right down there at the bottom. This is one of those: a misdemeanor murder. If Davis hadn't been linked with the kiddie-porn thing, it might have been different. Understand?"

She nodded. He'd looked like a "good" victim at first. But

now, because of an anonymous phone call and some singed pictures, he had become another unmourned piece of crap.

"Everybody knows what the score is, but they can't talk about it," Churnin said. "You can't even kid about it. Over a beer, one of the guys said he wasn't too hopped up about burned-up, shot-up kiddie diddlers. The only good ped was a dead ped."

"Catchy."

"Yeah, well, that refrain got back to the detective chief. So the glib guy is off the case, posthaste."

"And only the hardworking pure-of-heart remain on it?"

"They are working, Hannah, don't get me wrong. But I think there are some guys on the team who think he was absolutely right: let the human waste products get themselves flushed. Many other cases will be cleared before these three. That's my prediction."

"So nobody but Mrs. Roche thinks they're connected?"

"Oh, no. Everybody thought there might be a connection. It made sense. The Chester Molester CD-ROM is out a few months. People are all steamed up about these guys living in their neighborhoods. Every department in the state worries about vigilantes. And then, three weeks apart, there's Henry Charles fried and Freddy Roche shot. Three more weeks and Davis is dead. It looked weird. But the guys on the team weren't able to put the three together."

"Because Roche was the only molester on the CD-ROM?"

"Well, Seward was on it. But he's not dead," Churnin said.

"But someone could have been stalking Seward and mistook Davis for him. Davis was driving Seward's car, right?"

"Yes, but it still doesn't work."

"Why not?"

"Seward's picture was on the CD-ROM. Davis didn't look anything like him. Davis was ten years older, shorter, thinner. Plus, we talked to everyone who came to the Las Almas P.D. to look at the CD-ROM."

"They have to sign a log to view it, right? And fill out a form?"

Churnin nodded. "We interviewed them all—not that there were that many, maybe four or five a month since the first CD came out. There's no indication that any of them are involved in killing people. The other departments did the same thing."

"Did you talk to Dick Barker?"

"Freddy's neighbor? Yeah, we talked to him. Used to be with the L.A. County Sheriff's Department. A little bit of an asshole, but I can't see him taking parolees out."

"The CD-ROM couldn't have led anyone to Charles anyway."

"Right. He blew off his sex-offender registration years ago."

"So his being a molester had nothing to do with what happened to him?"

"I don't think so."

"He just pulled his van over near a playground because he was tired? Come on."

"I'm not saying he wasn't on the prowl. Santa Ana cops say the park's full of little kids during the day. But it changes after dark into creepazoid city, and he didn't know that. Between the gangs and the crackheads, vacationers are not welcome."

She thought for a moment. How else were these three men connected? "Is there any hint at all, other than from your informant, that Davis was actually a molester?"

"Nothing concrete. He hasn't got a criminal record, other than a drunken-driving charge. We talked to his wife. She says she never saw any telltale signs of pedophilia, but she said he was a real S.O.B. when he drank. Real Jekyll-Hyde type. And he was a kiddie photographer. At Sears, Kmart. Places like that."

"Does that instantly make him a molester?"

"No. But we found those Polaroids, or what was left of them. We don't know who shot them. It could have been Davis. We finally got some images off Seward's computer. Little boys in bathing trunks at the beach. Somebody using a telephoto lens."

"Cameras are easy to use these days. It doesn't take an expert."

"I know. It could have been Davis or Seward. Or somebody else shot them and sent them over the Internet."

"So all you really have are your informant's aspersions."

"He said things were getting nasty between Davis and Seward. Fights about money, fights about trust. It sounds possible. The neighbors didn't hear anything, but that doesn't mean squat. People there hold to the 'rat not, lest ye be ratted' ethic."

She nodded. "Any idea who this informant is?"

"Nope," Churnin said. "Called once, spilled this stuff, hung up. Hasn't called again."

They ate in silence for a few minutes. Hannah was mulling what she'd read in the newspapers. "There's something that wasn't in the *Times* story. The cop sources didn't mention any ballistics tests. Was the same gun used in both shootings?"

He smiled at her. "You're very good, you know?" He was getting drunk. She ordered tea for both of them, not wanting to be responsible for sending Churnin home tipsy. Girlfriends didn't dig that.

"I know," she said. "What about the guns?"

"They're still working on that. Freddy got lead bullets to the head and chest. All that bone, the bullets bounce around, so they're pretty mangled up. I'm not sure they'll be able to match either of them to a weapon."

"So somebody used a revolver?" A lead bullet was most commonly the ammunition for that sort of gun.

"Yup, probably," Churnin said.

"And what about Davis?"

"The bullet we got out of him was fully jacketed."

With its harder layer, it would have remained mostly intact, Hannah knew. Jacketed ammo was most often used in semi-automatic pistols, though there were jacketed revolver cartridges, too. "So it was a different shooter," Hannah said. "Or was it the same guy, changing ammo, changing guns?"

He shrugged. "Something like that. But guess what they found in the Oriental Dream parking lot?"

Hannah felt like a rookie investigator being quizzed by a grizzled partner. She remembered nights and days in the field, and that memory shook loose the answer. "A cartridge case?"

"Yes indeed. Very good."

Hannah knew that meant that Davis's shooter had used a semiautomatic pistol. With a revolver, the case stayed in the weapon after firing. But a pistol expelled the case.

"It doesn't really help that much," she said. "You don't know if it was one guy with two guns, or two different shooters."

"Right. There was something else about the cartridge case, though."

Hannah got the hint. Shooters were careful to wipe down the guns they used. But sometimes they forgot about the prints they left when they loaded the weapons.

"There was a print on it," she said. "But it wasn't Seward's."

Churnin gave her a nod for able deduction. "If it had been Seward's, our chatty cop would have told the *Times* about it."

"Do you know whose print it is?"

"No. It's inconclusive," Churnin said.

"Any weapons at Seward's house?"

"Not a one that we could find."

They ate in silence for a few minutes: more mirugai, some yellowtail tuna. Hannah refused to try *natto*, the fermented soybean paste that Churnin swore was a delicacy. The stuff looked like mucus. Finally Churnin gave a contented sigh and asked, in Japanese, for the check. He turned to Hannah.

"Any last questions?"

"Who prosecuted Freddy's molestation case?"

Churnin smiled. "I knew you'd want to go there, so I looked it up for you. A lovely hard-boiled gal named Cassandra Thrasher. She's a criminal defense attorney now."

"You think she'll remember the case?"

"Cassandra remembers everything. Anything else?"

"If this was your investigation, what would you do?"

"I'd try to keep an open mind," he said. "I'd look hard at Seward—he might be somebody's fall guy. And I'd talk to Freddy's former neighbors."

"Barker?"

"And the others."

"What else?"

"I'd hope that Henry Charles got well enough to tell me what happened that night. And I'd try not to let my pride yank me around."

"What do you mean?"

"I wouldn't let Marian Roche or the newspapers get me riled. Some of the guys are pissed off about being called incompetents, conspirators, and zealots. Nice word, zealot. Tell Marian it makes her sound very biblical."

"I will. And what happens when the guys are pissed off?"

"They dig in their heels. They want to prove that Marian Roche and the media are full of crap. So far, the evidence is going their way. At first, they saw three crimes with what looked like the same violent pattern woven into them. But they're good cops. More work told them that there was nothing there. Not all red fabric comes from the same loom, you know."

"Japanese saying?"

"No. I made it up."

"But what if they're missing something? What if there are patterns they haven't seen yet?"

"Well, the guys on the case are not going to be anxious to acknowledge them now. It would make them look like idiots."

"Even more 'obdurately fatuous.'"

"This is my point: some of the guys have to use a dictionary to find out just how much Marian Roche is insulting them. It makes them downright sulky."

12

It was after eleven when Hannah got home from dinner with Churnin. A light rain spattered the Integra's windshield as she pulled into the driveway. The house had a garage, but the rickety wooden structure was barely wide enough to accommodate the 1982 Chrysler LeBaron that Hannah had inherited, along with the house, from Mrs. Snow, her longtime landlady. To Hannah the garage looked to be on the verge of collapse, so she didn't park there. She ventured inside it once a month or so to make sure the LeBaron would start. Bobby's nephew had expressed an interest in buying it, but it would be a year before he even had a learner's permit. Hannah took pity on him and agreed not to sell it before he could make an offer.

In the living room, she thumbed through the mail and checked the answering machine. One message. In her Texas-tinged voice, Connie Westerland said she was just calling to say hello. It was her night off, and Ed, her no-longer-estranged husband, was coming up to Vancouver from Seattle that weekend. That got her thinking about Hannah, who must be wondering how a certain little boy was doing. Hannah had wondered, but cut the thought short every time. It hurt less when she didn't think about him.

"Well, Matthew's just fine, cute as can be," Connie said. "He's talking a blue streak lately, though we don't always know what he's saying."

Hannah smiled at the thought of it and felt the tightness in her chest. *Don't cry,* she thought. *Just stop it. Baby talk is not a reason for tears.*

Connie chattered on. "He seems to love the rain, which is good, because we've got plenty of it here. Martin and his wife said to tell you hello. They've got plenty of room if you want to visit. I hope everything's fine with you and Guillermo, and if you two want a vacation, you can . . ."

Hannah stopped the message and erased it. She didn't want to think about explaining the breakup to Connie, Martin, or anyone else. She looked around the living room, which needed dusting but was otherwise unnaturally neat. Hannah had been used to seeing Guillermo's law books, Matthew's toys, and Connie's half-finished crochet projects scattered around the room. Such clutter reminded Hannah that she was a part of a family. Now its absence made her feel empty.

She went into the kitchen and got the dust cloth. There wasn't any excuse for dirt—it wasn't a memento of anyone she cared about. She started on the coffee table, moved to the bookcase, and then to the Limbert server, which sat under a window that overlooked the driveway and side yard. She shifted the lamp, a Rookwood vase, and three novels she'd started and put aside. She glanced up as she dusted. Reflected in the window was a woman who looked tired, whose cheekbones were more prominent than ever. In three-quarter view, she looked like her mother, thin and overtired.

Then, out of the corner of her eye, she saw a ripple move through the middle of the thick, untrimmed camellia bushes that bordered the driveway. None of the other greenery rustled, so it wasn't the wind. The neighborhood had its share of cats, as well as other wildlife: Hannah had seen more than one opossum lumbering through her backyard. But even in the darkness, she thought she'd seen color among the leaves—something more vivid than an animal's fur.

She turned on the porch light and stepped outside. The rain had stopped, although clouds still hung low in the sky. A breeze blew up and died. Hannah turned off the light and closed the front door. She sat down on the top step.

After a few moments, Hannah heard the camellia's stiff leaves rattle. She peered around the corner of the porch and saw a figure emerge from the bushes. Off came a floppy crocheted beret, and although long bangs obscured a small face, Hannah thought she knew who this was: the girl she'd mistaken for a boy, last seen in the Plaza a month ago.

It was clear that she thought Hannah had gone back inside. She shivered from her shoulders down, shaking off the rain as a dog would. Huge jeans flopped around her feet. A black Raiders jacket hung to the middle of her thighs. She put the beret back on her head and sauntered up the street.

Hannah strolled after her, hands in her front pockets, as if this was her late evening constitutional, too. The girl didn't look back, but must have sensed someone following her. She broke into a hard run. Hannah took off after her.

The girl cut a nimble corner across a lawn and ducked under the thin, low branches of a weeping juniper. Hannah almost got her throat clipped as she followed. The girl didn't slow, but she did look back. The shift put her off balance. Hannah watched as her foot slid, probably in a patch of mud. She recovered, but it slowed her. Hannah sprinted then, and as she closed, she grabbed at the girl's black jacket. Gotcha, Hannah thought.

For a moment, she was right. She twisted a handful of fabric, jerking the girl toward her. But with two quick shrugs, the girl shed the coat and pounded away, rounded a corner, and disappeared into the park's green-tinged darkness.

Hannah's heart felt like a jackhammer, but she kept running, balling the jacket under her arm. There was something in the pocket: something round, but yielding, like a tired tennis ball. Hannah saw that the girl had paused at the far end of the park. In the bright lights of the basketball court, Hannah saw her talking to a man. He held the leash of a lean, hard-muscled mongrel.

The girl turned and saw Hannah. She grabbed onto the man's arm and screamed, long and shrill. The man's head snapped in Hannah's direction. The kid swung the man's arm pleadingly and then ran.

She'd done something shrewd. She must have told the man a tale that cast Hannah as her drunken, abusive mother. She pleaded for protection: oh mister, she'll hit me for sure. Hannah would never get past him without having to stop and explain. Detouring around the park meant minutes lost. Either way, Hannah figured she'd never catch the girl now. She turned and walked home.

She collapsed on the sofa and unbundled the jacket, which seemed big enough for the girl to use as a tent. In the left side pocket, Hannah found a packet of grape bubblegum and half a package of Marlboros. Despite the efforts of the boy Hannah had seen taking the girl's cigarette, her habit obviously continued. There was a scorch mark on the jacket's cuff. See, Hannah imagined telling the girl, it's a dangerous habit.

Hannah dug into the right pocket and extracted a stuffed animal—more exactly, its disincorporated head, which looked ready to be mounted as a tiny wall trophy. One plastic eye was gone. The other was dulled by age and hard play. There were only a few patches of plush left, and they were so dirty that Hannah could only guess at the original color. A golden tan, maybe. Dark, longer fuzz and two pits marked where the ears had been sewn in. Only black threads were left to show the former location of the mouth. Foam stuffing dripped from its throat. A plaything in extremis.

If Hannah hadn't seen it before, in a place and time she could never forget, she couldn't have said what the animal had been. But she knew what she held. A lion. For a moment, Hannah was back in the interview room. She could smell the burned coffee, hear the phones in reception bleating insistently. She could feel the sting of static electricity—a discharge of the room's tension—as she slid into a chair made for a first grader. She looked across the tiny table, into the girl's hazel eyes. They seemed far away, shadowed by her understanding of what she had lost and her fear of the losses still to come. Hannah knew how she felt: in the turmoil of the Barlow house, she had been that child.

Now Hannah realized her breathing had gone shallow. The room felt stifling. She lurched outside, where the rain had started again. She sat down on the porch and looked at the ragged toy trembling in her fingers. She took a steadying breath and whispered into the darkness.

"Janie?" She felt she could have added, "Come forth."

13

Bobby came back from Florida on Monday morning, nursing a head cold and needing a law-free day. He promised himself he could have it once he checked in at the office. Then he'd stop at the store, buy some bottles of good cabernet and a few pounds of oxtails. Then he would tackle the recipe he clipped from *Gourmet*. Garlic mashed potatoes would be perfect with it. If it was any good, he'd put it into the regular menu rotation for guests. Just thinking about the meal made him feel better.

Vera was on the phone when he came in. He waved, smiled, and pointed to Hannah's door—was she in? Vera scowled and tapped away on the keys.

The message was waiting on the screen in his office: *She's here, but something's wrong. You might want to try talking to her.*

Bobby thought he knew what it was. Hannah had tried to make it seem that she was coping with Matthew's departure and Guillermo's incredibly ill-timed, self-absorbed vanishing act. Bobby had attempted to talk to her about it, but Hannah said she didn't want to dwell on a moribund relationship. She didn't want to drag her personal problems into the office. Now, he guessed, the dam had cracked. He was relieved, in a way. He wanted Hannah to confide in him and told her that soon after Guillermo had moved out.

"We're not just business partners, Hannah. If something is making your life miserable, I want to know." He smiled reassuringly. "I'll know anyway."

She shook her head. "You shouldn't. Not if I'm doing my job right."

He didn't understand that thinking, but he didn't push her. He'd known her long enough to understand that Hannah sometimes dropped a curtain over parts of her life. Before they were business partners, they were friends. They talked freely about school, relationships, and families. But Hannah would only go so far with some things—her mother's pathetic, drunken death, which had apparently come after a fight with Hannah, for instance. And the last case she'd worked as a detective with the Las Almas P.D. That was also taboo, Bobby discovered. Those two topics shut her up tighter than a Kumamoto oyster.

She was on the phone when he came into her office. She motioned for him to sit down and continued talking. "Right. She would be eleven. That's sixth grade, but she might be in fifth. Might have missed some class time. Okay, I'll hold."

She looked up at Bobby and smiled. He had always thought her beautiful. Not in some supermodel way—she was too quirky and unself-conscious for that. Her beauty came from the contrast of pale skin with red hair, a sharp nose played off against a gentle mouth. More than that, it was the presence behind those features: intelligence, humor, and a carefully guarded vulnerability. Bobby had once been sorry he'd never been able to coax Hannah into bed. Now he thought their lack of sexual entanglement was a good thing. Their friendship had survived longer than a romantic relationship would have.

Today, Hannah looked too pale. Her freckles stood out more prominently than usually. Her cinnamon-dark, curly hair— Hannah's most wonderful feature, it seemed to Bobby—had been severely tamed—pushed off her face and pulled into a braid. She seldom wore a lot of makeup, but she seemed to be without it altogether today. She looked weary. Bobby knew she'd been fighting insomnia. He wanted to smack Guillermo. He'd thought about calling and telling him off, but he knew Hannah would never forgive him for meddling.

"You look tired," he said, as the hold on her call continued.

She nodded. "Stayed up too late."

"Hannah, have you thought about maybe seeing a doc—"

She held up a finger. Whoever she was talking to was back on the line. "Right. Jane or Janie Meister. Nothing? Okay.

Thanks." She hung up. "I can't believe how many school districts there are in Orange County."

Bobby stared at her for a minute. "Janie Meister?"

"I saw her, Bobby." Hannah's blue-green eyes seemed lit by fever. "I touched her and got this from her." She held up what looked like a rotting baseball patched with fake fur.

"What the hell is that?"

"This is Janie's stuffed lion, or what's left of it. She was inseparable from it. Still is, apparently. She's been hanging around my house. Last night, I ran after her. Nearly caught her, too. But she left me holding her jacket. This was in the pocket."

For a moment, Bobby couldn't think of what to say. "But you told me she was dead."

Hannah nodded thoughtfully. "I thought she was. As far as the world's concerned, she still is. I can't find any trace of her. No contacts with the police, nothing in social services or the school districts—so far."

"But they found her body."

Hannah frowned at him. "No, that's not right. They found the remains of a girl, between the ages of four and six. She and Janie had similar physical characteristics—height, hair color—but there was never confirmation it was her. The case is still open. I checked this morning."

"That means they still don't know it *wasn't* her, right?"

She shook her head, exasperated at his persistence. "Bobby, I saw her. You saw her, too."

"I did? When?"

"The morning we heard about Freddy Roche being killed, and I stormed out on you. She was there in the Plaza, with a bunch of other kids. Light brown hair, crocheted beret, carrying a skateboard. She was smoking a cigarette."

Bobby cautiously shook his head. "The only girl I saw smoking was a junior vixen with red lipstick and a bad attitude."

"That explains why you didn't notice." It didn't exactly sound like a joke to Bobby, but he smiled anyway. "It wasn't the first time I saw her," Hannah said. "At first, I thought she was a boy. She was across the street from my house. She's been *watching* me."

Hannah stared at him, daring him to explain that away.

Bobby broached the question gingerly. "When you last saw Janie, how old was she?"

"Five. She's eleven now."

"And this girl you saw, everything about her matches up to Janie?"

Hannah pondered that for a moment. "No. Not exactly. Her hair is lighter, and it's always in her face. She's tall for her age. But . . ."

"So this could be another girl. Someone who reminds you of Janie and had this thing in her pocket."

"No, that's not it."

"Have you talked to her?"

"I told you, she ran away."

Bobby nodded. "Why did she do that?"

Hannah stared at him for a few seconds and then looked away. "I'm not sure."

"I mean, you were someone Janie trusted. You believed her, and you tried—"

"Stop it." Her voice was harsh, and it caught Bobby by surprise.

"I just mean that Janie would have—"

"You don't know what you're talking about, Bobby. You weren't there six years ago, and you don't know what happened."

"Hannah, I'm just trying to give you another point of view."

"No. You're trying to tell me it's not her. Well, no one was more convinced than I was that Janie Meister was dead. I believed it, and I carried that death around with me for a long time. I wouldn't have believed it if someone had told me Janie was alive. But I saw her."

"And you instantly recognized her?"

Hannah shook her head and sighed. "I said she's changed. But this told me." She shook the stuffed-animal head at him as if it was some kind of fetish. He tried to take it, but she tugged it away.

"You *know* it was Janie because of a ratty chunk of stuffing?"

Hannah's lips tightened. He didn't know. He hadn't been in that room when Janie held the lion around the throat and middle, squeezing tight. The toy was an anchor in a world that was flying apart, threatening to carry her away. She could still see that patches of the lion's fur were matted by the girl's tears.

Hannah had used the toy as an opening, a way to connect with the huddled child. She whispered that lions were brave and strong. Weren't they? The girl nodded, almost involuntarily, as if it was a relief not to be asked the when, the where, and the tell us again what he did. Brave lions were a safe topic for her.

Hannah had stayed with it for a while, until finally the girl brought her face up out of the toy's soft comfort. She was pale beneath the red mottling on her face. Her expression asked if Hannah could make it all go away, awaken her from this bad dream, untie this knot. Hannah thought then, and a thousand times after, that she would have given anything to have that power: the ability to undo what had been done to her. Instead, it only got worse. Janie's journey was hard on the scruffy lion. It had lost vital parts. Had they dropped off? Or had someone ripped them away, taking away the legs that ran, the tail that twitched with anger, the chest that filled with the thunderous roar, until there was only the head—the place of memories? Whatever had happened, it was clear that the lion was a talisman, something that still held power for her. Otherwise Janie wouldn't have kept it. Hannah wondered if she would try to get it back.

The night before, Hannah had been afraid of letting herself understand who had run from her. Acknowledging that changed everything. Past seeped into present. Guilt thawed. The dead rose.

So she had tried other explanations for the toy's existence. It wasn't the same lion. There must have been thousands like the one Janie had. Maybe it was left behind at Orangewood and given to another child. Or someone had found it in an abandoned car, or in a house, or on the beach, long after a little girl's face was pressed down into the waves and held until she—

"Hannah?" Bobby was looking at her as though she should be hooked up to a Valium drip.

"Look, I put myself through all this already," Hannah said. "And the only thing that makes sense is that Janie didn't die, as everyone assumed she did. She's alive, and she's come back to

Las Almas from wherever she was. She's hovering around, trying to decide whether or not to approach me."

"Why is she so hesitant?"

Hannah rubbed her eyes. She's on the verge of tears, Bobby thought, but she won't let me see. He felt helpless in the face of her distress.

"I let her down once," Hannah said in a faltering voice. "I think she's afraid I'll do it again."

14

After that conversation, Hannah stopped talking to Bobby about the girl. For the rest of that week, she came into the office early and stayed late, behind her closed door. Any time he stopped by to say hello, she seemed to be hard at work. He didn't resort to asking Vera if she was turning in time sheets. That seemed like spying. Vera, sensing the tension between the partners, sent Bobby daily briefings on Hannah's mood. They read like storm warnings. "Calmer today." Or, "A little rough this morning, but I think it will blow over by afternoon."

A few days after their talk about Janie, he tried asking if she'd made any progress in finding her. She leveled him a look that said, "Don't dare broach this topic with me." He went into his office and brooded.

That continued into the weekend. He felt that his friend was slipping away from him, turning into someone else. The past had reached up and seized her, and he didn't understand why it was happening.

He'd heard only the briefest bits of the Janie Meister story from Hannah herself. Other pieces came from Ivan Churnin. Bobby had encountered him at a party thrown by a law-school friend who had joined the DA's office. Even Churnin's information wasn't firsthand, since he had come to Las Almas P.D. after Hannah's resignation. But on his third glass of Booker's, he shared what he'd heard.

"That kid's disappearance just about drove her crazy," Churnin said. "She ripped up a lieutenant's office, wailing like

a banshee that the girl was as good as dead. Acted like a real
head case. But she was right, I guess. The kid turned up dead.
And then she decided that it was her fault."

"Why?"

"She had a bad feeling about the family. She felt like she
should have done more with her intuition." Churnin shrugged.
"Maybe she should have. Maybe we all should do more, but
you've got to draw the line, or you go nuts."

On Sunday morning, Bobby called Hannah at home, pretending to need her help on a brief. But he got the answering
machine and hung up without leaving a message. He wondered
if he should just stay out of it. Maybe he should let Hannah
work through it. She would dig around, find out that the kid
wasn't Janie, and it would be over.

Wouldn't it? Maybe it wouldn't be that simple. Why was
Hannah fixated on the idea of Janie, anyway? He thought about
it while he got dressed and went outside to see how his new
dwarf lemon trees were faring.

The previous fall, Bobby had bought a house a couple of
miles away from Hannah's home. His place was a two-
bedroom in the Spanish style, not very different from the
duplex he'd rented in law school. The major improvement was
the area. In his old neighborhood, Bobby could count on a
gang-related shooting in his area at least once a month.
Hookers hung out at the mini-mart, talking shop while they
bought their lottery tickets and teasingly offered Bobby their
services—with frequent blow job bonuses. Bobby's car was
deprived of its radio and rims. Once, someone who could only
have been a desperate crankhead had stolen the law books out
of his trunk.

Now he lived a block away from Las Almas's mayor, who
had decided to plant herself in a gentrifying district called El
Cielo—heaven. It was still a name of wishful thinking, but Her
Honor's presence insured heavy police-car patrols. Bobby felt
safe for the first time in years. He loved being able to go into
his yard without carrying a golf club as protection. The only
war waged these days was against the snails in his planters.

He plucked half a dozen slimy creatures from the ground
around the lemon trees and thought of the changes he'd seen in
Hannah. She was anxious and short-tempered. Some mornings,

she looked as if she'd cried half the night and stared into the maw of darkness the other half.

But he knew why it was happening. In the span of a few months, Hannah had lost a baby she had come to love as well as Guillermo, the insensitive jerk. Not so long before that, her brother had died before her eyes. Her father's remarriage had pulled apart his already fragile relationship with Hannah. Bobby had read that you could assign points to those kinds of stresses. Go above a certain number and you were almost guaranteed emotional problems. Hannah, he thought, had probably crossed into nervous-breakdown territory after all that.

And then she sees this kid who reminds her of another lost person—Janie. The kid materializes near the office, at Hannah's house, like some kind of apparition. Hannah must have felt haunted. But she managed to turn it around. It would be tempting to imagine that you'd been given a second chance with someone you thought you'd irretrievably lost. If Hannah thought she could bring Janie back from the dead, why couldn't she regain Matthew, or her father, or Guillermo? Why not Michael, for that matter? All the abandonments undone, all the dead and lost recalled, restored. He wondered what Hannah would do, once she understood this girl wasn't Janie Meister. That she couldn't be.

He went inside and brewed a pot of coffee. Without letting himself think too much about the repercussions, he got out the local phone books. He knew Hannah's old detective partner at Las Almas P.D. was named Eddy. Something Eddy, not Eddy something. Eddy had retired a couple of years before. He was married to a woman with a weird name. Gudrun. That was it. But what was Eddy's first name? He ran his finger down the column of names, hoping one of the listings would jar his memory. And there it was: Devlin Eddy, with a Garden Grove phone number. Bobby wrote it down and stared at it for a long time before dialing the phone, imagining Hannah's face if she found out what he was doing.

Following Eddy's directions, he came to a cul-de-sac off Magnolia Street. The air hummed with the sound of the freeway. This was another seesaw neighborhood. Swinging low, Bobby thought. A remodeled house with a slightly garish, defiantly bubbling cherub fountain faced off with a near-shack that looked like an outlaw motorcycle gang's headquarters, complete with a decrepit sofa on the front lawn.

Bobby had assumed that former cops moved into well-patrolled, criminal-free communities. This could not be mistaken for such a development. The house next door to Eddy's looked like it was being scavenged, piece by piece. The door had disappeared. The windows were missing various essential components—glass, for example.

Eddy's own house was less disastrous. It was small, with a long, front porch, and lay deep in the shade of thick-leafed, towering avocado trees. The perimeter of the lawn was densely planted with flowering bushes. The voracious yard seemed to be gaining on a defenseless home.

A man sat on a folding lawn chair in the driveway, which was barred by a rolling chain-link gate. He smoked a thin, brown cigarette and read a magazine with a mostly naked woman on the cover. He put the magazine down and pushed back the gate when he saw Bobby getting out of the car.

He didn't look like Bobby's version of a retired cop. He was certainly nothing like Jimmy, Hannah's father. No bristle cut, no khakis, no well-defined muscles from a rigorous workout regime. Instead, Eddy looked as if he might have been a pledge for the biker fraternity down the street. His long, thin auburn hair was tied with a bandanna. He wore holey jeans and an aging denim work shirt with traces of embroidery. Sleazy Rider, Bobby thought. Coming closer, he was relieved to find that Eddy did not smell of booze or pot or a lack of personal hygiene. He did, however, reek of cigarettes.

Eddy extended his hand—clean, with short nails that appeared to be free of embedded dirt—and offered coffee, which Bobby declined. Eddy stared at him for a moment, sizing him up.

Bobby was used to that—people mentally putting a scale under his feet, a tape measure around his middle, wondering, "Jeez, how do you get to be that big?" Bobby wondered that himself sometimes.

Finally Eddy spoke. "You're still whipping up gourmet food for Hannah?"

"Occasionally." Bobby smiled. Eddy didn't quite smile back.

"I haven't talked to Hannah in, Christ, it's got to be more than a year now. She okay?"

Bobby shook his head. "Not really. That's why I'm here. I need to hear about that last case she worked on."

"Okay. But tell me something first. You do all that cooking because you think that's gonna get you in bed with her?"

Bobby suddenly felt he was back in high school, where he once underwent a harrowingly frank parental interrogation while his date finished curling her lashes. Lies didn't work then, but there was no reason to be coy now.

"I did hope so for a while, when we were in law school. I struck out."

Eddy nodded. "Yeah. I bet it's tough to get women when you're as big as a Frigidaire."

How novel, Bobby thought. An appliance joke. There wasn't one he hadn't heard. "You hungry?"

It caught Eddy off guard. "Why? You cooking?"

"If you have anything in your kitchen besides Gatorade and Twinkies," Bobby said.

"Funny guy. We've got all the staples. The wife's big on them. But don't think your cooking is gonna get you any of my sweet little ass." He waggled his finger at Bobby to show a wedding band.

Bobby laughed. "Okay. We'll keep it simple. I'll cook, and you'll talk about Hannah."

"She never tore up the lieutenant's office," Eddy said, lighting a cigarette and carefully blowing the smoke toward Bobby. "Threw a file at the guy, but that was it. Churnin always makes it sound like she took an Uzi to the place. I hear these things." He put down the cigarette and took another bite of the eggs Bobby made. He held up the empty ramekin. "What did you call this again?"

"Shirred eggs. Or baked *en cocotte*, if you prefer."

He nodded. "Pretty damn good. Those cinnamon muffins done yet?"

Bobby checked the oven timer. "About ten minutes to go. So Hannah didn't lose it?"

"Oh, she lost it, all right. She knew that creep Meister was going to run with his little girl. She tried to get somebody to stop him. I think she had half a mind to snatch the kid herself, because at least she'd be safe from her dad then. But she gave herself the career talk, I think."

"That she'd be blowing her job off the map if she did that?"

Eddy nodded. "She ended up blowing it anyway, once she knew the kid was dead."

"So Janie Meister really is dead?"

Eddy nodded. "That's what Hannah said. They found this kid's body—right age, right hair color, but there wasn't much more to go on."

"No DNA?"

Eddy finished his second helping of egg and wiped his mouth. "Cops up there might have taken a sample of some kind, I don't know. But what were they going to match it up to? The county didn't have samples from Janie for comparison. No parents to get a sample from. No sibs, either."

"What about dental records?"

"Janie had never been to a dentist, so far as Hannah could tell."

"So there wasn't any confirmation it was Janie."

"Hannah said she didn't need it. She knew it was her, just like she knew that S.O.B. father was going to run with her. He got up there to Oregon, something happened, and he killed her."

"That's when Hannah quit the department?"

"Shortly after. She thought a lot about it. Every cop goes through something like that. Some people can't handle it at all. Turn alcoholic or they off themselves. Other guys find a way to cope with their mistakes by keeping on, trying to do a better job the next time. I thought that's what Hannah would do."

"She didn't?"

"I don't think she could. It was like she'd been tested with Janie, and she failed. She felt like there was really no way to make up for it. Clearing murder cases, putting bad guys in jail—what was that going to do for Janie? She was dead, it was her fault, and nothing she could do could bring her back."

"She thinks Janie is back."

Eddy looked up from his food. "What?"

"Hannah thinks Janie Meister is alive."

Eddy put down his fork. "Holy Christ. What gave her that idea?"

The oven timer went off. Bobby took out the muffins and put them in front of Eddy. He ate while Bobby told him about Matthew's departure, Guillermo's desertion, and the appearance of the kid who seemed to follow Hannah. He mentioned the dismembered stuffed lion.

"That's it?" Eddy said. "This toy, which I don't remember, by the way, is the sole basis for her thinking Janie Meister is alive?"

He nodded. "She's so certain. It just seems weird to me."

"I'll say."

Out of habit, Bobby started washing the dishes. There was a sink full of plates and cups, many more items than he'd used to make breakfast. Eddy watched him, sighed, and started drying. As Bobby fished for silverware, his fingers found something odd. He pulled a narrow wedding band out of the suds and hastily resubmerged it as Eddy returned from putting away some plates.

"Where's Gudrun?" Bobby said casually.

Eddy didn't answer him. Bobby didn't push it, instead turning his attention to a foul broiler tray while Eddy noisily put away glasses. Suddenly Eddy put down the dish towel, pulled a short ladder out of the broom closet, and headed out the kitchen's back door. Bobby dried his hands and followed him across a patio, through the huge, overgrown yard. At the side fence stood an archery target. Something was affixed to the bull's eye—a picture of a smiling fortyish woman with short, blond hair. She had been shot full of arrows.

Eddy was climbing up the ladder when Bobby got to the garage. The ex-cop reached up into the rafters and pulled out a box. He glanced down at Bobby. "Catch."

Bobby threw out his arms and flexed his knees, ready for the weight of a boulder. What the hell was Eddy thinking? The box hit without harm. It felt empty.

In the kitchen, Eddy opened it and riffled through its contents. Just papers, from what Bobby could see: newspaper clippings and sheets of lined paper, covered with scratchy, cribbed handwriting.

"Notes for my great police novel," Eddy said. "The *War and Peace* of cop lit. Fucking brilliant."

"Did you get it published?"

"Haven't written it yet. Been busy."

"I can imagine," Bobby said, thinking of the arrow-studded picture. "What are you looking for?"

"I had a . . . here it is."

He handed Bobby a photograph, and although he'd never heard a description beyond hair color, he knew he was looking at Janie Meister.

She looked thin and small for a five-year-old. Her yellow sweater, embroidered with daisies and ducks, hung on her small shoulders. Bobby peered at the picture, trying to decide if her eyes were brown or hazel. He couldn't see them through her bangs' long strands, as fine as the bristles in a watercolorist's brush. Her hair was dark chestnut, but lusterless and dry. It's wrong, Bobby thought. A little girl's hair should shine. Janie seemed unconcerned about her dull hair and oversized clothes. She smiled shyly as she held a gargantuan tomato up to the camera.

He returned the picture to Eddy, who held it gently. "Hannah said it was taken at school. Some kind of gardening project."

Bobby nodded. "What's it doing in the box?"

Eddy started putting his papers away. "Oh, I had it in my wallet for a long time, just in case."

"In case she wasn't dead?"

"Christ no," Eddy said. "To remind me she was. And what could happen."

"What could happen if you fucked up, like Hannah did?"

Eddy glared at him. "I never thought Hannah fucked up. She worked harder than I ever did, cared more. I just was lucky I never had something like that happen to me. That's why I kept it."

"Does Hannah have this picture, too?"

Eddy shook his head. "This one was hers. I took this one away from her. Wasn't healthy for her."

"It kept Janie alive for her?"

"Something like that. I showed up at her place one day and found her staring at it. She also had her gun in her lap. That's all I needed to see."

Bobby sat down at the table. He suddenly felt shaky. "She was going to kill herself?"

"We never talked about it. I took the gun away. I took the picture. I took Hannah to Gudrun's, and we kept her with us for a couple of days. She didn't say a word the whole time, until breakfast that third morning. She asked for the picture, and I told her I couldn't give it back to her. She just nodded. Hugged me, hugged Gudrun. That was the end of it."

"Can I borrow it?"

Eddy stared at Bobby for a moment, as though weighing his intentions. "You going to go looking for her, too? See if you can figure out if it's Janie that Hannah saw?"

"Maybe."

Eddy shook his head. "Hannah finds out, she'll kick your ass."

Bobby knew he was right. "I can't stand by and do nothing, Devlin. I'm worried about her. I'm afraid she's . . ."

"Nuts?"

"Exhausted. Obsessed. Not herself."

Eddy put the picture in his shirt pocket. "I'll tell you what. Let me poke around a little. At least I know what I'm doing. No offense, but I don't think you can pull off being stealthy and inconspicuous." He smiled icily and added, "Big fella."

Bobby couldn't decide if Eddy was malicious or just socially awkward. But he decided to put up with him, for Hannah's sake. "You won't say anything to Hannah?"

"Not a word. And don't you, either. Where should I start looking for this kid?"

Bobby told him where Hannah had seen her—at the Plaza and in her neighborhood after dark. He reached for his wallet. "Look, there might be expenses. . . ."

Eddy threw him a disgusted look. "Put that away. You keep an eye on Hannah. I'll do the rest."

15

Hannah drove the streets between her house and the Plaza on Sunday morning, hoping that she might see Janie. She'd slept fitfully the night before and hadn't eaten since Saturday afternoon. Her head pounded. The sun seemed painfully bright in her eyes.

After a few hours, she decided she was wasting her time. Janie was playing a game that allowed her to be found only when she wanted to be. Today wasn't one of those days. Hannah went home, took three aspirins, and fell on the sofa.

The doorbell woke her. Bobby stood on her porch, a gourmet market's plastic bags dangling from his arms like oversized Christmas ornaments. She glanced at the mantle clock—it was after six.

Bobby grinned at her as he headed for the kitchen. "I went a little nuts at the store. Too much food for one person."

Hannah smiled. Bobby was sweetly transparent. He could figure what he needed for dinner within an onion's ounce and a steak's inch. This wasn't an oversight. It was a mission of mercy.

"Are you offering to restock my refrigerator?"

"I'm actually here to make you a fabulous dinner."

How did he know she hadn't eaten? "What have you got?"

"Well, I bought so much, I don't quite remember."

"Gourmet blackout."

"Honestly, Hannah, they have everything over there. Five kinds of mushrooms, potatoes in every color you can imagine, quail, squab, Kobe beef. Yak cheese—I swear to God. It's awesome."

Hannah leaned in the kitchen doorway and watched him unpack the bags. "What can I do to help?"

He smiled. "Take a nap for an hour? Read? Luxuriate in the tub?"

"You want me out of the way, in other words."

"I want you to take care of yourself."

She heard the undercurrent and readied herself to stop his lecture. "Bobby . . ."

"I mean it. Go pamper. I'll call you when dinner's ready."

She fell asleep in the tub, awakening only when Bobby knocked on the bathroom door. She still felt slightly foggy and limp, as though the hot water had melted her bones and steamed her brain. She dried off and put on black jeans and a white cotton sweater. Both felt a size too big.

When she came downstairs, she saw that Bobby had set the table with Mrs. Snow's good china and crystal. She thought one of her linen tablecloths was pressed into service, too, but it was hard to be sure. An array of plates covered it: a big romaine salad sprinkled with blue cheese, a loaf of hot French bread, and a huge platter of angel-hair pasta with a red sauce brimming with shrimp, clams, and scallops. He had uncorked and poured a bottle of Amarone. Hannah smelled its essence of spice and raisin. Her stomach growled.

Bobby pulled a chair out for her and started passing plates her way. As she ate and sipped at the wine, she warily waited for his heartfelt talk to begin. She knew how it would go: Hannah, you've had a bad few months. You're tired. You're vulnerable. Nobody blames you for being, well, not yourself.

She would interrupt at this point. Yes, it had been a bad time. But that had nothing to do with seeing Janie. She wasn't a figment born of insomnia and hurt. She was real.

But instead, Bobby talked about his trip to Florida and the real story of Mr. Spacy. He wasn't an idiot after all, just chronically jet lagged. He was literally zoned, his circadian rhythms wracked by transatlantic travel.

"He's carrying on an affair with a solicitor in Glasgow. He goes there as often as he can," Bobby said. "The zone-hopping means he can't keep his clock straight anymore. I told him either to get married or find a woman in eastern standard time. He's going to forget what side of the road he's supposed to be on some morning, and that will be it for him."

Hannah laughed. Bobby poured her another glass of wine.

"Hannah?"

She still was chuckling at the thought of Spacy in the throes of sleep-deprived passion. "What?"

"You have to start taking care of yourself."

She put the glass down. Here at last was The Talk. "I bathe daily."

"You know what I mean. You're not eating. You don't sleep regularly."

"Don't start with me."

"Let me just say this once. It wasn't your fault, what happened with that girl."

She turned her glass and didn't look at him. "So I've been told."

"You still don't believe it. You're carrying this around like a cross. You're crushing yourself."

"I'm being a martyr. That's what you're saying."

"Not in the sense of trying to get attention. But you're letting yourself drown in guilt."

Hannah didn't say anything, but seeing Janie like that, *knowing* it was her, did indeed feel like an undertow. In its grip, the rest of the world looked watery, out of focus. Janie was more alive to her right now than Matthew, or Guillermo, for that matter. But Bobby made it sound as though she had a choice about what was happening. She didn't. Pretending Janie was dead wouldn't make her go away.

"What do you think I should do?" She said it quietly, knowing that this was what Bobby needed to hear to stop worrying.

"Get some help. Talk to someone."

"I'm talking to you."

"I mean a professional."

"What else?"

"Try to get some regular pattern back into your life—sleep, work, meals. Your friends—stop shutting us out."

She picked up her fork and twirled it in the pasta. "I'm eating, see? And I let you in, didn't I? I'm not some kind of recluse."

He sighed. "You know what I mean."

She nodded. "I appreciate your concern. But I'm all right. Really."

"And what about this Janie thing?"

"She's a girl, not a thing," Hannah said. There was an edge to her voice.

"Okay, sorry. What about her?"

Hannah shrugged. "I haven't seen her again. I don't know what that means."

"You think maybe . . ."

"That I didn't actually see her at all?" It would be so much easier if she could convince herself of that. It was pointless to talk to Bobby about Janie. The only way to convince him she was alive would be to find her and bring her into the office. Until she could do that, she decided to let him think she'd dropped it. "Maybe."

Bobby seemed to take that as an admission of defeat. "I am sorry about Janie."

She forced a smile. "Tomorrow, I'm going to pick up where I left off on Roche. Michael thought he was okay, and I should have let that guide me. I'm sorry we didn't try to help him. Who knows what would have happened if we had?"

"Hannah, if I ever even remotely implied that his dying was something you could—"

She reached across the table and took his hand. She was always surprised at its solidity—it was like gripping a chunk of marble. Bobby was big, but he wasn't a marshmallow. "Stop apologizing for everything. I know there probably wasn't anything we could have done. But at least we can put Mrs. Roche's mind at ease. I'm going to Freddy's old neighborhood tomorrow."

He squeezed her fingers. "Good. Now let me do these dishes. You relax awhile."

She stretched out on the sofa and turned on the late news. She closed her eyes, just for a moment, enjoying the sounds of another person in her house. Tomorrow evening she would talk to Roche's neighbors. And after that, maybe she would spend some time in the Plaza. At some point, she felt sure, Janie would surface there.

•   •   •

Bobby left the clean dishes in the drainer and put the leftovers in the refrigerator. There was enough to feed Hannah for at least another night. He went to check on her.

The television still was on, but Hannah was sleeping soundly. She lay on her side, knees curled to her chest, hair falling over her face. He thought about waking her, but decided against it. She could use an uninterrupted eight hours, even if that meant waking up in the living room tomorrow morning. He put a note on the table—*Thanks for letting a friend lecture. See you at work.* He checked to make sure that the front door would lock behind him and let himself out.

The girl heard the door open. She had been at the house for more than two hours, lying at first in the shadows at the back of the lawn, watching the night sky and the shredded clouds. She listened for voices inside. She couldn't make out what they were saying, but she imagined that Hannah was talking about her.

After a while, when she could hear nothing but running water and the drone of a television, she got up and crept into the dugout she'd made within the camellia bushes. She sat cross-legged in her den and waited, prepared to hang out all night, no matter what curfew Jared had imposed. She wondered if the man would stay over. Would Hannah let him be on top? She contemplated that picture for a moment and then banished it.

After a few minutes, one of the neighborhood cats crept into the hiding place. The girl sat very still. The cat kneaded her leg for a moment. Then it curled up in her lap. She stroked the ratty fur until the cat began to purr. And she waited.

She had started to doze when she heard the big guy come out, whistling something under his breath. Good, she thought. Hannah had sent him home so she wouldn't have to look at his big naked body in the morning.

He unlocked his car door. The cat sprang up at the sound of the jingling keys, shaking the leaves and branches, digging his claws into the girl's leg. She bit her lip to keep from crying out in pain. The cat, preparing itself for flight, flexed its paws.

She cautiously looked out through the branches. The man stood very still, listening, his glance moving along the trees and bushes. In a minute, he'd be poking through the leaves. She nudged the cat, who obligingly leaped out into the driveway. The man let out a sighing laugh.

"Stupid cat." He started his car and left.

The girl waited a few moments and then crept onto the porch. From here, she could smell something wonderful: garlic, butter, sauce. She crouched low and then came up to look through one of the front windows. She saw the cloth on the dining-room table, the clean dishes gleaming in the kitchen's overhead light. She didn't see Hannah.

She tried to remember when she last sat down at someone's dinner table. It might have been at the foster home where she met Jared. She remembered him passing her a bowl of something like little green marbles.

"Brussels sprouts," he said. "They're not so bad. I'm Jared."

"Mae," she muttered. "They look awful."

"Try them."

She did, and instantly regretted it. She hated the rubbery leaves and their bitter, cabbagy tang. He laughed at her scrunched face. By the end of dinner, they were friends.

She and Jared tried to cook when they could, but since they lost the electricity, it was tough. When they were rich in quarters—the bounty of Jared's night job—they got by on fast food: burgers for her, bean burritos for the semivegetarian Jared. And fresh fruit. Jared was serious about fruit. He talked about sailors in the olden days, how they got sick with scurvy because they didn't eat enough citrus. For a while, if she whined about the bitter taste of the Dumpster-salvaged grapefruit or oranges he brought back, he would put on an eye patch made from a scrap of newspaper and nylon twine, and hobble around as though he were one-legged. He spat out phrases he'd picked up from an old pirate movie.

"Avast ye, little Mae, me matey, It's mutiny, aye, it is. It's to the scuppers you'll go. Arrgh."

Every time she asked, wide-eyed, "What's a scupper?"

"Ye little blighter, I'll keelhaul ye!" Then he chased her. She ran, giddy with laughter, looking over her shoulder as he hopped and blabbered his phony pirate talk.

They didn't play the game anymore. Once, soon after they'd found each other near the Plaza, she turned in mid-pursuit and flung herself into his arms, toppling him. She pressed herself into his hips, dipping to kiss him. He shoved her away.

"Don't."

She was stunned. "You said you liked me."

He nodded. "I do. You're family."

She stared at him. "So?"

"I'm like your brother, you know?"

"I don't have a brother."

"Brothers and sisters don't do that."

She frowned at him. "You don't care about me."

"I do. That's why we're not going to do that."

"You're queer," she taunted, hoping to hurt him.

"So?" He walked away, shedding his eye patch. She pretended to be mad, but she was mainly sad and confused. She'd ruined a good game and hurt Jared's feelings. She got him to explain a little later, about how brothers and sisters were, and she tried to be that way with him. It seemed to make him happy, but it felt odd to her. She had to rethink every word, every gesture. It was like learning to skate. She was learning to be the girl Jared thought she should be.

She heard sounds inside the house: springs creaking, someone sighing. Hannah hadn't gone upstairs. She was only a few feet away. The girl realized she'd been drifting again. Jared had tried to get her to stop that.

"You space out," he said. "It's dangerous."

She didn't think he understood. Space had been her only safe place, for a long time. She moved to another window and peered in. Hannah was turning in her sleep on the wooden-sided sofa. Draped on a chair next to the sofa was the black Raiders jacket. The girl's heart beat faster. Bert had better be all right.

She had borrowed one of Jared's flannel shirts for warmth. There was a flexible plastic card in the pocket, the kind the video stores used for rentals, issued in a name she didn't recognize. Jared showed her how to use it — sliding it between the door and the frame, maneuvering it so that it would spring certain kinds of locks. Not dead bolts. Just the easy locks.

"It's only for emergencies, Mae," he'd told her after a practice session. "Okay?"

She considered whether this was an emergency. It certainly felt like one. She had to get Bert back. She had never been without him, and it felt weird. She didn't like to admit it, but she had trouble going to sleep without his spongy roundness snug against her neck.

She surveyed Hannah's door and swore under her breath. There was a dead bolt, and if it wasn't locked now, it would be later. Someone like Hannah might even have an alarm system. Bert, she thought, you're going to have to wait, buddy. But I'll find a way to get you back.

She heard another sound inside—Hannah getting up, walking across the living room, approaching the front porch. She flattened herself against the shingles behind the screen door. But Hannah didn't come out. The girl crept back to the window and saw Hannah reading a note at the dining room table. When she finished it, she put it down and came back into the living room. The girl ducked so Hannah wouldn't see her.

She waited a moment and then rose to risk a peek. Hannah was sitting on the sofa again, her back to the window. She had the jacket in her lap. The girl held her breath as Hannah reached into the pocket and drew out Bert.

She hated it when anyone handled Bert. He'd tried to take Bert away from her once. She had to bite him to make him release Bert. But she got Bert back—everything but his tail. He managed to hang onto that. He cut it up before her eyes, telling her that's what he'd do to her if she ever tried sinking teeth into him again.

Now Hannah put Bert to her nose. The girl sat down, out of sight, and inhaled, too. She knew what Hannah smelled: old cloth and foam rubber. She sometimes thought she caught a trace of other smells in Bert. Oreos and the white paste from her kindergarten classroom. Her mother's perfume. The girl had dabbed the backs of Bert's ears with it once. It was something she'd seen her mother do, stroking the stopper along the skin at the top of her throat. The girl hadn't actually smelled the perfume recently, though. Maybe it really was gone. Like her mother.

She looked again. Hannah stared at Bert's worn and scraped face. She put her lips to the top of his head. The girl could almost feel the touch. Then Hannah put him back in the pocket of the jacket, laid it across the chair, and came toward the door. The girl slid off the porch as quietly as she could. She heard the dead bolt click shut inside. The living room lights went out.

Then, from the end of the block, she heard a whistle. Two

notes, one low, one high, like someone starting a fox hunt. Jared had come to escort her home. She hesitated for a moment. She wanted Bert back so much. Maybe the windows weren't locked, and she hadn't actually seen a security-company sign, so she could—

The whistle was louder this time, more insistent. Low-high, low-high, followed by his hoarse stage whisper: "Mae, come on!"

She brushed her hair out of her eyes and ran toward him. My brother. She mouthed the words as she ran. She liked the way they sounded.

16

Once she'd found the right street, Hannah could have picked out Roche's house even if she hadn't had the address. In the falling dusk, the new shingles, pale as naked skin, beamed out at her. The windows were dark. A rental agency's sign was stuck in the front lawn.

Roche had told them that his chief tormenters, Dick Barker and his wife, lived across the street. She intended to talk to them, but would save them for last. Maybe some of their followers had rethought their zeal for retribution since Roche's death. A touch of guilt could be a useful conversational opener.

Whatever had gone on here when Roche's past had been revealed, little residue of it remained now. It was just a quiet Monday evening in a nice Las Almas tract neighborhood, and at first, they treated her no better or worse than anyone who worked door-to-door. No one screamed at her when she told them who she was or what she was doing. There were no threats to call the police. Most of the people who answered her knock shook their heads and said they didn't know anything about protests, phone calls, shit-missiles, or firebombs. That included a couple who had been among the picketers photographed by the *Register*. A convenient memory lapse, Hannah thought.

But not everyone was an amnesiac. A gardener who lived three doors away from Roche invited Hannah in, swore her to secrecy, and revealed that he too was an ex-con—six years for armed robbery, but a flawless life after that. Even his own daughter, now a high school junior, had no idea. He didn't like what had happened to Roche, but he couldn't come out and side with him. Hannah understood, didn't she? She did, seeing how quickly that daughter's life could have been turned into an adolescent hell if daddy's past came out.

"Any thoughts on which neighbor might have killed him?" she asked him.

The ex-con shook his head. "Easier to figure out who wouldn't have."

No one answered at the next house, although Hannah could see lights inside. As she went on to the home next door to Roche's old place, she could hear the phone ringing inside. And as she knocked, the living room lights went out. No one came to the door. The suburban telegraph was on-line, tapping out a belated warning.

There was no point in continuing this way. She would try the Barkers. By now, they knew who she was and what she wanted. Barker opened the door on her first knock. He asked to see identification, but regarded her business card as though it might be teeming with anthrax. He didn't invite her inside. Instead he stood in front of his door, arms crossed, daring her to ask her questions. He was a thick-bodied man, just a couple of inches taller than Hannah. He had a florid complexion, slick hair, and a sneering face. He reminded her of a high school bully who used to pick on her brother, the latter who was at that time a boy too slight and sweet-natured to fight back. She thought she knew the kind of cop Barker had been: kick ass and take names. None of that community-oriented policing crap for him. She envisioned his gun collection. Way in back, there might be one he hadn't registered. Something he kept for a troubled day, when routine procedures wouldn't be enough to resolve the situation at hand.

But she wouldn't waste her time confronting him with speculation like that. Instead, she treated him like a good citizen.

"Mr. Roche thought that you orchestrated the neighborhood's opposition to him. I was hoping you might have some thoughts about who could have carried that too far."

Barker twitched his shoulder. "I didn't 'orchestrate' anything. I went down and looked at the CD-ROM when it came out. It's a good public safety tool, and I wanted to make sure my kids were safe."

"Your kids are in college, aren't they? That's what you told the newspaper."

His nostrils flared. She was pissing him off. "I meant all the kids around here. When I saw Roche's name on the disc, I thought it was my duty to tell my neighbors about him. Roche—the name fit him, didn't it?" He smiled, as if he expected Hannah to enjoy the joke.

She didn't react, but in her head she told him, "Yes, some names do fit—Dick." Out loud, she said, "You told them about Roche being a registered sex offender. Then what?"

"I walked with a sign in front of his house, on a public sidewalk, which I believe is my constitutional right," he said. "As soon as he moved down to the south end of town, I didn't care. I only worry about my backyard."

Hannah thought it interesting that Barker knew where Roche had moved. The cop brotherhood worked that way. As soon as Roche reregistered, somebody in the Las Almas P.D. had let him know.

"What about the phone calls and the manure, or the fire?" Hannah said. "Any thoughts on who might have done those things?"

"Look, I was a peace officer for twenty-two years. I'm clear on what's right and what's wrong, and I didn't do one thing that was illegal. But I understand that some people aren't quite as clear on those lines as I am."

"And their lack of clarity was not your problem?"

"I'm not my brother's keeper, if that's what you mean. I could only tell people that they should keep a cool head, not jeopardize their own freedom, not take the law into their own hands."

"Who did you say that to?"

"No one. I was speaking hypothetically."

"I see," Hannah said. She was about to ask Barker if his wife was home when she came out from behind him. He held his arm open, and she moved against the shelter of his broad chest. The glare she gave Hannah said she had been listening.

She was tiny, no more than five feet tall, with frosted blond hair, cotton-candy-pink lipstick, and a deep tan. An erstwhile beach bunny, Hannah thought. A Gidget who would pay for her sun-worshipping very soon in wrinkles and age spots.

"How could you represent scum like that?" The little woman's chin jutted as she spoke.

"Actually, Mrs. Barker, I never represented him," Hannah said. She paused. Should she let them in on her own distaste for Roche and her guilt about it? It might help. "I didn't like him much."

"Join the club," Barker said.

"But despite that, I think I should have helped him."

"Why?"

"He didn't deserve what he got."

"He deserved worse." Disgust curled Mrs. Barker's lip.

"Well, his mother doesn't agree. I'm working for her. She's quite upset, as you can well imagine. Being a mother yourself."

"We don't know anything about his killing," the woman said. "We just know he got what was coming to him."

"A bullet in the head? Even I didn't think that, Mrs. Barker. He'd already served a prison sentence for what he'd done."

She shook her head. "It doesn't change them. They just get out and do it again. They're—diseased. You can't cure them."

"Kelly . . ." Barker squeezed her shoulders.

Hannah wondered if she should press this. Kelly Barker seemed to have strong feelings about people like Roche. "Like mad dogs, you mean. You don't have any choice but to shoot them."

Kelly Barker didn't like being goaded. "You think you're clever, but you don't have any idea what it's like."

With that, Hannah saw it. Barker and his wife clicked into focus for her, as if someone had adjusted a lens. It wasn't about the Barker children, or Barker being Mr. Neighborhood Watch. It was about Kelly Barker as a child.

"No, I don't," Hannah said quietly. "Not the way a victim knows."

Kelly Barker was stonyfaced. No tears left, Hannah thought. Just anger. She wondered if Kelly Barker had personally vented her rage on Roche, or if she let her husband take care of it for her.

"I am sorry," Hannah said to her. "But I don't think Roche's death can make it stop hurting."

Kelly Barker looked at her with an expression of bitter triumph. "Not altogether," she said. "But it sure as hell helps."

• • •

The next morning, Hannah found a middle-aged woman waiting in the reception area for her. She had a funereal face—down-turned mouth, heavy-lidded eyes, and a deeply lined forehead. Her long, black hair had once been her glory, but now it was gray-streaked and put a grave frame around her mournful features. This gravity didn't carry over to her wardrobe: she wore a startling periwinkle suit. When Hannah raised a questioning eyebrow to Vera, the normally pleasant secretary turned to stare daggers at the woman.

The visitor ignored Vera's venomous look and put out her hand to Hannah. "Lisette Blackburn. I think Mrs. Roche mentioned me to you."

The name meant nothing to her. But then she recalled Mrs. Roche's dislike of Vera and her promise to send Hannah a "very good girl." No wonder Vera was glowering.

"Let's go into my office." She knew better than to ask Vera to bring coffee.

It didn't take long for Hannah to let Lisette Blackburn know that there was no position at Terry & Barlow for her. The woman smiled sadly and nodded.

"Mrs. Roche means well enough," she said. "She just doesn't understand that not everyone views the world the same way she does."

"How do you know Mrs. Roche?"

She blinked at Hannah in surprise. "She didn't tell you?"

"She just said that she'd send someone who would be a good replacement for our current secretary. She didn't even tell me your name."

"She should have explained," Lisette said with a little sigh. "I used to take her to visit Freddy."

"Visit him where?"

"I work—that is, I used to work—in a prison-outreach program. Your brother was on our steering committee."

Hannah nodded. "Freddy told me he met Michael at CMC."

"He went up there a half-dozen times, even when it wasn't convenient for him." She stopped, and Hannah knew what was coming. "I was sorry to hear about his death."

"Thank you," Hannah said. *Michael,* she thought, *for all your shortcomings, you managed to do some good. How terrible that you couldn't feel the redemption.*

"Well, Michael knew how it was. People who are incarcerated are cut off from their families so often. The prisons are in remote places, and people don't have cars, or baby-sitters, or the money for bus fare. We take people to visit their loved ones, to remind the inmates that they have families who are waiting for them, who want them to change their lives. Otherwise they despair, Ms. Barlow. They really do. And once they despair, there's no reason even to try to rehabilitate. For what? No one cares anymore."

"So you knew Freddy?"

She nodded. "We were very close."

"Not just part of your caseload, then."

"No. You can't be friends with everyone inside. There are manipulators there. They cozy up, and some of them want you to mule drugs. Some just enjoy twisting up your emotions. But Freddy was different. Freddy would have made it, if they'd just given him a chance."

"His neighbors, you mean?"

"Why couldn't they just leave him alone?"

"They were afraid of him," Hannah said.

"It's ridiculous. Freddy wouldn't hurt anyone. He never did."

"I think his victim might disagree."

Lisette's lips tightened. "You're right about that, of course. I just meant that he wasn't a violent man. He was trying to make amends, for a very long time."

"Amends? How?"

"I mean, changing his life. There was some medication."

Hannah nodded. "He told me about that. You know that Mrs. Roche asked us to find out something about Freddy's death?"

"She thinks that someone is stalking paroled molesters," she said. "Scary, isn't it?"

"Scary that she thinks that, or scary that it's happening?"

Lisette shook her head. "She gets these ideas, and you can't really talk her out of them."

"What other ideas does she have?"

"Besides the conspiracy? Oh, that I should be your secretary, or that Freddy was going to come home to live with her after the incidents in his neighborhood."

"What was so far-fetched about that?"

"Freddy was a grown man. He needed to be away from her. He'd struggled to do that for a long time. He stayed with her for a few days after he was evicted, but he didn't want to be there permanently. He said he wanted to move out for her protection, but I also think she smothered him. She always did."

"You helped him find a place?"

She nodded, looking down at her hands. They met in a ladylike fold, right over left.

"What do you think happened to Freddy?"

She shook her head. "I don't know, really. He didn't like going out at night alone since the incidents at his first house."

"Why did he go out that night? Was he meeting someone?"

Her head snapped up. "No."

"You sound very certain."

"Well, I just knew Freddy. I think it was ants."

"Restlessness, you mean?"

"No. Real ones. Freddy was very fastidious. I think he went out for bug spray."

"And someone followed him?"

"Maybe that, or it was just bad luck. A robbery, like the police say."

"Who else knew where he was living? You, the landlord, the police, who else?"

"His mother. But they weren't speaking right then."

"Why not?"

"Mrs. Roche was unhappy about him leaving her. She wouldn't say so, but she wanted him to stay her little boy. That's why we couldn't confide in her." Her voice caressed the pronoun that linked her to Freddy.

"You and Freddy couldn't confide about what?"

Lisette lifted her left hand. An antique ring, thick with garnets and seed pearls, glittered on the third finger. "Freddy and I were going to be married."

17

Bobby shook his head. "Reformed or not, Freddy's not the kind of guy you'd find at the altar."

It was an hour after Lisette Blackburn had left the office. Hannah had talked to her for a while longer about Freddy, and after she left, Hannah reassured Vera that she and Bobby were happy with her work. Then she sent Vera to lunch to cool off.

"I saw the ring," Hannah told Bobby. "Not a Tiffany solitaire, but nice."

"I don't know how much that proves," Bobby said. "He's not around, she can make up any story she likes."

That thought had crossed Hannah's mind. So had an image of an angry Lisette shooting Freddy after he told her he wasn't interested in her as a wife or lover. It seemed to Hannah that Mrs. Roche wasn't the only domineering female in Freddy's life.

"So what else did you find out about Freddy?" Bobby asked.

"Well, Lisette gave me his boss's name and number. Interesting that Marian didn't mention him."

"I didn't even know he had a job," he said.

"A friend of Marian's hired him." She checked her notes. "Caesar Pritzker. He has an antiques business in Laguna Beach—furniture and decorative objects. He had Freddy working in the shop. They had a stall at weekend swap meets from time to time. According to Lisette, Caesar only tolerated Roche because his mother was steering substantial inventory his way."

"How did she do that?"

"She's old, her friends are old. When anyone with a Heywood Wakefield dining room set or Murano glass or some other goodie was dead or dying, she'd let Caesar know. Then, when the time was right, she'd tell the bereaved family members how they could get rid of all the old crap in the garage. He got a jump on other dealers because he didn't have to wait around for the estate sales. And Marian Roche got a cut."

"Christ, that's ghoulish," Bobby said.

"But profitable, apparently. Unfortunately, Caesar and Freddy didn't get along," Hannah said. "Caesar had actually fired him once, but Marian told him she'd stop telling him about her dying friends if he didn't take Freddy back. So he did. It would have hit his business hard if he hadn't."

"Hard enough so that Caesar might have killed Freddy to keep his merchandise pipeline open?"

"That's what I'd like to look into," Hannah said. "Lisette doesn't know where Caesar was that night. She doesn't think the police knew how much they disliked each other. I thought I'd go by the store this afternoon."

Bobby nodded. "Sounds like a plan. I'm going to go out for a while. When Vera gets back, will you tell her I need her help with a filing?"

"Sure." She waited until she heard the outer office door close before she picked up the phone. She would talk to Caesar Pritzker. But first, she had other work to do. She had to find Mrs. T.

In that netherworld populated by fleeing felons, husband-dodging battered women, bill-skipping families, and—with any luck—once-dead children, there were still trails and way stations. A railroad also ran through the underground world, and one branch of it was run by the woman Hannah knew as Mrs. T. She helped abused kids and battered women disappear.

The nickname was a homage to Harriet Tubman, of course. Hannah had seen Mrs. T.'s real name many years before, a knot at the end of her thread of aliases. But she couldn't remember it now. She doubted if Mrs. T. thought of herself as anything but a title and an initial anymore.

What Mrs. T. did was frequently illegal, but that didn't seem to bother her. She was concerned with doing what was right.

Most of the time, family court judges ruled wisely in custody cases. But occasionally, a jerk in a black robe would blithely grant joint custody to a conniving asshole who was poised to run with the kid—just to spite the ex. As Mrs. T. saw it, she was just helping the weaker party beat the asshole to the punch.

It was a testament to her skill and judgment that she hadn't been arrested for obstructing justice, interfering with court orders, or out-and-out kidnapping. It helped that she had an unerring sense for a righteous case. She could sniff out a manipulative, lying mom like a bloodhound. Her compassion made people loyal to her. Parents on the run were sometimes found and arrested. But they never ratted out Mrs. T.

Most of her clients were women, but not all of them. A couple of fathers who had seen their ex-wives take up with scumbag boyfriends came pleading for her help. She made them go through the legal steps to get sole custody, but if that failed, she helped them climb aboard the Disappearance Express, too.

Hannah thought Janie might turn up on a spur of Mrs. T.'s railroad. She knew Janie couldn't be on her own at eleven. Someone was taking care of her. It might even be her mother. Six years before, Claire had been a woman in denial, someone whose escape came in the form of a wine bottle. But maybe, after the family took off from Las Almas, she woke up to what Meister was doing to Janie. Maybe she finally saw or heard something that broke the glass-and-booze barrier that kept her apart from life. She might have found the courage to side with Janie and run away with her. Meister would have gone after them, and Hannah didn't think Claire could have eluded him by herself. But Mrs. T. could have helped.

Police officers were supposed to keep their distance from her, lest they be accused of helping her. Mrs. T. trusted few people in law enforcement. She was, after all, committing crimes on a daily basis. But Hannah had been a cop she would talk to. Hannah had turned to her years ago, just after the Meisters had first disappeared.

Mrs. T. must have seen how distraught she was. She sat Hannah down in her suburban living room—big-screen TV, floral sofa, bland seascapes on the walls—pressed a glass of excruciatingly sweet iced tea into her hand, and made her drink all of it. She took Janie's picture from Hannah and photocopied it before giving it back to her.

"People like these Meister folks don't come to people like me," she said. "But I'll keep my ears open." Hannah, mute with anxiety, had nodded her thanks and gone home.

She hadn't talked to Mrs. T. since that day. She wasn't even sure she was still in the disappearance business. Now, as it approached three o'clock on a Tuesday afternoon, she began trying to find her. The six-year-old number she had was out of service, of course. Mrs. T. probably hadn't stayed at that house for more than a month.

Five hours later, after a circuitous trek that took her through divorce lawyers, a private investigator, a DA's child-support collections clerk, and two volunteers at abused-women's shelters, Hannah still didn't have a phone number for her. But she had an address, of sorts: a bench outside Victoria's Secret in the South Coast Plaza shopping mall. And she had Mrs. T.'s office hours: any Wednesday between two and five. If she wasn't there, the visitor should reach under the bench and feel around for a Post-it, which would describe the alternative rendezvous spot and time. Sometimes, if Mrs. T. had to leave the office unexpectedly, the note wouldn't be there. Then the needy visitor would just have to try again the following week. Persistence was an essential ingredient in getting an audience. Hannah was prepared to stick with it.

The next day, a few minutes before two, Hannah arrived to find Mrs. T. already at her post. She looked the same despite the passage of six years. She stood at medium height, with a medium build, a medium complexion, and moderately blond hair cut in a conservative, unremarkable style. She wore a white sweatshirt, jeans, and white Keds. Streams and eddies of shoppers moved past her, barely giving her a glance. She was as colorless as water, and Hannah wondered if she muted her appearance to serve her work, or if her looks had somehow determined her calling.

Today she had a stroller at her side. She was cooing to the baby in it when Hannah sat down beside her. "Your baby?" Hannah said. "Or are you just minding this one?"

She turned with a sweet smile, prepared to make mall-talk

with a stranger. But at the sight of Hannah, she laughed aloud and pulled her into a hug. "Good God, it's Hannah Barlow."

"Good to see you."

"This is my grandson. Baby-sitting is one of my chief joys in life."

Hannah nodded, feeling the start of a lump in her throat as she looked down at the boy, a chubby blond decked out in Sesame Street duds. She turned her attention back to Mrs. T. Now she saw the lines around her mouth, the crow's feet at her eyes. The blond strands were the product of good cosmetic chemistry. Hannah had never really known how old she was, and she still couldn't tell.

"Well, it's been a long time," Mrs. T. said. "You're out of the department and a lawyer now, I heard."

"I didn't expect you to keep tabs on me," Hannah said.

"Honey, anytime someone starts sniffing down my trail, all my little alarm bells trip. I got four phone calls about you yesterday in less than an hour."

"Are you still working?"

She tilted her hand. "Little of this, little of that. I'm pretty selective. I can't afford to spend any time away from this munchkin."

Hannah had never heard her voice any fear of jail before. "Is something wrong?"

She laughed. "No, not yet. But I think everybody's number comes up, sooner or later. There's a judge out in San Bernardino County that would just love to get me, the old coot. I won't give him the satisfaction."

"I came to ask a favor. I don't think it will put you at any risk."

"Tell me about it."

"Do you remember Janie Meister?"

Her eyes clouded. "I do indeed."

Hannah told her what had happened: Janie's reappearance in Las Almas. Hannah's theory that she might be with her mother, Claire, as both of them ran from Bill Meister. She described Janie in her street-kid guise.

"I hoped you might be helping one of them," Hannah said. "Or that maybe you'd heard something."

She shook her head. "No one's contacted me. I think I'd remember Janie. I've still got her picture in my files."

"She's changed a bit."

"Children do. I think that you can tell, though—the eyes, the smile." She paused. "But this one . . ."

"What?"

"I heard the little girl was dead."

Hannah felt that as a stab to the heart. "Who told you that?"

She took Hannah's hand and patted it. "It was gossip, dear. Word sort of came back, through people in your old department, some gals I know in county social services. You were pretty hard on some of them, I heard."

"No harder than I was on myself. We abandoned Janie. There was no excuse for it."

"We're human, Hannah. We make mistakes. Even you, even me." She smiled, and it felt like absolution. "But now you think she's alive?"

Hannah nodded. "She won't talk to me. She's run away."

"She's scared of something," Mrs. T. said. "Maybe her mom doesn't want her out, where her father could spot her, so she's sneaking out to see you. She might not even know if she can trust you."

"I thought of that."

"So you want me to see what I can find out? See where Mrs. Claire Meister is living? Any idea what her new name might be?"

"I don't know."

"What was her maiden name?"

"God, I don't . . . no, wait. I think I do." She shut her eyes and made the trip back to the interview room. She mentally opened the file that held Janie's case. "Higgins? I think that was Janie's middle name. Could it be her mother's maiden name?"

"I'll see what I can do with that. Now, how would I find Bill?"

"Bill? Why?"

"Well, have you considered that they all might still be together?"

Hannah hadn't. "Not possible."

"It is possible, believe me. What did Claire do for a living?"

"She wasn't working then. Meister didn't want her to."

Mrs. T. snorted her disdain. "Typical. So she probably doesn't have a lot of skills. Hard to think about getting away when you can't support yourself and your kid. That's why they might still be with him. What did Bill do?"

Hannah told her about CARNECO and Bill's slick sales patter. "I never knew for a fact that he was doing anything illegal," she added.

Mrs. T. nodded. "That's how the good ones operate. It's harder to track those guys these days. Big boiler rooms attract too much attention, so people like that work out of hotel rooms, apartments, even their cars, thanks to cell phones. But I know some people who might have heard if he's back in the game. I'll call you."

Hannah was only a little surprised that Mrs. T. kept up on the changing methodologies of criminal enterprises. Hers was a job that required varied skills. "Thanks. I don't know what you're charging currently, but . . ."

"You can owe me. I might need a good lawyer someday."

Hannah nodded, but didn't get up to leave. "Do you really think they might all be together still? It's so repulsive, I can barely think about it."

Mrs. T. patted her hand again. "Then let me, honey. I'm used to it."

18

Hannah made her delayed visit to Caesar Pritzker's store in Laguna Beach the next day. It was a small place a block off Coast Highway, with an antiquarian bookshop on one side and a designer florist on the other. Good company for a business like his.

She called before she left Las Almas and felt after hanging up that Pritzker would probably spend the forty minutes before her arrival practicing his speech about how much he loved and cherished Freddy. He was working in the display window when she pulled up: a short, thick man with ruddy skin and a bald head, fiddling with the arrangement of *objets* on a Nelson bench. He greeted her with a sigh of despair. "A horror, what happened to Freddy. I loved him like a son."

He offered her tea, and within two minutes, his alibi: he had been out of town when Freddy died. He was in Dayton, on the trail of a "significant" collection of Roseville pottery. He'd cut the trip short when Marian called to tell him the tragic news.

"She's my dearest friend—more than a friend, really," he confided. Unnecessarily, it seemed to Hannah. "She was devastated, of course."

Hannah nodded. "Even though she and Freddy weren't speaking?"

He waved a hand. "That happened all the time. Both of them are volatile. Freddy was, I mean."

"I understand you two didn't always get along, either."

He shook his head. "I got along. Freddy was the one with the problem. He didn't like having a boss. I actually insisted he show up on time, do real work. But we managed to reach an accommodation."

"You needed Marian's contacts, and he couldn't find anyone else who'd put up with him."

Pritzker raised an eyebrow. "If you want to be crass about it. He was taking care of things while I was out of town. I was actually very sorry to hear what happened."

"How long were you in Dayton?"

He made an expression of disgust. "Too long. I hate traveling, hate the planes, the hotels."

"Where did you stay?"

He gave her a slightly irritated smile. "You know Dayton?"

"Not intimately."

"The Marriott. And I had dinner at Jay's, a seafood place. Did Marian imply I hadn't gone?"

"No," Hannah said. "Why would she?"

Caesar huffed indignantly. "She sees conspiracies everywhere. Let me show you something."

He led her back to his office and took a stack of pictures from his desk. He held out one in which he, Freddy, and Marian Roche were at a table in some kind of Middle Eastern restaurant.

"It started out as a lovely evening." He smiled, showing very white and unnaturally regular teeth. A fence of rounded pickets.

In the picture, a belly dancer, her head cut off at the top of the frame, shimmied behind the diners. Freddy looked away from the camera, a profile in misery against the backdrop of the dancer's undulant flesh. His mother sat next to him. She clenched his hand with what looked like bone-crushing intensity. On the other side, Caesar's arm was draped possessively around Marian's shoulder. Hannah guessed him to be ten years younger than her. In his black shirt, with his red tie and red skin, he looked like a turkey vulture.

"Dinner didn't end well, I gather," Hannah said.

"No. Marian accused Freddy of having a secret affair with the dancer."

"Untrue?"

Caesar gave her an astounded look. "You know damn well it was. Marian refused to see what Freddy was about. She still does." He flipped through the subsequent pictures, and Hannah had a glimpse of antique-crammed rooms.

"May I?"

"These aren't important." But when she didn't relent, he reluctantly put the pictures in her hand. "Some shots of Marian's place. An inventory she wanted me to make. For insurance, and she asked me . . ." His voice trailed off as Hannah thumbed through the shots.

Marian Roche's house brimmed with things for which someone like Caesar would give his capped teeth: Oriental rugs, art pottery, silver, furniture. Very little kitsch, if you didn't count the dozens of snow domes assembled on the dining room table. But they might have a price beyond rubies, too, for all Hannah knew.

So although Caesar and Marian Roche were a team, making a killing on the deaths of her friends, Caesar was planning to be a solo act someday. He'd wheedled his way into Marian Roche's life and probably her will. Freddy's death put Caesar in line for a windfall. That was a good reason to confirm the details of Caesar's trip with someone other than Caesar.

For the next few days, Hannah turned not searching for Janie into a sort of Zen exercise. If the girl sensed safety, the absence of a pursuer, she might emerge. Hannah did allow herself quick checks from the corner of her eye, or glances in the rearview mirror. That didn't seem like chasing.

On Saturday, as the late afternoon skies alternated between sun and rainy shadow, her restraint paid off. As Hannah drove to the market for wine, cheese, and crackers—her version of sustenance when Bobby's leftovers had run out—she saw Janie.

She sat in the lower branches of a tree in the park near Hannah's house, using a veil of leaves for cover. Hannah, in her role as Zen student, resisted the urge to slam on the brakes. She drove on, but slowly enough that Janie had time to climb down and follow her if she wanted to.

Hannah finished her shopping in a few minutes. As she put the groceries in the back seat, she saw Janie idling by the KFC at the far side of the parking lot. Hannah drove home, sensing that Janie would follow. She put away her purchases, made lunch, made herself be patient. She'll be here, she thought. Just wait.

After she ate, Hannah went upstairs and ran the shower. If

Janie had arrived and was crouched in her camellia-bush hiding place, she would hear the rumblings of the ancient water heater. Hannah pushed back the bathroom window's curtain, and there was Janie, emerging from a small opening in the thicket. She stretched and yawned, dusted bits of leaves out of her hair, stuck her hands in her pockets, and walked up the driveway a few paces, as casually as she had that first night. Hannah turned off the shower and saw Janie tense as the pipes rumbled. She ran back to her hiding place, retrieved something, and sauntered toward downtown.

Hannah had already planned what to do when Janie finally showed herself. She put on a tan coat she hadn't worn in months and draped a shawl-sized scarf over her head. She grabbed the girl's jacket and toy from the sofa, pulled the Integra into the yard to clear the driveway, then slowly backed Mrs. Snow's LeBaron out of the garage. It had been in the darkness for so long that Hannah had forgotten what color it was—something close to metallic prune.

She put on her sunglasses and checked the effect in the rearview mirror. A sort of neo-Jackie O. look, but at least her hair and face were well hidden, and the weather made the outfit plausible. She wasn't sure, however, that she could drive slowly enough to follow a kid on foot without attracting attention.

But when she saw Janie a few blocks down the street, she was on her skateboard, which she had apparently stowed in the shrubs. She sped along the sidewalks, jumping curbs and weaving through a cluster of kids engaged in a game of street hockey. She glanced once at the LeBaron when they both stopped for a traffic light, but she didn't seem to recognize Hannah at the wheel. As they neared the Plaza, Hannah parked and followed Janie on foot. Her route led into Hannah's past.

She had spent countless Saturdays in this same kind of aimless, solitary wandering around downtown. She remembered how lost, confused, and lonely she'd felt in those years. She distanced herself from her mother's oscillating moods. She carefully gauged her father's amiability by the level of bourbon in the bottle before asking him for money, a lift to school, or permission to stay overnight at a friend's house. She wondered what Janie was thinking now, as she plunked down on a bench to let a moment of shifting afternoon sun warm her face.

The girl pulled a handful of change out of her jeans pocket, counted it, smiled, and tossed her skateboard to the pavement. She leaped on and pushed off, barreling into the street, forcing a Honda to screech to a stop. The driver beat on the horn and swore at Janie, who casually flipped him off. That was something Hannah hadn't had the nerve to do until she was fifteen.

Hannah ran a few steps to catch up, using the Saturday antique-browsing crowd as cover. Janie wove through the shoppers and made a hard right at a corner. Hannah knew where she was going: Sweet Stop, a place that still sold lemonheads, horehound drops, and Boston baked beans. Hannah also knew—from her one humiliating petty shoplifting experience—that the store had no back door. She waited for Janie to come out.

She emerged with a white bag, popping jelly beans into her mouth, skating idly along. A block later, a gray Volkswagen pulled up next to her. Janie waved to the driver. The car stopped, and Janie jumped in. Hannah ran back to the LeBaron.

For several blocks, there was no sign of the Volkswagen. The shopping crowds had thinned. Hannah took a turn onto one of the downtown's main drags. And there, at a Jack in the Box, she saw the car. Janie got out. The bug sped away, the driver tapping out a goodbye on its nasal, high-pitched horn. Hannah sat in the parking lot, which gave her a partial view of the restaurant's counter and dining area. Janie bought a large order of fries. She sat down at a table and began an almost ritualistic consumption of the fries. She dipped each in a coating of ketchup, rolled it in salt, and put it away in three bites. Only three, never two or four. High Mass went by more quickly than Janie's snack, Hannah thought.

When she finally finished, she stopped at the counter. The girl smiled at her and consulted her watch. Janie, frowning, thanked her. Hannah glanced at the LeBaron's clock. Miraculously, it still worked, and it read six-thirty. Janie skated more purposefully now, without stops for window shopping or pauses for food. She's expected somewhere, Hannah thought. Maybe it's time to go home.

Hannah followed her to a part of Las Almas that had been rezoned for apartments in the sixties. The bungalows had been bulldozed and replaced by cheaply built U-shaped complexes with central courtyards and swimming pools. Predictably, they turned to slums in a few years. At the entrance to one of these tumbledown places, Janie made a sharp turn and disappeared.

Hannah parked and got out. The building seemed too quiet and still. Almost Saturday night, but she heard no music. No one entered with shopping bags or party-starting six-packs. In the sheltered entrance, mailboxes lined the wall on the left. Plastered across the middle row was a notice: the building was condemned and next month would be demolished to allow for the widening of the I–5 Freeway. It would happen on schedule, Hannah thought. No preservation group would bother with a place like this.

She couldn't wander around the patio discreetly. Every apartment looked down on it. But she felt she couldn't leave without making some kind of contact. What good would more cat-and-mouse games do her? She'd tracked Janie to what was probably her home, temporarily anyway. Janie knew where to find her. It was stalemate. Someone had to advance the game.

She went back to the car, wrote her home phone number on a business card, and put it in the pocket of Janie's windbreaker. She tucked in the lion's head, too. Back in the entryway, she heaped the jacket on top of the mailboxes, knowing that Janie would spot it. And then she left, striving for a Zenlike acceptance of the fact that once Janie had her treasured lion back, she might never seek out Hannah again.

The girl waited inside the apartment, holding the door slightly ajar, wondering what Hannah would do now that she'd found out where she and Jared lived. She heard the echoing footsteps around the mailboxes, heard them leave and return, heard the final clang of the gate. What was up with that? Why had she come back?

She went downstairs and immediately saw the jacket. She felt herself shaking as she reached for it, not knowing what she'd do if Bert wasn't there. But he tumbled out of the pocket, along with a white card. She caught him before he hit the ground. His eye stared at her, reproaching her for her carelessness. She was shaky with gratitude and relief. She looked at the card and had time to stuff it in her pocket when she heard the footsteps behind her. Jared was weighted down with a garbage bag full of sopping-wet jeans.

"Did she follow you?"

She nodded. "Yeah, but I didn't know that until I was nearly home."

"You'll get better at it. Practice is what it takes."

"What next?"

He shrugged. "Not sure. We'll see what she does."

"What do you think she'll do?"

He sighed. "Maisey-Daisy. Don't get all anxious. You got some quarters still?"

Almost every night, Jared got onto his bike and went to work, punching out the locks of parking meters with a screwdriver and hammer. A full coin canister held sixty or so dollars in change. If the lock wouldn't yield, and if they were particularly hard up, Jared would clip the head of the meter with pipe cutters and bust it open in the privacy of their apartment. It kept them going. The criminal aspects bothered Janie a little at first, but Jared insisted that it wasn't wrong at all.

"But it is stealing, right?" she asked.

"No more so than making people pay for time. Time doesn't belong to the city, does it? Even Einstein didn't own time, right?"

She nodded. "Time's free?"

"Fuckin' A," Jared said.

It was enough to get by on, but they still had to economize. They washed their clothes in the apartment bathtub, since the water hadn't been turned off yet. Then they carted them, dripping wet, down the street for drying.

She pulled her last quarters out of her pocket and gave them to him. "I spent some on candy and fries," she admitted.

"That's okay. Did you eat any veggies today?"

"Don't fries count?"

"No. We'll go to see Carl later."

They watched a rerun of *The X-Files* in the laundromat while their jeans tumbled. They changed in the bathrooms and stopped by the Plaza to see which of their friends might be around. Jared knew guys from his group-home days to whom he turned for various favors—I.D.s, telephone calling-card numbers, and if he was truly needy, a loan now and then. But his homies weren't there, so they went on to Carl's Jr. by themselves.

Jared watched the guy in faded holey jeans and a denim shirt with pearly buttons on the pockets. He had thinning brown hair and a bandanna that reminded him of something a golden retriever would wear. He was sucking on a big Coke and intently reading a swinging-singles magazine. But he didn't fool Jared. He'd been trailing them since the Plaza, maybe even since the laundry stop. Jared wasn't sure who sent him, but it didn't matter. He had a pockmarked face and squinting eyes. He'd stuffed a pack of smokes in his pocket. Jared bet his breath reeked of cigarettes. He had a sudden flash of his father's face, shrouded in smoke. Daddy turned up at the strangest times in his head. His first impulse was always to smash his nose into his spongy brain.

Maisey-Daisy sat down with a plate of salad dripping in ranch dressing. He didn't say anything to her about the guy. She would freak out, and then the guy would know he'd been spotted.

But she noticed his distraction anyway. "What's wrong?"

"Nothing," Jared said. He watched her tear through the array of vegetables: corn, garbanzo beans, and red bell pepper. She color-coordinated her food—all yellow and scarlet, this time. "Get something green. You've been skimping."

She sighed. "I hate lettuce."

"Come on. Humor me."

She scowled at him. "Okay. But you have to play cards with me later."

"Deal. Get me some broccoli while you're there."

She went back to the salad bar, and Jared watched as the guy slurped the last of his Coke, threw away his trash, and left. Jared knew he'd be waiting for them outside somewhere.

19

When Hannah came back from playing what might have been her endgame with Janie, she found a cryptic message from Mrs. T.: "It's Operation Silver Dollar. Call Rudy Podesta."

Hannah recognized the name: Podesta, a retired Newport Beach Police detective, occasionally played pool with her father. He had to be in his seventies by now — what was he doing on the job? Hannah didn't have Podesta's number, and he wasn't listed. She would have to get it from her father, which meant running Estelle's gantlet. She steeled herself for the encounter.

Estelle shouted her hello over a grating metallic background noise. She was forever buying kitchen gadgets from television ads. The counter usually brimmed with blenders, dehydrators, juicers, and several iterations of the Veg-O-Matic.

"Estelle, it's Hannah." She had to shout, too. "Is Dad there?"

The noisy appliance went off. Estelle let the silence hang for a moment, as though that was supposed to be a form of punishment. "I told him how rude you were to me. I'm not sure he'll want to talk to you."

Hannah wished, not for the first time, that her father had stayed a lonely widower. "Let him decide that, all right?"

The receiver fell to the counter. Hannah could hear clicks — the tiny, strappy stacked-heel sandals Estelle favored — as she marched out the back door. Jimmy was doubtless in the garage, fiddling with some project. Hannah never was quite sure what occupied him out there.

After a few moments she could hear the phone being lifted. "You sure can make Estelle mad."

Hannah remembered when his voice was as clear and vibrant as a fast-moving river, a reflection of his restless, charged personality. But with age, it was as though the channel had been clogged with mud. He sounded thick and sluggish lately.

"It's mutual, Dad. She gave me a bad time about Guillermo."

"He call you yet?"

"No. I don't think he will."

"And you're not calling him?"

"I don't have any idea what I'd say."

She could almost see her father shaking his head. "Sorry, sweetheart."

She didn't want to talk about relationships with Jimmy. He was hardly one to teach her how to keep love fresh. His marriage to Hannah's mother, before her death in a drunken stupor when Hannah was seventeen, had been an intermittent slugfest. She didn't know if he and Estelle duked it out, but she doubted it. Her mother's death had taken the fight out of Jimmy. It had certainly put him off the bottle—for a few years, anyway.

She cleared her throat and put the conversation back on course. "Listen, Dad, I called to see if you had a number for Rudy Podesta."

"Rudy? Sure. Hold on." He came back and read the number to her. "I haven't seen him in a month or so. Why are you calling him?"

There was something about the tone of his voice—the sound of a father prying, a shadow of interference—that rankled. "It's a work thing, Dad."

"And we don't talk shop anymore?" It wasn't like Jimmy to fish around for ways to keep Hannah on the phone. She wondered if he and Estelle had been fighting.

"I'd love to, but I can't right now. I'll call back soon, okay?"

"Sure. Fine." He sounded almost surly, and before Hannah could ask him what was going on, he'd hung up. She considered calling back right away, but the thought of having to talk to Estelle twice in one day made her change her mind. She called Podesta instead.

•   •   •

As Podesta came into the Belmont Shore brew pub where they had agreed to meet for dinner, Hannah saw that he'd retained his looks despite advancing age. At seventy, Podesta still had his wavy silver hair; a neatly trimmed moustache; a smooth, tanned face; and a marked resemblance to César Romero. He'd always had a reputation for being a lady's man, and Hannah felt sure that hadn't changed.

He kissed her on the cheek as he sat down. He still ran every morning, he said. His spartan meal order—minestrone soup and green salad without dressing—testified to his desire to stay trim. He didn't even seem tempted by the brewery's Top Sail Ale. Hannah had one, deciding to postpone concern about fat until she was closer to Podesta's age.

Podesta sipped his iced tea and dropped his voice to tell Hannah that he could only discuss Silver Dollar with her if she swore not to blab about it. She swore, and Podesta smiled.

"I know I can trust you because of your law enforcement background and your impeccable taste in fathers and friends."

"Which friends?"

"That Mrs. T." He smiled dreamily.

Hannah was amazed. She always imagined that some awful personal loss had led Mrs. T. to her life's work. She assumed that a vow of celibacy went along with her secretive existence. Wrong again.

As Podesta slowly grazed through his meal, he told her how he could help—as a favor to Mrs. T. Operation Silver Dollar was a sting, using retired police officers and some AARP volunteers to catch investment-fraud telemarketers. Podesta called them the leeches.

"Some of the poor souls who've already been scammed agreed to let us use their phone lines. We just sit back and wait for the calls."

"The con artists haven't moved on by then?"

"No, because these poor old people's names get floated in the underground as easy marks. Their names are like gold."

"They make up a sucker list," Hannah said.

"Yes. And the hell of it is that some people are so desperate to make up their losses that they'll invest again. And lose, of course."

"Worse than Vegas," Hannah said.

"Absolutely. No showgirls, no Siegfried and Roy. Well, in

this case, that list is how these cons will get their comeuppance. Once a call comes in, it gets routed to me or someone else on the team. We playact that we're these susceptible souls and record the calls so the U.S. attorney can build cases."

Hannah nodded. "Do you think Meister might turn up in your net?"

"Good chance. I remember CARNECO. That was a real slimy shop. There's a guy in Costa Mesa that's got a little version of it going — Coast Financial Services. He's been in the game forever, likes to reuse talent he trusts. Meister might hook up with him."

"But how will you know it's him? He won't use his real name."

"You'd be surprised how many do just that, or make up some variation. He might be Tony Meister, or Bill Master . . . it will be something close. It's too hard to keep making up new names. 'Who am I today?' You know?"

"This is all okay with your bosses? I don't want to muck up your investigation."

"Not a problem. We've got hundreds of these creeps we're working to indict. I already told my supervisor that a child molester might crop up. She said she'd be willing to let another agency pick him up quietly, if we can do it without blowing the rest of the sting. It would be great if it works out for the little girl."

"I hope it does."

He wiped his moustache and reached for her hand, patting it much as Mrs. T. had. "Now, why doesn't a pretty girl like you have a date on a Saturday night?"

She couldn't help smiling. She wondered if he had been collaborating with her father. "Well, Rudy, I don't know. I do have plans for tomorrow, though."

"Brunch? A nice run along the beach? Church?"

"No. I'm going to visit a pedophile who's charged with murdering his roommate."

He guffawed. "It's a relief to know some young people still honor the Sabbath."

20

As Jared and Mae walked home from their Saturday-splurge dinner, Jared scanned for the guy but didn't see him. He knew he was there, though. Mae was whistling something under her breath, oblivious to their tail. Jared undid the padlock on their front door, installed to ensure that the building's other squatters—particularly the nutcase downstairs—couldn't walk into the apartment and help themselves to their stuff. They didn't have a lot: his old bike, two army surplus sleeping bags, Mae's backpack, and Jared's voluminous duffel bag, which held his meter tools and baseball bat.

While Mae brushed her teeth, Jared tried to peer out into the dark spaces beyond the patio. He could almost feel the guy down there, watching the apartments, wondering which one he and Mae were in. As soon as they lit the candles in the living room, he would know.

"Cards?" Mae stood in the hallway, shuffling the deck they'd bought at a thrift store for a nickel. She loved beating him at gin, hearts, any game at all, but only if she really won. He played sloppy once and let her win. She knew immediately what he'd done, and she went into a royal snit over it.

"Why don't we just turn in?" Jared said.

She stared at him in amazement. "It's not even nine. God, I might as well be back at Orangewood."

He thought for a moment. "Okay." He decided that it wouldn't matter if the guy saw the candles. Jared lit the vanilla-scented votives they had lifted from a coffeehouse, and they played gin until Mae beat him three times straight.

"Loser, loser, three times a loser!" She grinned at him.

He feigned irritation, but was glad to see her happy. She'd had a spell of bad dreams recently. She would sit bolt upright, shrieking through clenched teeth, but still asleep. She was hard to wake and seemed to have no memory of what had terrified her. No memory she would talk about, anyway. He wanted to help her, but it was taking a long time. He wondered if he shouldn't find some other place for her to stay, where she would be safer. Then he realized he couldn't let her go.

"How about reading to me for a while?" Jared said.

She shrugged. "I don't feel like it."

"Come on." He worried about how little school she'd had, but neither of them could figure out how to get her into a classroom without attracting attention. She faked silent reading pretty well, but when she had to do it aloud, she mispronounced some words and didn't recognize others. He liked reading—it let him get away. It taught him stuff he needed to know. He wanted her to have those tools.

"Please, Maisey?"

"Only if you stop calling me that."

"All right. What book?"

She smiled darkly. "I've got another Poppy Z. Brite."

He shook his head. He'd thumbed through some of Brite's splatterpunk books, which Mae shoplifted with regularity. Brite's characters—white-trash New Orleans vampires and gay cannibal serial killers—weren't for him. As far as he was concerned, they weren't for her, either, but if he tried to take them away, she'd just dig her heels in. At least Brite used words that Mae wanted to look up—probably in hopes that they were dirty or gross. Jared made her write the unfamiliar ones down in a notebook, along with the definitions. But that didn't mean he wanted to hear Brite's graphic, sickening scenes read aloud.

"Maybe later. What about that book I got for you?" Jared had boosted a book of stories for her from a used bookshop downtown because there was a picture of a little mermaid on the cover. She had once said she liked the Disney video she'd seen as a kid.

She rolled her eyes. "Jesus, Jared. It's for babies."

"Just one."

"Oh, okay." She rooted it out of her backpack, sat down on

the floor, and flipped to a story. She wrinkled her nose disdainfully. "What's a match girl?"

"Don't know. Read it and we'll see."

Halfway through the story, when the freezing girl struck a match and saw her dead grandmother in the flame, Jared told her to stop. He was trying to keep the tears out of his eyes, but it was a struggle.

"That's good enough," he said. "We'll finish it tomorrow."

"She's not going to see her grandmother, is she? Grandma kicked a long time ago."

"Probably. I don't know," Jared said. He managed to wipe his eyes without her seeing. "I haven't read it."

"Why are kids always freezing to death in old books like this? Can't they break into someplace warm for the night? That's what we'd do."

He didn't answer her right away. "Not all kids are like us. Let's get some sleep."

She wouldn't admit it, but she didn't like sleeping in a room by herself. So even though having someone so close made Jared uneasy, he let her put her sleeping bag next to his. In the dark, he thought he heard her crying. He started to reach out, but the sick wave swamped him, and he pulled his hand back. He thought soothing thoughts for her, hoping they would touch her, even if he couldn't. He heard her shift and sigh, a sound she sometimes made when she held Bert close. Soon her breathing steadied and deepened.

Jared lay there, listening to her. He was glad it was nearly their last night in the apartment. He looked forward to a shower with hot water and a real bed. It had been a long time— months—since he'd had that. Almost a home.

The building was becoming too dangerous a place for them. People didn't pay much attention to a boy his age being on his own. But Maisey-Daisy was another matter. People noticed girls. And while she could act tough, it was like she slipped into a bubble sometimes, unaware of what was happening around her. She was like a sleepwalker, and that was dangerous, too. By this point in her life, she should not only have known Hannah was following her, but should immediately have spotted the seedy, smelly-breathed guy, too. Daddy, he thought, she didn't see you, but I did.

He told himself he shouldn't bad-mouth his foster sister,

even to himself. She was young—and a girl, after all. And she needed Jared. He felt a sweet sting of affection at the thought. He would protect her. He was committed to her. He smiled in the dark. Hell, he had nothing but commitment.

21

Hannah sat down on the other side of the Plexiglas and watched Mike Seward as he picked up the phone. If he'd been lined up with a half-dozen other men, and Hannah had been instructed to pick out the child molester, she probably wouldn't have chosen Seward. That was the problem with some criminals: they refused to fit their stereotypes.

In Seward's case, it was the eyes, which were not dim and shifty, but a clear olive green with long lashes. They were set in a small face framed by limp, unwashed black hair. Avoiding the showers, Hannah thought.

Seward smiled pleasantly at her, untroubled by the artifice of using a phone to talk to someone who sat a few feet away. "Freddy's mom wrote to say you might come by."

Hannah didn't like the sound of this. Marian Roche had no business making her contacts for her. And she'd never mentioned that she knew Seward. "You know her? And Freddy?"

He nodded. "Oh, yeah. I hadn't talked to him in years. Wrote to him a couple of times when he was up at the Men's Colony. Haven't seen him since he got out. But I called his mom when he died. Shame about him."

"Being murdered, you mean?"

"Well, not quite. That was a merciful release."

Hannah hadn't expected that. "You have an unusual definition of mercy."

"Not really. He was a zombie at the end. Brainwashed into poisoning himself."

"The Depo-Provera?"

"It's the most effective kind of extermination, you know, the kind where the state makes the victim hate himself. And the next thing you know, he's dead by his own hand. The state is off the hook. If this was happening in China, Amnesty International would be all over it."

"Freddy Roche didn't kill himself. And he was hardly a political prisoner," Hannah said.

Seward stared at her in astonishment. "He most certainly was. I am, too. We have been jailed and tortured because of the people we love."

Children, Hannah thought. She had kidded with Podesta about going to visit a pedophile. She didn't know Seward took the term literally. He obviously had no shame about sex with children. He thought it was a bold political statement.

"I thought Freddy was trying to change," Hannah said. "His engagement, for instance."

Seward stared and then collapsed in laughter. "His *what*?"

"He was engaged, supposedly. To a woman he met when he was in prison."

"Oh, Jesus. I know the one you mean. She's dreaming."

Hannah thought so, too. She made a mental note to call Lisette. There was something odd about this engagement.

She waited until he was done hooting and shaking his head. "If you knew Freddy, do you know Henry Charles, too?"

Seward's amused expression soured. "Henry Charles was a sick freak who raped little girls."

"Is. He's not dead yet."

"Too bad."

"So you do know him."

"I know he never, ever loved children. They're like fodder for him. Just something that he chews up. There's no feeling there."

"So not every child molester is a pedophile, by your definition."

"Many people—most of them—claim to love children. People who deny children their rights don't, not really. Forcing a child to deny his feelings, keeping him from exploring his sexual nature for eighteen years—now, that's real child abuse."

Hannah was already tired of the twisted revisionist screed. It was like listening to a Holocaust denier argue that Zyklon-B was a simple little cure for lice. "Mr. Seward, help me out here. How well do you know Henry Charles?"

Seward shrugged. "I know people who know Hank."

"Did Cotter Davis know him?"

Seward shook his head. "No. Cotter Davis was a pathetic old fart who was in the wrong place at the wrong time."

"And you didn't kill him?"

"No way. My lawyer is going to shred the DA's case. I'm good on this one. Innocent, one hundred percent."

"You didn't have a fight with Davis over pictures?"

"Look, I don't know who this supposed police informant is, but he's lying."

"So there was no pornography in your house?"

"Well, Cotter had copies of *Penthouse* and *Playboy* in his room. Does that count?"

Hannah wasn't going to let Seward use his political discourse to avoid the issue. "Let's not waste time, Mr. Seward. If you talked to Marian, you must know what I'm doing here."

He nodded. "Yeah. She doesn't buy that Freddy was killed by a robber."

"Right. So save the First Amendment speech. All I want to know is whether someone made up a story about you having pictures of boys. You had none at all?"

He stared at her for a moment and then put down the phone. He reached down and pulled out a piece of paper and pencil, which he apparently had hidden in his sock. He scribbled something and pressed the paper against the plastic barrier. She leaned in to read the small, neat handwriting: *Not by the time the cops got there.*

He didn't want to take any chances on the call being monitored. Hannah nodded. He scribbled some more and put it up for her to read: *Cotter didn't know anything. Wasn't even a boy-lover. Just a sad old guy—no family, no friends.* He balled up the paper until it was no bigger than a marble, and swallowed it. He hid his pencil and picked up the phone.

"And now he's dead," Hannah said.

"Because of me, but not the way the police say."

"How, then?"

"Somebody *thought* he was me."

"You don't look anything alike."

"You're assuming that the assassin knew what I looked like.

What if he didn't? Cotter had my car. He was wearing my jacket. He took it from my closet—didn't even ask, by the way. So it sort of serves him right." He smiled, but the expression was nervous. Pinpricks of sweat covered his forehead.

"You said an assassin did this?" Hannah said.

He came closer to the barrier and whispered into the phone. "We know someone is after us."

"Who is 'us'?"

"You know." He made quotation marks with his fingers. " 'Monsters.' 'Freaks.' "

"What makes you think so?"

He sat back. "I met some friends at a bar, for a meeting."

"What kind of meeting?" She knew it wasn't going to be Kiwanis.

"PPRI. Panlove Political Rights International."

"Panlove as in 'universal'? Or as in 'Peter'?"

He glared at her. "You making fun of me?"

She shook her head. "No." But she felt queasy, imagining a PPRI meeting agenda: a picture swap, followed by a talk on techniques for luring children into sex. Then cake and ice cream.

"After the bar closed, I walked to my car," Seward said. "I'd parked a few blocks away on a side street."

It was more discreet to do it that way, Hannah thought. He wasn't supposed to be consorting with other pedophiles.

"It was dark. The street lamps made pools of light on the sidewalk. Very quiet out, at that hour." Seward's voice had become soothing and melodious, with a storyteller's power to enthrall. It was innocent enough now, but she imagined how he used it with his victims and felt her skin turn cold.

"For the first block, everything was normal. You'd hear dogs and the wind. But after a while, I felt like I wasn't alone. It was just a feeling, at first. Then I heard something. I turned around, and there was nothing there, but then the leaves on some bushes were moving. I heard a few footsteps. Then they'd stop. I got pretty scared, so I ran." He put the phone down. When he looked up, Hannah saw the fear in his eyes.

"Then what?"

He couldn't hear her. But he'd read her lips, and he raised the phone to continue. "I got in my car and tore ass out of there."

"Maybe someone overheard your meeting and decided to scare the hell out of you."

He shook his head. "This was a place that we know. They leave us alone. And we're careful about what we say."

"So it was your imagination, then."

"No. The same thing happened to another guy, that same night, at almost the same time. No attack, just someone letting him know he'd been seen with us."

"Did you tell the police?"

He shook his head. "Too complicated. And they wouldn't believe me. I'm not sure my lawyer believes it, either."

"So you agree with Marian. Someone is stalking pedophiles," Hannah said.

"Somebody knowledgeable about us. What we believe." He wet his lips and went on. "Do you know the date of the attack on Henry Charles?"

"Late April," Hannah said. "That's all I remember."

"April twenty-fifth. It's significant. Do you know what happened on that date?"

"No."

"Do you know the name Charles Lutwidge Dodgson?"

It sounded familiar, but Hannah was too slow with the answer to suit Seward. "You'll know his pen name: Lewis Carroll. Who was Alice Liddell?"

"She was the model for *Alice in Wonderland,* wasn't she?"

He nodded. "The girl who inspired two books. The girl he loved. Read the books closely. It's all there."

Seward stopped abruptly. Hannah shifted her glance and caught her own expression of revulsion reflected in the plastic barrier. Was there nothing innocent in the world? Did a children's tale have to be marred by a salacious back story? She willed her face into neutrality, but Seward saw her reaction.

"He did love her, Hannah, make no mistake."

"What does Lewis Carroll have to do with Henry Charles?"

"It's the date. April twenty-fifth was the day Dodgson and Alice met. We chose that date to celebrate our way of life and love—Pedophile Liberation Day."

"Is this your own private holiday, or do other people celebrate it, too?"

"Word gets around. The Internet has been invaluable. People honor the day in their own ways. But some very sick person used it as the day to liberate Charles from this world. Not that I disagree with the target, but it could just as easily have been me."

"You don't think the date was a coincidence?"

He shook his head. "I would have thought so, until Freddy was killed, and Cotter got shot. Someone chose April twenty-fifth to start a campaign. Look, I'm not crazy about jail. It can be a dangerous place for someone of my . . . inclinations. But for the moment, I'm glad I'm here. I'm safer than Freddy and Henry Charles were."

22

It was late afternoon, touched by unseasonable rain and a cool wind, when Hannah left the jail. She was thinking about Alice Liddell and the holiday proclaimed in honor of Dodgson's obsession with her. How did Alice remember the day she met Dodgson? What was her childhood like after that? Thinking of the literary Alice and her tumble into a mad world, she drove home. She took down the locked gun box that had resided on an upper shelf of a linen closet since the day Matthew had come to live with her. Her father, with his unerringly inappropriate instincts, had chosen the occasion to give her a Glock Model 17 semiautomatic pistol.

"You said you need to protect the little guy, right? This sweet Austrian beauty will do the job." He gave her a goofy grandfatherly smile.

"I was talking about socket plugs and cabinet latches, Dad, not heavy artillery," Hannah said. But she had thanked him before he could pull a hurt expression. Then she promptly locked the matte-finished pistol away, wishing it a *gute nacht*.

She put it in its shoulder holster and returned to the apartment building where she had seen Janie the day before.

This time, the building's tall metal gate was shut and secured with a new lock. There was no foothold on the fence that would enable her to climb over it. Hannah peered into the breezeway's shadows. She couldn't tell if the jacket was still sitting on top of the mailboxes. To find out if Janie had taken her offering of trust, she would have to find another way into the building.

Hannah walked down the weedy strip that separated the building from the one next door.

At the back of the building was a parking lot and another gate. This one was unlocked. More precisely, the lock had been beaten into submission. Someone was determined to make the building home for as long as possible.

As Hannah walked the perimeter of the courtyard, she saw apartment doors standing open. Inside, there were bare kitchens, their floors etched with the outlines of missing appliances. Carpeting held the impression of sofa feet. Ghosts of picture frames hung on walls that had been navajo white but now were deserted tan.

As she passed one closed apartment door, it flew open. She instinctively stepped back. A thin man with tangled hair leaped out at her, glaring. His jeans, nearly black with grime, hung low around his hips. He was bare-chested, with leathery skin and scrawny arms. He ground his teeth. Hannah couldn't tell if he was crazy, high, or both.

"Not going," he said. His eyes took in the bulge under the side of her thin linen jacket, registering the gun's presence. He didn't back off, though. He grumbled defiantly and shifted on his bare feet. Hannah thought she understood: he'd taken her for a cop, or someone hired to clear the building.

"Okay," she said. It was clear he wasn't armed. She held her hands away from her body to show him she wasn't inclined to draw down on him. "I'm not here to move you. I'm just checking the mailboxes."

He squinted at her as if she were the crazy one. "They don't bring mail here."

"I know. I left something out there. I want to see if it's still there. You can watch, make sure I don't take anything that's not mine." She didn't want to leave him behind her, in case there was a weapon in the apartment he'd commandeered.

He nodded and followed her. Hannah tried asking him if he knew any of the other people who were staying here, but he didn't seem to hear her. He'd tuned to some other station in his head.

When they came to the mailboxes, Hannah saw that the jacket was gone. But if the building was inhabited with nearly naked men, someone other than Janie might have taken it to keep warm. She ran her hand along the top of the boxes, wondering if the animal's head had been left behind. At first she felt nothing but dust. Then her hand connected with some papers, and they fluttered to the ground: a newspaper and a postcard mass mailer, the latter had something written on it.

Before Hannah could pick it up, the scrawny man snatched the card from the ground. He frowned as he looked at it.

"May I have that, please?" Hannah said.

"Thanks, Hannah." He held onto it.

Hannah stared at him. "How did you know my name?"

"It says that: 'Thanks, Hannah.'" He handed the paper to her. "You Hannah?"

She looked at the note. Finally, a connection. "It's from a girl I think lives here," Hannah said. "I returned her jacket to her."

He nodded, but Hannah wasn't sure it was in answer to her remark.

"She's about eleven, light-brown hair. Have you seen her?"

"Gone," he said. "All gone. Except for him. He's staying." He nodded to a downstairs apartment that still had drapes over its windows. Another squatter, Hannah guessed.

"You want to see her place?" Without waiting for Hannah's answer, he headed for the stairs that led to the second floor. Hannah followed him to a door that stood open. A white candle, burned down to a now-hardened puddle, was waxed in place on the kitchen counter. There were fast-food cartons on the floor.

Hannah checked the bedroom. It also was empty, except for a book—Hans Christian Andersen stories. She took it with her. The bare-chested man was outside, leaning back against the second-floor railing.

"When did she go?" Hannah asked.

He shrugged and shook his head. "This morning?"

"Was she alone?"

He shrugged again. "We're all alone."

Hannah was about to ask him for a less existential reply when he suddenly grabbed her by the arm and threw her against the stucco wall. The rough surface raked her cheek.

"Don't come back here, Hannah!" He screamed the words. His breath reeked of alcohol and rotted meat. His body smelled worse. "It's my house now! All mine!"

He dragged her toward the stairs with one hand and thrust

the other under her jacket, reaching for the Glock. Hannah spun out of his grasp, shoved him down, and kicked him in the stomach. She fled down the stairs, losing her footing as she ran but catching herself on the railing. He got to his feet and stood at the top of the stairs, panting, shifting, flexing his hands, staring at her as though her head had sprouted vipers.

"Go!" He threw up his head, elongated the word. Howled it.

Hannah ran, glancing back once to be sure he wasn't following her. She'd misread him, seeing the scruffy mutt and not the rabid dog. Was she losing all her instincts?

When she got to the car, she locked the doors and sat there for a moment, quickly surveying the damage to her face in the rearview mirror. The stucco only had scratched her—a little concealer would cover it. She twisted the mirror back and as she started to pull away, she stopped and cautiously got out.

What caught her eye was a skateboard, peeking out of the bushes. Hannah hadn't paid enough attention to Janie's board to know if this one was hers, but this apartment house was a twin of the one she'd just left. This one was also posted for demolition, but the building's gate stood open. Maybe Janie's move had been a short one.

But Hannah wasn't going in there now. She would let the bare-chested manager cool off. The next time she visited, she would be more cautious. She would be ready to draw the Glock.

Hannah drove by the twin buildings on Monday, but the topless psychotic was on patrol, flapping his arms and howling. She didn't want another confrontation. If he was this whacked-out all the time, maybe Janie was staying away, too. Patience, she thought. Wait a couple days. If he leaves, Janie might resurface.

She tried to concentrate on work, finishing a summary-judgment motion in one case and dashing off a letter to a pissy opponent in another. She called Lisette Blackburn, but got her answering machine. She wrangled enough information out of a desk clerk and antique-store owner in Dayton to confirm that Caesar Pritzker had told the truth about his visit, although his actual time of departure was hazy. Finally Hannah managed to get an impromptu appointment with Cassandra Thrasher, the lawyer who had prosecuted Freddy Roche for his lewd acts with a child. If Hannah hurried, Thrasher said, she could give her twenty minutes right away.

Now that Thrasher was no longer working for county wages, she could afford an office with a view. Hers was in Orange, in a high-rise that overlooked the Crystal Cathedral. Hannah looked out at the church as she waited for the lawyer to come back with coffee. Against a sky dulled by smog, the building had none of a crystal's faceted radiance. And it reminded Hannah less of a cathedral than of the skeleton of a new ride at Disneyland.

Thrasher arrived with two mugs, holding an unlit cigarette between her lips. She motioned Hannah to a chair and lit up, in defiance of any number of anti-smoking laws. Hannah liked her immediately.

Her auburn hair was styled in an unmoving pageboy— evidence that the reign of Queen Aquanet had not yet ended. She wore an expensive St. John Knits suit and foot-wrenching pointed red pumps. Hannah bet she was divorced, drank her bourbon neat, and played poker with a bunch of wisecracking public defenders on Friday nights. Maybe she even took one home, occasionally.

"Freddy Roche." Thrasher's voice sounded like a rake on gravel. "A creep. And now a dead creep. You believe in karma?"

"If it exists, it doesn't work fast enough to suit me."

"It worked plenty fast for Freddy. David Alvarez can finally sleep nights."

"That was the victim?"

Thrasher nodded. "You want to hear about the case?"

"Please," Hannah said.

Thrasher told Hannah what she already knew from the newspaper story. But the press hadn't reported the case's aftermath. "Roche went to prison, but that didn't help David much, or Anita," Thrasher said.

"That's David's mother?"

Thrasher nodded and stubbed out her cigarette. "She blamed herself for what happened, for not seeing what Roche was up to. David blamed her, too, in a way. He wouldn't go to school, wouldn't go to counseling. He quit church, took up pot. Found some bad friends to hang with. When he slugged Anita for trying to stop him from leaving the house, he wound up in Orangewood. You know Orangewood?"

Hannah nodded. The county's home for abused and neglected kids, which sometimes sheltered troubled children like David Alvarez—the ones not yet sufficiently criminalized to belong in the Juvenile Hall next door.

"He ran away from Orangewood and from a couple of the group homes they put him in," Thrasher said. "Anita was heartsick."

"Is he still in the system?"

"No. He seemed to pull up from the spin he'd gone into. He went home to Anita's about a year ago, just after he turned sixteen. They'd each got some counseling. I think the kid might have gotten a little Prozac, too."

"So he's all right now?"

Thrasher shrugged. "I guess so. Haven't heard from them in quite a while. I don't think Anita quite understood my career shift. I hope for the best for David, but I'm not sure you ever get over being a plaything for someone like Roche."

"How do I find David and his mother?" Hannah asked.

Thrasher had already written down the address. "Anita's probably still punishing herself for what happened. But it could have been any kid. Roche was good with children. He knew how to talk to them, how to woo them. It was scary, how well he understood what they needed."

"Anything I should pass along from you?"

She shrugged. "Sure. Tell David I send him a big hug. I don't think he'll accept it, though. He never really forgave me, either."

"For being a defense attorney?"

"No. For prosecuting Roche."

Hannah understood. As long as the molestation was a secret, David could deal with it in his own way—pretend nothing was wrong, or wish for it to stop, or even try to make it stop. But once there was an arrest and a prosecution, it was out of his hands. And then all eyes turned to him. A molested girl got sympathy. But boys were sometimes considered complicit in their abuse. If he'd been a real male, the schoolyard gossips undoubtedly said, he'd have fought back, kicked that guy's ass.

So that meant David was a fag, a homo, a queer. He liked it. If not, why didn't he fight back—or at least tell? If those were the messages David got, Hannah wasn't surprised he'd turned angry and uncontrollable. She wondered if he'd decided to bide his time until he could focus his rage through a pistol sight and empty it into Roche's skull and chest.

23

The Alvarezes' house was near the neighborhood where Hannah had last seen Janie, but a few blocks out of the freeway's ever-growing path. The bulldozers wouldn't roar through here until the state needed a twenty-lane road. Maybe ten years from now, Hannah calculated. She wondered again if it wasn't time to move. Soon Orange County would be utterly buried in asphalt and traffic.

She had telephoned from her car, asking Anita Alvarez if she would be willing to talk to her about Freddy Roche's death. There was a long pause, and Hannah prepared herself for the kind of cajoling she'd done with other reluctant witnesses.

But Anita surprised her. "Sure," she said crisply. "Why not?" She confirmed her address and hung up.

From the look of Anita's street, Hannah constructed a picture of its residents. They worked overtime just to keep up with the rent or mortgage on these thousand-square-foot houses. Getting ahead, moving up to a bigger, better house meant a second or third job. Getting robbed or burglarized could really set a family back, so they weren't taking any chances with security. The houses were ringed with fortifications: burglar bars, barking dogs, and tall fences. Hannah also knew there were defenses she couldn't see—metal baseball bats behind the door and guns in nightstand drawers. She wondered how vigilant Anita Alvarez was.

Anita met Hannah at the door in a white shirt and black pants. She wore a Vons Supermarket name tag. She motioned Hannah to the white Haitian cotton sofa, which was lumpy, thready, and ready for retirement. The small living room was awash in everyday clutter. Framed ski-resort posters hung on the walls. A bookcase held some paperback mysteries and romances, as well as a few self-help books. A tabloid show played on the television, but the sound was muted. At the back of the living room, the drapes were pulled back to reveal a sliding glass door that opened onto a small yard. It was a patch that barely deserved its name. There were no plants, apart from a rectangle of dying grass, which had a deep dip at its center. No time for gardening, apparently.

Anita sank into an armchair, stifled a yawn, and took a sip from a pink coffee mug.

"Sorry. I did a double shift." She rubbed her eyes. Hannah wondered if she was divorced, widowed, or never married. Thrasher had never mentioned David's father. Raising a son alone would be difficult, no matter what the circumstances. Hannah guessed that she and Anita were about the same age, but the years had acted like a pumice stone on Anita, wearing her face down to a flat expression. She was skinny and stoop-shouldered, as though she'd been hauling boulders for years.

"I could come back, if this isn't a good time," Hannah said.

She shook her head. "There's no good time to talk about Roche. When I heard he was dead, I told my David, 'Thank God.'"

Hannah wondered about David's reply. Did he rejoice? Or was it a more muted response, since he knew already, having been the agent of Roche's death? And where was David? There was no sign of another car outside and no trail of clothes, books, and shoes that usually marked a teenager's after-school molting ritual.

"Actually, I wanted to talk to David, too," Hannah said. "Is he here?"

Anita's eyes strayed from Hannah's face to the yard. Hannah's glance followed. Was David out there?

"Ms. Alvarez?"

Her eyes had gone vacant. She got up and put her fingers to her throat, as though she had to push the words up to her lips. "I guess Mrs. Thrasher didn't know."

"What, Ms. Alvarez?"

"David is dead. Killed himself. With a rope. " She stared into the yard, and Hannah knew now why it looked so bare and why the earth dipped in the middle. Anita had cut down the tree he'd used to hang himself. And the conversations she had with David were only in her imagination.

She wouldn't sit down. She wouldn't listen to Hannah's apology. She finally agreed to let Hannah make some fresh coffee, but she hovered nearby, lining up sugar, cinnamon, and cream. She stopped Hannah at the tap and pointed her to the bottled water. Hannah thought issuing orders must be a way to shore up normalcy, to keep a stranger's pity from pouring into your ears. She understood and let Anita build her dam of bossiness. Letting an outsider see your weakness would just add a soupçon of humiliation to the pain.

Finally, Anita drooped into one of the cane-backed kitchen chairs. "I have no sadness about Freddy Roche," she said. "It's justice."

"When did David die?"

"Ten months ago. Five weeks after he came home." Hannah was sure that Anita could also recall the hours and minutes since his death. "He pretended to be all right. That was the only way they'd let him come back to me. I was afraid he was putting it on, but he wouldn't talk about it, and I didn't want him to leave again." She stopped and sipped the coffee. "One day, when I was at work, he went to Home Depot and bought rope. Our neighbor loaned him a ladder. David told him he needed to clean the rain gutters. We don't have rain gutters, couldn't that idiot see that, after fifteen years next door? Jesus!"

Anita slammed her cup down and went to a cupboard. "I'm going to have a drink." She pulled down a bottle of Johnnie Walker Red Label and two tall glasses. "You want some?"

Hannah nodded. If it helped Anita, she wasn't going to make her self-conscious by refusing to join her. "With some ice and water. Please."

"He didn't leave me a note. But I know why he did it."

"Because of Roche," Hannah said.

She nodded. A bitter expression twisted her mouth. "How do you get over something like what Roche did to him? He thought that there was only one explanation for why it happened. He thought he'd done something to lure Roche."

"I'm so sorry."

She fought back tears. "He was a good kid." Anita sloshed several shots into her glass and, before Hannah could stop her, filled hers to the brim, too. No ice, no water.

Anita was silent for a moment. Hannah imagined her reviewing the too-few days she'd had with David. Every morning since, she awakened to her son-starved life, an existence that was at once pale and dark. Hannah didn't know how parents could go on after their children died the way David had. She wasn't sure she could be as strong. But maybe they did what she had done after Janie's disappearance: pretend. Just act like life could be lived. Fake it, and hope that was enough to keep you going. Wait for the colors to seep back into the world. Maybe they never would, for Anita.

"My sister said I should get married again, have another baby," Anita said. "She has a little girl. But I can't, you know? Because it's just too . . ." She stopped and shook her head.

Hannah nodded. She was on notice now. How could she bring a child into a world that she knew was mined, where people like Freddy Roche lay just under the surface, waiting for a child's misstep?

They drank the scotch, and Hannah waited for Anita to say something. She finally looked up from her glass. "You know what that little shit did after my boy died? He sent me a sympathy card. I don't even know how he found out that David was gone. Through the church, maybe."

Hannah couldn't imagine what Roche had been thinking. "A sympathy card?"

"Honest to God. I kept it because I thought he might be up to something. Stalking me, trying to scare me. I didn't know. Now I don't have to worry. You want to see it?"

"Yes," Hannah said.

Anita came back with it. The cover was drenched in images of violets. The poem inside was pure treacle: heaven and clouds, God and angels, the loved one above watching loved ones below. Hannah was dumbfounded at Roche. Was it like tone-deafness? Couldn't he feel the guilt he should have felt? Didn't he understand that David was dead because of what he'd done? How could he have thought he deserved to share Anita's grief, to be a brother in bereavement?

Hannah handed it back to her. "I don't know what to say, except that I'm sorry for what you're going through."

She tilted her head and peered at Hannah. "You seem nice enough. Pretty normal. So why do you care who killed him?"

After seeing the card, Hannah wasn't sure she did. But Marian Roche still cared, and that's who she was working for—in this world, anyway. She told Anita that Marian had hired her.

"His mother." Anita spat the words out.

"She doesn't believe he died in a robbery. She's distraught, and I'd like to help her, even if it's only by showing her there's no other explanation for what happened to him."

Anita shook her head. "She never came to court, you know that? She didn't want it thrown in her face, that she brought up a monster. But she knew it. What kind of mother raises a child molester?"

It seemed pointless to wonder about Marian's role—if any—in shaping Freddy's perversion. All that mattered was what he had done. She looked up to see Anita staring at her. "I don't give a shit about Mrs. Roche's pain, and I think it might be time for you to go," Anita said. "You have absolutely no idea what it's like, trying to get back your child once someone like Roche has had him."

Hannah shook her head. "That's where you're wrong."

Anita's demeanor changed abruptly. She sees it, Hannah thought. That thing that we share. "Why am I wrong?"

It might have been the effect of the scotch, or the need to convince someone that Janie Meister was alive, but Hannah started talking about her. She told Anita everything, from the interview room, to the body in the surf, to the girl who parted the camellia branches and disappeared into the night. She talked about trying to find Claire, the drunk. And Bill Meister, the scam artist.

"But you said he had a nice house, a great car. You don't get those with three-card monte," Anita said.

"He probably hadn't worked that con since kindergarten," Hannah said. "He was on to better things. He had a company with a nice name and an address in Newport Beach. Bill's work might be my best hope. With any luck, that's the way he'll get arrested."

"It won't be for what he did to his daughter," Anita said.

"Probably not initially," Hannah said. "But it's better than nothing."

"He still around Newport Beach? I always thought they were all crooked down there. How else do you afford those boats, those houses?"

"I don't know. He could be anywhere now."

"What's the company called? My mom gets these calls sometimes. I don't want her to fall for him and his kind."

"CARNECO was the name. It folded. Tell her to look out for Coast Financial Services. Better yet, don't let her invest over the phone at all."

Anita nodded. "She does bingo, lotto, slots. She always thinks she's going to stumble into wealth."

"It's a nice dream sometimes," Hannah said. Anita tried to pour more scotch, but Hannah put her hand over her glass. She'd already had too much. "When Roche got out of prison, did he try to see David?"

Anita's chattiness dried up at the sound of Roche's name. "No."

"There was no contact, at all, other than the card?"

"Well, I let him know there would be trouble if he ever bothered my boy again."

Hannah wondered if the scotch had addled her head. Had she heard Anita right? She asked her, as neutrally as she could: "So you knew where to find him."

She caught the implication. "Mrs. Thrasher handled it. I wrote a letter, she got it to him. I didn't threaten him, if that's what you mean."

Hannah nodded. "I see."

Anita smiled a little. "And I didn't kill him, either. That's what you're thinking. I talked to the police already. You can ask them. I was working that night. Half a dozen people were with me, the whole time."

"But you did find out where he lived, didn't you? After he sent the card."

Anita shook her head. "He wasn't that stupid." She left the room and came back with the card's envelope. There was no return address. "I didn't know where he was," she said. "But I'm glad someone figured it out."

24

As Hannah drove away, she watched Anita in the rearview mirror. She swayed slightly, waved goodbye, and walked woozily back into the house. She seemed untroubled by Hannah's questions about her hatred of Roche. She even seemed to enjoy her position as a likely suspect. Hannah called Thrasher's office to see if she would confirm that she sent Anita's letter to Roche, but she had already gone home.

If Anita had been working that night, she couldn't have killed Roche. Hannah considered the other possibilities for a moment. Could she have hired someone to do it? Such people existed, though most of the hired killers she'd heard about lately turned out to be undercover cops who promptly arrested the hiring party. Assuming Anita found a bona-fide hit man, he would want cash—a substantial amount of it. Anita didn't seem wealthy. And even if she did have money, and if she had put someone up to killing Roche, it didn't explain Charles and Davis. It only made sense if she or David had some connection to them. Was the connection Mike Seward? He seemed to prefer boys, so maybe he victimized David, too. Perhaps that was a secret David kept, finally telling his mother at the end of his life. Anita said there was no note, but she could have destroyed it and sought private vengeance against Seward. Could she have mistakenly shot Cotter Davis instead?

That scenario had a sort of logic. But it didn't explain Henry Charles. Seward said he knew people who knew Charles. Did he mean David and Anita Alvarez? She wondered what could have pulled the mother and son into Charles's universe of vans and vagrancy and the molestation of a little girl. To find that out, Hannah decided she would have to visit what was left of Henry Charles.

The burn unit at St. Luke's Medical Center was its own quiet world, locked away behind windowless doors and accessible only after a conversation with a voice on an intercom. Hannah waited in the reception until a nurse in pale-blue scrubs tepidly greeted her.

"Visiting hours are over in ten minutes," she said. Her name tag identified her as Dawn, although she was nothing that rosy and gentle. Dawn had sallow skin, tired gray eyes, and a body big and rawboned enough to qualify her for a job as a titty-bar bouncer. But when she spoke, her voice was low-pitched and soft, a tender sound that could slip through the interstices of pain.

"You're not a member of Mr. Charles's family." She said it with mournful certainty, brushing back her mud-colored bangs.

Hannah explained who she was. "I'm looking for family."

"Maybe we can help each other out."

Hannah looked over the slots that held gowns and masks in the reception room. "Do I need to put something on first?"

"No. You won't be getting close enough to touch him." Dawn led Hannah down a hall. They passed the hydrotherapy room, with its aluminum tub and overhanging pallet used to lower the burn victim into the water.

"How is he?" Hannah said.

Dawn tilted her head one way, then the other, the seesaw of life and death. "We're doing what we can."

"You know about him—what he did?"

Dawn nodded. "A fair number of our patients are outsiders. They're here because they blow themselves up in their meth labs, or get drunk and light their mattresses with cigarettes. Or they're poor, and the burglar bars turned on them. It doesn't matter to us how they got here. We just try to help them get better."

"Is he going to get better?" Hannah was sure she'd heard the question endless times. She probably knew, perhaps from the day a patient came in, whether he would be going home or not. But predicting death? It wasn't likely.

Dawn's big shoulders allowed themselves a tiny, less-than-confident shrug. "People do survive, even with burns like his. Sometimes. Our unit secretary probably knows more right now than I do. I've been off for a couple of days."

As they passed one of the half-dozen patient rooms, a nurse shifted a fabric-covered screen that had blocked the door, giving Hannah a glimpse of a strange bed. It was suspended between a pair of tubular circles, almost like the rings of a hamster's wheel.

Dawn pointed to it. "It's electric. It lets us change their positions and dressings without touching them."

Now Hannah focused on the patient, who could be either a man or a woman. A man, she decided. His hair was burned away, and the head was swollen to the size of a basketball. The skin was a ragged patchwork of colors: red, brown, and a painfully naked pink. His bandaged arms were splinted, swathed in netting, and suspended from a crossbar. Hannah guessed the pose helped air circulate, but it made him appear to be falling endlessly backwards. He trembled uncontrollably.

"I doubt you recognized him, like this," Dawn said softly.

Jesus, Hannah thought, *it's Hank Charles. He'll be lucky if he doesn't survive.*

"If it turns out he does have family, I'm not even sure we'd let them in here," Dawn said. "He's medicated, really out of it. And with thirty pounds of fluid retention, the burns, the dressings—even their own wives and mothers can't recognize them most of the time." She left the doorway and Hannah followed her to a counter. Dawn greeted a woman there with a smile.

"What's up, Andie?"

The unit secretary looked up from the chart she was reviewing. She was barely twenty, Hannah guessed, with blond hair and a nose so upturned that it gave her the look of a cereal-box pixie. She smiled tentatively at Hannah and Dawn. "Not much. What's new with you?"

"I need Henry Charles's chart, please."

Her pleasant expression drained away. She handed the file over with another glance at Hannah. She fidgeted with her pen while Dawn flipped through some pages. "Not a lot of change while I was gone?"

Andie shook her head. "No. He's stable."

"This is Ms. Barlow," Dawn said. "She's trying to find

someone who knows Mr. Charles or something about his family. Some other child molesters have died, right, Ms. Barlow? It's funny the police didn't mention that when they were here."

Hannah nodded. "It looks like he was the first. That we know about." She tried to make eye contact with Andie, but she wouldn't look up. Hannah talked to her anyway. "No one has visited, Andie? Still no word about family?"

She hesitated. "Well . . ."

Dawn sighed. "Thank God. Did they come in yet?"

The girl finally turned her eyes to Hannah's. Why was she so uncomfortable? "No one came in," she said. "Nobody will."

"But there is family?" Hannah said.

"Sort of," Andie said.

"As in distant?"

"As in an ex-wife."

Dawn frowned. "What's going on? How do you know, if no one came in?"

"She's my aunt. My mom's sister." Andie addressed Hannah now, which seemed preferable to looking at Dawn, from whom Andie had been keeping secrets for nearly six weeks. "My mom didn't want people to know."

Hannah wasn't surprised that the young woman knew Henry Charles. Even a city the size of Las Almas was webbed with relationships that connected unlikely people.

"Would your aunt talk to me?" Hannah asked.

Andie considered that for a moment. "I don't know."

"Could you give her a call?"

She nodded uncertainly. "Okay."

"Cripes, Andie," Dawn said quietly. "You sure know how to keep a secret."

An uneasy smile flickered and died on Andie's lips. Hannah wondered how much time she and her family had spent with Charles before he was discovered. "This isn't the kind of thing you want people to know," Hannah said softly.

The secretary riveted her eyes to her charts and didn't reply. It was all the answer Hannah needed.

Andie agreed to call her aunt during her break and try to arrange a visit for Hannah. Hannah waited in the cafeteria, wondering if the girl would change her mind. But after half an hour of drinking very strong black coffee, she saw Andie approaching. The girl put a slip of paper on the table. Hannah read it: Laurel James, with an address and phone number in Anaheim.

"She can't see you until Thursday," Andie said. "She said she'll be ready by then."

"What time?"

"It doesn't matter."

Hannah wondered what rituals Laurel James needed to perform before she could bring herself to talk about her ex-husband. Maybe she lit a fire, for purity. Andie shifted uneasily, as if she were eager to get away. She's opened up a tightly sealed box, Hannah thought, the one crammed with demons. She's afraid that she won't be able to close the lid again.

"Should I ask her not to tell your mom?" Hannah motioned for Andie to sit down.

She stayed on her feet. "That would be great. It's not that Aunt Laurel's got anything to be ashamed of. She didn't know what Hank was doing. He was good at hiding it. From my mom, from everyone."

"You never told her, then? About what happened to you?"

Andie blinked at her, startled. She started to walk away, but then stopped and returned. She bent close, so only Hannah would hear. "Who told you?"

"No one. It's this case, along with some things that happened a long time ago," Hannah said. "They've made me good at picking up the cues."

Andie nervously plucked at the sleeve of her scrub shirt. "I was here working that night when they brought him in. It was so eerie. It was like someone *knew* about me. Like they did that to him for me."

"Do you have any idea who that could be?"

She shook her head. "It wasn't me. I was on shift from six that night."

"I didn't mean that," Hannah said, although she had.

"Look for someone he hurt," Andie said. "But that doesn't narrow it down much."

25

Hannah devoted most of Thursday morning to reading over the stories on Henry Charles that she'd pulled out of NEXIS. She stopped to call Lisette Blackburn, but got the answering machine again. Lisette was dodging her, she decided. She'd sensed that Hannah didn't quite believe the engagement story. She tried to get an address, but it was unlisted. She made a note to ask Marian about her.

Then she steeled herself for a call to Cassandra Thrasher. She took in the news of David's suicide in silence. Then, under her breath, she muttered, "Fucking bastard Roche." Finally she confirmed that she had given Anita's letter to Roche's attorney to be passed on. Anita Alvarez was telling the truth when she said she had no idea where to find him, Thrasher said. Hannah thanked her and turned back to the news-story printouts.

As with David Alvarez's case, Charles's victim and her family were not named in the stories. But the phrasing led Hannah to believe they must have been the Charleses' neighbors. The girl would be a teenager now, closing in on adulthood. Hannah could try going door-to-door in their old neighborhood, as she had in Roche's, but that seemed too intrusive and blunt. Laurel James might know where she was, but Hannah wasn't sure she would tell her.

She wondered if someone in the girl's family had set Charles and his van on fire. Could anyone be so patient? Could someone postpone vengeance for ten years before exacting the price in fire? She imagined Charles's victim: too small to run, to fight back. The stories were not graphic, but hinted at an incident of penetration. Hannah was sick at the thought of it. The girl was torn and split in incomprehensible ways. This man had the power of pain. He had probably warned her of the horrible consequences that would come if she told. Fear froze her, then shattered her. If she were the mother of a child tortured that way, she could wait until hell was a shrieking blizzard for the chance to get even with Henry Charles.

In that moment, she suddenly saw Janie as that victim. She wasn't any different from the girl Charles had raped. What would she do to avenge Janie? It was a question she hadn't let herself ask before. For so long, Janie was dead, and that was all that mattered. She hadn't contemplated revenge on Bill Meister because nothing she could do to him could bring Janie back.

But now Janie was resurrected. Was it time to mete out the punishment Meister deserved? Maybe Rudy Podesta and the U.S. attorney shouldn't be the ones to deal with him, she thought. Maybe I should do it. It made her heart race. She was thinking the thoughts of the person who'd shot Freddy Roche and Cotter Davis and set Henry Charles on fire. For just an instant, Hannah saw the avenger as someone just like her— someone tortured by crimes insufficiently punished, haunted by failures to protect a child.

She ignored Vera's puzzled look, left the office, and walked out into the summery morning. She sat down on one of Grove Street's benches and closed her eyes, trying to see the difference between herself and the person who thought like her, the person who inhabited a dark world of private vengeance. The line was blurred, and she couldn't easily sharpen it. She felt herself standing on one side, and then, so easily, shifting to the other. She imagined finding Meister, trailing him, cornering him. The Glock was in her hand, and he was trapped. Pleading . . .

She felt like she was sinking, the water closing over her head, keeping her from breathing. She opened her eyes and stood up, feeling light-headed for a moment. She had to stop those thoughts before they turned to plans, and plans became action. Those thoughts pointed her down dark roads. They led to places where she couldn't turn around, couldn't come back. Dead ends.

●　　●　　●

The door to the apartment opened as Hannah knocked on it. In the dim, heavily curtained living room she saw a hardwood floor, a bookcase, a sofa, and a trestle table that held a sewing machine. She heard music on the stereo, a recorder playing something piping and sprightly, with a hey-nonny-nonny chorus in four-part harmony. But she wasn't sure anyone was home.

"Ms. James? It's Hannah Barlow."

Hannah heard the swish of heavy fabric brushing the floor. Then a voice came from behind the door: "By the pricking of my thumbs, something wicked this way comes."

It was a woman, using plummy, theatrical tones. The portentous lines were Shakespeare's, but Hannah couldn't remember which play. She waited to see if Laurel James—if that's who it was—had anything to add to her weird greeting. Hannah decided she'd been invited in.

An imperious woman, dressed as Elizabeth I in middle age, stood behind the door. She was not beautiful, but she looked powerful, nearly goddesslike, in her elaborate makeup and costume.

The wig she wore was a fiery red, worked into tight curls. A wide, starched white ruff sat under her chin, cupping a heavily creamed and powdered face. There were pools of rouge for cheeks and petals of scarlet for a mouth, all painted on a mask of thick white makeup. The eyes were black and glittering and seemed to be peering out at her from deep inside limestone caves.

The woman seemed to inhabit the clothes more than wear them. The hoop-stiffened, cone-shaped skirt, worked in layers of burgundy brocade and silk, looked like it wouldn't fit through the front door. The brocaded bodice was as flat as a board, and Hannah guessed there was an unforgiving corset behind it. How could she breathe in that thing?

"Laurel James?"

She swept a hand from wig to knee. Rings glittered on every finger. "A poor lone woman."

Dressed like the virgin queen, employing the language of that day. Was Laurel James an actress? Or had her marriage driven her mad? Andie hadn't warned her of that possibility.

"Are you going to a costume party?"

She smiled sympathetically at Hannah's puzzled expression. "You look as if you held a brow of much distraction."

Hannah wasn't quite sure what that meant, but she did hold the beginning of a headache. "I'm not much for Elizabethan English, Ms. James."

She nodded. "Speak plain and to the purpose . . ."

It sounded like another quotation, and Hannah had had enough. "Okay, your highness. Here's one for you: 'Our revels now are ended.' *The Tempest*, I think." Hannah started to leave, but Laurel motioned for her to stay. Her smile threatened to crack the makeup's shell. "You know the bard!"

"Not like you, apparently."

"His language is so beautiful. 'Speak the speech, I pray you, as I pronounced it to you, trippingly on the tongue.' "

Hannah was briefly transported to senior-year high school English. She hadn't minded the class, but she'd hated the pedant nun that taught it, and Laurel was just about that tiresome. "What's the costume about?"

Laurel smiled beatifically. "For six weekends a year, I have the privilege of being Elizabeth Regina."

Now Hannah understood. "A Renaissance fair of some kind."

"I've done it for several years, but it's my first time as Elizabeth. I was Mary Queen of Scots one year."

"Not a role you can live with for long," Hannah said.

Laurel laughed delightedly. "The season begins soon, and we have publicity pictures to take, so I was going through my costuming for the right look." She paused. "I'm sorry if I overdid the quotes. But they do help put me in character."

Hannah considered the fantasies Laurel James might have chosen to escape her identity as a child molester's wife. Compared to those, dressing up like the queen of England and spouting Shakespeare seemed benign enough. "If you're busy, I could come back," Hannah said.

She pushed up a gold-threaded sleeve and checked the chunky digital watch on her arm. "Will an hour suffice?"

Hannah nodded. " 'Tis enough, 'twill serve." The phrase was out before she could stop herself. It had turned into a demonic parlor game.

Laurel James beamed at her. "I just lost a lady-in-waiting. Are you interested in the job?"

Hannah shook her head. "Corsets and I don't get along."

With a regal moue of disappointment, she nodded. "Then you wouldn't like the bumroll either. Give me a minute to change."

When she returned in a sweatshirt and jeans, she seemed to have shrunk. She curled herself on the sofa with a mirror, tissues, and a jar of cream. As she wiped the thick makeup away, a timid, middle-aged face emerged. In contrast to the haughty tones she used as the speechifying monarch, her real voice was soft, sometimes halting.

"You're trying to find out if what happened to Hank is related to those shootings?"

Hannah nodded. "The police talked to you about the fire-bombing?"

She nodded. "It was a shock. I didn't know he still lived around here."

"Did they ask you if your ex-husband knew the other two men?"

"I told them I didn't know. I haven't talked to Hank in years."

"Do the names David and Anita Alvarez mean anything to you?"

"Not at all. Are they suspects?"

"Not in Henry's case, no."

Laurel glanced up tentatively. "He's not dead yet, is he?"

Hannah shook her head. "I gather it's just a matter of time, though."

"Maybe it will finally be over then." She didn't sound convinced of it.

"When did you last see him?"

"At his sentencing." She stopped as she smeared cream on her face and wiped the luscious mouth away. Her own lips were thin, and they trembled with the effort of talking about Charles. "I wanted to see him get what he deserved. Leah's grandmother stood at the courtroom doors and shrieked at me. Called me whore-slut-bitch. Like it was my first name."

"Leah was the victim?"

Laurel nodded. "Leah Gabally. The family thought I was covering up for Hank. Or that I was 'in denial.' I heard that a lot, that day. But I loved her. I would never have left Leah alone with Hank if I had known."

"You had no idea that he was . . ." Hannah reached for the words. A pervert? A sicko?

"Abnormal?" Laurel shook her head. "I was eighteen when we got married. Sheltered. Bookish, but ignorant, really. My father thought Hank was good enough—the best I would ever get, given my looks, he said. I didn't know men could be what Hank was. It makes me sick that I ever shared a bed with him. Thank God I couldn't have children."

"What do you do now, Laurel? To live, I mean." Charles had once worked in an oil refinery, but went out on a disability sometime in the early 1980s, the stories said. Laurel had been described as a housewife.

She shrugged. "We lost the house. Hank was always plopping his money in some bad investment, so there was nothing left by the time he went to prison. I wanted to move anyway. I thought I'd baby-sit again, but I couldn't. I was afraid someone would find out about what had happened. So now I clean houses and teach some costuming classes to pay the bills. Living is what I do at the fair."

That added up to about 120 hours of life a year and numb existence the rest of the time, Hannah thought. Andie had been right about Hank Charles hurting a lot of people. "Did the police ask if you had any thoughts about who threw the bottle of gasoline?"

Laurel nodded. "I told them it wasn't me, because that was what their question really meant."

"What about the girl's family? Could the Gaballys have done it?"

"I told the police I didn't think so. The family was in ruins. Her parents blamed each other for what happened to her, there was a custody fight, and you know the rest."

"Just that Hank seemed to serve a lighter sentence than he deserved."

"You don't know why Hank didn't do more time?"

Hannah shook her head.

"It didn't get into the papers in a way that connected it to Hank's case," she said. "Leah's mother killed herself. Took a room at a hotel in San Diego and jumped from a fourth-floor balcony. Leah was with her, but it was never clear whether

Leah jumped after her, or if she took Leah along, intending to kill her. Leah survived. Barely. The father took off with her. He told the DA he didn't intend to put his daughter through the trauma of a trial after that. The prosecution case was in shambles. The DA took a plea bargain from Hank's lawyer."

Hannah was stunned into silence. Laurel nodded at her expression. "Horrible. Every day I think about Leah and her family. Should I have known what Hank was doing? Why didn't I know? Could I have stopped it?"

The questions were all wrong, Hannah thought. Laurel James wasn't responsible for what Charles had done. But she shouldered guilt, as did Leah's mother. Women could soak up blame like that, absorbing the poison through every pore. She doubted that Charles himself ever felt guilty at all. Maybe now, when the pain medication ebbed, he might feel the vaguest sense of regret, but it wasn't the same thing.

If Laurel inverted blame that way, Hannah couldn't see her throwing a flaming bottle into Hank Charles's van. Laurel could play Ophelia—addled and self-destructive. But would she lash out murderously at Charles? Hannah didn't think Lady Macbeth—purposeful and keen for blood—was in her repertoire. But she could imagine Laurel killing herself if her jeweled, playacting world ever lost its power to blot out the more recent past.

"What about Leah's father?"

"Moved back to wherever his people were—Pennsylvania, somewhere. The police implied that they'd talked to him. They didn't think he was involved." She fidgeted with a tissue. "I don't feel like I've helped much."

"I'm grateful you agreed to talk to me." Hannah wrote her home number on the back of a business card. "In case you do think of anything else, call. If you remember any friends who might have a grudge. Or co-workers. Maybe relatives?" She wondered if Laurel even knew about Andie.

"He didn't have friends," she said.

Hannah nodded. She wasn't surprised.

"But there is something else. Maybe I should have called the police at the time."

Hannah waited, but Laurel seemed hesitant to go on. "I'm not here to judge you, Laurel."

"I didn't see it with my own eyes. I just heard it, second-hand." She stopped dead, shaking her head. "I should have called someone."

"About what?"

"A friend of mine saw him one day, about five years ago. It would have been right after he got out of prison. She only caught a glimpse. She wasn't sure it was him. He was getting on a bus. He had a tripod and an expensive camera with him. He never took pictures when I knew him. Stupid waste of time, he said."

The room seemed to grow darker, colder. "Was he alone?"

Laurel sank against the back of the sofa and put a hand to her forehead. "There were two children with him. A girl and a boy. My friend wouldn't call the police, wouldn't get involved. But I should have. Now I have bad dreams about them, too."

Hannah blinked away the images that flooded her mind. Photographs were the link that attached Charles to Seward and perhaps to Roche. Children as chattel, their pictures as currency.

26

Seward was smiling when he sat down in the booth and picked up the phone, pleased to be visited again. He didn't see that Hannah was seething.

Hannah yanked the receiver from its cradle. "You said you didn't know Hank Charles. What's the truth?"

His smile faded, and he shifted in his chair. "I didn't lie to you. I said that I knew people who knew him."

"It was more than that. You traded pictures with him. You don't care for girls, but Charles wasn't as particular. He'd take any child that he could find, boy or girl. And you were a customer for the boy shots, weren't you?"

He leaned in and cupped his hand around the phone. "I've got a hearing coming up. This murder charge won't hold up, but I don't need any other static."

"Okay. Let's talk about Freddy Roche, since his problems are over. Did he and Hank Charles swap pictures?"

"Could have."

"What about you and Freddy?"

"We never swapped pictures," he said. He wouldn't look at her. And she knew why.

"No. You swapped the real thing."

He glared at her. "I'm not going to talk about this."

"You're going to have to talk to somebody about it, or you're going to go to prison for Cotter Davis's murder. You know something about who's behind these attacks."

He wet his lips. "Okay. I wanted to swap with Freddy. There

was a boy I would have liked to have, if he'd let me. But he didn't want to share."

"David Alvarez?"

He shook his head. "This is one the cops never found out about."

"Go on." As he hesitated, she addressed the departed Freddy. You damn liar, she thought. You made everyone think you were different from the other pedophiles. You even fooled Michael. You made it seem that there was one boy, one slipup. You sanctimonious monster.

"There was a park that Freddy and I used to go to," Seward said at last. "Lots of kids hung out there. There were basketball courts, roller-skating paths. Nice private bike trails. A couple of blocks away, there was a McDonald's and a video-game arcade." He made it all sound like a trout farm, a lake thick with catch. "I saw Freddy with this boy more than once. He was ten or so. Thin, with thick hair, big eyes. Just a beautiful boy. An angel, honest to God."

"Did Henry Charles know this boy?"

Seward didn't answer her. His right hand had dropped below the counter ledge. His eyes closed, and his face slid into vacancy. This was the look Henry Charles must have worn, but his was tinged with sadism. And it was how Bill Meister must have appeared, when he reached for his daughter. All of Hannah's rage welled up, and before she could think about it, she was on her feet.

"Stop it." She smacked the plastic barrier with her palms. "I didn't come here to watch you jack off."

His eyes flew open. He slammed the phone into the receiver and stumbled away from the booth. A deputy ran into the corridor, but by then, there was nothing to see but Hannah's overturned chair.

Late Monday afternoon, Hannah sat brooding in her office. I'm losing it, she thought, the phrase she'd heard in her head all weekend. Once I could have stilled that repulsion, curbed someone like Seward and still gotten what I needed from him. All it takes is the ability to distance yourself.

But her objectivity was gone. Everywhere she turned, she found victims. Andie. Kelly Barker, Roche's neighbor. Leah, raped and nearly killed. David Alvarez, hanging from a tree. And now there was the "angelic boy" that Roche wouldn't share. Their stories echoed Janie's story. In the moment that Seward slipped his hand into his pants, he became Roche, Charles, and Bill Meister. If not for the Plexiglas. If she'd had the Glock . . .

She stopped the picture from completing itself. Seward dead wouldn't do her any good. He had information she needed. If she was going to find out who had attacked Charles, who had killed Roche and Davis, and what connected them all, she would have to control Seward. That meant she had to control herself, and it wasn't going to be easy. She glanced at her watch. It was nearly seven. Most of the day had disappeared while she brooded. She had planned on going by the building where she'd found Janie's skateboard. She had just over an hour before nightfall.

She looked up and realized Bobby was standing at her office door. She had no idea how long he had been there, watching her think of victims like Janie and of what it would be like to kill Mike Seward. He had the worried countenance of a bloodhound, sniffing the air for a hint of her emotional state.

"Can't talk, Bobby." She pulled out her purse and keys. "I've got a client meeting tomorrow to prep for. I've got to go check some things at the law library." It was a blatant lie, and she realized she'd told it with ease.

"It won't take a minute. Have you heard from Devlin Eddy lately?"

The name took her by surprise. "Eddy? No. It's been quite a while. Why?"

He shrugged. "I ran into him a couple of weeks ago. He said he was going to call you, see how you were."

She knew where this was going. "And you told him I wasn't doing well, I suppose."

"I told him you'd like to hear from him."

"Well, I would, but he hasn't called me. Look, I've got to go."

He seemed on the verge of saying something else, but stopped. "Okay. See you later."

Hannah put down her purse. "Are you all right?"

He nodded. "Sure. I'm fine."

It sounded unconvincing, and had she really been herself, Hannah thought later, she would have pursued that conversation. She would have cajoled the truth out of Bobby. But she was single-minded now. Janie was all she cared about.

27

Even from the street, Hannah could hear the clattering skateboard wheels. First, they spun, speeding fast, faster. Then there was silence—the rider catching air—and a smack as the wheels hit ground. She waited before going into the apartment's courtyard, listening for the psychotic ravings of the seminaked landlord. But there was only the sound of the skateboard, racing, airborne, falling, racing again.

Hannah brought the Glock and added the frame of mind to use it this time. She slipped on a denim jacket to cover the holster and gun and went into the courtyard.

In the near-dusk, the skateboarder was silhouetted against the white bottom of the drained swimming pool. She skated its length, turning the board up along the banked sides before dropping down to the bottom again. Hannah sat down on the edge of a planter full of weeds and watched her. Her brown-and-blue-striped T-shirt was too big. The jeans flapped like slack sails against her legs. She had a green burlap knapsack on her back and wore dirty, white platform sneakers, thickly doodled with a blue felt pen. She had abandoned the tricolored Rasta beret and wore her hair in two topknots on either side of her head, like some punk milkmaid.

As she skated, she bit her lower lip in concentration. Finally, as she finished a long swooping curve along the pool's side, she looked up and saw Hannah. For an instant her control faltered, but she leaned in, recovered her balance, and coasted to a stop. She kicked the skateboard onto its tail and carried it out of the pool. A few paces away from Hannah, just out of reach, she gave Hannah a sideways glance from under the long fringe of her bangs.

"Hey." Her voice was low and husky, and Hannah didn't remember it being that way six years before. Maybe it wasn't natural. She might push it into a deeper register because it sounded cool.

Hannah forced herself to adopt a disinterest she didn't feel. "Hey yourself."

Janie nodded her acknowledgment, behaving as though there hadn't been a chase, as though they were friends who saw each other every day. She looked down and gave the skateboard a little kick. Her shyness, if that's what it was, gave Hannah a chance to study her. She knew what she wanted to find, so she tried to see clearly, stripping away filters of memory and wishfulness. Were the hazel eyes Janie's? The hairline, the nose? The expression of distance and wariness?

It was impossible to say. She hadn't seen Janie Meister for six years. She thought it was her. But maybe she was kidding herself. Maybe she just saw what she wanted to see.

"You got your jacket?" Hannah said to her.

She nodded. "Yup."

"And your lion."

"Oh, yeah. I didn't really notice he was gone. But thanks, anyway."

"You thanked me already. I found your note."

She nodded. "Well, you know, you didn't have to bring the jacket back."

"No? What about your lion? It looked like you've had that toy a long time."

"Sort of. It's pretty ratty. I actually was going to throw it away."

"Really? Why would you do that?"

She rolled her eyes. "I'm a little old for it, don't you think?"

Hannah shrugged. "I don't know. Does he have a name?"

She hesitated for a split second, as though the name was a secret. "Bert. He's Bert."

Was that a name she'd heard from Janie before? Hannah didn't think so. She only remembered a conversation about the lion's courage and strength. "Why Bert?"

"The guy who played the lion was Bert somebody. You know, in the movie."

Hannah ventured a guess. "*The Lion King*?"

"No. That was a cartoon." There was an implied "duh" at the end of the sentence.

"Right," Hannah said.

"I meant *The Wizard of Oz*."

"A good movie. A great tornado."

She looked supremely bored with the conversation. "Well, it was no *Twister*."

"The flying monkeys scared me when I was a kid," Hannah said.

"God, why? They're completely phony. And not scary. At all." She shrugged, all sangfroid and maturity.

Hannah nodded. Janie knew what to be scared of. She was a street kid. She'd seen more than she should for someone her age.

"How old are you?" Hannah asked.

"Thirteen."

Not if she was Janie, Hannah thought. She's added two years.

"How about you?" The girl smiled at her. Her teeth were a little crooked, but looked like they'd been brushed within the last few days. And her clothes, though baggy, looked relatively clean.

"Well, I don't get carded anymore," Hannah said.

The girl looked over Hannah's features. "Forty?"

"Not yet." Hannah knew the girl was trying to get a rise out of her.

"Women are always pretending to be younger than they are," she said.

"And girls always say they're older."

She smiled slightly. "That's because people treat teenagers like criminals. No matter what you do, someone thinks you're up to something."

"Adults forget what it's like to be young," Hannah said. "You were born in eighty-seven?"

"Nineteen eighty-five." She said it without hesitation. She'd trained herself to spit out a thirteen-year-old's birth year. Maybe that was part of the camouflage the Meisters imposed on her while they were on the run.

"I think we know each other," Hannah said, after a pause.

There was no point in stalling anymore. If the girl was going to run, anything could set her off.

"Yeah?"

"You're Janie, right?"

The girl shook her head. "Mae."

"Not Janie Meister?"

"No." She said it very quietly, looking down at her feet.

"Mae what?"

"Wallace."

Hannah nodded. "Okay, Mae Wallace. Pleased to see you. But didn't we meet once, a few years ago?"

The girl took off her backpack, sat down on the ground, and crossed her legs. "I don't think so. Not that I remember." She traced the cracked cement with her finger, like a palm reader assessing a lifeline.

Hannah waited for a moment. She didn't want to hit this point too hard. It would quickly deteriorate into a volley of yes-you-are, no-I'm-not. Then Janie would run. "Why were you hanging around my house?"

She shrugged. "The other night, you mean? I wasn't. I was just taking a walk."

"Not that night. I mean the first time I saw you. You were sitting across the street, remember? You weren't walking then."

The girl nodded. "Your neighborhood is pretty. Lots of trees. And I was taking a walk. But I got tired."

"The other night, why did you run away? People are allowed to walk in my neighborhood. It's a free country." The teenager's mantra.

This time the girl couldn't restrain herself. "Duh," she said, clicking her tongue. Then she shrugged again. "It's like I was saying: people get all crazy about kids." She frowned at the injustice of it. "I mean, most of us don't do anything really bad, but people think we're all gang bangers or something and call the cops on us. I thought that's what you were going to do."

"No," Hannah said. "I hadn't planned on that."

"Anyway, you got your exercise that night." She grinned down at the ground.

"Yes I did," Hannah said. "Mae?"

She looked up too quickly, as if to convince Hannah that this was her name. "What?"

"If I tell you some things about the time we met, do you think you might remember better?"

"Well, we didn't meet. But go ahead, if it makes you happy."

"It was kind of a scary time for you."

"*I* was scared?" She said it as though that was simply impossible. Flying monkeys brought her no fear. What could Hannah be talking about?

"You needed to be strong. And that's tough when you're a kid."

She nodded, allowing that kids—some kids—could be scared. "When was this again?"

"You were five. You had Bert with you. Do you have him here now?"

She stiffened as though this question threatened her. "I think he's at home." Hannah was fairly sure that was a lie. He was nearby somewhere, probably in the backpack. But she wasn't willing to take Bert out now. That would only reinforce the echoes and shadows and memories of the interview room. She would be Janie again.

"Well, anyway, you showed Bert to me back then, and we talked about how strong lions were. And how brave. We talked about how you could be those things, and that's how you would get through the scary time."

"Oh. Did she?"

"She?"

"This girl you're talking about. Did she get through the scary time? Was she okay, then, after you had this little heart-to-heart talk?"

Her voice had the tang of sarcasm. Janie, Hannah thought, it is you, but you can't let yourself be that girl. You're angry. You know damn well it didn't work out right, and you're telling me so. You're telling me I fucked up.

"No," Hannah said, "She wasn't okay. I let her down. But she had her lion."

She nodded. "Big help."

"I think it probably was. Anyway, Bert looks a lot like him. That's why I thought you were her." Even though she was making Janie a character, someone other than the girl sitting on the pavement and fighting down her rage, Hannah found it hard to go on. "When I saw him, I was glad to know he was still with you. He hadn't let you down. I'm sorry I did."

The girl looked up, face brimming with anger. Hannah imagined her reliving everything that had happened in the last six years, placing Hannah in the continuum of blame, considering whether to forgive her or not. Mae—Janie—broke the gaze first, and the moment's crackling heat disappeared, gone as fast as a lightning strike. "No reason to apologize." There was nothing but bland disinterest in her voice now. "It wasn't me."

Hannah nodded. She knew she couldn't push her anymore. Hannah gestured to the deserted building and its undraped windows, which gaped vacantly at them. "So, do you live here?"

The girl shook her head, got up, and sauntered around the planter. "God, no. I just like it because of the pool and stuff." She turned back to Hannah. "Who was this girl again?"

"Janie Meister."

"She lives around here?"

Hannah nodded. "I think so. She used to live near the Plaza. I saw you there one morning."

She nodded. "Right. I saw you with some guy."

"That's my law partner."

"He's huge, isn't he?"

Hannah smiled. "Pretty big. A good guy."

"Are you sleeping with him?"

"No."

"Good. 'Cause I think he could flatten you."

Hannah didn't say anything. Janie was flicking anger and insult at her, little jabs of a rapier's tip. She was determined not to parry. She wouldn't give Janie an excuse to storm out.

The silence went on for a moment. The girl stared intently at the rubber sides of her shoes. Finally, she looked up. "So this Janie girl. Were you a friend of her family's or something?"

"No. Her family was messed up. I was trying to help."

The girl nodded. "There are a lot of messed-up families." Her eyes traveled the windows of the building as though she'd seen dysfunctional clans in every one.

"Do you live with your family?" Hannah said.

"Kind of. With my mom."

"Here in Las Almas?"

"I've moved around a lot, you know?" She managed to not quite answer the question.

"Where have you lived?" Hannah asked.

"Oh, San Diego, Arizona, Nevada."

"With your mom and dad?

"My dad's dead."

"I'm sorry to hear that, Mae." Hannah wondered if it were true, or only the girl's wishful thinking.

She sat down next to Hannah and dusted the knees of her jeans. "Listen, don't keep calling me Mae, okay? I know you're talking to me. There's no one else here."

"You're not crazy about your name?"

"Not very. It sounds like an old lady. Janie's an okay name."

Hannah took that in. Was it an invitation to hear her true name spoken? It was more dangerous for Hannah to do that. It reinforced her wish that this girl was Janie. "What if I called you Janie, then?"

She shrugged. "I don't care." A moment later, she nodded. "If you want. Okay."

"So, Janie: Do you live with your mom?"

"Yeah. She's kind of tough, but she's okay."

"She's tough on you? How?"

Janie frowned. "Well, I don't mean she hits me or anything. She's strict."

"Really? You seem to do whatever you want, go wherever you want to go. You're not even in school, are you?"

"We do home schooling." She reached into her backpack and pulled out workbooks: Spanish, Math and Spelling. They were dog-eared and soft from constant carrying. She had been working on the same courses for a while.

"Don't you miss being in a classroom, where you can make friends?"

Janie shook her head. "I'd rather be with my mom. She's great."

Hannah found it hard to listen to the fantasy the girl had constructed. Even if she wasn't Janie, even if she really were someone called Mae Wallace, Hannah doubted if she lived with a strict, loving, home-schooling mother. The girl flitted around town on her own, at all hours. She was probably malnourished. Her clothes hung on her.

"Where do you and your mom live?"

Janie pointed vaguely north. "Over by downtown."

"It will be dark soon. Why don't I drive you home? I'd like to meet your mom."

"She's at work right now." She fiddled with her backpack. "But I should go anyway."

"How about some dinner?"

Janie eyed her suspiciously. "Like what?"

"Well, whatever you want. As long as it's not five courses with French wine, I think I can handle it."

"Mom's on a PETA kick, and I'm pretty tired of veggies." She bit on her fingernails for a moment as she thought. She seemed to be savoring her carnivorous options. "Meat's okay?"

"Sure. We'll get you some animal protein. Any place in particular?"

"Just someplace where the fries are good." She picked up her skateboard and smacked the dirt from the seat of her jeans. Then she gave Hannah a tiny smile, free of any sarcasm or anger. She was just a kid desirous of cheddar, ground beef, and some matchsticks of potato. The expression's purity made Hannah's heart ache.

They were just past the archway, about to get into Hannah's car, when they heard a whistle, high and low. It came from somewhere behind the courtyard, perhaps in the building's parking lot. Janie froze.

"I've gotta go." She dropped the board, jumped on it, and sped away in the direction of the summons.

"Janie!" Hannah ran after her, swearing under her breath. Who had whistled for her?

The girl rushed headlong down a walkway and veered right. She was on a path that fronted a set of apartment doors at the back of the building. Hannah was closing in on her. Then, from the corner of her eye, she saw one of the doors thrown open. The psychotic landlord, Hannah thought. She reached under her jacket for the Glock.

It was too late. In a blur of motion, the figure barreled out and tackled her, smacking the gun from her hand. She fell sideways, her head cracking against the pavement. With the stabbing pain came pinwheels of light. She didn't see the source of the second blow, but it came down hard across her right cheekbone. A hand tugged at her shoulder and side. And faintly, nearby, she heard a high-pitched laugh, starting at glee and then spiraling up toward hysteria. She felt her lips forming Janie's name. Then the pain overtook her, obligingly wiping away all sound, all sight.

28

Bobby was sipping a Rioja, playing an old Joni Mitchell album, and deboning a chicken for a late supper when the phone rang. It was after ten, and no one but Hannah or his family called him that late. He still was holding the knife when he picked up the receiver and heard himself addressed as Robert Terry. Only strangers called him Robert.

The stranger spoke in a calm, measured voice. Its dispassion horrified him. He made her repeat what she'd said. His hands were shaking as he put the receiver down, and he dropped the knife, nicking his thumb as he grabbed for it. He trembled so much that he couldn't bandage the slit in the plump skin. The blood trickled, the cut throbbed, and all he could think of was Hannah. He stanched the blood with the sleeve of his Douglas sweatshirt and held it there as he drove to the hospital.

He thought he would faint when he saw her. She was in an examining room, sitting up on the padded table in a short-sleeved blue-and-white cotton gown. The right side of her face was brutally scraped and bruised. The skin circling her right eye was swollen, and a thin cut crossed her cheekbone. Her hair was pulled back, emphasizing the thinness of her face. Her legs and arms were bare, pale white where they weren't bruised. She looked unbearably fragile, and he felt his throat tighten. Her dirty pants and shirt lay heaped on the chair. The jacket was torn at the elbow.

She smiled weakly at him, shaking her head. "Don't worry. It looks worse than it is."

He steadied himself and found his voice. "My God, Hannah. What happened?"

She bit down on her lip. "I found Janie at one of the apartment buildings they're tearing down near the freeway."

"Shit," he said. "She did this?"

"No, of course not. We were talking, just about to leave, when somebody whistled to her. I chased her. Somebody jumped me—a guy I saw there earlier, I think. A shirtless nutcase."

Bobby looked at her clothes and then back at her. She seemed to know what he was thinking and shook her head. "He didn't do anything else, other than take my purse and my gun. I found the purse when the police came—out in the gutter. The money was gone. So was the gun. And my car keys."

"What about your car?"

"It's gone, too."

Bobby shook his head. "Jesus Christ."

"Bobby, don't. Not now."

"Goddamn it, Hannah, listen to me." His relief at seeing her—not dead, not raped, just shaken and bruised—was replaced with anger at her bullheadedness. "When are you going to wake up? You've convinced yourself this street kid is Janie, and what has that got you? She set you up for a mugging. Now she has money, a gun, and your car. God, Hannah, I tried to warn you."

"I don't need this from you." Hannah's voice shook.

"What did you tell the police?"

"That somebody jumped me."

"But you didn't tell them about Janie, did you?"

She shook her head. "Not yet. I'm sure we'll be talking again."

Bobby stepped closer and took her hands. Her nails were broken, some well below the tips of her fingers. "Hannah, you have to let this go. Even if it really is Janie. Can't you see that?"

She didn't answer him. She felt like her personality had been sliced in two. There was the Hannah who woke up on the ground, picked herself up, and shakily dusted the grime from her clothes. That Hannah had been able to think straight, amazingly enough. She walked out to the street, saw that her car was gone, flagged down a guy in a pickup, and convinced him to call 911.

The other Hannah was the one who had been knocked to the ground and still lay there, dazed. Desperation had crowded out that Hannah's good sense. What was she doing chasing Janie down in a place that had already shown itself to be dangerous? She had tunnel vision. She only saw that she had to save Janie. Everything that Janie had become—however bad that was—could be traced back to what *she* had done. The Hannah whose mind wasn't tracking, whose feelings flamed up like lit brandy, was the one still determined to make amends, no matter what Janie might have done. And that was the woman sitting here now, aching and stiff. The rational Hannah was probably down in the business office, making sure her insurance carrier got the ER bill.

"Hannah?"

She opened her eyes. Bobby was frowning at her. "The Janie you knew is dead, one way or the other. You have to realize that."

Hannah closed her eyes and tried again to superimpose the features of five-year-old Janie onto Mae Wallace's almost-adolescent face. The two began to fit, and then they slid apart. She was suddenly light-headed. She swayed and felt Bobby's solid, blocky hands on her arms, steadying her. Opening her eyes again, she read the expression on his face, and that scared her even more than her feeling of bifurcation.

"Do they think you can go home?" Bobby's eyes were watery, but he was determined to ignore the tears. So she would, too.

"If somebody keeps an eye on me," she said.

Bobby nodded. "That's what I'm here for."

At home, she rinsed her face and arms cautiously, sucking in a breath at the sting of the soap. She avoided looking in the mirror. In her room, she slid into fleece-lined sweatpants and a shirt. Even that was an effort, and her legs began to shake. She sat on the edge of the bed until the weakness passed and then dug through her purse in search of the painkillers she'd been given at the hospital. Her fingers felt fat and numb. In frustration, she upturned the purse, spilling it onto the bedspread. She found the pill bottle, but realized that something other than her gun, wallet, and keys had been stolen. She'd had an atomizer of Chanel No. 5 cologne in the purse, an extravagant gift from her sister, Theresa, who barely could afford her own rent. It was gone.

"Hannah?"

She went into the hallway and looked down the staircase. Bobby stood there holding a tray. "I made tea. I could bring it up."

She shook her head. "I want to be down there, with you."

She settled herself on the sofa and covered herself with one of Mrs. Snow's crocheted granny-square afghans. The cut on her cheekbone throbbed. Closing her eyes seemed to lessen the pain, so she did that. When she opened them, she found Bobby standing over her. "You're hovering," she said.

"I was thinking—I could call Guillermo, if you want."

"No." She spat it out and instantly regretted how rude it sounded. She reached for his hand in apology. "Thanks, but no."

"You're sure you don't want to go up to bed?"

She shook her head. "I still feel jangled. I won't sleep. I'd rather just lie here."

He sat down on the edge of the couch and squeezed her hand. "There's something I need to tell you."

"What?"

"Devlin Eddy's involved in this. He was . . . helping me."

Hannah blinked at him. "Helping you do what?"

He let out a breath and shook his head. "Goddamn it."

"Bobby, what's going on?"

"He was following that kid. I went over there and told him what you were doing. He was worried about you, too. He had this picture of Janie. He told me—"

"What the hell did you think you were doing?" Hannah's face flushed.

"Making sure you were okay."

"No." Hannah shook her head, even though the motion hurt. "That wasn't it. You were looking for a way to prove it wasn't her. But Eddy didn't know her. He wasn't working the case. What the hell, Bobby? You had no right."

"Hannah, listen. The point is that I haven't heard from him. I've called his house, but there's no answer. I've gone there a couple times, and there's no one home. Ever."

Hannah felt a chill up her back. "What about Gudrun?"

"Well, he wouldn't say anything, but I think maybe she left him."

"Have you told the police you can't find him?"

"Not yet."

"Call them. Now."

Bobby nodded. "He wanted to help you."

Hannah squeezed his hand, trying to reassure herself as much as Bobby. "He's probably fine."

"Right. Took off for Vegas to forget his broken heart."

Hannah smiled slightly. She didn't want to tell him that Eddy hated gambling. He hated impromptu trips. And he never left town without programming the phone to forward his calls to wherever he was.

Near dawn, Hannah heard the noise of a car outside. It was before six—too early for a visit from the police. She sat up and was assaulted by a pain that felt like it was splitting the back of her skull. She groaned and lay down again, feeling the room spin around her.

An hour later, she woke up and eased herself to a sitting position, giving the pain its due respect. In return, it permitted her to stand. She went to the window. Her Integra was parked in front of the house.

Hannah went out into the damp morning. The car was coated in dew and seemed undamaged. Opening the doors could disturb prints, so she contented herself with peering inside. The keys were in the ignition. A scrap of grayish, coarse-grained paper, printed with a phrase in Spanish—*Me gusta mucho*—lay on the passenger seat. On it, in the same hand that had printed *THANKS, HANNAH*, was another message: *SORRY*.

She went inside, woke Bobby, and called the police.

Later, after she sent Bobby to the office, assuring him it was safe to leave her alone, the investigators showed up. They checked the car and told her that her gun wasn't in it. The door handles, steering wheel, and stick shift had been wiped clean of prints. Hannah felt an odd sense of relief: the prints' absence distanced Janie from the theft. They asked Hannah about the note. Contrition was not a usual element in car theft. She told them she didn't know who had written it.

• • •

Hannah stayed home the next day. The pain was waning enough that she could have worked, but when Bobby called, she told him it was a vanity issue: she looked like the losing end of a bout with Muhammad Ali. But the truth was, she felt ashamed. Of mishandling Janie. Of putting Eddy in danger. Bobby told her he'd made a missing-person report, but hadn't heard from the detective yet.

She spent the rest of the day trying to decide whether to talk to a therapist about her fixation on Janie. She thought she knew what would happen: she would be told to let Janie go, either by admitting that she was dead, or—at best—that she was a petty criminal who'd set her up for an assault and robbery. She would have to distance herself, for her own psychological and physical protection. But distance meant that Janie became quarry for the police or the social workers. She tore up the list of names of therapists she'd compiled from the phone book, took a pain pill, and went back to bed.

When the phone rang late that night, she didn't hear it. At the other end of the line, Mrs. T. sighed and left her a message.

29

Hannah sat across the street from the Valley Palm Nursing Home in Pomona, an inland city that teetered between the seediness of downtown decay and the grail of suburban redevelopment. On this stretch of Holt Avenue, the score was seed ten, suburban glory zero. The nursing home Hannah had under observation stood between an old motel and a row of disreputable-looking bars. She checked her watch—7:55 A.M.—and hoped Mrs. T.'s information was good.

One of Mrs. T's multitudinous sources—a woman who ran an employment agency for medical workers—had produced the lead. She'd placed a woman as a nurse's aide at this convalescent hospital two months ago.

As the applicant filled out the agency paperwork, she hesitated. She told Mrs. T.'s source that she'd like to use her maiden name. The woman was attuned to such concerns. Sure, she'd said. She'd waited for a moment. Bad husband, huh? Ms. Clarice Higgins nodded. Well, just in case there's some mismatch with Social Security, put down your other name, the agency owner said. Just for the file, just between us, because honey, I know how it is. She'd smiled the smile of womanly understanding. And, reassured, the applicant wrote that her married name was Meister. Based on that conversation, Mrs. T. didn't think she'd stuck with Bill Meister.

Nevertheless, Hannah wondered whether this was the right person. Pomona was an hour away from Las Almas on a light-traffic day. If Janie was telling the truth when she said she lived with her mother, it meant that Claire was making a very long commute to work. Mrs. T.'s message said Clarice worked the graveyard shift, and had told the agency she'd supply her address and phone once she started working. But she hadn't done that yet.

Hannah's cellular phone trilled.

"Are you in Pomona?" Mrs. T. sounded like she'd been up for hours already.

"Yup. No sign of her yet. Did she mention any children in her interview with the agency?"

"No. Maybe she's keeping that to herself."

"Or she doesn't know where Janie is," Hannah said.

Mrs. T. hesitated. "Well . . ."

"Is there another option?"

Mrs. T. didn't respond for a moment. Hannah knew what she was thinking: the third option was that Janie was dead. Finally, Mrs. T. sighed. "I'd better let you go. It's just now eight."

Hannah hung up. The sun was already beating down on the wide stretch of blacktop. The air smelled dusty, slightly pungent. The smog was sleeping in, though, saving up its strength for an afternoon onslaught. Hannah sipped her coffee and waited. At five after, the home's double doors opened.

When Hannah last saw Claire Meister, she was wearing one of the uniforms of the upper-middle-class Orange County mother: flat, black leather loafers whose lack of ostentation telegraphed their quality and price; designer-du-jour jeans; a thin cashmere turtleneck, topped by a black lambskin jacket; gold earrings; and a diamond to dazzle the rival wives.

Hannah remembered hating each element of that carefully orchestrated ensemble on the day she interviewed Claire Meister. She felt Claire's betrayal of her daughter in every garment, in every piece of expensive jewelry. To live as she did, she needed Bill Meister and his money. She needed to live with her eyes closed, blind to an income picked from pockets of elderly dupes. She certainly couldn't permit herself to see what Bill was doing to Janie. What Claire ultimately cared about was the nice-looking family, the house, the clothes, the cars, and the appearance of rectitude and success. As long as it all *looked* right, everything was all right.

Now, as she stepped outside, Claire blinked in the bright sun. Like the other aides ending their shift, she wore white pants and a pastel tunic. There were white leather clogs on her feet and a nylon lunch tote in her hand. Her hair was a ragged mess, no longer coiffed and colored with streaks of wheat and sunflower gold. Where it wasn't brown, it was gray. She was heavier and seemed to have aged fifteen years, not six.

She waved as her coworkers walked to the parking lot. One turned to say something. Hannah rolled down her window in time to catch the end of the question: Did Clarice want a ride?

She shook her head and sat down on the bus bench. When her friends had pulled away, beeping goodbye on the horn of a yellow Maverick, Claire stood up. She waited for a gap in the morning traffic and hauled herself across the street to the Tune Up, a bar that advertised itself as opening at six A.M. Hannah locked the car and followed her.

Claire had taken a place at the bar and was sipping a bottle of Coors when Hannah came in. There were booths along the side of the room, and Hannah sat in one of those. Claire didn't notice her. The bartender raised his chin to prompt Hannah's order. She pointed to the coffeepot. Claire called for a second beer.

"Tough night?" The bartender held the bottle as if he needed a correct answer before he could open it.

Claire nodded. "Mrs. Cartwright."

"Shit," he said, popping the cap. "You said yesterday that was coming. How old was she?"

"Eighty-five."

"Well, here's to her." He lifted his coffee cup, and Claire raised her bottle.

It wasn't until after her third Coors, when she was unsteadily making her way to the bathroom, that she finally noticed Hannah. It was a glance, nothing more. Hannah imagined that her shiner, even veiled in powder and concealer, altered her looks. She knew she felt different. Vulnerable. Punchable.

On the way back from the bathroom, Claire glanced again at Hannah. She seemed to be peering through a beery fog. She walked on as if nothing was wrong, but at the last minute grabbed her lunch bag from the bar and hurried for the door. Hannah was already on her feet. She took Claire by the arm, spun her around, and deposited her in the booth. The coffee slopped into its saucer as Claire's bottom smacked the seat with a thump.

The bartender stopped drying glasses. "Hey, sweetheart, you and your friend should go easy on the furniture."

Hannah shot him a stern look. To him, the shiner apparently made her look formidable. He shrugged deferentially and added, "Please?"

"Two coffees here."

Claire ventured a look at Hannah and then stared down at the table.

"You've changed a little, Mrs. Meister," Hannah said.

Claire frowned. "You've mixed me up with somebody else."

"No, I haven't. You're using your maiden name, but you're still Claire Meister, minus the nice clothes and the upkeep from the gym and salon."

She looked up at Hannah's black eye and bruises. "What happened to you?"

"Nothing for you to be concerned about. Let's talk about Janie."

The bartender put the coffee in front of Claire. She tried to pick up the cup, but her shaking hands stopped her. She put her fingers to her lips and whispered: "No jail, please. No."

Hannah was about to tell her she wouldn't call the police, not right away, when she realized that she was frozen in time for Claire. She thought Hannah was still a police detective. Why should she correct that notion?

"Okay, Claire. For the moment, let's not think about jail. Let's discuss your daughter and your husband."

Claire managed a sip of coffee on her second try. "I can't talk about it."

"Why not?"

"He'll kill me."

Hannah considered that for a moment. Bill Meister was certainly capable of murder. "Are you still with him?"

"No."

"You're divorced?"

"No. But we're not together." As she sat silent, refusing to advance the conversation, Hannah looked closely at her. She was red-eyed from her night shift and the morning beer. Her face was as pale as dough and just that soft. She wiped some sweat away from her hairline. The talk about Bill was scaring her, and that was just what Hannah wanted.

"Does he know where you are?"

"He said he'd know if I told," Claire said. "He said he'd find me."

"How long since you saw him?"

She shook her head as if it was useless to keep track of time. "A long while."

"Do you really think he's keeping tabs on you?"

She bit at her thumbnail for a moment. "Yes."

"Does he know you hang out here?"

"I don't think so."

"Good. So we're in a safe place. Can they make us breakfast?"

"Sure. Scrambled eggs with Tabasco and chorizo. That's good here."

"Perfect." Hannah signaled the bartender and placed the order, along with toast and juice. "You'll eat a little, and we'll talk."

"Okay." She scanned Hannah's face. "It is you, isn't it? Hannah Barlow?"

"In the bruised flesh."

"Somebody beat you up." Claire said it confidently. She didn't mistake the injuries for a fall or a bump into a door. Hannah hadn't thought much about what Bill might have done to Claire. She had only considered Claire's failure to protect Janie. But Claire probably wasn't so much evil as weak and dependent. That nature had cost her a child, as well as whatever punishments Meister meted out.

Claire was still assessing Hannah's damaged skin. "A fist? No. Gun butt."

"Both, I think," Hannah said.

Claire took that in. "Those will fade, eventually. In the meantime, there's some makeup you can get. Dermablend. It covers everything. No one will know."

"Thanks," Hannah said.

The food came, and after a few bites, Claire put down her fork and started to talk.

30

"Bill convinced me we couldn't stay in Las Almas. You were out to get him, and you weren't going to let up. He would never see Janie again, if you had your way." She looked up cautiously to see Hannah's reaction. "That's what he said."

Hannah thought Bill had made her sound like a wild-eyed fanatic, but it was close enough to the truth. She nodded for Claire to continue.

"I couldn't believe he'd done anything to Janie. Bill was a good father. Bought her clothes, toys, took her places, just the two of them. Two peas in a pod." She smiled weakly, and Hannah saw the shadow of her jealousy in that expression.

"I was scared to leave. I knew it was wrong to run, but Bill said it was no more wrong than what you people were doing to him. I sat down with Janie, one last time, after everything was packed, to see if she would tell me the truth. She wouldn't talk to me about it before that. So I asked. I told her it had to be the truth.

"She said it had happened, on those mornings in her room. I just panicked inside. What were we going to do if Bill left us? There was a mortgage, house payments, the way we lived. I didn't have a job. . . ." She took a sharp breath, feeling the choice again. Her reanimated panic came at Hannah in small, slapping waves. "Then, just like that, Janie started crying. She said she took it back. It wasn't true. She'd made it all up, because of the cat. She pleaded with me to believe her."

Hannah remembered the story: Bill said he'd promised Janie a kitten. She'd been whining about wanting one, and he'd given in, during a moment of weakness. But then he'd changed his mind. She'd have to wait until she was six. And the tale of molestation was her supposed revenge.

Hannah never believed that version, not for a moment. Claire shouldn't have, either. Janie only recanted because she saw Claire weighing who she needed more: a breadwinner or a daughter. Janie felt her panic, just as Hannah did. She understood that if she told the truth, Claire might choose Bill over her. So what were her choices? If she wanted Claire, she had to take Bill, too. Hannah felt a surge of fury at Claire. She shouldn't have wavered, not for a second.

"That was it." Claire sighed. "Janie insisted it wasn't true, so what else could I do? She hung onto me. She didn't want to leave, she said, why couldn't we stay? But if we didn't leave together, Bill would have left alone. I just knew it. I couldn't risk that."

On that first night, as they drove north, Janie had whimpered constantly. She wouldn't see her friends again. Where were they going? Bill clenched his teeth and kept driving. Claire got into the Vanagon's middle seat and sang Janie to sleep.

The interminable I–5. A weepy, grim breakfast in Pleasanton. A few days around Sacramento, where Bill made whispered phone calls in the night as the three of them stayed in a tiny motel room, using fake names. Janie was bored and restless. Carsick, for the first time in her life. She would eat a little and then throw up. After a few days, Claire began asking where they were going, only to hear Bill say he hadn't decided, and shut up about it. It wasn't relocation, she realized. It was blind flight.

So the easiest thing to do, after the day's driving, was get a six-pack and drink. She wasn't so anxious after a beer or two. The ritual began with two beers after five, then three after four. Soon, she bought two six packs when they stopped for lunch. Bill claimed to be helping her drink them, but Claire lost count of how many he put away.

She liked to drink in the car, though Bill didn't permit it often. A beer buzz, the motion of the vehicle, and the drifting radio stations soon put her to sleep. She had red wine with dinner, and she slept again. They were on the road for about three weeks, moving every few days: a side trip to Reno, then west into the Bay Area. They went from Oakland to Novato, then up the state's rocky, beautiful north coast. After Eureka, Janie's carsickness grew worse. There was a day's rest at Crescent City. Then they came to Brookings, just across the Oregon border.

She woke up one morning in a motel room, not sure where they were this time. The rooms began to look alike after a while—the same peach walls, the same laminated counters, the white shower curtains. She looked at the phone, because sometimes the area code on the dial gave a clue. This one didn't register with her. She put on her robe, opened the door, and leaned out into the smell of salt. Seagulls spiraled overhead, screaming.

She remembered then. Oregon still, somewhere on the coast. Bandon, maybe? She went back inside. Janie and Bill must have left for their morning walk while she slept. They would bring back fruit and milk for breakfast. Claire took a shower and a quartet of Advil. It was the red wine that gave her such raging headaches, she decided. She would have to switch to something else. A nice *fume blanc,* perhaps.

She opened the closet door to get fresh clothes from her suitcase. Each of them had a bag—blue for Claire, black for Bill, pink for Janie. Only the blue one was there. She stared at it, as though it owed her an explanation for where its companions had gone.

Now she looked outside again. The Vanagon was gone. She sat back on the bed and tried to summon up an explanation. The store was too far to walk. Okay, yes, that was it: they'd taken the van, and they'd be back soon. It was a little after nine in the morning.

Claire got dressed, keeping her eyes off the emptiness in the closet. She sat on the bed and flipped through the TV's channels. At eleven, she walked down the road and found the grocery store. They had not seen her husband or daughter there. She went back to the room and stared at the phone. Who could she call? What would she say? She waited. She went back to the store, cheerfully lied that yes, they'd come home. She paid for her six-pack of Bud and drank it. And waited.

At eleven that night, Bill came back alone. She was asleep. He sat her up and told her it was an accident. Her heart cramped—they'd been at the hospital? Was Janie okay? She was babbling now, out of fear. He shook her and told her to shut up.

Janie had a tantrum. She could be wild, Claire knew that. They were at the beach, and she'd thrown a screaming fit. He tried to hold her because she was going to run into the road. She twisted violently away from him. There was a popping sound in her neck. Claire could still remember how he paced in front of her, his arms folded like some kind of history teacher reciting a lesson. He stopped and looked down at her.

"She's gone, Claire, and we're never going to see her again. Nobody is."

That was when she knew. She didn't know how she could understand it all at once—every lie he'd ever told, everything she had overlooked or explained away about Janie. It was like a white light had gone on over his head. It illuminated everything, and in its glare, she saw her daughter, violated and murdered.

She let out a sob and grabbed for the phone, but Bill was too fast for her. He picked it up and shoved her back on the bed. Didn't she see what would happen if she told? She would be arrested, too. She was to blame, as much as he was. She knew what was going on. She had always known—it was the way she wanted it. If she had only given him what he needed, he wouldn't have had to go to Janie.

He was going to leave. She could have the Vanagon, if she wanted, but she probably should sell it. He peeled several hundreds from his wallet and threw the bills at her. It would be enough to get her to some town and find a place to stay. She could get a job then. He assumed she was fit for some kind of work. Fast food, maybe. Probably not stripping.

The sound of his voice, as it slid over the death of their child and into cheap insults, pulsed in her ears. She thought she might explode if he didn't shut up. She lunged at him, slapping and punching.

He picked up the telephone receiver and cracked it across the bridge of her nose. When she fell to the floor, he kicked her until she felt she couldn't draw a breath. It had been years since he'd beaten her like that. She started to scream, and he fell on her, all his weight against the cracked ribs. He brought a pillow down on her face.

She came up out of the airless darkness to see him standing

over her. He'd be back to finish her off if she ever called the police, he said. He would know where she was, what she was doing. He had friends, and his friends had friends. They had good reason to protect each other. He dropped the pillow on her and left.

Hannah had listened without interrupting her. She had an idea of what Bill was doing with this story of Janie's death. It was only that—a story.

He had to get rid of Claire. Motel rooms offered little chance for him to get Janie alone. Eventually, Claire would stumble in on them. He worried that Janie would get over her terror and tell Claire the truth. Her continual sickness would finally prompt Claire to take her to a doctor. He was tired of hauling Claire around, when Janie was all he really wanted.

But Bill had to be sure that Claire wouldn't send the police after him. That's what she would have done if she thought Janie was alive. Claire had to believe Janie was dead and that she was partly to blame.

Claire tried to take a bite of her now-cold eggs, but she finally dropped the fork and reached for her juice. "I could use a shot of vodka in this," she muttered.

Hannah ignored that, but signaled for more coffee. "What did you do then?"

"I knew I should go to the police. It was my fault, too, what happened."

"But you didn't call them?"

She shook her head. "I couldn't stand being locked up. Years and years in prison? I couldn't do it. If they would just execute me, that would be one thing. But it wouldn't be execution. It would be a cell. Being locked up? I couldn't."

"You knew they found a child's body," Hannah said.

She nodded. "It was a couple of weeks after Janie and Bill disappeared. Gaviota Bay was sixty miles away from where we had been staying."

"And you thought it was Janie?"

"I knew it was. Until then, I thought maybe Bill was lying to me. I stayed in the motel for a while, hoping Janie would come back. But when I heard about the body being found, I knew she wouldn't. I left."

"And never tried calling the police? Not even so they could catch Bill?"

"I know it was selfish. And wrong. I should have called the police, for Janie. But . . ."

Hannah knew the reasoning she was using, the mind-feint that let her slip from what she owed Janie. Her daughter was gone. Would it bring Janie back if she surrendered herself to the police? No. And if they found Bill? She would still be dead. So what was the point?

"I did start to call, more than once," Claire said, eager to exculpate herself. "But I always got scared."

"So you just forgot her?"

She shook her head. "I never did. The dreams—so awful. After a year or so, I couldn't handle them anymore. I was afraid and sad all the time. I tried taking some pills, but they wouldn't stay down. Couldn't even kill myself."

Hannah restrained herself from suggesting that she try again. Claire's excuses made her furious. But she thought of Bill beating her and of the hold he still had over her. "And so what's your life now?"

"I work. I move about every eight months or so. People always ask too many questions. They won't leave you alone."

"But Bill always finds you?"

She nodded. "I've gone for months thinking I've gotten away. But I can't. He called last week. It was like always. He didn't say anything. He just breathed for about fifteen seconds, and then hung up. It's to remind me not to call the police."

She didn't doubt it was Bill. But was he tracking Claire—or was he searching for Janie? Obviously, Janie had gotten away from him at some point in the last six years. Maybe he called because he thought Janie was with Claire, or was trying to get back to her. For the first time, Hannah realized that she was in a race. She had to find Janie before Meister did.

She realized she was staring at nothing. Claire looked troubled. "You okay?"

"Want a ride home?"

Claire frowned suspiciously. "You're not arresting me?"

"Not yet."

Claire's one-room apartment had a few pieces of furniture, but no more than would fit into a rental truck. Framed pictures sat on the dresser, including one that showed the whole, perfect

Meister family, taken when Janie was about three. She sat on Bill's knee. His hand supported her at the waist. Claire and Janie held hands. The girl's smile was toothy and silly. To Hannah, the picture telegraphed a word: "before."

Claire tossed her keys on the coffee table and sank onto the sofa bed. "God, I'm wrecked." In a moment, she was snoring softly.

Hannah turned back to the pictures. Two of Janie's school pictures flanked the family portrait, duplicates of the one Hannah had had until Eddy had taken it away. Janie wore a daffodil-yellow outfit. Her smile was barely a smile at all. Janie, after. Hannah picked up one of the frames and slipped the picture out. She shook Claire by the arm until her eyes opened.

"May I borrow this? Evidentiary purposes."

It made little sense, but Claire was too groggy to appreciate that. "Sure, sure," she said. She closed her eyes again. "Something weird happened a couple days ago."

"What?"

"I thought I saw her. On a bench, across the street from work. I even went outside for a better look. But a bus pulled up, and when it left, she was gone."

Hannah didn't say anything.

She tried to focus on Hannah's face. "It couldn't have been Janie, right?"

Hannah gave her shoulder a squeeze. "Get some sleep now."

She nodded drowsily and closed her eyes. "That's what I thought." Soon she was snoring again.

Hannah watched her. Was it an apparition, a product of a guilty conscience? Probably. The specter of Janie surely haunted Claire on a daily basis, in one form or other. But what if she hadn't imagined this visit?

She found the phone amid a clutter of unwashed glasses, and dialed information. Sure enough, Clarice Higgins was listed, address and all. Not the smartest move, but maybe Claire was trying to leave a trail. If some part of her wasn't convinced of Janie's death, this was a way to assure she could be found. Hannah imagined Janie going through phone books in libraries and dialing information from phone booths. She could have figured out that Claire had reverted to her maiden name. Hannah estimated it was a two- or three-hour bus ride from Las

Almas to Pomona. Janie could have done that. She also could have convinced her Volkswagen-owning friends to drive her out here. But given the timing, Hannah guessed that her Integra was the car that had made the trip.

Hannah thought about waking Claire to tell her about the girl in Las Almas. But she finally decided against it. In the bar, she'd held back because Claire didn't deserve hope, not after the way she'd failed Janie. But now there was another reason: Bill Meister. If Claire didn't know Janie was alive, she couldn't compromise her safety, not even if Bill showed up and tried to pummel the information out of her.

She stopped at the manager's apartment on the way out. What she was about to do didn't always work, but it was usually worth a try. Most apartment managers had a little busybody in them. It made them good at their jobs. So she introduced herself as Clarice's cousin, gave the manager fifty dollars, and asked her to call if Ms. Higgins gave notice, or even if she just seemed to be going away for the weekend.

The manager pocketed the money and nodded. "Keeping tabs on your cousin? What's the problem?"

Hannah shrugged. "I lost her once. I don't want to do it again."

31

She had intended to go straight to the office after leaving Claire's apartment, but from the freeway, she saw that wrecking equipment had converged on Janie's apartments, as she now thought of the buildings. She pulled off the freeway and inched up the block, looking for a parking place amid the trucks.

The site was behind chain-link fencing now, and the building where Hannah had been mugged was already gone. But the crew hadn't started tearing down Janie's last-known home. The men milled around, smoking, joking, and swigging soft drinks. Break time.

Hannah sighed. Her most reliable compass for Janie's whereabouts was about to be rubble. She got out, and that was when she saw the patrol car on the far side of the site. Next to it, an unmarked unit was pulling up. She recognized the men who got out as homicide detectives. And she saw where they were going: the apartment that the psychotic landlord had pointed out to her, saying, "All gone. Except for him. He's staying."

Bobby heard the outer office door open. Hannah hadn't been in all day, and he knew, somehow, that it was her. He heard her speak softly to Vera, and then she was at his door. She was pale and had a sleepwalker's slow gait. The expression on her face was haunted. He was afraid even to ask, but he forced himself. "What?"

She looked for a moment as though she might faint. He got

up to help her, but she waved him back. "They were demolishing the apartment building where Janie had been staying. They found a man's body."

"Oh, God," he said. "Eddy?"

She nodded, and that was all she could manage.

She told him how she ran past the demolition workers and followed the detectives to the apartment. The stench nearly knocked her over. The uniforms stopped her from going in, but from the doorway, she had a glimpse of jean-clad legs and shoes—the cheap, liver-colored plastic Payless specials Eddy favored. Then, as they were pushing her back, one of the detectives took a picture from the dead man's denim shirt. Janie's picture. The one Eddy had taken away from her. Hannah swallowed back the burning pain in her throat, the sensation that wanted to vent itself in a cry. She motioned for one of the uniforms and told him she knew the victim.

"His wallet was gone," she told Bobby. "He had been there at least a week. I told the homicide guys about your missing-person report and that Eddy had been on the force. They'll have his fingerprints on file. They said they'd call me as soon as possible. They have to find Gudrun first."

Bobby felt like he'd been plunged into a dream. This was all his fault. Hannah had to be thinking that, too. "Hannah, if I'd thought that anything like this would happen . . ."

She shook her head. "Don't. You said it was his idea to follow Janie."

"I was going to do it. He said I wasn't equipped for the job. Too big to be inconspicuous."

Hannah nodded. It sounded just like him. She had known Eddy for what seemed to be forever. Though they'd drifted apart recently, she still counted him as a friend. It didn't seem possible that he was dead. Eddy had saved her from despair over Janie. He had taken the gun out of her hands when she thought dying was the only way to end the pain she felt. Now he was dead. Because of Janie. She felt on the verge of crying, her eyes burning, her throat tight, but the tears wouldn't come. The mounting losses—Matthew, Guillermo, Janie—had drained her.

"Janie couldn't have done this." She didn't realize she'd said it until Bobby responded.

"Why not?"

"He was bludgeoned, they think. An eleven-year-old girl couldn't do that to someone Eddy's size."

"This happened next door to where you were attacked, probably around the same time, right?"

Hannah nodded.

"Both times, Janie was there," Bobby said.

"You don't know that she was there when Eddy was killed."

"He was following her, Hannah. I can surmise it."

"Janie wasn't the one who beat me. I'm sure of that."

"She has friends, you said. They might be kids, but they're obviously old enough to rob people, beat them, and steal their cars. That's major-league gang stuff, not the work of some tag-crew wannabes."

Janie, she thought, what have you become?

The call came from Jerry McCabe, the Las Almas watch commander who'd told Hannah about Freddy Roche's death. The man found in the building was identified through fingerprints as retired Las Almas Police Detective Devlin Eddy, age forty-eight. He had been beaten to death with some kind of wooden cudgel, perhaps some two weeks before. His wife, from whom he'd been separated for three months, was coming back from Munich, where she was visiting family.

Hannah thanked him and hung up. Her finger was shaking as she punched in Bobby's number.

The next day, although she was in no mood for it, she went back to see Seward. Vera had given her his message when she'd come into the office the day before, but in her shock over Eddy, she hadn't read it until later. *Sorry,* it said. *Let's talk.*

She saw his eyes widen as she sat down. She knew that the skin around her eye was turning the shade of a greengage plum. She doubted that even Claire's recommended makeup could have hidden that completely.

"Jesus! Who . . . ?" Seward's question stalled.

"The same person who stole my car, I believe." She was determined not to discuss it with him and gave him a look that said so.

Seward fiddled with the phone cord. "About the other day. You've gotta understand. In here, it's really tough. I just kind of got carried away, and I—"

"Wait a minute, Mike," she said. She didn't want to hear a discourse on how difficult it was to deal with sexual urges in jail. But she had to manage her temper. She needed to win him back. She had seen Eddy soften up a suspect this way, but it only worked with the truly narcissistic types. She hoped Seward was one of them. "I was the one who was rude. It had been a tough day, and I was not being as sensitive as I should have been. I'm sorry. Okay?" She offered the performance up to Eddy's memory. His funeral—too hastily arranged, Hannah thought—would begin in two hours.

Seward seemed surprised. There wasn't much contrition in jail, she supposed. "Okay." He smiled magnanimously. "No problem."

She nodded. "Good. Why don't you pick up where you left off? There was this little boy you liked, but he was Freddy's. A kid about ten?"

"That's right," he said.

"And Freddy was having sex with this boy?"

Seward shrugged. "You're making it sound dirty."

She thought he was pushing it, but she gritted her teeth. "You know what I mean."

"Their love was consummated, I'm sure. Freddy let me know that much. But he was weird about the kid. He wouldn't talk about him."

"That was something you did with him? Talked about your boys?"

Seward smiled suggestively. "Don't you talk to your friends about your lover, recount your special times?"

Hannah dodged the question. "Did Hank Charles know this boy?"

Seward rolled his eyes to underline his dislike of Charles. "God, I hope not. But I did see Charles a few times, hanging around the park. The old buzzard."

"What became of the boy?"

"I don't know. Sometimes when they grow up, the relationship changes, but they still see their old friends."

"Was it like that with this kid? Do you think Roche found some way to stay in touch with him?"

"He wouldn't say. He thought I would try to get him for myself."

"What was the boy's name?"

"I don't even know that."

"Come on, Mike. You couldn't wheedle that out of Freddy? I thought you were good at getting people to trust you." Christ, she thought, I'm flattering a pedophile. Eddy would reel with laughter at the sight.

He preened slightly. "Well, Roche was jealous. He kept me away from him." He glanced around and then smiled secretively. "But I know one thing."

"What?"

"Freddy took pictures of him. Before they carted his ass off to jail."

"Didn't the police find them?"

Seward slowly shook his head. "Freddy had a hiding place." He sang the words, as an obnoxious schoolboy would.

"Where?"

"If I tell you, you have to promise to do something."

Hannah steeled herself against the annoyance and disgust that were creeping up her gullet like battery acid. "What?"

"Bring them here. I miss seeing pictures."

That tore it. "Jesus."

He didn't seem offended. "Do we have a deal, or not?"

"What kind of pictures are these?"

"Beautiful ones."

"Is the boy recognizable?"

"Yes. Clearly."

Hannah wanted to vomit. But what choice did she have? This boy could be the link: he was Roche's victim, Seward's desire and, possibly, the model for Hank Charles's camera. Tell him what he wants to hear, she told herself. She could always lie and say the pictures were gone. "Okay. Where are they?"

Seward smiled. "Do you know where Marian Roche lives?"

"Don't tell me she was saving them for him."

"Marian doesn't even know they're there. You'll have to get into the garage."

"And then where do I look?"

"Beats me. Think of it as a treasure hunt."

Hannah stared at him, feeling the blood pound at her temples. "Goose chase, you mean."

"No. Unless Marian stumbled on them and threw them out, they're there. Freddy told me he hid them in there. I swear it."

"How do I know this outing isn't punishment for our earlier disagreement?"

Seward sighed. "Look, I've wanted to see these for a long time. Would I bother if I didn't think they were there?"

"I don't know." Hannah started to get up, but Seward still held the phone to his ear. He motioned her to sit down.

"What?" Hannah said. Her patience felt tissue-thin.

"Tell me what happened to your face."

"So you can gloat?"

He shook his head gravely. "Women and children shouldn't be hit. It's a rule I live by."

These ethical enunciations nauseated her. But she had little to lose by talking about her injuries. It didn't hurt to remind herself how stupid she'd been. So without offering the details of Janie's past, she told him what had happened: how the girl ran, how she chased her, and how she was attacked.

She couldn't bring herself to look steadily at him as she talked. She did glance up once or twice, just to make sure he wasn't enjoying himself. Each time, she found him nodding earnestly.

"The worst part was her laugh," Hannah said, remembering the sound of Janie's staccato giggle. "I was beaten bloody, blacking out from the pain, and she's laughing as though it's the funniest thing she'd ever seen."

She looked up again. Sweat dripped from Seward's forehead. "You're making it up," he said. "That last part."

"That she laughed? I wish I was."

He shook his head. "I can't believe it."

"What?"

"There's something I didn't tell you about that night, when someone followed me. Something I heard."

"Go on," Hannah said.

"It was a child. Whispering first—something I couldn't make out—and then laughing. This weird, eerie giggle. It scared the shit out of me."

"A kid laughing scared you? I don't believe it."

He furrowed his brow. "It wasn't happy laughter. This was a laugh that meant there was a secret I wasn't in on. It meant something was going to happen. This was her game, and I was *it*. That's why I ran."

"Did you tell the police?"

"Are you kidding? They would have told me it was my guilty conscience."

Hannah was inclined to think that's just what it was: the ugly psychic residue of Seward's crimes had taken a shape that night and gone after him, like something from a science-fiction movie. But she humored him. "How do you know it wasn't a delusion?"

"If I felt guilty about anything—which I don't—wouldn't I have heard a boy? Isn't that who they say I victimized?"

Hannah shrugged. "Yes, I guess that's right."

"It wasn't a boy."

Hannah studied him. His eyes were fixed on hers. He held the phone so hard that it quivered in his fist.

"How can you be so sure?" Hannah said. "Kids' voices, when they're young—"

His harsh laugh interrupted her. "You forget who you're talking to. I know children's voices, Hannah. I listen to them. I *really* listen. I'm certain it was a girl. She was enjoying how scared I was."

"That doesn't mean it was the same girl who laughed at me."

He looked at her, incredulous. "You're checking up on dead molesters. This kid is chasing me. My roommate is murdered. You get beat up, and we both hear a girl laughing? That's no coincidence."

Numbly, Hannah hung up the phone. Seward was shaking his head like some kind of mechanical doll, saying words she couldn't hear. But she could see them on his lips. "It's not," he was saying. "It's not."

32

A week had passed since Eddy's funeral, and as Bobby made morning coffee for the office, he tried to tell himself that the pitiable service was responsible for Hannah's constant distance and moodiness. The ceremony had depressed him beyond words, and he barely knew Eddy.

He was cremated after a brief service at a mortuary chapel. Gudrun had refused to wait a few days so that the Las Almas P.D. could arrange a full-fledged ceremony to honor one of its own. According to some of Hannah's department sources, Gudrun had shrilly informed the brass that police work had brought her husband nothing but misery, and here was the final proof of it. She went out of her way to avoid Hannah at the service, but bluntly told Bobby that he was responsible for her husband's murder. It stunned him. Hannah seemed to read his mood. On the way home, she told him to stop beating himself up. Gudrun might be projecting her own guilt, thinking that if she hadn't flown off to Germany, leaving her wedding ring in a sink full of dirty dishes, Eddy might not have filled his days with a quest. That helped, until he remembered Gudrun's picture on the archery target. That should have told him how reckless and unbalanced Eddy was. Not the right man to tail a lying street kid with dangerous friends.

Bobby had encouraged Hannah to take a long weekend after the funeral, and she had. But when she returned to work at midweek, she promptly disappeared from the office for hours at a time. He knew what she was doing. It infuriated him. If anything should have snapped her out of her delusional search for Janie Meister, it was Eddy's death. He told Barry Kimberling, the Las Almas homicide investigator assigned to Eddy's case, about the girl Eddy had been following. He stressed the link between Eddy's murder and the attack on Hannah. Kimberling told Bobby that Hannah didn't buy the theory. She said she had no reason to believe the girl who called herself Mae Wallace was involved in either incident. Bobby was furious. Why was she protecting the girl who'd been involved in her former partner's murder? This was not the Hannah he knew.

Now Bobby watched as she dragged herself into the office. She was thinner than ever, her jacket hanging on her shoulders. Her hair was pulled back in a braid from which twists and tendrils sprang. She looked brooding and distracted. Vera tried to hand her messages, but she didn't seem to see or hear her. The phone in her office rang, and as Vera moved to transfer and answer it, Hannah snapped that she would get it herself. The door slammed behind her.

Vera turned to Bobby, a look of distress etched on her face. "Do something." Her soft voice cracked.

He wanted to hide in the comfortable disorder of his office and pretend that Hannah would be herself again, come Monday. But he knew that wasn't going to happen. And he knew that when Vera overcame her dislike of direct address, it was time to listen. He tapped on Hannah's door. No answer. He tried again, and Hannah, sounding exasperated, called for him to come in.

She was on the phone, scribbling on a pad as she talked. "What name was he using? Masterson? Right—not so far from Meister. And he's in Sunset Beach? Or was—right. Thanks." Her voice was excited. She hung up, studying her notes intently. Then she glanced up, seemingly surprised to find Bobby in front of her.

"Was that about Janie?" He asked it expecting her answer to be an outright lie.

"In a way," she said. "I've got a line on her father."

Bobby nodded. He was examining her face. The bruises seemed to be gone, but the skin under her eye still looked puffy and tender.

She continued, oblivious to his stare. "Meister got into a

money hassle with one of his telemarketing friends and got his arm broken. He just left the hospital."

"Great," Bobby said sarcastically.

If she caught the undertone, she was ignoring it. "I don't think I told you. I also found Janie's mother."

"And what about Janie?"

She frowned and shook her head. "I don't know where she is. But now I have to keep tabs on Meister. If he's after Janie, I have to—"

"Hannah, sit down."

"Not now." She rummaged through the papers on her desk until she found her keys. "Meister could be close to finding her."

"Now, Hannah. We need to discuss some things."

She sat down. Bobby wasn't usually someone who issued commands. "What things?"

"Hannah, it has to stop. I know that this has been a rough time for you. Matthew, Guillermo, but most of all, Eddy."

She flung her keys onto the desk. "Let's not forget who got Eddy involved in this, Bobby."

"Goddamn it, Hannah, it's not a blame contest."

She put her hand to her forehead. "I'm sorry, but . . ."

"You promised me you wouldn't get wrapped up in finding this girl. But you did anyway. You got hurt, Eddy's dead, and even those two lessons haven't taught you anything. Now you have to let it go."

"Are you *ordering* me?" She stared at him, incredulous.

"I'm pleading with you."

"Bobby, you don't understand. I'm close to finding one of Roche's victims—someone who could be a link to everything that's going on. Including Janie."

Bobby gaped at her for a moment. "Hannah, that's nuts."

"It sounds strange, I know. But Seward said he heard—"

"Stop." He shook his head. "I don't want to hear any more about this kid. I just hope that she'll be arrested and tried for her role in what she did to Eddy—and to you. She used you, Hannah. She let you believe that she was Janie because it made you vulnerable. That's all." He paused. He couldn't remember ever feeling so hurt and angry, the two strands wound so tight that they threatened to choke him. "And as to Roche and his mother? You were right when you turned his case down, and

I'm sorry that some misplaced sense of responsibility to Michael helped Marian Roche talk you back into it. She doesn't begin to pay our bills. We have other clients who need you. I need you. Our practice is going down the tubes because you're not *here*—even when you're physically behind that desk."

"What are you saying?"

Bobby sighed. He'd lost sleep in his dread of this moment. He loved Hannah—as a friend and as a partner. "I think we can go another ten days or so before the wheels start to come off around here. But no more than that. If you're still obsessing about this a week from now, if you haven't backed off and let the police handle it, I'm going to take steps to dissolve the partnership."

Hannah stood up. She was on the verge of rage, but Bobby now felt only heaviness in his heart as he looked at her. The beating, weight loss, and exhaustion had changed her. She barely looked like herself. But the shift in personality was worse. She was knife-edged and unpredictable, as dangerous as a shard of glass.

"You've picked this moment to give me an ultimatum?" She was shouting at him. "Jesus, Bobby, you pompous—"

"Stop it, Hannah." He said it quietly, too sad to scream back. "Don't try to make me the problem."

She picked up her purse, shoving in her notes and wallet as she talked. "Maybe we shouldn't wait a week. Maybe we should call it quits right now. I need a partner who is a friend, not some martinet who meddles in my life and gets my friends killed."

"I'm not responsible for that, Hannah, and you know it."

"Fuck you." She pushed past him. He heard her tell Vera that she might not be in for a few days. Bobby winced at the sound of the office door slamming behind her.

33

Before her fight with Bobby, Podesta had told Hannah that Meister—registered as Bob Masterson—was staying at a motel in Sunset Beach, an unincorporated town between Seal Beach and Huntington Beach. The community, marked by a Polynesian restaurant at one end and a Jack in the Box at the other, was not nearly as lovely as its name. But on a sunny Friday afternoon in summer, it had its appeal. Hannah put on her sunglasses and the Angels cap she kept in the trunk of her car. She felt anonymous behind them. The Dermablend also helped, covering bruises that changed shades daily, like mutant sunsets. Thus camouflaged, she found a spot from which she could watch the motel for Meister's return. The air was warm. She could smell the ocean and feel the breeze that came in off the water.

It had been a miserable, soaking winter, full of floods and landslides. So although it was a workday, the beach was thick with people determined to reclaim their sunning rights after so many months' denial. She scanned the crowds, but didn't spot Meister. She tried to forget what Bobby had said.

But what if he was right? What if the pursuit of Janie was destroying her? It had killed Eddy, there was no denying that. She realized that it was her own guilt that kept her from feeling the full impact of Eddy's death. If she thought too much about it, she would have to admit he would be alive if it wasn't for her. More exactly, because of her quest to find the truth about Janie.

It couldn't have been Janie herself who'd killed him. She

knew that much. She also didn't think Janie could have stalked Seward, no matter what he thought he'd heard. There was no way that she could have been involved in setting fire to Hank Charles. There was no connection to him. Nor was there a link from Janie to Davis and Roche. Janie was an eleven-year-old kid who lived on the streets and perhaps had violent companions. Hannah suspected that one of them had beaten her, because it was the best way to complete the robbery. Janie had obviously regretted what had happened, or she wouldn't have apologized in her note and the car wouldn't have been returned. Seward wanted Hannah to think something even more sinister about Janie, but he was a freak, pulling a head trip on her for his own amusement.

Hannah closed her eyes for a moment. Suddenly, the arguments she was making to herself sounded ridiculous. Desperate. She wanted to believe anything except the obvious: the girl, whoever she turned out to be, was a hair's breadth away from feral. A leader, perhaps, too young to commit crimes independently, but perfectly capable of planning and directing them. Hannah saw her with a flash of clarity as a miniature pirate queen. Then she closed her eyes to shake the picture away. I'm losing it, she thought. I really am.

When she opened her eyes, a man was locking his motel-room door. And although she hadn't seen him in years, she knew him immediately.

Meister always was a peacock, and he looked the part today in a Hawaiian shirt of indigo and hibiscus red. His khaki shorts were crisp. He had an enviable tan, which ended abruptly at the snowy cast on his left arm. His hair was streaked blond. Behind his owlish sunglasses, his blue eyes would still be strangely pale, like blue chalk, ground and dissolved in milk. He smiled to himself, wearing an expression of ease and confidence that Hannah wanted to smack from his face.

He strolled past her without a glance, his attention trained on a woman in an enormous sun hat, leaf-green blouse, and long, loose white pants. She laid out a plaid blanket, and he sat down next to her. She soothingly stroked his plastered arm. But her eyes were riveted to the water. Hannah followed her gaze out into the lapping surf.

A child of about six, dark-haired and sleek as an otter, emerged from the waves. She ran to the woman, laughing, teeth chattering. The woman folded her into a beach towel and held her in her lap. Meister reached over and caressed her head.

Hannah realized that she was holding her breath, frozen by the sight of Meister fingering the girl's silky hair. He petted her as he would a cat, for his own sensuous enjoyment. The girl leaned against his knee. Hannah shuddered.

After a few minutes, he got up and ducked into the shade of the woman's hat to kiss her cheek. He left the beach, heading for the street. As he passed, Hannah glanced away. The woman packed up her bag. The girl laughed as she pounced on her striped beach ball to deflate it. Hannah wanted to run to the woman and tell her what this man was. But it would take time to explain it all, to make her see the danger. If she did that, she would lose Meister. She made her choice, hoping it was the right one.

During a lag in the traffic, Meister bolted across Pacific Coast Highway and walked into a juice bar. Hannah dawdled outside, pretending to use the pay phone. She had assumed Operation Silver Dollar was keeping close tabs on Meister, but she didn't see any obvious signs of a tail. Maybe he was too cautious to be watched closely. She reminded herself that Meister had no reason to bolt. If he was on Janie's trail, he had every reason to stay.

Inside, Meister read the newspaper while he waited for his smoothie. He tried small talk, but the counter girl ignored it. After a while, he tossed down his money and took a table in the back while the blender whirled. Hannah couldn't stand too long outside without being conspicuous, so she entered, placed an order, and watched him as discreetly as she could.

Meister went into the men's restroom and made a phone call when he came out. Then he sat at his table and stared out at the traffic. The girl poured out his drink and slapped a service bell. "Order's up, Will."

He snatched the drink, tossed a nickel in the jar, and walked outside. He paced in the sun as Hannah waited for her drink.

"He's a regular?" Hannah asked.

"For a couple of weeks," the counter girl said, punching the blender's buttons. "Smooth talk. Lousy tips."

A cab pulled up and honked. Meister got in, and the car headed south, down Pacific Coast Highway toward Newport

Beach. Hannah ran to her car and followed. The dearth of cabs in Orange County made the job easy.

At Newport Boulevard, the cab turned inland. After several miles of bumper-nudging traffic, it delivered Meister to a five-and-dime store in an old Costa Mesa strip mall. Hannah arrived just as the door closed behind him. A garish coin-operated rocket ride still sat outside on the sparkled sidewalk. But the store's windows were soaped to near-opacity. Hannah was sure that whatever was going on inside, it didn't involve goldfish, knitting yarn, or Butterick patterns. Dime stores were going the way of the heath hen.

She got out of her car, staying a little distance away from the store. There was a sign in large, red handwritten letters on the door: Coast Financial Services. Through some of the soap swirls, she could see light and movement inside. The door opened and a man in jeans and a yellow terry-cloth shirt stepped out, propping the door with his body as he took a puff on a thick cigar. Now Hannah could see more: desks and phones. And Meister. He was pacing. The decentralized, low-key telemarketing scam that was supposed to be safer obviously hadn't worked out for him—the cast on his arm made that clear. He appeared to be falling back on an old-fashioned boiler-room operation, presumably run by a kinder, gentler con artist of long years' acquaintance. She heard one of the phones ring. Meister answered it. The cigar-smoker tapped off his ash and closed the door.

After a minute, the light inside went off. Hannah got in her car and started it, ready to follow Meister and his friend. But no one emerged. She went to the door and peered through the swirls. No one was there. She tried the door. Locked. And then she realized what had happened. It was a store. It had a delivery entrance—and exit.

Around the corner, she found the fading sign that marked the store's delivery door. There were no cars there, but there were faintly delineated parking spaces. Water, freshly dripped from a car's air conditioner, puddled on the ground of the space closest to the back door.

In her car, she called Rudy Podesta. "Have you got someone tailing Meister?"

"No reason to," he said. "We assumed that he wasn't going anywhere."

"I think you're wrong. Something scared him. He's taken off."

"Back to the motel?"

"I seriously doubt it."

"Shit, Hannah, did you blow my arrest?"

Hannah was speechless for a moment. "Hell, no Rudy. Your assumptions did." She stabbed the phone's power button. She'd lost Meister. And since she'd lost Janie, too, she had no way to warn her that he was back in Orange County. Why had he run? She knew she hadn't spooked him. But something had.

34

Jared couldn't stop laughing. "Freaked him *out.* 'They're watching you, Bill, and they're gonna getcha.' He really lost it, didn't he?"

The girl shook her head. "I couldn't hear what he said."

"He panicked. It was great."

Jared wove through the traffic as she tracked the forest-green Saturn and its two occupants. They briefly lost the car as it turned into the parking lots of South Coast Plaza. But she knew where the passenger liked to shop, so they just waited outside the men's department entrance to Nordstrom. The Saturn came back and picked him up. She glanced away as he got in. Now all she could see was the back of a blond head. But there was no doubt. She had no trouble keeping track of the car, either. She knew the years and models. Vans, trucks, classics—she knew them all on sight.

"Are you watching?" Jared must have sensed that she was drifting off.

She sighed in exasperation. "Of course. They're turning left."

They followed the Saturn as it turned onto Harbor Boulevard. A few blocks later, the car stopped abruptly at a used-car lot that advertised a massive Fourth of July weekend sale. The passenger got out, and the Saturn pulled away.

She sank back in the seat. Recently, when the pictures of him had gushed into her mind like black water, she'd made them stop by telling herself that all the bad things he'd done, he'd done to someone else. She didn't even know him, because she was Maisey-Daisy, Jared's sister. But then she saw the flaw in her reasoning: He might be somebody else's father. He might be doing horrible things to some other poor kid. She discovered that the thing that really worked was to see him dead. It wasn't enough just to imagine that he had died. She had to see him lying there, cold.

At the foster home, she attended a funeral for the real kids' grandfather. That was what the foster mother called them: "my real kids." The girl supposed that made her one of the fake kids. At the viewing, she sneaked a touch as the old man lay in his open casket. His hand was cold and rubbery. She liked to think about the passenger that way: chilly and immobile. She could scratch him and spit on him, do anything else she wanted to. Lying against a little satin pillow, tied down by death, he could not touch her. Or anyone else.

The fantasy evaporated as he walked past their car. He wore a loud shirt and tan shorts that flapped against his legs as he strode down the row, examining the price stickers. She forced herself to sit up and look at him. Because maybe it wasn't him. How did she know for sure he wasn't dead somewhere? Anything could happen in three years. The sun was setting, and the windows of the Volkswagen were a smoky gray that made it hard to see. She rolled the glass down a little.

He was standing next to a white Toyota Celica. The tiny vertical lines between his eyebrows compressed like an accordion as he examined the car. She knew the expression—annoyance, soon to become whip-stinging anger. Stop whining. Yes, you do. Because I said so, goddamn it.

Suddenly he pulled off the glasses and hunched down to read the sticker. Watching him, she felt herself rising and sinking, slipping out of gravity's hand, the way she had once on a roller coaster as it had peaked and plunged. His eyes were so pale, so cold. He could bring a little sun into them when he needed to, when he wanted something from someone—like her mother, for instance. But she knew their real power, how they could pin you with their freezing laser. How they sealed you in an ice cave.

He looked that way the day they went to pick out a kitten. That's where he told her they were going: to see his friend whose cat had just had a litter. She'd made a little nest in a closet and had her kittens, now how about that? She had wanted a cat for a long time and he promised that this time she really could have one. She should have known just by looking at him that it was a lie. The white glacier slid into his eyes when he lied.

There were no kittens. There wasn't even a house. Just a man in a white Ford Econoline van with a camera. Her father said she should pick out a kitten, and he'd be right back. She thought he looked upset. Why would cats make him sad?

The man had a camera. He smiled, cooed at her, admired her dress, tried to get her to laugh and pose. But Camera Guy was looking at her the way her father did, when they were alone. As soon as her father was gone, Camera Guy stopped smiling.

She shook her head, trying to forget. Her father always said, when she resisted him: listen to me—this is what daddies do with their daughters. But Camera Guy wasn't her daddy. He hit her—hard—when she wouldn't kneel down. She cried and screamed, and he hit her again. Then she knew nothing would make him stop. After a while her father came back, and the men fought because her father saw that Camera Guy had hit her. That was not part of the deal, her father screamed.

She cried all the way home, though he tried to soothe her. Sorry, he said. Sorry, sorry. He would never let that happen again. There was a problem, he told her, something about a flood and a gold mine. That was what made Camera Guy mad. That was why he had had to leave her there. It had been wrong. No one should have a special time with her like he did, he said.

She hadn't understood much of it. It was the only apology she ever had from him, but it was all backwards, like writing in a mirror. He was sorry that someone else had hurt her. But he wasn't sorry about hurting her himself. It was crazy talk, and it made her feel like she was spinning away, being washed down a drain.

Now she felt herself shaking, the kind of shaking that would lead to an eruption of tears. She couldn't do that now. So she thought about what had happened to Camera Guy. The explosion, the fire. She could hear him screaming, disappearing in the flames. She could still smell the gasoline, feel the wall of flame that erupted in the street. She recalled the ripple of relief that coursed through her. But then came the backlash of sick fear and panic.

She closed her eyes to center herself. She was coming back

to the car, the street, this day, and the late afternoon. She could smell something sweet, some flowers in a strip of dirt that bordered the car lot.

When she opened her eyes, he was no longer examining the price tag. He was standing, glasses off, staring out at the street. At Jared's car. He squinted. He blinked. He put his glasses on and started walking toward the car.

Jared saw him coming. "Damn it!"

He shoved her down, swung the wheel, and jammed the accelerator. She banged her knees on the dash, heard horns blat and brakes screech. Crouching, knees pinned by the dash, she clenched her eyes shut. She felt Jared swing the car left and right, jostling for a place in the thick traffic. The wind blew down on her. Why had she opened the window in the first place?

"Did he see you?" Jared's voice was harsh.

"No." The denial came out too quickly. "Maybe. I'm not sure."

"Shit."

"I'm sorry," she said.

"You can get up now."

She eased herself up into the seat. She wanted to look back, but she knew she shouldn't. "We have to be careful," Jared was saying. "We have to make sure he doesn't know we're following him." Jared apologized for being rough. But his voice came from very far away, because she had gone deep inside now. She was slipping away, heading for the place where she was alone, the only one, not touching, not touched. Just not.

35

Hannah listened to the dying doorbell chime and the approach of footsteps inside the Spanish castle that Marian Roche called home. A tiny metal portal in the middle of the front door swung open and Hannah saw one of the old woman's eyes—narrowed and slightly bloodshot—peering out at her.

"I called your office numerous times in the last week and you were never there." Her voice was muffled by the oak door. "Is a personal visit supposed to erase that?"

"I was out talking to people about Freddy, Mrs. Roche. I wanted to finish some of that before getting back to you."

"Well?"

"There are a couple things we need to discuss. May I come in?"

The eye crinkled in suspicion. The peephole snapped shut and the front door opened. In contrast to her neat appearance on the day she hired Hannah, she now looked like a woman who spent her time in close proximity to her bed. Although it was nearly noon, she still wore a white bathrobe and some red crew socks. Her thin peach-pink hair was a disheveled tangle around her shoulders. "What is it you want to talk about?"

"I've been trying to reach Lisette Blackburn, but haven't had any luck. Do you have an address for her?"

Marian padded to a desk and copied something from a day planner. She all but threw it at her. "What is it you want from Lisette?"

"Some . . . follow-up questions."

Marian clicked her tongue. "She didn't take your job?"

"I didn't offer one. But she did tell me that she and Freddy were engaged. She said she and Freddy were keeping it from you."

"Oh, that ridiculous woman." Marian rolled her eyes. She hadn't stenciled in her eyebrows yet. Without them, her face was less of a caricature. "He liked her well enough. But she wasn't right for him."

Hannah nodded. So Seward said. And Caesar Pritzker, too. But they hadn't meant it as Marian did. "So you don't believe it?"

"No, of course not. Freddy had no secrets from me. What was the second thing you wanted?" She was impatient, although it was clear she wasn't going anywhere.

"I need to look through your garage for some things Freddy might have left here."

She frowned. "The garage? The things he brought over when he moved into that unwholesome shack are up in his room."

"He also might have left some things earlier, before he went to prison, Mrs. Roche. The garage is where I'd like to start."

She shrugged. "Well, I suppose. If you tell me what you're looking for, I could help."

Hannah knew she couldn't tell her. Marian Roche would cold-cock Hannah before she would let her dig up evidence against her boy, even if he was dead. But Hannah didn't intend to be stopped. She was angry at herself for losing track of Meister on Friday. She was frantic at the thought of his finding Janie. She imagined her now as someone lost in a labyrinth, a place peopled with molesters and other assorted monsters. Any thread, however unlikely, that might bring her closer to a hint about Janie's whereabouts was worth pursuing. That's what the pictures might be, and if they were here, she would find them. Marian wasn't going to stop her.

Hannah smiled pleasantly. "I'm not sure quite what I'm after. I think I'll know when I find it. May I have a look, please?"

Marian clearly was displeased, but motioned for Hannah to follow her. They stopped in a spotless kitchen so she could retrieve a key from a drawer. Marian ushered Hannah out a back door and into an overgrown yard. Rosemary blanketed a low stone planter, and a thickly planted citrus grove at the back of the yard scented the air. A fenced strip, devoid of grass, ran the length of the deep lot. Suddenly, an amped up Doberman dashed into view. The dog froze at the sight of Hannah and then began a fusillade of full-throated barks.

"Baby, you silly girl, hush," Marian crooned. Hannah doubted the beast could hear anything but her own doggy fury. She hoped the wire-mesh fence was strong.

Marian unlocked a door that faced on the yard. The door for cars must be on the opposite side, facing an alley. She flipped a switch and an overhanging bulb dimly illuminated the interior. There was a new Cadillac Catera parked smack in the center, surrounded by neatly labeled boxes, stacked three and four high—fifty or more of them.

Marian smiled thinly at her. "Make sure you put everything back as you found it."

Hannah examined the sides of the boxes. Someone had labeled them with their contents—Lladró figurines, Russel Wright dinnerware, Murano glass—and the packing date. If the notes were accurate, all the loot here had arrived long after Freddy went to prison—Marian's inventory, accumulated from her dying friends, Hannah supposed. There was enough to keep Caesar in stock for a long time. She selected three boxes at random and slit them open with her penknife. She found dishes, glassware, costume jewelry, and bric-a-brac, just as the labels said. She gently laid the pieces on the floor, removed the crumpled newspaper that cradled them, and upended each box. All empty. She checked under flaps for envelopes. Nothing hidden there. She sighed. Going at it methodically, she would be there for hours.

Hannah surveyed the rest of the garage. Unlike some she'd seen—her father's garage, for instance—this one was finished. Its wooden studs and horizontal strips of heavy black insulating sheathing were plastered over. In her father's garage, pictures in an envelope could easily be slipped between the studs and paper layers. But not in Marian Roche's garage. The interior finish looked at least thirty years old. There was no sign of recent cutting and patching.

She looked under the car—no sunken safe. She was running out of options. She could open all the boxes. She could move them all, to be sure they didn't conceal something hidden in the perimeter of the concrete floor. She sighed. The boxes probably weren't the answer. So what had she missed? She examined the walls, and as a final check, she looked up.

It was something she'd learned on architectural tours of old downtown areas. The lower-floor facades changed with the years, so if you wanted to see what the past really looked like, look up. See the shape of the building, the details, all the stuff that the lower-floor merchants didn't bother with, because they only cared about catching customers at eye level.

The upper reaches of the garage ceiling weren't plastered—she was looking at the underside of roof shingles, and there was nothing tucked away up there. But as she scanned the space, she thought she saw something at a corner where the low-wattage light couldn't reach. She had brought a pen-sized flashlight, which she now pointed up into the darkness. There was a two-foot gap at the top of the wall—an opening to something. But what?

Hannah went into the backyard for another look. The garage seemed wider out here than it did inside. There was apparently another room in the building, a section that wasn't accessible from the garage itself. She walked around the corner and saw a second windowed door. Peering in, she saw a lawn mower, a potting bench, and various garden tools—clippers, shovels, and trowels. The storeroom had a dropped ceiling, which must serve as the floor to an attic space above. That gap she saw in the garage was its entrance. She tried the storeroom door. It was open and there was a ladder in the back corner.

When she emerged with the ladder on her shoulder, Baby whimpered, growled, and then launched into a dramatic Dobie aria. Hannah ignored it, hoping that Marian was deaf to most of the animal's uproar by now.

She propped the ladder against the garage wall, checked it for steadiness, and climbed up. In the flashlight's beam, she could see little but dust, some old wooden window cornices, and a few cardboard boxes. But in the far corner there was a breadbox, its green enamel flaking away. She tested the attic floor. It seemed sturdy enough.

"Okay," she whispered to herself. "Let's explore."

She crawled through the dust of years, stopping twice as sneezing overtook her. The floor jiggled in response to the violence of the fits. She imagined herself falling, then being impaled on the branch cutters she saw in the tool room below. Marian would barely bat an eye, she thought. Snack time for Baby.

The cardboard boxes turned out to be Marian's picture depository. It surprised Hannah. She would have thought that Freddy's precious childhood merited better treatment than this. But as she looked more closely, she realized that this was pre-Freddy. These were old black-and-white shots of a young woman and a rotating cast of men. She recognized the strawberry blonde as Marian, decked out in slinky dresses, swimsuits, broad-shouldered suits, and platform shoes. The men were in uniform, bathing trunks, wide-shouldered jackets, and slouchy hats. She hugged them on piers, outside movie theaters, and in front of muscular Studebakers and plump Fords. Marian might have had to ration butter and meat during World War II, but there was obviously no shortage of men in her life. She wondered which was Freddy's father. Then she wondered if Marian knew.

By the time she reached the corner where the breadbox sat, Hannah felt like a spider's dinner. She had wiped the webs off her face, but they clung to her hair. Something tickled the skin under her collar, and when she slapped at her neck, a balled-up spider dropped onto her knee. It unfurled itself and skittered away. Hannah, not normally a bug-bothered person, shuddered. The attic's heat, dust, and wildlife were getting to her. She picked up the breadbox, which rustled as she turned it. It was hinged at the top, but the lid didn't want to yield. She was sweating now, the dust on her face turning to a grimy slick. She turned and shuffled awkwardly back to the ladder on one hand and two knees, cradling the breadbox like a football.

The lid wouldn't come off, and as she turned the box, she saw why: it had been glued shut. She took the box to the toolroom, ignoring Baby's growls. Hannah glanced back at the house. Marian, still in her bathrobe, stood at the dining room window with a wineglass in her hand, pretending not to watch her.

She closed the toolroom door, put the box on the potting table, and looked around for something to pry it open. In one of the worktable drawers, she found a screwdriver. Good enough. She jammed the blade between the box and its lid. Wiggling it, she tried to break through the bead of dried glue.

Instead, the wall of the box bent a half-inch. She tried the lid again. It wouldn't budge, but with a few more assaults on the side of the box, she had made a gap big enough to slip her hand carefully inside.

She felt plastic, with something soft under it. She gently tugged and out came a freezer bag. There was a small pair of underwear inside. She turned the bag over. A lock of straight brown hair, tied with a blue ribbon, nestled against the white cotton fabric. She pulled out another bag. Another pair of underwear, patterned with airplanes this time. Another strand of hair—ashy blond.

There were a half-dozen bags in the box. Hannah laid out Roche's trophies and stared at them. Through the plastic, she pushed down the waistband of one and looked at the tag: size ten. Goddamn it, Freddy, she thought.

She shook the box. There was something else inside. She scraped her hand on the raw edge of the metal as she pulled out the last of Roche's treasures—a white envelope containing a dozen pictures. Not Polaroids. No need for privacy and stealth. These were pictures that wouldn't raise an eyebrow at a photo lab, which is where these seemed to have been developed and printed.

The four-by-five prints showed a boy that Seward had described: a child of ten or so with straight, thick, light-brown hair that fell below his ears. His eyes were the light green of cat's-eye marbles. The pictures seemed to be taken in a park. In the top one, the boy's shirt was off. His tan skin gleamed with sweat. He smiled and cradled a fresh, scuffless basketball in the crook of his thin arm. A gift from Freddy, no doubt.

She flipped through the rest of the pictures. The boy ran, posed like a muscleman, clowned with an ice-cream cone. At the bottom, there was a shot of Roche and the boy together. Roche had his arm over the boy's shoulders. Like his young friend, he was shirtless. Although Roche was thinner then, it still wasn't a pleasant sight. Even worse was the oleaginous smile on his face. Hannah wondered if Henry Charles had been the photographer.

The pictures were not erotic, but Hannah knew what they meant to people like Roche, Charles, and Seward. She felt queasy at the thought of bringing Seward any of the photographs—no matter how innocent they seemed. She looked through the ribbon-tied tokens, trying to match a shade of hair to the boy in the pictures. None seemed right. Roche might have had other hiding places for these prizes. Perhaps he didn't get close enough to this secret boy to take a trophy. Hannah wanted to believe that, but Seward had seemed certain that Freddy had counted the boy as a conquest.

She looked at the best close-up of the child. His smile was open, trusting. She wondered how slowly and subtly Freddy worked to win his trust. How long was it before he brought the boy home on some innocuous errand? How long before handshake turned to hug, to lingering touch. She was sure that Freddy took his time. He wasn't a Henry Charles, relying on force and threats. Freddy was patient. Seduction was a pavane, a stylized dance where every step was something to cherish and savor.

There was something familiar about the boy, but she couldn't imagine where she might have seen him. The most probable contact was some time in her career with the Las Almas P.D. Any boy befriended by Freddy Roche probably had a precarious home life. She might have seen him on a domestic call, an abused-child report. She closed her eyes for a moment, waiting for a memory to drift up. Nothing came. Hannah decided that she couldn't trust every intuition. She still wasn't sure if Janie was Janie, or a trick of her guilty mind. Perhaps she was reaching again for connections that didn't exist.

In the garage she found a brown paper bag and put the breadbox inside it. She planned to leave through the alley, deposit the bag in her car, then return to tell Marian she'd struck out. No unpleasant scenes that way.

But halfway down the alley, she heard the gate open behind her. Marian stood there, holding Baby by a black leather collar. Marian had finally gotten dressed and was now wearing a red velour jogging suit and an elaborately decorated pair of Nikes. Baby stared at Hannah. The dog's lip slowly receded to show the milky-white blades of her teeth. Marian, who slipped her fingers out until only one held the dog back, smiled unpleasantly. "She wouldn't hurt you. Unless I told her to. Bring that here to me."

Hannah didn't relish being food for Baby. She walked back to the gate. "Put her away. Then we'll talk."

When Baby was penned, Hannah took out the plastic bags

and lined them up on the wrought-iron table in the middle of the yard. She fanned the pictures of the angelic boy and stepped back so Marian could see what she'd found.

"What is all this?" Marian picked up one of the bags and turned it, as Hannah had. She frowned at the lock of hair. Hannah waited for realization, which was sure to be followed by protestations of Freddy's innocence. Instead, in a split second, Marian scooped up the evidence and bolted into the citrus grove. She was fast, and Hannah swore under her breath for underestimating her.

Hannah lost her briefly in the greenery. By the time she emerged onto a back patio, she saw the plastic bags laid out on a barbecue grill like so many chicken breasts. Marian was flicking a lit match onto them. They melted, smoked, and caught fire. Now she was ready to drop the pictures onto the flames.

Hannah snatched them from her. Two of the prints tore as they struggled. Marian made small, angry grunts as she scratched Hannah's arm and tried to bite her. Hannah had a sudden, surrealistic feeling that she would have been better off fighting Baby. The sickening stench of the burning plastic and human hair filled the air. Finally, with a twist of Marian's matchstick arm, the pictures fell to the ground. Hannah snatched them up. Marian lunged for her, but Hannah pushed her away.

"Don't, Marian, or I swear I'll really hurt you." Marian sank to the ground, panting. She sat there on the gravel, staring silently at the photographs in Hannah's hand. "These things might lead to Freddy's killer," Hannah said. "Isn't that what you want?"

Marian struggled to catch her breath. "He didn't do anything. It was Seward. What Lisette said. All lies, all filthy . . ." She broke down in sobs and gasps.

Hannah helped her to a chair, but the old woman angrily pushed her away once she was seated. Hannah stood quietly for a minute until she collected herself. "Marian, what did Lisette say?"

"Nothing," she snapped. "Forget it."

"And what about Seward?"

She shook her head. "Forget it, I said. Get out before I turn Baby loose."

Hannah would have liked to press Marian, but she took the Baby threat seriously. As she got in her car, she could hear Marian crying, and soon the dog started to howl. She listened to the bathetic counterpoint. She supposed she should feel some sympathy for the old woman, but it was difficult. She watched Marian when she was confronted with Freddy's mementos. She instantly understood what they meant. But they evoked no pity or shame. She just wanted to destroy them, a selfish attempt to preserve her only illusions.

At a stoplight Hannah picked up one of the photographs and studied it. The boy would be about sixteen or so now. Would this picture mean something to Lisette? Is that what Marian had let slip? Hannah decided to make an unannounced visit.

No one answered the knock at Lisette's door, which is what she expected. She jotted a note on a business card—*Marian says you lied—what did you say?*—and inserted it between the door and the jamb.

At home she put the angelic boy's pictures on her desk next to the photograph of Janie. She looked again at Janie's notes—one on a workbook page, the other on a piece of junk mail. She turned the advertising mailer over. She hadn't paid attention to what it was, but now she stared at the words in capital letters: HAVE YOU SEEN ME? She looked at the missing child pictured, gone ten years now, and knew what she would do next.

36

Ivan Churnin was on the phone when Hannah came into the detectives' bull pen. Monday morning, eight A.M., and already he was at work. He waved her to a chair and hung up.

"I was just calling you," he said. "Henry Charles died last night."

"They expected it," Hannah said. What she thought was something else: thank God. Maybe now Laurel James and her niece would have some peace.

"We've talked about him in the past tense since day one, if you want to know the truth. But now he's officially dead." Churnin's glance seemed to linger on Hannah's face and its concealed bruises. He knows all about what's happened to me, she thought. It's not his case, but it doesn't matter. They all talk.

He leaned back in his chair. "Is this just a courtesy call?"

"No, business."

"Oh. I thought perhaps you were on your way to tell Kimberling the truth about who beat the hell out of you."

Hannah shrugged. "I told him what I know. Which is almost nothing."

"Being uncooperative won't help us catch the guy who did that to you. It's probably the same guy who killed Eddy, you know. Is there some reason you don't want us to find him?"

"Of course not."

"Kimberling is right down there, corner cubicle. Never too late to come clean."

"Ivan, look at these." She laid out the pictures she'd brought of Janie and Roche's boy.

Churnin tapped Janie's photograph. "This is the same as the picture in Eddy's pocket."

Hannah nodded. "It's Janie Meister. Eddy was following her. Didn't Kimberling tell you that?"

"No. What I know about Eddy is thirdhand. Kimberling doesn't trust me. He thinks I'll leak stuff to you." He frowned at Hannah. "Wait. Janie Meister? How could Eddy be following her? She's dead."

"I thought so, too. But I've seen her and talked to her. She just won't admit who she is."

"You're certain it's her?"

"No. I think it's her. I need to be sure."

He nodded warily. "Okay. I'll save my questions about her secret to resurrection for later. Who's the boy?"

"He was mixed up with Freddy Roche. Both these pictures are five or six years old. I need to know how these children would look today."

Churnin nodded knowingly. "And you heard that the National Center for Missing and Exploited Children trained one of our guys to use age-progression software."

"But he won't do it for civilians. He'd do it for you."

"All right. Tell me about the boy. Mixed up with Freddy?"

"One of his victims."

"I thought there was only one."

"That's the one the police found out about. I've seen some evidence that implies another six or so victims. Including this boy." She told him about the underwear and locks of hair and how Marian had turned them into burnt offerings.

Churnin didn't say anything about the nature of the mementos, but Hannah knew he'd seen worse things in a molester's treasure chest. Of Marian, he said only that she could make a hell of a ruckus for an old gal.

"Age doesn't slow some people down," Hannah said. "Look at Strom Thurmond."

"No thanks," Churnin said. "Tell me what you know about this boy."

"Almost nothing. I don't even know his name. But Seward wanted him. And Hank Charles might have taken some of these pictures."

"The boy's a link, then?"

Hannah nodded. "Maybe."

Churnin flipped to a number in his Rolodex and picked up the phone. "Let's see what Sean Yates can do for us."

Yates, a soft-spoken, graying property-crimes detective, decorated his work space with reproductions of Eakins's portraits, Cassatt's mothers and children, and his own sketches of felons. Churnin said that Yates had been an art major in college before deciding that his true calling was police work. He'd turned his skills to composites, reconstructions of victims' features from skeletal remains, and other works of forensic art. Yates looked at Hannah's pictures and shook his head.

"The computer programs work pretty well, but they don't work miracles." It obviously was a talk he'd given before. "I can't just scan in these pictures, push a button, and have the computer spit out perfect current portraits. You've got a starting place, but I need more to work with."

"What else would help you?" Hannah said.

"Ideally, good pictures, shot in roughly the same pose, of the parents of these children, at the age these kids would be now. That gives me an idea of how their faces changed as they matured."

Hannah and Churnin exchanged a look. "I might be able to get something for the girl," Hannah said. "I don't have anything for the boy. I don't even know his name."

He shrugged. "I have a file of kids' pictures that I use as a sort of cut-and-paste archive when I don't have anything else, but the outcome won't be as precise."

Hannah nodded. "I'll try to get pictures of the girl's parents for you." If they even exist, Hannah thought. She had wondered once what had turned Meister into the man he was. She hadn't extended that to picturing him as a boy.

Claire kept the chain on as she opened her apartment door, but even through the crack, Hannah could see the array of beer bottles on the counter behind her. All were empty save one, which was half full and dewy cold. It was just before noon.

"You here to arrest me?" Her breath had the yeasty smell of a brewery.

"No. I need to borrow some pictures. Of you and Bill, when you were eleven or so. Do you have anything like that?"

She squinted at Hannah, as if that might make her request

clearer. She let Hannah in and motioned for her to sit down. Her hair was lank. She wore a black T-shirt and baggy pink leggings that made her legs look like they were melting. "You want pictures of us as kids? What for?"

Hannah had struggled with this throughout the drive to Pomona. Should she tell Claire about the girl? If the child turned out not to be Janie, Claire would go through the agony of losing her all over again. If she was indeed Janie, Hannah could be putting the girl in danger by telling Claire about her. The choice wasn't easy, but Hannah knew what she should do.

"Sit down. I'll explain, but first, do you have any pictures like that?"

Claire rubbed her hand across her mouth and leaned against the sofa's arm. "I used to have some. But when we left Las Almas, we left a lot of stuff behind. I didn't want to, but—"

"Bill didn't want you dragging a bunch of memorabilia around."

"Right." She had the befuddled look of someone whose brain was stewing in beery juices. "I had a picture album, but I can't remember whether we . . ."

Hannah bit her tongue. It was no time for a lecture on the evils of alcohol, but Claire's drinking made everything harder. "Why don't you take a quick shower? I think hot water does something to stimulate the memory."

She nodded, and then looked intently at Hannah. "Is this about Bill?"

"No," Hannah said gently. "It's about Janie."

Before Hannah could explain, a wild fear came into Claire's eyes. Hannah could almost follow the racing suspicions. She never gave up hope of Janie being alive, no matter what Bill told her. But if pictures were needed, it could only mean one thing: there was another body, this one really was Janie, but they needed pictures for reconstruction, recreations. It wasn't an entirely logical chain of thought, but Claire's panic was understandable.

Hannah reached for Claire's hand. The woman recoiled and Hannah realized that touch seldom brought Claire comfort. "It's not that," Hannah said. "I think Janie is alive."

"It can't be." Claire's eyelids fluttered. She wanted to believe, but was afraid to.

"Bill lied to you," Hannah said. "He wanted Janie all to

himself. He told you she was dead so you'd feel terrified and guilty. So you wouldn't follow him."

She seemed about to break down, shaking and prayerfully holding her fingers to her lips. She whispered from behind them. "Is she all right?"

"When I saw her, she seemed fine." That was the best Hannah could do. It was true that Janie was physically well, albeit underfed. But Hannah couldn't vouch for the health of her mind, or the state of her soul. Hannah struggled to deny Janie's involvement in Seward's stalking, in Eddy's murder, and in the attack on herself. But she sensed Janie's spirit in all those events, as though she were a violent muse.

"Did you know all along? And you didn't tell me?" Claire came unsteadily to her feet, angry and agitated. "Goddamn it, I want to see her."

Hannah reached up for her hand and pulled her down. "Listen to me: I didn't tell you before because of Bill. I think he's trying to find her."

Her eyes widened. "He's here?"

"I saw him in Orange County not long ago. I thought that if you knew where Janie was, Bill could try to force you to tell him. Understand?"

She nodded. If there was one thing she grasped, it was Bill's brutality. "What are the pictures for?"

Hannah explained the age-progression process. "With a picture that's age-progressed, we'll have a better idea if the girl really is Janie. I can't rely on my memory, and the girl has denied being Janie."

"Let me see her. I'd know my own daughter."

"Maybe you would. But I don't know where she is right now. She's a runaway, Claire."

"But someone is taking care of her, right?"

"I don't know that anyone is."

"God, my baby." She stared at the pictures on her dresser. "She's—"

"Not a baby anymore, but still young. The pictures, Claire?"

"Oh, Jesus, why can't I think?"

Hannah indicated the beer bottles. "Those don't help."

Claire's face colored. "If I don't have a drink or two, I have bad dreams."

"If Janie's alive, that bad dream is over. You have a reason to stop now," Hannah said.

Claire nodded vaguely, but she also seemed to be weighing if that was reason enough for sobriety. Christ, Hannah thought, she's hopeless. "Go take a shower. Is it okay if I look around?"

She nodded. "Go ahead. The closet is as good a place to start as any."

Hannah found two cardboard moving boxes, dragged them out, and sorted through them. She found some of Claire's clothes: tailored wool pants and a green silk dress, both of which looked too small for her now. There were a few sheets of stationery, their edges browned and brittle. A stump of a votive candle, perhaps burned down as Claire prayed for her daughter, or herself. But there was no sign of a photo album. Claire came out of the bathroom, drying her hair, just as Hannah pulled out a child's book with an embossed gold-foil spine. It wasn't L. Frank Baum's original *The Wonderful Wizard of Oz*, but a highly illustrated simplified version for very young children.

Claire gasped. "Oh God, I thought that was gone."

Hannah held it out to her. "Janie liked the story, didn't she? She still has a stuffed lion."

Claire's eyes widened. "Bert?"

Hannah nodded. "Bert."

"Then it really is her," Claire said. She sat down and gently ran her fingers over the book's cover. She began turning the pages. Some of them seemed stuck together. Claire carefully parted the edges and looked up. "One weekend, it wouldn't stop raining. Bill was away on business. Janie was about four, and she was just in love with the story. She was bored and cranky, so to pass the time, we turned the characters into people she knew. Like Dorothy did, in the movie?"

"I remember." In its doppelganger casting, the film's Wicked Witch of the West was also Miss Gulch. In Dorothy's fevered dream, the hired hands at Uncle Henry's Kansas farm became the Tin Woodman, Scarecrow, and Cowardly Lion.

"We glued in pictures," Claire said.

"Of you and Bill?"

She nodded. "I was Glinda, the good witch."

"And Bill?"

"The wizard, of course. But Janie didn't think adults belonged in a kid's book, so I used old photos." She stopped at a page. "Here. I was about twelve, I think."

It was a school picture. The girl smiled brilliantly, her eyes wide, her face open and happy. Claire looked incapable of such joy now, and that saddened Hannah. But there was something worse about the picture: Claire as a child looked nothing like the girl who called herself Mae Wallace. Had she been telling Hannah the truth when she'd said she wasn't Janie Meister?

Hannah asked, "Where's Bill?"

Claire turned a few more pages and stopped at a photograph of a boy whose thin neck and prominent Adam's apple hinted at the imminent arrival of adolescence. The picture had been pasted onto the body of the great and powerful wizard. The boy looked warily into the camera's lens, as though afraid of exposing the soul behind the pale, vulnerable eyes.

Claire ran her finger across the picture. "I don't know all of what happened to Bill when he was little. He said it was the past, and it was done with. But it wasn't, was it?"

Hannah shook her head. The past had cycled itself into the next family, the next generation. Not every victim became a victimizer, but some did. It seemed to her now that Bill was one of them.

"I'll call you when the progression is done," Hannah said.

"You don't have to," Claire said. "I know it's her."

37

Yates scanned the pictures into his computer and sat down with a sigh. With a few keystrokes, five-year-old Janie and her parents appeared on the computer screen.

"This doesn't happen instantaneously," Yates said. An attempt to discourage kibitzing, Hannah supposed.

"Just show Hannah how you do this," Churnin said. "Then we'll leave you alone."

Yates nodded. "Okay. The CompuAge software lets me simulate the changes in the child's face as she ages. All the growth takes place below the eyes, by the way. So let's grow this little one up some. Watch."

They waited as the computer digested Yates's mouse-clicked commands. Janie's face disappeared. When it reemerged, her face had subtly changed. It was less soft. There was more definition in the cheekbones and chin. But she looked odd, as though she'd been stretched in a fun house mirror.

"Don't worry," Yates said. "I'm just getting started. Now, the program has a filter in it that allows me to merge features from the mother or father with the child's face. It's a little bit science and a little art."

"Show her that part, Sean," Churnin said.

"Right. Here's dad at twelve, right?" He called up Meister's image. "And here's your little girl, at—what is it, six?"

"Five," Hannah said, staring at father and daughter side by side.

"Okay." You can see that there's a similarity in the shape of their mouths, more so than with mom. I'm going to assume that as this little one grew up, her mouth changed as dad's did, and that at eleven, she looks more like dad at that age. Let's say it's . . . seventy-five percent similar, okay?"

With a few mouse clicks, the image began to rearrange itself. A ghost of the eleven-year-old skateboarding girl's features settled onto the stretched template of Janie's face. Hannah felt her pulse race. She had assumed that Janie would look like her mother, but she had been wrong. Except for the eyes, she looked like Bill.

"How long does it take to do the whole thing?" Hannah said.

"Best case scenario? Eight hours or so. I'll try to work fast on both of these. Give me till tomorrow morning."

"Nine o'clock, straight up?" Churnin said.

Yates nodded. "Now go away and let me get this right."

In the morning, Hannah held the fresh color laser print and felt the hairs rise on her neck. It was like looking at Janie through a strange prism. Her street-grown wariness had been filtered out. It seemed that Yates and his software had rewritten her life, restoring the comforts and reassurances of a normal childhood. It showed in her eyes and her smile, in those places where it was absent in the real Janie. If only this Janie, living in a software-tweaked cyberworld where she went to school and Girl Scouts, ballet classes and soccer practice, could step out of the picture and take the place of the feral child Hannah knew. If only.

Yates shifted in his chair. "Well? How'd I do?"

Hannah held the picture a moment longer. She had to see only with her eyes now, not her heart.

Churnin cleared his throat. "Hannah, is that the girl who's back from the dead?"

She handed the picture to him. Please, God, let me be right. "She isn't quite this healthy or happy. But it's Janie."

"How about this one?" Yates handed her the age progression of Roche's secret victim. "It's the best I could do with what I had."

Hannah looked, and the realization hit her like a blow to the chest. Yates couldn't have known the boy was blond now, so the hair was still light brown. Apart from that, he had captured the teenager Hannah had seen plucking a cigarette from Janie's mouth one morning near the Plaza. That's how Janie survived on the streets. Roche's boy had grown up to be her guardian angel.

The age-progressed picture captured his strong jaw, but because it focused only on the face, it missed the breadth of his shoulders and the strength that they implied. Hannah knew she was looking at the person whose blow had split her cheek. Guardian angel? Maybe a fallen one.

"Do you know him?" Churnin asked.

"Not by name," Hannah said. "But I saw him once, at the Plaza." She waited to see if Churnin would make the next leap.

"Are these kids together?"

"I think they are."

"Do they have something to do with the killings?"

Something? Everything. The boy had settled his score with Roche. He had probably killed Eddy because he viewed him as a threat to Janie. His connection to Henry Charles was still murky, but from what Laurel James had told Hannah, he could have been Charles's victim, too. After prison, Charles had widened his choice of prey.

But there was something missing: an explanation for Cotter Davis's death. Hannah decided that Seward lied when he said he hadn't molested the boy. He must have—that's why the boy was stalking him six years later. But why had the boy mistaken Cotter Davis for Seward? He must have had Seward's image seared in his brain, if he was his victim.

And what was Janie's role in these deaths? Was she the audience? The jury? The cheerleader, urging the boy to right all the wrongs for kids like themselves? She wanted to think that Janie didn't know what the boy was doing. But Seward's stalking story made it difficult, as did her own experience. She and Seward had both heard Janie laughing at their pain and fear. But telling Churnin any of this would instantly make Janie a suspect.

Churnin leaned toward her. "Talk to me, Hannah. What's going on?"

"The boy may be involved. I don't know about Janie. She's just eleven, Ivan."

"Do you know where they are?"

She could only guess. There were deserted buildings all along the path of the freeway expansion, but they succumbed to the wrecking crews daily. There were motels, but where would

two kids get the money? She knew an answer for that—
prostitution. She suddenly felt sick.

Churnin took her silence for guile. "Hannah, don't hold out
on me. If you know something, tell me."

"I have no idea where they are, Ivan."

"Have you joined the vigilante team over this girl?"

"No."

"I'm going to distribute this picture to the next watch. Does
this boy have a car?"

"Try a gray Volkswagen," Hannah said.

Churnin sighed. "You could have volunteered that, you
know."

"It's speculation, Ivan. I saw Janie get into one when I was
following her. I don't know that it's his car."

Churnin ran his hand over his shiny head. "No bullshit,
Hannah. You call me if you hear something, or you 'remember'
anything else."

"I will." She meant it . . . at that moment, anyway.

She found a message from a perplexed-sounding Lisette
Blackburn at home. She didn't know what lies Marian was
talking about. Hannah was unconvinced. She went to talk to her
in person and finally found her at home.

"I'm sorry I didn't call sooner," Lisette said, opening the
door to her. "My uncle died up in Fresno. I just got back."

Her living room apartment was decorated with reproductions
of Spanish religious paintings and eight-by-ten pictures of
Freddy Roche—in a prison visitor's area, in Caesar's shop, in
his last little house, trying to look happy. There were no
romantic engagement photographs, Hannah noticed.

Hannah showed her the age-progressed picture of Roche's
undiscovered victim. "Do you know him?"

She stared at it for a long time, as though it was a puzzle with
pieces missing.

"Lisette?"

She shook her head. "It's strange. I think I do. But I'm not
sure."

Hannah took out one of the original pictures, taken of the
boy at the age of ten. "How about now?"

"Oh, yes. You should have shown me this first. He was a boy
Freddy liked."

"The way he liked David Alvarez?"

Lisette sighed. "I don't want to talk about all that. Freddy was sorry. Dredging it all up now doesn't do any good. It doesn't change anything."

"That's right," Hannah said. "This boy still has to live with what Freddy did to him, assuming he's still alive. David Alvarez isn't."

Lisette glared at her. "Don't you think I know that?"

"Do you know his name?"

She shook her head. "Freddy just said he was very sorry about how he'd treated him. He recognized that he'd hurt him. He won his forgiveness."

"How do you know that?"

"Freddy said so."

"Do you know where he lives? Anything about his family?"

"No. I only know that he forgave Freddy. That's what I told Marian—that one of Freddy's victims had forgiven him."

Hannah nodded. That's what had upset Marian. She would never acknowledge that her son had any victims. "How did Freddy contact him? Letters of some kind?" She was thinking of Freddy's sympathy card to Anita Alvarez.

"Oh, no," Lisette said. "The boy came to see him."

"When?"

She frowned, as if trying to recall the date. "Well, it was a couple days after Freddy moved into his new house. I made a cake for them. I was going to stay, because Freddy wanted me to be there. But then he decided they should talk alone. That's why I didn't recognize the boy from this other picture, I guess. I didn't actually see him."

"Go on."

"Freddy called me when he'd gone. He said he'd made a clean slate of it. And when the boy saw how he had changed, he forgave him. For everything."

Hannah felt a frisson at the words. "What did 'everything' entail?"

"The touching. And the other . . . physical things. What happened with the pills, that one time."

Hannah knew she should be past any shock or revulsion at Roche and his tactics. But she had imagined seduction, not sedation. "Roche drugged him?"

"Once." Lisette frowned and fiddled with her ring. "Freddy's life was out of control then. He was in debt to someone."

"You mean, a money debt?"

"I assume that was it. He wouldn't talk about it. But this man—this sick, sick man—had Freddy take pictures."

"As he sexually assaulted this boy?"

Lisette nodded. "Freddy was horrified. He didn't know what the man had in mind. But he felt trapped. The man would have snitched him off, he said. It was around the time Freddy was arrested for what happened with David. If the police found out there was another boy, his prison time would have skyrocketed."

The man was Seward. Hannah knew it. He wanted the pictures to rekindle his memories of the rape. The photographs of the act itself were probably long gone. Perhaps they were what Seward had burned before the police had shown up. It also explained how the boy had mistakenly shot Cotter Davis. He'd never seen Seward. He had been drugged, unconscious throughout the attack. But when he awoke, he must have known something horrible had happened to him. Hannah imagined Roche's reaction: he probably considered him tainted after that, like a piece of spoiled meat. He cast the boy off.

Lisette waited for Hannah's next question, seemingly oblivious to the picture she'd just painted. "Didn't you tell the police this?"

Lisette shook her head. "There was no reason to. Freddy said the boy was angry at first, and that's understandable. But then he saw how sorry Freddy was. How he'd changed. They cried. There was forgiveness. And when the boy left, he was radiant, Freddy said."

Of course he was, Hannah thought. He'd seen his prey up close, heard him confess a horrible crime, as yet unpunished, and understood how vulnerable he was. How could Lisette miss the connection between the visit and Roche's death, just three or so days later? Could anyone be so naive, so out of touch with people and their reactions? And then she understood. No one could be, not even Lisette.

"When did Freddy ask you to marry him?"

Lisette's glance skimmed the Freddy-bedecked room. She looked down at the garnet and pearl ring on her finger, then covered it from Hannah's sight.

"Well, it was a while ago. I don't remember the date."

"Where were you? What did Freddy say, exactly? Was he down on bended knee?"

Lisette's face colored. She wouldn't look at Hannah. "Stop it."

"You brought it up, didn't you?"

Lisette looked up at her. "Yes." It was barely a whisper.

"You told him you loved him. You said you wanted to be with him forever, isn't that right?"

She nodded, eyes still trained on the hands that hid her ring.

"I imagine he said he couldn't do that," Hannah said. "He told you it wouldn't be fair to you. He didn't love you in that way."

"Why are you trying to hurt me?" Lisette's voice was remote, a little delayed in its transmission from her private fantasy world, which Hannah had begun to destroy.

"Lisette, I just want to understand why you didn't tell the police about this boy. Even if you didn't know his name, a description could have been—"

"His name is Jared West," she said.

"So you did know," Hannah said.

Lisette looked up, anger flaring in her eyes. "Freddy deserved what he got. He hadn't changed at all. I could see how he looked when he talked about Jared. But he let me think . . ." A stifled sob kept her from finishing.

Hannah understood. Lisette thought Freddy was using her, and maybe he was. But in the end, he told her the truth. He couldn't marry someone he didn't love. Lisette would never be what he wanted. Although Hannah didn't want to give him credit for it, there was a kind of nobility to that.

Hannah reached for Lisette's hand. "You have to tell the police about Jared, no matter how angry you are at Freddy."

She shook her head. "I can't. They'll want to know why I didn't tell before."

"I know a detective there who won't care about that."

Lisette dabbed at her eyes. "I need to be alone and think about it. Just until tomorrow. Would that be okay?"

"Not longer than that."

"All right." She uncovered the ring. "He did give this to me, you know."

Hannah nodded. "It's beautiful."

She smiled crookedly. "When I saw the box, I really thought . . . Then he said it was a thank-you gift. For helping him find the house."

It must have been an awful moment, Hannah thought. She imagined Freddy, blundering into yet another misunderstood gesture, seeing the look on Lisette's face, and knowing how he'd hurt her. He must have known it was something he couldn't make right.

Lisette slipped the ring off her finger and held it out to Hannah. "Take this."

Hannah shook her head. "Lisette, I don't think . . ."

"I can't wear it anymore," she said. She dropped it into Hannah's lap and left the room. Down the hall, a door softly closed.

At home, Hannah turned the ring over in her hand. She had paged Churnin twenty minutes ago, determined to keep her word to him. Now they had a description, a name, and a motive. Jared had had every reason to kill Roche. Freddy might have shared him not only with Seward, but with Charles, too.

She suspected that Seward had known all along who was behind the attacks. He'd undoubtedly known Jared by name. He might even know where he lived, then and now. But to tell the police any of that meant admitting a crime—the rape of a child—that would put him in prison for a long time. He was gambling, hoping that Jared would be caught in a way that didn't implicate him. That was probably where Hannah came into play.

The phone rang. Hannah grabbed for it, hoping it was Churnin. But it was Laurel James who stammered a hello.

"Can you meet me? I have to show you something." She read Hannah an address and hung up.

The U-Lock Self Store was a sprawling tribute to America's inability to throw anything away. When closets, garages, attics, and basements couldn't hold the detritus anymore, did people throw things away, or engage in the retail recycling know as the garage sale? They did neither, Hannah thought. Instead, they rented storage rooms and filled those, too.

Laurel James met her at the office and led her to a room-sized locker. She fumbled with the key. "I don't come here often. I keep most of my new costumes at home. So I wouldn't even have found it if I hadn't needed to find a garter, and I . . . there." The lock clicked.

She pushed the door open and ushered Hannah inside. The room was hot and airless in the July night. A rolling coatrack stood in one corner, bristling with velvet and brocade dresses and skirts. Boxes lined another wall. The lid was half off one that was marked STOCKINGS, PARTLETS, CHEMISES.

"What did you find?" Hannah said. There was nothing obviously out of place.

"Hank and I had this storage room for years. The police searched it after he was arrested and took anything suspicious then. I didn't even think he had a key anymore. But he must have made a copy. This was in the accessories box."

She handed Hannah a black leather photo album, secured by a strap and brass lock. Hannah remembered what Laurel had said about her husband: when she knew him, he never bothered with pictures. Then her friend had seen him later with camera gear and two children.

"I couldn't find a key," Laurel said. "He must have had it with him when . . ."

Hannah nodded. She slit the leather tongue with her penknife and opened the album. Dozens of pictures filled the pages, neatly arranged with four to each side. All of them were girls, ranging in age from about four to seven. Hannah flipped through the album, steeling herself for the moment when she would come to the horror show. But there didn't seem to be any of those shots. It was just like Roche's trophy pictures: if someone didn't know Charles's deviance, these would seem innocent enough. There were girls eating ice cream, playing on the beach, smiling from the backs of swaybacked, earnest ponies. Some posed solemnly before a backdrop of shag carpet—the inside of Charles's van, Hannah guessed. In all of the shots, the girls wore white undershirts with thin straps—Hank's particular fetish, apparently. It meant he'd undressed them. She imagined Hank Charles touching the girls as he took off their clothes, then touching their pictures later, reliving his violations of them, over and over. She turned the page, sickened.

Janie Meister stared sadly at her. There were four images of Janie wearing that thin, white undershirt. In this close-up, she could almost see the pale skin beneath the cloth. Her eyes were puffy from tears. She couldn't imagine it. How had Charles gotten hold of Janie? Meister, of course, but she couldn't imagine why he had shared his daughter. It wasn't like him. He guarded her jealously. She felt a wave of sickness and closed the book.

Laurel watched her expression anxiously. "These were the new victims, weren't they? More victims, after he got out of prison."

Hannah nodded. "I know one of them."

"Oh, God," Laurel said. "I'm so sorry."

"I need to keep this," Hannah said.

Laurel nodded. "Please. Take it."

Jared might have murdered Roche and intended to kill Seward, Hannah thought, but he wasn't the link to Henry Charles. Janie was. She must have recognized him and his van as soon as she'd seen them. She knew them as a prisoner knows her cell. Hannah couldn't let herself imagine Janie gloating over Charles's death. It wasn't possible for the child she knew six years ago to cock her arm, throw a bottle with a blazing wick, and then laugh about it. But Janie now? Hannah remembered the wild giggle. She imagined how it sounded to Henry Charles as fire seared his lungs and charred his skin.

Laurel was talking, but Hannah couldn't quite hear her. Hannah had believed that she could save Janie. But now she wondered what there was to save.

"Ms. Barlow? Are you all right?"

Hannah looked up. "It's hot in here. Let's go outside."

Laurel locked the storeroom behind them. "You knew Henry died?" Hannah nodded, still feeling sick. "Andie called me to tell me." Laurel sighed, sounding relieved. "There are three fewer monsters now."

Hannah heard the words and understood what she had not fathomed before. Together, a dead girl and an angelic boy were collecting on debts owed them. They tallied the damage done to their bodies and souls and kept the totals in their memories. But the debt was only three-quarters paid. A bill was still outstanding. She thanked Laurel for her help and ran to her car.

"You think this little girl killed Henry Charles?" Churnin stared at Hannah, trying not to show his disbelief. He had answered his page immediately this time and met Hannah at her house. As they stood on the porch in the hot night, Hannah showed him Charles's photo album. She imagined Janie watching, hearing everything. It felt like a betrayal to talk to Churnin about her, but Hannah knew she had no choice.

"He hurt her, Ivan. Just like Roche and Seward hurt Jared West. These two kids killed three of the people who violated them. But there's still Meister. Jared and Janie made sure he got away from me the other day. He might think he's hunting Janie, but it's really the other way around. They didn't want him arrested, because he's theirs. He's *it*."

38

Five days after Hannah told Churnin about Jared and Janie, she sat restlessly in the waiting room of the men's jail. She checked her watch: it had been forty minutes since she asked to see Seward. She was determined to get him to tell her everything he knew about Jared West. If she could find him, she would find Janie, too. Seward seemed to be the last chance. Claire had heard nothing from Janie. Hannah and Churnin talked daily, but neither could come up with a lead on her, or Jared. The streets seemed to have swallowed them.

"Hannah Barlow?" A deputy at the desk scanned the room and motioned Hannah to the desk when she stood up. "You can't see your guy today. He's not here."

Hannah tried to imagine where he'd be. Not in court, not on a Saturday.

"Is he sick?"

The deputy smiled, thinking he was tweaking a pathetic woman in love with a pervert. "What do you think?"

"I mean, why isn't he coming down? What's wrong?"

"From his standpoint, nothing. He bailed out on . . . let's see . . . Thursday."

"That's not possible. He was in on a homicide charge. Isn't that half a million bail?"

"That's it." He scrolled through a page of electronic records. "But it looks like he got a hearing, had bail knocked down to two hundred and fifty thousand. And somebody posted a property bond for it, plus the bondsman's ten-percent premium. Twenty-five grand. He's got some generous friends."

Another deputy overheard them. "You talking about Seward? Only inmate I ever knew who wasn't happy to get out."

And Hannah knew why. "But you bailed him anyway?"

The deputies exchanged a glance and a shrug. "Look," the first deputy said, "this isn't the Ritz-Carlton. If bail is posted, out he goes."

Hannah mulled it over on the way to the car. She knew that a bail bondsman wouldn't tell her who had put up property to spring Seward from jail. But she didn't have to ask. As far as Hannah knew, Mike Seward only had one contact with that kind of money.

She rang the bell at Marian Roche's now-encumbered Spanish castle, waited for a minute, and rang again. Baby growled and gnashed in the backyard. No one came to the door. Hannah went back to her car and waited, hoping to see a curtain twitch. Nothing. If Marian was home, she wasn't seeing visitors. Hannah couldn't fathom why she would help Seward. It didn't make sense.

It was a short drive from Marian's jasmine-scented neighborhood to the less pleasantly perfumed area that Seward called home. He lived in a neighborhood nicknamed Autotown, where garages and body shops dominated several commercial blocks. Hannah had patrolled there, years before. That was during Las Almas's hard times. Fistfights, petty thievery, and gunplay were weekly occurrences in Autotown. Just a few businesses managed to limp along, probably doubling as chop shops after midnight. Now some of the garages had reopened. The nearby residential streets had fewer seedy brown-bag drinkers on the corners and more kids playing on the sidewalk. She saw a woman planting geraniums that were brilliant pink. Some of the driveways she saw were slick and grimy, but at least that meant people could afford cars and the oil changes that kept them running.

Seward's house, maintained in a state of benign neglect, sat on a raised lot with a low concrete retaining wall at sidewalk level. She climbed the stairs, knocked, and started counting. By twenty, no one had answered. There wasn't really much likelihood that Seward had come home, not if he was trying to avoid Jared. If Marian had paid his bail, she also might have helped him get a room somewhere. Hannah left the porch, trying to decide who else would help her find him. There was little hope on the weekend of locating the public defender who'd drawn Seward as a client. Marian was her only chance.

She walked down the lawn, stopping to peer over the gate that crossed Seward's steep, filthy driveway. He didn't confine himself to oil changes. From the look of it, every conceivable car fluid had been drained onto this concrete pad.

Hannah started down the driveway but stopped midway. Perhaps she was leaving too soon. If he'd stopped at home for clothes, maybe a neighbor had seen him or talked to him. She stared at the driveway, considering whether a round of door-knocking would be worthwhile. A trickle of dark fluid oozed its way down to the gutter. Hannah dipped her finger into it. She smelled it. This hadn't leaked out of a car. It was blood.

39

In Marian's dream, Freddy was having a new house built for her. It overlooked the ocean, and there, they could be left alone. Although it was late afternoon, the carpenters were still hammering away, making so much noise that she had to yell down for them to stop.

Marian awoke with a start. The pounding emanated not from her dream, but from her front door, and it started again as she lay there on the living room sofa, feeling drowsy and sticky with sweat. She considered whether she should answer this time. Then she heard the voice: "I know you're there, Marian."

That obstinate, mulish Barlow woman. Marian was sorry she'd ever gone to her.

"If you don't let me in, I'll go to the police," Barlow shouted. "Right now."

Her heart fluttered at that. But she stilled the impulse toward panic. No one had the right to talk to her that way. Certainly not a lawyer in her employ. She ran her fingers through her hair and stood up. The floor reeled, and she had to steady herself. Only one glass of wine at lunch tomorrow. The hammering started again.

"Just a moment, for God's sake!" Who did Hannah Barlow think she was? She lifted her chin and opened the door, ready to deliver a lecture. Maybe she would just dismiss her, which she should have done before.

Barlow was dressed properly this time, not in jeans and a T-shirt, but in a navy pantsuit and cream blouse. Her eyes were narrowed in a fierce expression that unnerved Marian for a moment. She feigned bravery. "I can't countenance this behavior of yours," Marian said. "You're fired."

Barlow smiled icily. "That's fine, Marian. You're going to need a lawyer, and I'm delighted to hear that it won't be me."

She felt her stomach dip at the threat, but told herself that's all it was. She ventured a laugh. "Why on earth would I need a lawyer?"

"Because you bailed Mike Seward out of jail."

Marian was dumbstruck. How had she found out?

"Come on, Marian, it was easy," Barlow said. "Mike Seward didn't know anyone else well-heeled enough to make bail for him. But now you have a serious problem."

Marian glanced across the street and saw the Morgans' nanny playing in the front yard with the twins. She was covertly watching Marian and her guest.

"You'd better come inside," Marian said. She felt woozy from the wine and Barlow's onslaught.

The lawyer was watching her. Marian felt naked, as though Barlow knew everything about her. She might even know about the fencing she'd done for Freddy and Seward. She knew, from the day Barlow found the breadbox, that she'd been wrong to think she could control her.

"Admit it, Marian. You put up bail for Mike Seward," Barlow said.

Marian nodded. "Yes."

"Why?"

She shrugged. "A friend came and—"

"Whose friend?"

She hesitated. It was all so confusing, suddenly. It had sounded right and reasonable at the time, when the visitor sat in Marian's living room, took her hand, and told her the words she wanted to hear, above all other words: Freddy was innocent.

"Marian, this is more serious than you can imagine. Who did you talk to?"

She disliked being lectured to by someone young enough to be her granddaughter. She drew herself up to show displeasure. "It's not a crime to bail someone out of jail."

Barlow nodded, as though Marian had said something eminently sensible. "You're right. Bailing out someone isn't a crime. But murder is."

She felt her knees weaken. "What?"

"Mike Seward is dead. I found him in his garage. His throat was cut."

Marian stared straight ahead. She heard a strange buzzing in her ears, as though they were being invaded by needling insects. "I don't believe it."

Barlow shrugged. "I don't care what you believe. It's what happened. It will take the police a while to get a court order to compel the bondsman to tell them who got Seward out. If you don't talk honestly to me, I'll give you up right now."

Marian put her hands to her mouth. "You're horrible."

"I don't have time to be genteel, Marian. Tell me why you bailed Seward out."

"What about the police?"

"Am I still your lawyer?"

Marian understood—attorney-client privilege prevailed, as long as Barlow was working for her. "Very well. You still are."

"Then tell me how you got involved in this."

"My visitor said that if Seward was out of jail, it could be proved that Freddy was innocent of the crime for which he went to prison."

"Who is this visitor?"

"I can't say."

Barlow came out of the chair and grabbed Marian's arms just below the shoulders. She could almost feel her skin bruising. She winced and gasped. "You're hurting me!"

"Don't play games. No one else is." Barlow relaxed her grip. "Tell me who it was."

Marian felt terrified and helpless, but it wasn't only because of Barlow's rough handling. She was beginning to realize what she'd done. She was trembling, but she knew she couldn't give in. "No."

"You're only postponing the inevitable, Marian. The police will question you."

"It couldn't be worse than this. They won't assault me."

"That's true. But you'll be in a very small room, not this nice big house. They won't touch you. They'll pound your mind instead. They will tell you things about your son, show you pictures, that will turn your stomach. I've spared you that."

Marian felt her throat closing down. She couldn't speak. She barely could breathe. Barlow knelt next to her, her voice softer now. "Why are you protecting someone who's using you, Marian? Whoever it is, they don't care about you. They don't care if you're indicted and tried and sent to prison, all by yourself."

Prison. Marian had seen the place they'd kept Freddy, the thing that wanted to look like a college campus but which had a fence topped with razor wire and guard towers outfitted with rifles. She knew what Freddy had gone through—all the indignities and the cruelties. She realized that they didn't let prisoners dye their hair. No makeup. No jewelry. No wine or Drambuie there. Just Pruno, that horrid moonshine crap Freddy and Seward joked about making.

"It was Anita." Her voice quavered. Its weakness sickened her.

"Anita Alvarez?"

Marian nodded.

"You know her?"

"Yes." She felt as though she might be sick.

"From church," Barlow said, almost as if to herself. "You and Freddy went to the same church as the Alvarezes."

She nodded. The nausea was passing. "I quit going, because of her. She was awful to me, after Freddy went to prison. She berated me in front of my friends after services one day. But then she showed up here a week ago and told me she had been wrong."

"Wrong about what?"

"About Freddy. He hadn't molested her son, she said. Her son had lied."

Barlow was silent for a moment. "That's not possible."

Marian nodded fiercely. "It's the truth. She said that before her son killed himself, he told her that he lied to protect another man. He's the one who molested him, not Freddy."

"And this man was Mike Seward?"

At last, Marian thought, she understands. "Yes."

"If that's so, why would you want him out of jail?"

Marian sighed. It was complex, but she would try to explain. "There was no way to prove it, don't you see? David was dead. Anita's testimony wouldn't be enough. Seward would deny it."

"So?"

"So, he would have to be persuaded."

"Seward would be persuaded to confess?"

It sounded foolish now, the way Barlow said it. Marian nodded. "Anita said so."

"Who was going to elicit this confession?"

Marian lowered her head. Above all, this was what she wasn't to talk about. Anita made her swear she wouldn't. It was an easy promise to make. Marian didn't know who it was.

"Marian? Who was going to get Seward to talk?"

She shook her head. "Someone . . . forceful."

"Forceful?" Barlow sighed. "And you didn't guess what would happen?"

Marian felt affronted. "Of course I didn't think someone would kill him. That would have defeated the purpose. You're quite stupid if you can't see that."

"Maybe I am," Hannah said. "But the police are who you have to convince. I don't think they'll buy that story."

Marian felt her face burning with anger. "I don't care. It's the truth. I don't know who was going to make him talk."

"But once he was done with Seward, Seward would turn himself in?"

Marian nodded. "Freddy's name would be cleared."

"Oh," Barlow said. "I understand it now."

"I should hope . . ." Marian stopped. Was Barlow mocking her? "Understand what?"

"Why you were so determined to burn the underwear and pictures I found. You thought they would muddy up Seward's confession. No matter what Seward said, there were your son's trophies."

"No!" She knew she sounded querulous and silly. She so wanted to believe in Freddy's innocence. There was nothing else in her life now. "Seward planted them here. He was the one who told you about them, wasn't he?"

"Yes, because Freddy told him where he'd hidden them. You're kidding yourself, Marian. Anita didn't dupe you into getting Seward out so he could confess."

"Are you saying she cut his throat? It's not possible. She's a slip of a woman."

Barlow got to her feet and picked up her purse. "She didn't have to do it herself. She had help."

Marian shook her head. "I don't understand."

"You will." Barlow scribbled a name and phone number on one of her cards and handed it to her. "I suggest that you pay a call on Detective Churnin at the Las Almas P.D., Marian. Before he comes looking for you."

40

Hannah stood on the porch of Anita Alvarez's house, her finger pressed to the doorbell. A light burned in the front window. Accumulated bills and letters spilled from the mailbox. All of it told her that Anita Alvarez was gone, along with the children she had been hiding. Hannah knew why they were together, but wondered how the union had been made.

She was about to knock again, as futile as that was, when she saw the woman next door watering her lawn. Although the evening was cool, the woman wore only an old, sagging tube top and baggy denim shorts. The spray from her hose was aimed straight ahead, but her head was turned to monitor Hannah.

Hannah raised a hand in greeting. "Anita's gone?"

"You a friend?"

Hannah shrugged. Best not to define the relationship so soon. Wait and see how the neighbor reacted.

"Three days now," the woman said. "I thought about picking up her mail, but finally said to myself, 'Fuck it, Cissy. She doesn't tell you where she's going? Just bolts like that, expecting you to pick up after her? Who needs it?'"

Hannah nodded. She was going to take advantage of whatever Anita had done to antagonize her neighbor. "So you don't think she's on vacation or something?"

Cissy shook her head. "I think she's long gone. You go around back, you'll see the mess she left. Gate's not locked."

Hannah thanked her and walked into the backyard. The drapes were open and the working-woman's disarray she'd seen in the living room three weeks earlier had grown into a mountain of debris. Anita had swept through her own house like a tornado.

"Fuckin' mess, huh?" Cissy was standing behind her, arms folded, shaking her head in disgust.

"Were there a couple of kids staying here?"

"Oh, trouble times two," Cissy said. "Coming and going at all hours. Anita didn't seem to care." Cissy ran her eyes down Hannah's navy suit. "You trying to find those kids?"

Hannah nodded, trying her best to look like the social worker, or whatever official the neighbor wanted her to be.

"Anita hasn't been the same since David died," Cissy said. "My husband loaned him the ladder, you know? How were we supposed to know he wanted to kill himself? His own mother didn't know." She shook her head.

"It was a terrible loss."

"Yes ma'am. But Anita, she went crazy."

Hannah knew she was right. There was no other explanation for what had turned her into an accessory to murder.

"You need to go in there, go ahead." Cissy gestured to the sliding door. "Track's all funky and there's no alarm or nothing."

"Thanks." Hannah hoped that none of her neighbors would offer breaking and entering tips to someone lurking around her house. Cissy was right about the door. After a few minutes of rocking and tilting, she had it off the track. She could hear the splash of Cissy's hose on the walkway out front. She was watching Hannah's back.

Inside, Hannah sorted through the disorder. Anita had flung clothes everywhere in her hurry to decide what to take and what to leave behind. In Anita's room, dresser drawers had been turned out. In the smaller of the rooms, a suitcase with a broken lock lay on the bed, along with more discarded clothes. Some of the jeans and sweatshirts were years old. They were too small for Jared. David's old clothes, Hannah decided.

On the chair were things she recognized. A Rasta beret, baggy jeans, and a blue-and-brown-striped T-shirt. She pressed the shirt to her nose. Chanel No. 5. Now it was Janie's scent.

Her skateboard was under the bed, along with her Raiders jacket. Hannah dug through the pockets. Bert was gone, but

Janie had left one of her notes behind. What this time, Hannah wondered. What came after thanks and sorrow?

She hadn't written Dad or Daddy. Just BILL, followed by an address on Main, a street that existed in virtually every one of Orange County's two dozen cities and towns.

41

Bill Meister felt the Courvoisier envelop him, as though it was a deep, warm bed into which he could sink and sleep for hours. He rolled the drink on his tongue and savored its sweet sting. He held the glass up to the light, bathed in its amber glow, and ran his tongue over his lips. For the first time in ages, he felt the situation warranted the utterance of his pet phrase.

"To the good life," he whispered. The television was on, tuned to MTV, with the sound muted. He'd wolfed down a room-service dinner of steak and stuffed baked potato. And now all he had to do was get a good night's sleep before his outing to Disneyland with a special little girl. Her mother had wavered, until he sprang for the works at her favorite day spa. She'd loved the idea, as Bill knew she would. Things were building slowly, slowly. A few more hours alone with the girl, and he could have her. Bill shivered with anticipation. He sang his motto this time, in his Andy Williams voice.

It had been the bad life for a long time, and the cast on his left arm marked the lowest point. The pain had been indescribable, searing. He had never felt anything so excruciating in his life. How dare someone violate him that way—over money, of all things.

He stopped to remember how long he had been on the plunge that culminated in his injury. Three years, though it seemed longer. It began with his arrest in a boiler-room bust outside Tucson. Then, the next domino: the loss of Janie. As they were carting him off to jail, he knew he'd have to stash her somewhere. He couldn't risk the police finding her alone at the house he'd rented. Left alone with cops, she'd babble everything.

So his single phone call from jail went to Ronnie Djokovich and his clan. He knew they were fifth-generation cheats, but he had no choice but to trust them this time.

"Get my daughter and keep her till I get out," he told Ronnie, who owed him. Big time.

"Cool, man," Ronnie said, stuck in the seventies as usual.

Meister did an easy year in jail, affably answering to one of his several aliases. When he got out, Janie was gone. She'd just run away, the Djokoviches told him with a shrug, as though she were a stray mutt who'd slipped the leash. He was sure that was a lie—Ronnie's wife, Emilia, had the look of complicity about her. But she wouldn't fess up to hiding Janie somewhere.

Ronnie took him aside for a chat as Meister started browbeating Emilia: "Look, man, the kid's already nine, you know? In a couple years, she won't pop your cork anymore. So what's the big deal? Plenty girls around."

Meister had resisted the urge to punch him. Janie's age wasn't the point. She had been his, his alone, for three years. Then he'd gone a year without her. He damn well wanted her back.

Finding her was no easy thing. He thought about using the police. He'd drummed the name Mae Wallace into her head and insisted she carry around her fake Social Security card. He had a set of documents that showed him to be her father, Bill M. Wallace. But he was leery of sitting down with some detective to report little Mae missing. What if there was some warrant or other floating around out there? What if Claire got her head out of the bottle and told the police about him and his tale of Janie's death? It was unlikely, because he made it his business to check up on Claire from time to time and put the fear of God into her. But anything was possible. He decided then he would have to find Janie on his own. Now, two years later, he finally had a line on her. Meister congratulated himself on his persistence. Nobody cared about Janie like he did.

A few weeks ago, he'd finally found out from one of Ronnie's former pals that Emilia had sent Janie to live with her sister's family. And where did Emilia's sister live? Santa Ana, not five miles from Meister's old house in Las Almas. The sister dodged and lied when Meister confronted her. But then he threatened to drop a dime on Emilia and Ronnie's very lucrative lonely-widower scam. Since it trickled down and benefitted the sister's own family, she finally came across with the story.

"Janie told Emilia *everything*," the sister said, eyeing him as though he belonged under a bridge. It turned out that Janie arrived at her house just two weeks before Meister got out of jail. She stayed for maybe six months. Then she said she was leaving, going to look for her mother.

"You let her go?" Meister regarded this as gross negligence on the part of someone left in loco parentis. "She's eleven, for God's sake."

Emilia's sister shrugged. "And she's not my daughter. Thank the Virgin and all the saints." She let go a wad of saliva, nearly spattering Meister's white nubuck Allen-Edmond saddle shoes.

Meister figured a kid Janie's age couldn't go too far. He actually thought he'd seen her in Costa Mesa, on the afternoon he'd bought the Celica, but decided it was his imagination. She was probably in Southern California, probably even in Orange County. His plan was simple: wait for Janie to call Claire. She was a smart little girl. Eventually she'd track her mother down.

He tossed back the last of the cognac and reached for the bedside notepad. He'd had Claire's phone number for several weeks and had called it a couple of times, just to make sure it was her and that she hadn't skipped. It was her, all right—that scared-sheep voice. Drunk the first time, but not the second. Still stupid, he thought. Using her maiden name? An idiot would know better. He'd swung by her apartment a couple of times, but didn't see Janie. He planned on paying Claire a formal visit soon. And once he had Janie, he'd find a permanent solution for Claire. He should have done it a long time ago, in that Bandon motel room.

The knock on the door startled him out of his plans for her. Only the little girl and her mother knew where he was staying. He peered through the peephole, and what he saw made him feel faint. And then he was furious.

The convex glass distorted her so that she looked like a doll in a fishbowl. Pink barrettes decorated her hair. Her spangly pink dress had a tight bodice. The skirt was so short that the tips of her thumbs barely grazed the hem. She wore white patent-leather shoes and white socks dripping with crocheted trim. When she looked up at the peephole, he saw the thick globs of mascara clinging to her eyelashes. She smiled slightly, then let the tip of her tongue flick across her teeth. She was wearing pink lip gloss. He shook at the sight of her, tarted up like a Lolita whore.

Meister fumbled at the lock, threw open the door, and grabbed her. Her arm was small, and his hand still fit around it. But she was taller now, heavier. She dug her heels in and wouldn't budge.

Her smile trembled. She knew how much trouble she was in, the little bitch. "Hi, Daddy."

"Get inside." Now he could smell it—she was wearing perfume, something rich and womanly. It made his stomach heave. Ronnie was right. She was on the verge, even now. "Goddamn it, get inside." He stood behind her, shielding her from anyone who might be coming down the corridor, and shoved her into the room. She collapsed on one of the beds, a smirk on her face. She smoothed the dress over her long, shaved legs. Shaved. Christ, it was too much. She'd probably had her first period by now. He felt nauseated at the thought. He wasn't sure he felt anything, even with the little-girl illusions she'd put on to tempt him. The thought stopped him. Tempt him?

The door closed behind him. He turned and saw them, both holding guns. He stumbled backward, toward the window, eyes trained on the weapon closest to him. He watched it go up and come down in a blur, until it wasn't a thing but only a sound and a feeling, a thud that fell across his temple. The room dissolved in a gray surge with a sound like the surf. And atop that, skimming the edge of the wave, was another sound. Even in the pain, he smiled to hear it. Despite everything, Janie still had a little girl's laugh.

42

Hannah dialed Churnin's pager as she drove home. During the red lights, she ran her finger down the map book's index. She had ruled out several of the county's Main streets because they had too few or too many digits to match the address Janie left. But there were still a dozen towns left. And if this was a Main Street in Los Angeles County, she would never find them in time.

Then she remembered Claire's story and what she'd seen herself: Meister liked the anonymity of motels and hotels. She flipped to the hotels listed in the index, and there it was: Luxury Suites Hotel. On Main Street in Irvine. The address matched. She dialed the number. If Rudy Podesta was right, Meister would be registered under a name similar to his own. If he wasn't Mr. Masterson, the name he'd last used, it would be something close to it.

"Luxury Suites Irvine. How may I direct your call?"

"Could you ring Mr. Master's room?" She mumbled the name, hoping to force the operator to guess at what she'd said.

There was a pause. "Um, did you say Mr. Mastin? Will Mastin?"

"Yes. Thanks," Hannah said.

After twelve rings, the call bounced back to reception. Hannah hung up. Shit. Where was Churnin? As if in answer, the phone rang.

"What now?" Churnin growled.

•   •   •

The manager let them into Meister's room. The television was off, but its top was still warm. A room-service cart held the remains of a steak dinner. Neither bed had been slept in, although the spread of the one closest to the door was rumpled. There was no suitcase in the closet. A litter of toiletries, including a razor and a toothbrush, lay on the bathroom counter. It wasn't clear whether Meister had left against his will.

Churnin turned to the night manager, who clearly hoped that this would turn out to be nothing. "The car he listed on the registration card," Churnin said. "Is it here?"

"It's gone, sir. But the boys said they didn't bring it around for him. He must have taken the key from the valet's cupboard."

Churnin thanked him and told him not to clear the room.

"So the guest will be back?" the manager said hopefully.

"I wouldn't count on it," Churnin said. "How'd he pay for the room?"

"Credit card."

Churnin and Hannah exchanged glances.

The manager caught the meaning. "Great. I should have known we were being ripped off when he ordered a whole bottle of Courvoisier."

In the lobby, Hannah and Churnin sat down for a moment. "Either they found him, or he got spooked again and ran," Hannah said. "But I have no idea where he'd go, or where they would take him."

"We have an unmarked car at Anita Alvarez's house," Churnin said. "She hasn't been back. We've put out her license plate and description, and now we can do the same for Meister's car."

"It may be that Meister is trying to find Janie. He'll be surprised when he finds she's not alone."

"Of the two, he's the one I'd be worried about. Janie and her pal have quite a track record. Meister hasn't killed anyone."

"That we know of."

"Touché. Go home. I'll call if we find them."

"I feel helpless," Hannah said. "I shouldn't have let Janie get away."

"Not your fault," Churnin said. "She doesn't trust anyone."

"Except Jared."

Churnin nodded. "I got some Juvie Court stuff on him. He did some time in Orangewood and foster care. Ran away a bunch and got arrested a couple times."

"Serious charges?"

"Nothing violent—shoplifting, joyriding. The dependency files said Mom abandoned the family—Jared and his little sister and their dad—when Jared was eight. Then dad threw him out, a couple years later."

"He threw him out when he was ten? Was that how he wound up with Freddy?"

"Other way around, seems like," Churnin said. "But that wasn't clear at first. Children's Protective Services found Jared, wandering around half-starved, it sounds like. He claimed he ran away, but wouldn't give an address. When they finally ran one down, Dad was nowhere to be found."

"His father took off?"

"Yup, with the sister. Then, about a year later, she turned up at Orangewood. She said daddy dear threw Jared out because he didn't want a 'stinking fag' in the house."

"Jesus. He told his father about Freddy and Seward, and that's what his response was?"

"That was it. Jared, meanwhile, told the social workers he didn't know what his father was talking about. They had some exam results that indicated he might have been sodomized. He wouldn't discuss it. Denied anything happened."

Hannah shook her head. "Then what?"

"He started running away. Trying to find his sister, the files said. She got adopted after a year or so. But they didn't want a 'troubled' boy like Jared. Thought it would interfere with their bonding if he came around."

He and Hannah stared at each other for a moment. Churnin shook his head. "Some hand the kid got dealt."

She nodded. Every time she thought she'd heard the worst thing an adult could do to a child, someone came up with an even more hateful variant. Roche had driven David Alvarez to suicide. Jared and Janie turned their rage out, spewing it in bullets and fire. But she was afraid they were just as doomed as David was. How could children survive lives that adults worked so hard to ruin?

Churnin and Hannah walked to the parking lot. "By the way, Mrs. Roche called me," he said. "She's pretty freaked out about

Seward. Complained about you, too, counselor. Battery and verbal intimidation. Didn't want to file anything formally, though."

"Lucky me. Seward wasn't a humanitarian, but she helped them hunt him like a rabbit."

"Did she know that's what she was doing?"

Hannah shrugged. "She says not. I don't know whether to believe her."

"All for Freddy," he said. "Anything but admit her son was just as bad as Seward was." They were at his Volvo now. "You have a gun, right?"

She had hoped this wouldn't come up. "Jared got it when he knocked me out."

"When Janie set you up, you mean?"

She sighed. "I'm not sure that's what happened."

He shook his head. "This kid, she's really used you."

"No worse than people used her. It's what she knows. I could have done something, a long time ago, to stop that."

Churnin grabbed her hand. "Hey. Listen up. You weren't her mother. You weren't her guardian. You were just trying to do the best job you could. It wasn't your responsibility then. It isn't now. You can't think about her as a little girl anymore. If you do, she's going to be the end of you." He lifted his pant leg and pulled a pistol from an ankle holster.

Hannah stared at the gun. "No."

Churnin shook his head. "If it comes down to it, Hannah, you're going to need this."

"She's eleven, Ivan."

"So? That didn't matter with Henry Charles."

"I'm not him. She wouldn't hurt me."

"What about Jared? Eddy found out what Jared does to people he thinks are Janie's enemies. Does that change your thinking at all?"

She took the gun and went home.

She stared at the television, her solace for insomnia now that she lived alone again. She tried to let the images lull her, but it wasn't working.

It felt strange to worry more about killers—because that was what Janie and Jared seemed to be—than Meister, their potential victim. She knew they were trying to save themselves. But they'd chosen a bloody way to do it.

They swung the scythe indiscriminately. It caught molesters like Roche, Charles, and Seward, but it also cut down others, like Devlin Eddy and Cotter Davis. Jared and Janie didn't seem to realize that killing even a thousand molesters wouldn't end the breed. More would spring up from the bloody ground to take the place of the ones who died before them. And the ghosts of Roche, Meister, and Seward would always haunt them, no matter how much blood they spilled.

The phone rang. Hannah glanced at the VCR—it was just after two in the morning. She muted the television and picked up the receiver. But she heard only silence.

She swallowed hard. "Janie?"

More silence, followed by an infinitely small voice. "Help me."

"Where are you?" Hannah said.

"He's looking for me, and he's getting close. Please come and get me."

Hannah's throat tightened. She knew who *he* was. She remembered how confident she'd felt when she met Janie for the first time. She tried to bring that strength and reassurance into her voice now. "Tell me where you are. I'll come right away. Then I want you to call nine one one."

"No!" She shrieked the word. "No police, or social workers or foster homes or any of that crap. I just want you to help me." Then she added, bitterly. "You owe it to me."

Hannah knew what she should do: call 911. Call Churnin. But she was pierced by the sound of Janie's voice and the claim she so rightly stated. Debts had to be paid. "Where are you?"

"Home." She hung up.

Hannah stared at the images on the TV screen for a moment. She could only think of one still-standing residence that Janie might call home.

43

It was as she remembered it, but time destroyed the charming veneer the house once had. The clapboards were peeling and the shutters had fallen from the front windows. Drought killed the lawn. The tree was browning. Even the sale sign, which advertised the house as a bank-foreclosure bargain, was hanging aslant on its metal stake. Hannah looked up and down the street from her car, seeing no one. The house was dark. She checked to make sure her flashlight and phone were in her purse. She got out of the car.

Suddenly, Janie appeared on the lawn, dressed in an oversized white T-shirt and white jeans. The cuffs were rolled and the pants hung low on her narrow hips. She seemed to shimmer in the darkness. She backed away as Hannah approached.

"Are you all right?" Hannah said.

"Sure." Janie's hair fell in curling cascades, as though she had just come home from a dance. Like Hannah, she glanced up and down the street.

"Did someone follow you?" Hannah said.

She shook her head.

"Let's go, then. We can talk at my house."

"No." She turned and ran toward a gate that led to the home's backyard.

Hannah hesitated for a moment. Something was wrong. But she wasn't leaving without Janie. Not this time. She followed her.

As Hannah pushed open the gate, she saw a playhouse, a scaled-down replica of the Meisters' house. Janie leaned against it, staring up at the stars. "I couldn't tell you right away."

"That you were Janie?" Hannah said.

She nodded. "When Mom left, Bill told me I had to be Mae. He said bad people were chasing us, and Mom was on their side. Without new names, we'd be caught. They'd take him away, and I wouldn't have anyone. Big threat."

"I'm sure it was, back then."

"I was little. You remember."

"Look, Janie, we have to go. If your father—"

"In a minute. I just want to tell you something."

"It's cold. We'll be more comfortable at my house."

Janie ran a hand down the side of the playhouse. "This used to be my favorite place. He couldn't touch me here. Anybody in their house could look out and see what was going on in my house. So I'd sit out here for hours. Until it was dark and Mom made me come in."

Hannah sat down on one of the picnic benches nearby. Short of dragging Janie into the car, what could she do? She seemed to feel safe here—of all places. "What did you want to tell me, Janie?"

She smiled. "It's weird to be called that. No one does."

"Not even Jared?"

She lifted her eyebrows in surprise at hearing his name from Hannah. "He just started. He didn't think it was safe before."

"Why not?"

"It's complicated. Never mind."

"What does Anita call you?"

"Who?"

"You can drop that. I know about her."

She shrugged. "She made stew for me the other night. Real stew, not that canned Dinty Moore junk."

Hannah nodded. Anita had created a family for herself, equal parts nurturance and revenge. Have some stew. Help me kill the man who ruined my son.

"Tell me about Jared," Hannah said.

"What about him?"

"You met him in a foster home?"

She nodded. "Bill went to jail for a while. To make sure the cops didn't find me, he stuck me with his friend Ronnie. What a jerk." She saw Hannah's expression and laughed. "Nothing happened. Ronnie's just a crook, not a perv. But he was going to send me back to Bill as soon as he finished his year in county." She let out a sigh. "I couldn't handle that. So I told."

"And he believed you?"

"Maybe he believed me, but he didn't want to piss Bill off. Emilia was the one who helped me. That's Ronnie's wife. She sent me down here to her sister, the nutcase. Had some kind of weird statue that she thought talked to her and cried bloody tears. What a freak."

Hannah listened to the calm Janie tried to impose on the story. Everything was casual, manageable. She hated to imagine the reality of Janie's last six years. "What happened then?"

"I ran away. And the cops picked me up, and then it was Orangewood, and then I was in the foster home, which was kind of a dump. But Jared was there. Only for a little while, unfortunately."

"How did you wind up on the street?"

"The social workers sent me back to Emilia's sister. Didn't even really ask me if she was or wasn't my aunt, like she'd said. They didn't give a shit, really. Anyway, Emilia's sister, the statue freak, couldn't have cared less if I stayed around. So I told her I was going, and she's like, 'Fine, who cares? Filthy *puta*.'"

"She didn't do anything to help you?"

"Nah. Her kids were cool, though. They gave me some money and the phone numbers of some people I could crash with, out in Indio. But when I was getting ready to hitch out there, I saw Jared at the Plaza. He knew stuff. Places we could stay. He told me what a dive Indio was. He got me to do homework and junk. Made me give up pot, which was sort of a drag. But I understood what he was doing. Straighten up now, party later. You know?"

Hannah nodded. The most responsible person in Janie's life was a sixteen-year-old killer.

"What about your mom?"

Janie's brow furrowed. "What about her?"

"Have you tried to see her?"

She shrugged. "Not exactly. But I know where she is."

"You went out to Pomona, didn't you? In my car."

She nodded. "She was going into a bar at eight in the morning. So she's still fucked up, I guess."

"That's because Bill told her you were dead."

Janie frowned. "What?"

"That's why she didn't look for you. He told her he'd killed you."

Janie stared at Hannah for a moment. "Bastard."

"She didn't abandon you. That's what I'm getting at," Hannah said.

"No?" Janie laughed, a sound tinged with the sharpness Hannah had heard when she lay beaten on the ground. "Well, she didn't protect me, either. Now I know what she was supposed to do. They teach it in school: good touch, bad touch. You know the drill."

Maybe Janie was right. Claire wasn't perfect. But who else did she have? Jared and Anita were accomplices, not family, homework assignments and beef stew notwithstanding. For a moment, Hannah visualized herself caring for Janie. She tried to shake the notion away. It echoed of Matthew and the jury-rigged home she'd made for him. She lost him in the end. But would that have to happen with Janie? She felt the idea taking root, and she fought it by focusing on Claire. The girl's mother. The denial queen. The alcoholic.

"Your mom has a lot of problems," Hannah said. "But I think most of them began with Bill. If she could stop drinking, she might be all right."

"Yeah, like that's going to happen in this century." Janie fiddled with the ringleted ends of her hair. "Did you talk to her?"

"Yes."

"Did you tell her you'd seen me?"

"Yes, but not where. I was worried about what would happen if your father showed up."

"Did she . . ." Janie stopped. "No. Never mind."

Hannah knew what it was: a question she wasn't sure she wanted answered. "Did she want to see you?"

Janie nodded.

"More than anything," Hannah said. "How about you?"

"I don't know," she said. "It's been a long time."

"Let's go home, Janie. There's time to think about all that later."

She didn't refuse, but she didn't move, either. "I need to say I'm sorry about something."

"What?"

"That day, when we talked, and I ran? And Jared . . . you know."

"When Jared beat the shit out of me."

She nodded. "Sometimes, when I see someone get smacked around—an adult, like you—I can't help getting a little rush from it. In some weird way, it feels good to see that you're not the only one who gets hurt. I might feel guilty later, you know? But at that moment? I can't help how good it makes me feel."

Hannah tried to imagine the world Janie knew, and she realized she couldn't, not really. Hannah's own childhood was no fairy tale. There was her parents' unsettled marriage, her mother's mood swings, her father's drinking, and the devastation that had come after her mother's bloody death. But despite all that, no one violated her. She hadn't lived on the streets. She couldn't feel the jolt of relief that Janie felt, watching a beating. But she thought she could understand the reaction, at least intellectually. It was a variety of schadenfreude: joy at the misfortunes of others. Janie was willing to admit that she felt a rush seeing someone struck. But would she confess to rejoicing in a death, too?

"Janie, where is Jared now?"

"Don't know. We had to split up for a while."

"Why was that?"

"I'm not going to talk about it." She snapped the words and turned away from Hannah. There was only one anchor in Janie's life, and it was Jared. She wouldn't speak against him.

"Okay," Hannah said. "So he's gone, and you were alone. You got scared that Bill was close to finding you. Why did you think that?"

She turned back and nodded. "Sometimes I think about him, and it creeps me out."

"But you haven't seen him?"

She shook her head.

"Are you feeling okay now?"

"Sure," Janie said.

"Then let's go. It's cold out here."

Janie nodded, but again made no move to leave. "Those guys—you know, the ones who tried to hurt Jared?"

Hannah felt herself go still. Tried to hurt Jared? "You mean Roche and Seward?"

"They're dead, right?"

"Don't you know?"

"I guess I do. But I wasn't there. He wouldn't let me go."

"Yes, they're dead."

She nodded. "He wouldn't say much about it."

Hannah wanted to feel reassured, but knew that Janie could be lying. She decided to push a little. Sooner or later, she would have to find out how culpable Janie was. "Had he already started stalking them when you met him?"

Janie shook her head. "Thinking about it, maybe. But he wasn't doing anything. We had been hanging together about a week when we saw Henry Charles driving around. I thought I recognized the van, and then when I saw him, I knew for sure. It freaked me out, and Jared wanted me to tell him what happened."

"Charles molested you?"

"Bill let him." She shook her head. "I don't think he wanted to, but he did." She was silent for a moment, and Hannah was glad that she could not be in Janie's head, remembering all that. "I didn't know his name then, so I called him Camera Guy." She glanced at Hannah. "When he was done, he took pictures."

Hannah nodded, but didn't tell Janie that she'd seen some of them.

"Jared told me we could find out his name, what was going on with him, maybe turn him in to the police. He knew a kid from Orangewood who was in a cool foster home, with his own room, a computer, and modem. It was great. We went over there, put in some search terms. It took a while. But then a newspaper story about him came up. We found out he only spent a few years in prison for what he did to another girl. Jared said that was typical, and if we called the police to tell them about me, probably nothing would happen. You know that . . . how really *great* cops are at protecting kids."

The indictment rang in Hannah's ears. "So what did you do?"

"We weren't sure what to do. Then Jared found out on the Internet about the molesters' holiday. He thought we should celebrate it.

"By killing Henry Charles?"

Janie acted as though she hadn't heard that. "Jared read this other thing, that there was a law that let people find out if molesters were living in their neighborhood. All their names are on a CD-ROM. I just laughed when I heard about it."

"Why?"

"Well, it's so stupid. I knew where the molester was in my neighborhood—he was right down the hall. So what good did that law do kids like me? I told Jared that. He said: 'Let's make our own law.'"

"What was it?"

"If somebody had molested a kid and hadn't been punished for it, we'd take care of it. Jared called it Janie's Law. I liked how that sounded. That other girl, the one they named the law and the CD-ROM for?"

"Megan."

"Right. She had to get murdered before they named a law after her."

"How would Janie's Law take care of molesters?"

"We scared that Seward guy and some of his friends after one of their meetings. And Anita helped with Roche. She called some of his neighbors and told them they might want to check the CD-ROM."

"But that wasn't all you did."

Janie shrugged. "At first. We wanted to scare them. Stop them, maybe."

"Which was it with Charles?"

She regarded Hannah with a serious look. "You can't scare people like him."

"You had to stop him, then."

"Jared stopped him."

"You didn't throw that bottle?"

"I got scared. I held on too long."

The scorch mark on the Raiders jacket, Hannah thought. All this time she'd thought it was from Janie's cigarettes. But it was the bottle and its burning wick. "And then Jared decided to punish Roche for what he did to him?"

Janie frowned. "He never did anything to Jared. He tried, but Jared beat the hell out of him."

Hannah nodded. Jared couldn't tell her that he had been as victimized as she was. Jared was the hunter, never the prey. "What about Seward? Had he tried to mess around with Jared, too?"

"Oh, no. He'd hurt some other kid Jared knew."

"So Roche died for what he did to David Alvarez, and what he tried to do to Jared?"

"That's it."

"How did he find Roche and Seward?"

Janie shook her head. "I don't know. He wouldn't tell me. They weren't my cases, he said."

"You weren't the victim," Hannah said.

A look of revulsion crossed Janie's face. "I hate being called that."

"Okay. You weren't someone who'd been hurt by Roche or Seward."

"Right. Not like David and the other kid."

"Did you know David?"

"No. But Jared did, from a group home they were in together."

"And that's how Jared found out about these molesters?"

"Kids talk sometimes in places like that," she said. "It's sort of like jail, I guess. 'What are you in for?' Kids do that. Not usually boys. But sometimes."

"And they talked to Jared."

"Jared is so easy to talk to. When we were in the foster home together, I let kids know that they could go to him, if they wanted. It was okay to talk to him, because he understood how it was, for kids like us."

"Kids who'd been molested."

"Right. He knew because guys had tried to hurt him, too. Plus, he could keep a secret. Kids didn't have to worry about it turning into stuff for court, or the psychologist, or the cops, or the defense attorneys. Plenty of kids had been through that whole thing. If they talked to Jared, that's where it stopped. But if they wanted Jared to help them, he would."

"With Janie's Law."

She nodded again. "By the time he left the group homes, he'd learned some things."

"Like what?"

"How to protect himself."

"How to get guns, you mean."

"Whatever he needed. There was a guy who'd loan him a car if he really needed one."

"The gray VW."

"Yeah. It's a cool ride. I'd like to have one someday. But the old kind, a real one. Engine in back, where it belongs."

Hannah nodded, her heart sinking. It was as though the normal, almost-adolescent Janie—who wanted a classic Bug, daubed on Chanel perfume, and rode a skateboard—had survived. But she was trapped in the hardened amber of the streets, her father's violations of her, and these killings. Hannah wondered if she could help Janie break through that chitinous layer and take back her life. The first thing was to make sure she was separated from Jared. She only hoped that Janie was telling the truth; that she wasn't a participant in what Jared had done.

"So with a car and all his other tools, Jared decided to punish the molesters who'd hurt you and David and this other kid," Hannah said.

"Right," Janie said.

"Okay. Explain something to me."

Janie nodded, looking almost happy to oblige. Jared had shifted the power, leveled the field. Janie seemed to take pride in that.

"Roche went to prison for what he did to David. Wasn't that punishment? How did Janie's Law apply there?"

Janie gave her an incredulous look. "David killed himself. Nobody ever punished Roche for that."

Her calm explanation chilled Hannah. Violations of Janie's Law were not limited to the state penal code. Moral crimes were punishable, too.

"What about Cotter Davis, Janie?"

"Who?"

"The man who got shot because Jared mistook him for Mike Seward."

Janie shivered and stood up. "It's cold out here. Let's get inside."

Hannah thought of pressing the question, but didn't want Janie to take off. Janie was physically safe, away from both Jared and Meister, and she didn't intend to lose her. "Okay. I'll make some tea at home."

"Not your house. Mine. It's time." Before Hannah could speak or grab at her, Janie bolted across the back lawn and into the darkened house.

44

Inside, only the moonlight lifted the darkness. Hannah could make out the kitchen sink and the white cupboards. She heard Janie's fast footsteps moving deeper into the house. She turned on the flashlight and followed its narrow beam. It caught a flash of white clothing as Janie turned at the top of the stairs.

Hannah ran after her, feeling the twitch of fear in her thighs. She took out Churnin's gun and suddenly felt herself propelled back in time, to the night shifts, silent-alarm calls, and the sick uncertainty she felt as she wheeled around a dark corner. You never knew if you were coming up on a cat, a kid, or a tweaked-out burglar who would shoot and shoot until you were a bloody pulp. Her flashlight's beam found Janie at the end of the hall. She stood with her hand on the doorknob. "This was my room." She opened the door and went into the darkness. Then Hannah saw a match flare inside. It bobbed and bloomed as it touched a wick. Hannah followed her, pushing the door wide open with the gun's barrel.

The candle flames flickered, and what Hannah saw made her think of the Easter vigils of her childhood: a darkened church and a crucifix wrapped in purple cloth, which would soon be pulled off in recognition of the resurrection. Here, in the middle of a room decorated with a wallpaper frieze of Sesame Street characters, was a figure hooded in a black pillowcase. He balanced precariously on a white stool. His left arm was immobilized in a cast and shackled to the right arm with a length of twine. There was more rope above: a white nylon cord stood stark against the dark fabric and then disappeared up into the rafters. Hannah followed the snaking rope with the flashlight. It was looped and tied around the exposed beam that ran the length of Janie's room.

Meister wavered on the tiny platform, which was barely wider than his feet. He gripped its edges with his bare toes and let out a muffled, panicked whimper. He was gagged. He swayed and Hannah rushed to steady him. Then she heard the slide of a pistol. She turned.

More candles sputtered to life, and in their glow, she saw Jared. He sat back on his heels, eyes cast prayerfully down, the good altar boy. Her Glock was in his hand.

He looked like a kid who would have graced the yearbook's starring pages. His blond hair was cut close to his head, as though he played water polo. His khaki pants were class-president pressed. A white long-sleeved shirt was radiant from bleach. Perhaps this freshness was Anita's work, a way of turning Jared into her lost son. But Hannah didn't think so. She sensed that Jared was on his own quest for purity. He cleansed himself as he cleansed his world. He might shoot and stab, but he always washed the blood away, down into the sewers, down where the monsters lived. Down where they died.

Janie huddled next to him. And near her stood Anita Alvarez, a revolver trained at Hannah's head. She was wearing a silky, leaf-green blouse and white pants. Hannah realized she'd seen them before. On the beach, Anita's hat shielded her from more than just the sun. The child who frolicked in the waves must have been Anita's niece. She couldn't risk being a mother again, but she was willing to use the girl to lure Meister, to track and trap him. She smiled at Hannah. "Put your gun down."

Hannah did as she was told. Anita picked it up with the fluency of someone used to being around weapons. She patted Hannah's pockets, took the cell phone, and backed away. "Thanks, Hannah." She gestured to Meister. "We wouldn't have found this piece of shit without you."

Hannah felt her face redden. Anita had managed to get her stupidly, chattily drunk. It was all calculated, and Hannah hadn't seen it. "And what was your role, Anita? Did you get Jared the guns? Both of them? How about the knife he used on Seward?"

She shrugged. "He found that on his own. Some cable-shopping show."

"But you're pissed at your neighbors for letting David borrow a ladder? Hypocrite."

"Be quiet, Hannah. You're here at Janie's invitation. So use your party manners." Jared's voice resonated in the bare room. It was deep enough to make him sound like a man of thirty. He had the bearing of a slightly pained young university professor anxious to get on with the class work. "Are we ready? Janie?"

Janie was staring up at the black void above Meister's shoulders. In addition to heightening Meister's terror and claustrophobia, the hood served another purpose: Janie was spared the sight of those glacial eyes. She trembled slightly and reached for Jared's hand, but he stood up, stepping away from her touch.

"Janie," Hannah said. "You can't let them do this."

She stared at Hannah uncomprehendingly. "Why not?"

Meister wriggled and tried to shriek through his gag.

Jared cleared his throat. "Bill? Shut up or I'll fucking shoot you." No histrionics. Just a flat statement of purpose. Meister froze, but Hannah could see the shallow breathing that rippled his shirt. His legs trembled.

"Janie has the right to see her torturer punished, right?" Jared asked.

Hannah sensed that an interrogation had begun. "Yes. After a trial."

"Come on, Hannah," Anita said. She sounded surprised that Hannah wasn't cheering at the sight of Meister trussed, hooded, and ready to stretch a rope. "You told me yourself how horrible Bill Meister was. He'll never be punished enough by a court. You know that."

"No court has had a chance," Hannah said carefully.

"Right." Jared smiled. "Because you screwed that up, didn't you? You let this prick go. You could have stopped him, and you didn't. Some justice."

Hannah watched as Jared tightened his grip on the gun he'd stolen from her. Was she here as a witness, or a defendant? In Jared's mind, Hannah might be the next to mount that small, white scaffold. Perhaps he planned to shoot her with her own gun. It would be a tidy scene for the police to read: she had executed Meister and then killed herself. All because of Janie.

Any number of people could believe her capable of that, given her behavior in the last weeks. Bobby certainly would. Only Churnin might have some doubts.

"Janie?" Hannah heard the hoarse sound of fear in her own voice. She willed herself to stay calm, for the child's sake.

Pulled out of her thoughts, Janie looked up hazily. "What?"

"It's true that I failed you," Hannah said. "I've regretted it every day since."

"Just imagine how much Janie regretted it," Jared said.

Janie was silently exasperated for a moment. "Jared, let her talk, okay?"

Hannah expected him to flare up at a challenge to his authority, but he just shrugged. "Fine."

"I believed everything you said, Hannah. I thought everything would be okay, because you said it would."

"I'm so sorry," Hannah said.

"Easy to say," Jared interjected.

Janie gave him a fierce shut-up look. "Well, if Bill is gone, won't everything finally be okay?"

"What he did to you was terrible. He deserves to be punished." She paused, remembering her own vigilante fantasies. It was all very well, in a dark moment, to wish Meister dead. But it was another thing to witness—and sanction—a lynching. "But not like this."

Jared sighed. "See, this is the problem. She wants you to forgive this piece of garbage, Janie. People put all the pressure on the victim—sorry, I know you hate that. People say, 'If you forgive, then we all can forgive. And you can get on with your life!' That's such bullshit. People like Janie can't get on with their lives. They keep paying, because the monsters never pay enough."

"The prison sentences are too short. You're right," Hannah said. "But this isn't the way to do this."

"Jared," Anita said. "I thought you said she was all right with this." Her expression was turning uneasy. She had assumed Hannah was part of the court, one of the true-believing witnesses. She thought Hannah's initial shock at the sight of Meister would fade. She didn't pick up on the other nuances in the room, including Jared's hatred for Hannah, whom he saw as yet another adult who had failed Janie. She didn't understand that Hannah might die next. Maybe Anita and her conscience—if she had any conscience left—were Hannah's way out of this.

"Did he tell you I would go along, Anita? I do care about Janie. I also care about you, and your son, and Jared, too, because of what—"

"Shut up," Jared said. "This isn't about me."

"Five people are dead, Jared. That's all because of you."

"Five?" Janie frowned and counted. "Jared?"

Jared ignored her. "Do you feel sorry for Henry Charles, Hannah? After what he did to Janie and the other girls? He did a few years in prison, got out, and went back to raping children. Nobody bothered keeping track of him. Except us."

"You can't pretend what happened was a bad thing," Anita said.

Hannah shook her head. "I can't mourn somebody like him. But his being a monster doesn't make this right."

Anita shifted uncomfortably. It might have been a trick of the candle, but she seemed to be receding into the shadows. Good, Hannah thought. Dwell on how sick this is, Anita. Keep thinking about what you're doing. "Jared," Anita said, "maybe we—"

"Hang on, Anita." He waved her interruption away with the gun. "Hannah's apparently got a few ethical concerns. Is what we're doing wrong? Well, let's look at that. No more lives will be ruined by predators like Bill. We've saved the state some long, drawn-out trials. We've cut down on expensive prison bills. Since you've got a nice house and pay taxes, it's probably important to you, Hannah. You know that none of these guys would stop on their own. Prison doesn't change them. It's just a little time-out they put up with, until they can get back to their game. Bill sure hasn't changed—Anita said you saw how he was with her niece."

"I saw."

"So, what we're doing is just what a bug zapper does. Pest control."

"What about Freddy Roche? He was trying to change."

Jared smiled at her, an expression chilled by cold hate. He was too thin, the skin drawn tight across his cheekbones. The gentle face in those six-year-old photographs was stripped down to loss and anger. He was angelic now only in the way an avenging seraph would be. "Really? You think Freddy was reformed? Did you *know* Freddy?"

"What are you getting at?"

He shook his head. "It's not important."

Hannah turned to Anita. "What about you, Anita? You still think this is right?"

Anita swallowed and looked down at her feet.

"Go ahead, Anita," Jared said. "Tell her what you think." Hannah tried to read what that meant. Did he encourage Anita because he actually believed he could make Hannah complicit in their kangaroo court? Maybe it didn't matter if Hannah agreed, not if Jared was going to kill her right after Meister's neck was snapped.

"I'm doing this for all the victims," Anita said. "Jared told me you—"

He interrupted Anita again. "See, Hannah, the guilty people get away with the horrible things they do to kids, and no one cares. Bill didn't go to jail for what he did to Janie, but because of his swindles. David was so sick at what Freddy did to him that he killed himself. When I heard, I couldn't believe it. He's dead, and Freddy Roche is alive? That's so wrong."

"And then there were the other boys," Hannah said. "No one ever made Freddy pay for what he'd done to them, the kids the courts never found out about. Seward got away with that, too, didn't he?"

Their eyes locked. Jared's narrowed, asking the question: do you know? Hannah stared at him, leaving him to guess the answer. "Exactly," Jared said at last, quietly. "They got away with it. Because kids were afraid to tell."

From the corner of her eye, Hannah could see Anita relax slightly. Hannah sounded like a convert. Anita imagined they would all witness Meister's death, pronounce themselves satisfied that rough justice had been delivered, and leave the body to be found. It could be viewed as a suicide, if the police were so inclined. But Hannah wasn't done with Anita yet. She didn't think she knew everything Jared had done.

"So you were the stalking horse," Hannah said to Jared. "You let Freddy Roche find you."

He nodded. "I thought I'd see what happened. Anita and Freddy went to the same church. She let him know that I was around. She told him that it was too late for David, but that I was willing to accept an apology for what he'd tried to do to me. Three cheers for the healing power of religion."

"Jared," Anita cautioned. "It's still not a good idea to say too—"

"Hannah's okay with this, right Hannah? You won't say anything."

You won't leave me alive to say anything, Hannah thought. She dodged the question. "What about Seward? How did you find him?"

"Roche knew where he was," Jared said. "He told me. Just before he died."

"But you screwed up with Seward, Jared. You killed his roommate, someone who'd never hurt a child."

"Davis? He probably was one of the undiscovered molesters. A kiddie photographer? Alcoholic? Lived with Seward? Birds of a feather, I say." Jared shrugged, as though what he'd done was no more serious than crushing an ant.

Hannah flicked a glance to Anita. She looked away. Jared believed these justifications. But did Anita? Was she asking herself what she'd stumbled into because of her need for revenge?

"What about Devlin Eddy?" Hannah said. "He was my friend, my partner at the Las Almas P.D. He was no secret pedophile. Why did he die?"

Janie looked up. "Who?"

"The fifth victim, Janie. Jared beat him to death."

Anita's grip on her gun slackened. "You killed a police officer?"

"I had no idea who he was. I thought maybe Meister sent him," Jared said impatiently. "He was creeping around, following us."

"So that's an automatic death-penalty violation under Janie's Law?" Hannah asked.

"It was a mistake," Jared said.

"You didn't tell me about him," Janie said.

"I didn't want to upset you," Jared said. "I was protecting you. Let's get this done."

Janie ignored him. She looked up at Hannah. She hoped she saw a shift in the girl's eyes, a dawning realization of how confused and volatile Jared was. She would need time to see it fully. Hannah turned to Jared. "You called the police after

Davis died, didn't you? You implicated Seward. What was that about?"

Jared tried to engage Janie, but she wouldn't look at him. So he answered Hannah. "Somebody had to look like the suspect. I was thinking that Seward could get the death penalty if he was convicted of killing Davis. And he did have pictures of kids, you know."

Hannah nodded. Time to reveal Jared's secret pages. She was sorry she had to. "He had your pictures, didn't he?"

Jared stared angrily at her. "Shut up."

"I didn't see them. Not the ones you're thinking of."

"What's she talking about?" Janie said.

He can't bring himself to be one of the violated children, Hannah thought. Killing people is easier for him than saying what Seward and Roche did to him.

"You saw some of Seward's pictures the night you followed him, didn't you?"

Jared was off balance, not knowing what she would say next. "He had some when he came out of the bar that night, after his meeting. That's how we knew *he* wasn't reformed."

"But getting him arrested seemed like a mistake. You couldn't trust him to keep quiet, could you?"

"No," Jared said. "I saw that later. He could have told the police that I knew him and Freddy. It was a link."

Janie shook her head. "Wait. Jared, you said you didn't know Seward."

Jared's face reddened. His story was slipping. Soon Janie would realize that he couldn't have fought off his attackers, no more than she could have. "Janie, be quiet. We didn't think Seward would talk, but we didn't know. He had to get out of jail. Anita took care of that."

"And you took care of Seward."

"One less pest in the world." Jared tried to smile, but the expression faltered. Maybe slitting Seward's throat was too much for him. A firebomb, a gunshot, even the beating he gave Eddy couldn't have matched the abattoir he created in Seward's garage.

"I know Seward wasn't sorry for anything. But I don't understand about Roche," Hannah said. "He wanted forgiveness. You didn't have to give it to him. You could have just followed him and shot him. Why did you go talk to him?"

Jared glanced at Janie. She nodded. "Go ahead. I want to know why, too."

"I don't think—"

"Jared, it's my law, isn't it?"

Jared seemed to think about that, and Hannah realized how much he needed Janie. For justification, for comfort, for someone to whom he would be a hero and not a victim. Finally he shrugged. "Okay. I just wanted to hear how he'd try to justify himself. He cried and said he was sorry. He told me all the things he was doing. The shots, and all. And I started believing him."

"That means you stopped, too." Janie said it quietly.

"He couldn't keep it up. I could see he hadn't really changed."

"How?" Hannah said.

Jared's mouth twitched with disgust. "He was crying, wringing his hands. It was making me feel weird. I was getting ready to go. He tried to take my hand. I wouldn't let him."

Hannah realized that no one touched Jared, and he touched no one, not even Janie, whom he obviously loved.

"Go on," Janie said.

"He said that he was wrong to do what he'd done—tried to do—with a little kid. But wasn't I sixteen now? Grown up enough to choose my own . . . company."

Hannah closed her eyes. Freddy, in his self-involved stupidity, had assured his own death.

"Okay?" Jared said it fiercely, turning to Hannah. "Get it now?"

Hannah found herself nodding. Jared said, "Ready, Janie?"

Janie looked up. She seemed distracted, and Hannah knew she was sifting through Jared's story, finding all the false notes and inconsistencies.

"Jared, wait . . . ," Hannah said. She felt like Scheherazade, talking to keep death at bay.

"No," Jared said. "We've kept Bill waiting long enough. And Janie, too." He leaned down to her. "Go ahead. Just shove the stool, and come back here to me. It will all be over in a minute."

Hannah hadn't realized what Jared was doing until that moment. He wouldn't be the executioner this time. It was Janie's turn. "Jared, for God's sake."

He looked back at her, exasperated. "What now?"

"If you want to avenge yourself and David, and even Janie, that's your choice. But she's eleven. If you care about her, why are you trying to turn her into a murderer?"

"You haven't heard anything I've said, have you? This is justice that Janie will never have otherwise. It's what she wants." He knelt next to the girl. "Haven't you told me how much you hate him, how much you want him dead?"

"Of course she feels that way," Hannah said. "But what about the consequences for her?"

"I'll tell you the consequences," he said. His face burned red now, two deltas on his cheeks. The flames of the candle danced around him. "No more fear. No more nightmares. He will never, ever have the chance to hurt her again."

"He couldn't hurt her from prison, either." She turned to Janie. "Janie, listen to me."

"She's just trying to confuse you," Jared said. "Everything will be okay. Anita's got papers to prove we're her kids. She's got cool passports that no one will ever know aren't the real thing. We'll go to Mexico and eat lobster and it will be great. We speak the language, and we can go to school, and all this will seem like a bad—"

"Jared, please." Janie was close to tears.

Jared stooped and hesitantly touched her shoulder. It seemed to take a tremendous effort to make that physical connection. "It'll be okay, Maisey-Daisy. It doesn't take long."

Janie didn't answer, and Hannah took the opportunity while she had it. "Maybe Jared has thought about the consequences another way, Janie."

"What way?" Janie wiped her eyes. Her hands were shaking.

"Maybe what he's thought is this: 'Janie's a kid—just eleven. If she gets caught, the worst thing that happens is she spends a year in Juvenile Hall then goes to the Youth Authority until she's twenty-one. That's it. Ten years. Big deal.'"

"Shut up," Jared said. "I wouldn't ever do that."

"Wait," Janie said, frowning at Hannah. "What do you mean? Jared's a kid, too."

"But he's sixteen, Janie," Hannah said. "He would be tried as an adult. He could get life in prison. He might even get the death penalty." She looked to Jared, who was seething. "Did you factor that into the plan, Jared? Just in case Janie was questioned not just for Bill's death, but for all the killings? Callous, but smart."

"Goddamn it." Jared put his finger on the trigger and shoved the gun into Hannah's chest. Anita screamed.

"Stop!" Janie shrieked. "Everyone shut up!"

Hannah and Jared glared at each other, but they were silent. Jared took a step back. Anita slid down the wall until she was huddled on the floor. Meister stood motionless. He didn't even seem to breathe.

After a few moments, Janie whispered, "Hannah?"

Hannah kept her eyes on Jared and his gun. "I'm listening."

"Can you promise me that if Bill goes to prison, he'll never get out?"

Jared snorted a laugh, which Janie ignored. She stared raptly at Hannah. "Ever?"

Hannah could see that Janie already knew the answer. Child molesters don't go away forever. For years on end, yes. But not forever. She didn't know what a court would do with Meister. It would be a spin of the justice wheel, which was more reliable than roulette, but not by much.

"Christ, Janie," Jared said. "She can't even guarantee they'll convict him."

"Jared, please," Janie said. "Hannah?"

"They would convict, Janie. I feel certain of that." It was a lie—she wasn't sure of a conviction. People didn't want to believe in incest. Old cases made juries nervous. But she wasn't going to concede that now. She would lose this case on the spot.

"But what about the sentence?" Janie's face seemed to glow, waxy pale, in the candlelight.

"I can't honestly tell you they'd send him to prison forever."

Janie's face darkened. "I thought so." Her voice was cool.

"But for a long time, Janie. Long enough that you'll be grown when he gets out. You won't have any reason to be afraid of him then."

Janie nodded. "But I'll still be his daughter, won't I? He could try to see me."

"The courts could stop him. And you'd have a family by then. You'd have people who would protect you."

"I have that now," Janie said. "I have Jared and Anita."

Jared stiffly put his arm around Janie. She seemed to melt

into his touch, and Jared smiled. "See, Hannah, I've kept my word to Janie. I've done more than you ever promised to do." His lips brushed Janie's forehead. "Let's do this and go."

"It's wrong, Janie," Hannah said. "It's murder, and you don't want that on your conscience."

Janie stood unsteadily and walked to where Meister stood.

"Be better to him than he was to you," Hannah said. "Killing him won't make the pain stop. Jared has lied to you, Janie. He didn't just kill Roche and Seward for David's sake. He wasn't angry at Roche for what he tried to do, or what he wanted to do. It was what Roche did, him and Seward. Things happened to Jared that gave him nightmares, Janie. Ask him if he's stopped having bad dreams about Roche and Seward, now that they're dead. Ask him."

She turned to Jared. "Is that true? Did they hurt you, too?"

"Janie, it doesn't matter."

"You told me you made Roche stop before . . ."

His eyes softened, looking at her. He had wanted to be invulnerable for her. "I made them stop, didn't I? Does it really matter that it was this year, instead of six years ago?"

Janie shook her head. "You were a little kid."

"Right."

"But when they were dead, the dreams stopped, right?"

"Sure," he said. There were no tears in his eyes. But his voice was hoarse, scraped raw by the lie he told Janie in that one word.

Janie lowered herself to the floor. "I can't do it," she whispered.

Jared's face reddened, but he held back the anger. "It's okay. I'll take care of it."

"Jared," she said, reaching to take his hand. "Wait. I don't . . ."

He straightened, ignoring her, and glared at Hannah. "And then it'll be Hannah's turn."

"No!" Janie grabbed for Jared's arm, but he pulled away from her.

Hannah's heart was hammering. Anita struggled to her feet. "Jesus, Jared, you didn't say anything about that."

"You told me what she did, Janie," Jared shouted. "She made you a bunch of promises and then threw you back to him."

"Goddamn it, Jared!" Anita yelled. "We're not doing this.

I'm willing to believe Davis and that policeman were mistakes. But this is wrong." She snatched for the Glock in Jared's hand, as if she had control over him, as if he were her little boy, playing with a forbidden toy.

Hannah yelled for her to stop. Jared pulled away from Anita. She lunged at him. And in that instant, the gun went off. Anita fell, the blood spreading like a slow flood across her blouse. Her eyes darted wildly, searching for help. Then the lids fell shut. Janie clamped her hands over her mouth and stared up at Jared.

"Jesus," he whispered. He dropped the gun. For a moment, he seemed frozen by shock. Hannah took a breath. It was over. She reached down for the weapon.

Jared sprang at her. His elbow caught her in the throat and she toppled, gasping, against the wall. He grabbed the gun and pulled Janie up by the arm. Then he kicked the stool out from under Meister's feet and ran.

45

Janie's keening cries carried up the stairs and echoed off the floors and walls of the empty house. Hannah gasped for a breath and lunged for Meister's swinging body. If the knot had been placed right, his neck would have snapped instantly. But Meister was lucky. He only was strangling slowly. From under the hood, she could hear his desperate gurgles. He kicked wildly.

"Goddamn it, I'm saving you," she croaked. Pain seared her throat. She could only imagine how Meister felt.

She lifted him enough for the rope to slacken. The kicking stopped. She hooked the overturned stool with her ankle and righted it under his feet. Then, standing on the tiny platform with him, she reached up and loosened the badly tied noose. Jared had missed out on Boy Scouts, and thank God for that, she thought.

Meister and Hannah tumbled to the floor together. Hannah pulled off his hood and stripped the duct tape from his mouth. He gasped and coughed. His eyes rolled. Hannah sat back on her heels for a moment. After hating him for so long, she actually felt a twinge of pity for him. But it disappeared as she looked into those cloudy blue eyes. She took the rope down from the beam and tied his ankles with it. He tried to retch out some words. She stopped him.

"Lie still," she said. "Somebody will be here."

She moved to Anita, felt for a pulse, and found none. She reclaimed her gun and cell phone and punched in 911. "There's been a shooting," she said. She gave the location, hung up, and ran downstairs.

Outside, there was no sign of Janie and Jared. She got in the car and idled it for a moment, trying to decide where to start the search. If they were going to Mexico, they'd take the I–5 south. It was two hours to San Diego and then just another fifteen miles to the border crossing south of there, at San Ysidro. She kept her lights off and circled the block, heading for the freeway on-ramp. The route took her past the site of the demolished apartment buildings, and there, in front of the place Janie and Jared had called home, she saw a gray Beetle. Two figures were in the street next to it. It looked to her as if Janie had collapsed in the gutter. Jared hovered over her.

She fought down a panic that felt like a rope around her chest. She coasted to a stop, got out, and crept toward them. She only heard the hum of traffic from the freeway. She strained to hear Janie's voice, but couldn't.

Hannah came up behind them, stopping a few feet away. Jared still was bent over Janie. Now Hannah could see that the girl was crying, silently. He was trying to get her to stand up. Hannah's Glock was still in his hand. He was shaking, and Hannah was afraid he would accidentally fire it again. He was no longer the measured executioner. Now he was a terrified kid, and she wasn't sure which was more dangerous.

"Jared." She put all the authority she could muster into her shout. "Put the gun down now."

He whirled to face her, dragging Janie to her feet and holding her in front of him. She screamed, but there was no one there to hear her. Jared stabbed the air with her gun. "Stay back."

Hannah held Churnin's gun steady, training it on Jared's head, her best target. "Let's take it easy, Jared. Janie's scared."

"We're going to be okay," he said, tugging Janie up until her head was at his chin. "We've got our passports, and we're getting out of here. You aren't going to stop us."

"God, Jared." Janie whispered it like a prayer. She looked up at Hannah, terror and confusion on her face. She had seen Jared kill Anita and threaten to kill Hannah. What would he do to her if she tried to run? She squeezed her eyes shut, as if that could make this night disappear.

Hannah softened her voice. "Jared, let Janie go. Don't make this worse."

"No. We're staying together."

"You won't get far. You certainly won't get into Mexico. I can help you with the police. After what Roche and Seward did to you . . ."

"As if anyone cares about that!" Jared shouted. "They'll call it my abuse excuse. Besides, what proof is there? I could have made it all up. That's what Roche tried to do with David—make him look like a liar. What about Davis and your friend? And Anita? What's the excuse for what I did to them? Shit, they'll probably just shoot me on sight."

"Jared, with the right lawyer . . ."

"Look." He shook his head in disgust. "You don't care about me. You only care about Janie."

He's right, she thought. Janie has a chance. Jared probably doesn't, not now. She imagined how Jared's life might have gone if his mother hadn't deserted him. If Roche and Seward hadn't used him. If his father hadn't rejected him. She tolled the losses: family, safety, every vestige of innocence. And she saw what sprang from the losses: murderous rage, first focused, but now diffuse, scattershot. Jared had become another sloppy, indiscriminate killer. It must disgust him, she thought, because he tried so hard to keep this mission pristine.

But even as his surgical strikes turned into a bloodbath, he'd kept his love pure for Janie. He still thought he could hold her above the flood he'd created. It was madness, Hannah thought. They would both drown in what he'd started. He must suspect that. But he still wouldn't let Janie go.

"I care about you because Janie does," Hannah said. "You've done a good job of keeping her safe, despite everything else."

"You know I'll always take care of her," he said.

She nodded. "I know you want to."

"I'm doing a better job than you ever did." He unlocked the car and swung Janie toward it, pushing her toward the backseat. She seemed to weigh heavy on his arm. The fight had gone out of her. "We'll write," he said to Hannah. His smile was only partly ironic.

"Jared, you won't get six blocks from here. The police are on their way."

He paused, listening for sirens, shrugging in dramatic perplexity when he heard none. "Who told them, Hannah? Not Meister. Not Anita."

As he spoke, Hannah shifted her attention to Janie. She wanted to infuse her with strength, give her permission to leave Jared's world, a place that had been safe, in its sad, warped way. But there was nothing safe about it now. The look in Janie's eyes—frightened, wary, but alert—seemed to say that she understood that. Hannah saw Janie rise in Jared's arms. He seemed to think she was getting into the car on her own. Hannah thought she might be ready to break his hold. Come on, Hannah thought, run as fast from him as you ran from me that night.

But then she hesitated and turned to look at Hannah. Hannah read the expression: she wanted to leave, but she was loyal to Jared and afraid for him. What could Hannah offer?

"If you let her go," Hannah said to Jared, "I'll let you go."

"No," he said. "I need her."

As solace, Hannah thought. As an appreciative audience. As protection. As everything, because that was what she was to him. "She'll only get hurt," Hannah said.

"Are you saying I can't protect her?"

"Everything has changed, Jared. This isn't like hiding out from the truant officers."

"Goddamn it, I'm not an idiot. Now shut up and back off." He lifted the Glock, and as he moved, Janie slid from his arms.

But she didn't run. Instead, she grabbed for Jared's hand, twisting the gun, trying to pry it from his grip. The move surprised him, and in that moment, he lost control of her and the weapon. It was turning, slipping. His finger was still on the trigger.

As the struggle played out before Hannah in silence, it could have been a children's wrestling game. Janie was no match for Jared's strength, but he was too tentative, almost gentle, fearful of hurting her. By not wrenching her hand away, a moment came when her finger slipped into the trigger guard.

"No!" Jared screamed it, twisting the gun so that it wasn't pointed at her. But now it was nuzzling his chest. As Janie, frenzied, tried to pry Jared's fingers off the gun, she squeezed the trigger. The pistol's crack seemed deafening. Hannah could smell the acrid cordite in the air. Jared slumped against the car door. Janie screamed.

Hannah pulled Janie away from Jared. She laid him on the ground. He focused on Hannah for a moment before the consciousness dimmed in his eyes. Hannah felt his pulse ebb, rally, and die. Her mind raced. She had to do what she could for him. She ran for her phone and hit 911 again. She gave the cross streets. "There's been a shooting. Send an ambulance. Fast."

She hung up, imagining what would happen next. In her mind, she saw the police arrive, heard Janie's babbled explanation spilling out before Hannah could stop her. Then a montage of grim bureaucratic scenes: detention hearing, trial, acquittal on the grounds of accident or self-defense, assessment of Claire as an unfit mother, assignment to a group home, and where did Janie come out at the end of that, two or three years later? Hannah thought she knew. Wrecked. Twisted. Even more lost.

She told herself not to think. Just do what you should have done six years ago: the right thing, if not the legal one. She saw the phone booth on the corner, and the idea sprang from that.

Hannah pried the gun from Janie's hand, wiped it with her shirt, and then clutched it as tightly as she could. She set it aside. She took the packaged handwipes she kept in the glove box and wiped Janie's limp hands clean. She threw the bloodied cloths on the ground. Janie didn't question any of it. She leaned against the car's bumper, turning herself so she couldn't see Jared. She wasn't crying. She didn't rock, or keen. Hannah took her by the shoulders.

"Janie? Listen to me."

Janie's eyes were cloudy, turned to view some other world. But when Hannah shook her again, she came back. "I killed him."

"It was an accident. I saw what happened."

"But there's Bill and Anita. The police won't believe anything I—"

"I know," Hannah said, interrupting. "That's why you're not going to talk to them." She reached for the band of Janie's blood-spattered shirt. "Take that off."

Janie blinked at her. "What?"

"Do it."

Janie slid out of the white T-shirt and handed it to Hannah. Hannah took off her blouse and threw it around Janie's shoulders. She unzipped her jeans, stepped out of them, and gave them to Janie. She stared at Hannah, uncomprehending.

"What are you doing?"

"Give me your pants. Put my jeans on."

"But . . ."

"Don't argue with me. We don't have a lot of time."

Janie did as she was told. Hannah held out her house key. "You know the way from here?"

Janie nodded, but Hannah could see her confusion. She pressed the key into the girl's hand. "When you get there, take a shower. Throw my clothes in the washer. You can run the washer, right?"

She nodded.

"Okay. A woman will be there in a little while. Older than me, blond hair. She's going to look after you for tonight."

Jane paled. "A cop."

"No. Definitely not a cop, or a social worker. You can call her Mrs. T., and you can trust her. She's great at helping people."

Janie looked dazed. Hannah took her hand and held it tight. "Don't go with anyone but Mrs. T. She'll call you Mae, and she'll come to the back door. Okay?"

"But what about the police?"

"You're not going to see the police."

"Ever?"

"Not if we do this right."

Janie shook her head. "I don't understand."

"You have to trust me. Can you do that?"

Janie didn't answer right away. It seemed to Hannah that in the course of a few seconds, the girl was reliving their history together, beginning in the so-called child-friendly interview room, moving to the tree-shadowed darkness of Hannah's neighborhood, and winding up here, near the courtyard that now lay under rubble. Janie must have felt uneasy, but she had little choice but to trust Hannah. She nodded quickly, and Hannah felt a flood of relief.

She helped Janie to her feet. Hannah looked at the girl wearing her clothes, seeing her both as Janie and as herself. Hurt and abandoned, but not broken, not lost forever. She pulled Janie close, and the girl didn't resist her arms. "It will be all right. I promise you."

Janie searched her face and tried a faltering, unconvincing smile. "Okay."

"It's the truth, this time. Stay off the main streets."

The girl nodded, turned, and ran into the night. Hannah only had a few minutes before the police would arrive. She ran for the phone booth. The next call couldn't be made on the cellular.

46

Churnin sat back in the wooden chair and cradled his head in his hands. Hannah, seated on the other side of the table, could see the tape in the recorder turning slowly. The video camera, started by Churnin, was now running on its own, recording them in a medium shot. Hannah had surrendered the stained shirt and white pants as evidence. Now she wore a borrowed flannel shirt and a pair of jeans—clothes Churnin's girlfriend had left in his Volvo. No jailhouse orange for me, Hannah thought. Not yet, anyway.

"Tell me one more time," Churnin said.

Hannah nodded. They'd been at it for more than three hours. Bright morning sun washed the window of the interview room. "The whole thing?"

"Pick it up from the point where you saved Bill Meister's scrawny ass."

"I got the rope off, laid him on the floor, and made sure he was breathing."

"The cockroaches always survive, it seems."

Hannah avoided what might have been bait. "Is he going to be all right?"

"Sure. He goes into federal custody today. They get first crack at him for the mail fraud. Then we'll see about possible state charges. But without his victim? I don't know how that will go. Anyway, Meister was alive. What next?"

"Anita was dead," Hannah said. "Jared had run with Janie, but they said they were going to Mexico, so I went to the nearest southbound on-ramp. I saw the car that Jared had been driving, and then I saw him and Janie. He was standing over her."

"Hitting? Threatening?"

"I think he was trying to get her back into the car. She must have tried to run away from him."

"And you barreled in there and shot him?"

She shook her head. She had told the story twice already, and it was getting easier with each repetition. Churnin knew there was something amiss. He might even have known exactly where her lies lay. But he hadn't tried to trip her. Not right away, in any case. She hewed to the truth as much as possible. "No. He was holding her, and I tried to convince him to let her go."

"He was holding the gun to her head?"

Hannah waited for a moment before answering him. She tried to gauge the look on his face. Was he now trying to give her a justification for killing Jared? Or was he trying to catch her in a lie?

"No. I don't think he intended to hurt her. But he was panic-stricken. He'd just shot Anita Alvarez."

"That was an accident, you think?"

"I know it was." There was no reason to malign Jared now. His intentional killings were bad enough.

"What happened then?"

"Janie got away from Jared. And that's when I rushed him. I tried to get the gun away. It went off."

"This is your own gun we're talking about?"

"Yes. A Glock Model Seventeen. My father gave it to me."

"You had your finger on the trigger?"

"We both did."

"He would have killed you if he'd gotten control of that weapon?"

Hannah thought for a moment. On this point, her concocted story and reality coincided. "I think so."

"And what about Janie?"

"She ran."

"Do you know where she is now?"

"No." That was the purest truth she'd spoken in five hours.

Once Janie was gone, Hannah checked to make sure the pay phone could take an incoming call. She paged Mrs. T., who called back less than a minute later. Hannah started laying out her plan.

"After I've talked to the police, I can meet you and Janie somewhere. Just let me know where to—"

"No." Mrs. T. said.

Her tone was so implacable and flat that it took Hannah aback. "What?"

"Hannah, if I'm going to do this, you can't know anything. You can't see Janie, you can't talk to her. No contact. Disappear means disappear."

"But who's going to take care of her? You can't. They would just follow you to her."

"I won't be with her. As we speak, I've dispatched someone to get Claire. She and one of my minders will be with Janie."

"Claire?"

"Yes."

"Jesus, she's a raging alcoholic."

"Maybe she's willing to change."

"You can't do this."

"Well, I won't take the girl without your permission, but if I'm doing it, I'm doing it my way. That's the deal."

"Goddamn it, Mrs. T., how can you even think—"

"Listen to me." Mrs. T.'s voice was sharp, and its edge silenced Hannah. "She is Janie's mother. I'm about putting children back with their parents, not giving them away to other women, even deserving ones. Even good, lonely ones. Got it?"

"This isn't about me." Hannah started to argue her case, but she found she couldn't go on. Because it was about her and having someone in her life. She heard sirens now. So did Mrs. T.

"Well, Hannah? What are we going to do? Doesn't Claire deserve another chance?"

"What if I think I deserve a chance?"

"Then I can't help you."

Hannah saw the flashing lights, half a block away. She couldn't risk being caught on the phone. "All right." She hung up and went back to where Jared lay.

Churnin walked around the table and leaned over Hannah's shoulder. "Why is it that I don't think you're telling me everything?"

Hannah turned to look at him. "Do you think I'm being uncooperative?"

"Nope." He started a slow stroll back to his chair. "We've searched your house, and they're going through your car now. There's no sign of the girl. It was really Janie Meister, wasn't it?"

"Yes. You haven't found her?"

Churnin sighed. "No. We found her mother's place, though. Thanks to you."

Hannah had given Churnin Claire's address. She told herself she had no choice, since he'd figured out that Hannah knew where she was as soon as she brought the Meisters' pictures back for the age progression. But that wasn't the only reason. She hoped the police might pick Claire up before Mrs. T.'s contact did. That would spoil her plan. Then Mrs. T. might have to reconsider Hannah's proposal. She tried to sound calm as she asked Churnin: "And was Claire there?"

"Nobody was there. Miss Higgins split without her stuff. Left lots of pictures of her daughter, though."

Hannah felt a pang of disappointment and hated herself for her jealousy. Janie wasn't a prize to be won. She'd been crazy to consider running with Janie. Did she actually think she could disappear into Mrs. T.'s underground with the girl? And do what? Work at a Dairy Queen in Pahrump?

"Claire loves Janie," she told Churnin. As she said it, she realized she had no right to the girl. None. Her eyes stung.

"You think they're together?"

She nodded. "Janie must have hitchhiked out there to her. Or she called, and Claire picked her up somewhere."

Churnin drummed his fingers on the table. He glanced up and caught Hannah rubbing her eyes. "You okay? Want something? Coffee?"

"I'm fine, thanks."

"All right, then." He opened a folder in front of him. "Let's see what we've got here." He read something for a few moments and then looked up at her. "There was gunshot residue on your clothes, but not your hands, Hannah. Why was that?"

She knew this would come up. Even though she wore Janie's clothes, which were stained not only with blood but with traces of gunpowder, there was no way to get the residue on her own hands, short of firing the gun again. And that presented its own problems. So the only thing she could do was account for the lack of evidence—as best she could.

She shrugged. "I told you. I had that boy's blood all over my hands. I couldn't stand it. I had some witch-hazel towelettes in my glove compartment. I used them."

"Yeah. We found them. But it's pretty fastidious for an ex-cop, even for a female one."

"I've changed, Ivan. Blood gets to me sometimes."

"Still, there should have been some gunshot residue on your skin."

"I don't know what to say about that."

"It's odd. Because your fingerprints are on the gun."

"And the trace-metal detection test—what did that show?" She knew what the technician saw after spraying Hannah's hands and examining them under ultraviolet light.

"We saw the outline of a Glock."

"I told you I was holding it," Hannah said.

"Right. But it doesn't mean you shot it, now does it?"

"Did I really shoot Jared West? Is that what you're asking? I told you I did."

"It would be nice if Janie Meister could corroborate that," he said.

He knows, she thought. "I would like nothing better than to have Janie here. You know that."

Churnin turned off the tape recorder. Then he got up and switched off the camera. "This is just us. Is she with you? If some gung-ho Juvie Court judge insists we go looking for her at your house next week, will we find her there? Is there hair and fiber evidence in those clothes of yours that's going to make a liar out of you?"

"I don't know what to say. As God is my witness." And here, she had to stop. Christ, crying in front of Churnin. She couldn't allow it, but she couldn't stop it. "I don't know where she is."

He watched her silently for a moment. "You shouldn't lie to me, Hannah."

"I'm not lying. I don't know where she is."

"Tell me who shot that kid."

"I told you."

"Say it again, Hannah."

"I shot him. It was an accident, but I shot him."

He tapped the desk with his pencil. "If I find that girl, and I hear differently, it's going to go badly for you, Hannah. I've bent over backwards to help you. I don't deserve this shit."

He didn't deserve it. But she had no intention of giving him the truth and letting him decide what to do with it. He would have to go after Janie, then. He would have no choice.

"I've got nothing to add, Ivan. Do I need to call my lawyer now?"

"They're still mucking around with your car. Collecting fibers, whatnot. Call Bobby for a ride if you want. But you don't need him for anything else."

"We're through?"

"For the moment. Meister told us what he heard—Jared West's confession, you trying to talk them out of killing him, how Jared wanted to kill you. That puts the other deaths to rest."

"And what about Jared's death?"

"All in good time. I'll tell the DA what we've got. What you said. What you didn't say. It's up to him. Election's coming, and I'm sure that will be a factor in his decision."

Churnin was letting her know that it might not matter to the DA who shot Jared, or why, or how, as long as the surface of the story was presentable. There was a definite advantage not to look too closely: the Las Almas P.D. could legitimately claim five homicides cleared and a serial killer stopped. So what if the evidentiary pieces didn't fit without a bit of trimming, as long as they made a believable garment? Without Janie, there was nothing to disturb the weave. There was also no good reason to search for her. She was probably with her mother. The only possible objections would come from Bill Meister, and he was in no position to bleat about a parental abduction.

Hannah got up. "Thanks, Ivan."

Even though the recorders were turned off, he bristled. "I'm just doing my job."

"I know that."

"And in a few minutes, I'll have to talk to the media. When Marian Roche finds out she was right about the serial killer, she'll start thinking up more big words to torture us with."

On Monday, Hannah went to the office at her usual time. She found Bobby pacing the conference room, flipping through

stacks of discovery documents, and swearing under his breath.
Vera sat at her desk, thumbing through *Vogue*. It looked like an
old one, and Hannah was willing to bet it was an issue from the
fifties. The picture her coworkers made was as serene as it
could be, and Hannah felt a wave of comfort. Bobby spotted
her first. He looked wary, and Hannah understood entirely.
She'd put him through hell in the last ten weeks.

She paused in the doorway to the conference room. "Can I
talk to you?"

He shrugged. "Sure. Let's get it over with."

Vera watched them covertly as they went into Bobby's
office. Hannah shut the door. "May we have this conversation
as attorney and client?"

Bobby's face went white. Hannah thought for a moment he
would launch into a litany of questions. But to his credit, he just
nodded. With the cloak of privilege around them, she told him
everything that happened early Sunday morning.

"So Janie's with Claire? This is the same Claire who looked
the other way while Meister abused their daughter?"

"It wasn't my choice," Hannah said. "They're in Mrs. T.'s
world now. I hope she'll make Claire toe the line."

"You still don't know where are they?"

Hannah shook her head. "I might never know."

47

The letter came eight months later, on the day that Guillermo called Hannah to ask if they could meet for coffee and talk about a fresh start. Hannah counted the months: more than twelve since he'd walked out. She was ready to hang up until he admitted that he'd been a pigheaded, selfish asshole. Those very words. Hannah thought he was fishing for a demurrer and a return apology. She didn't give him either one.

"I agree completely. Particularly with the anal characterization."

She expected Guillermo to hang up. But instead, she heard him laugh. "See? Common ground already." Then he added: "How about it, Hannah?" They set a date for Monday evening at the Diedrich Coffeehouse near the Plaza.

Hannah opened the letter after they hung up. Her address had been typed, and there was no return information on the envelope. She expected to find a real-estate come-on inside. Someone was always trying to convince her to sell Mrs. Snow's house. But not this time, unless agents were writing their letters in red felt pen on blue-lined, three-hole-punched composition paper.

The letter's author always had a gift for succinct communication, and this was no exception. She had written directions to the Indian Cove campground, just off Highway 62 in Joshua Tree National Park. Next Sunday, at ten in the morning. Hannah was relieved that it didn't conflict with Guillermo's coffee hour. He would have found himself sitting alone with his cup of Huehuetenango Guatemala.

•   •   •

On Sunday morning, Hannah made the two-and-a-half-hour drive into the desert, arriving twenty minutes early. Joshua Tree could be an eerie place of lunar rockscapes, lonely canyons, and the almost-human Joshua trees with their up-reaching, prayerful arms. She remembered that years before, a little girl from Huntington Beach had disappeared from the Indian Cove campground, setting off a nationwide panic over child kidnappings. Two years later, hikers found her remains nearby. How strange to think that another lost girl would soon appear— alive—in the same spot.

Hannah was looking for a shaded parking place when she saw a kid lying atop a picnic table, basking in the sun. She slowed and then stopped.

Janie wore purple-rimmed sunglasses. Her head was turned slightly away, so that Hannah saw just the curve of her cheek, wisps of very dark brown hair, and a mouth set in a serious expression. She had headphones in her ears, and she kept the beat with one foot as she tugged the other one close to her chest. With a red felt pen, she had drawn loopy daisies on a pair of white canvas slip-ons. On this warm March morning, she wore a pair of baggy purple nylon running shorts and a flowered T-shirt. Her hair was long now, braided neatly and thrown over her shoulder. Her skin had a coppery glow, highlighted on her arms by fine golden hairs. She had painted her short fingernails tangerine. She glowed like an earthbound sunrise, illuminating the red-and-tan boulders around her. She pulled out a Marlboro and lit it. Hannah shook her head. Some things didn't change.

Hannah watched her take a drag. Then Janie bellowed a chorus of whatever was playing in her ears. Beastie Boys? Beck? Hannah couldn't tell.

She felt suspended in a net of conflicting feelings: she would like to go on watching Janie, unobserved. That way, she could preserve the fantasy that after only a few months, she had been healed of six years of privations and losses. Another part of her wanted to tap her shoulder, hug her, stub out that cigarette, and hear everything that had happened in eight months—the good and the bad.

"She's changing, every day. Sometimes I don't even recognize her."

Hannah turned. The soft voice sounded like Claire Meister's, but like her daughter, she was transformed. Claire's hair was cut short and dyed black. Contact lenses darkened her eyes. She was much thinner, and her face no longer had the pale, sickly bloat Hannah had seen over breakfast at the Tune Up.

Hannah reached to shake Claire's hand, but instead Claire pulled Hannah into an embrace. "I can't even say how grateful I am."

Hannah thought of how she tried to rob her of Janie and stepped out of Claire's hug. "Is it all right for you two to be here?"

"You mean has Mrs. T. given her blessing? She said we shouldn't stay too long." Claire lit a Newport and shrugged at Hannah's displeasure. "I know. A new bad habit."

"I guess I shouldn't ask where you're living."

She shook her head. "Mrs. T. said we're going to move pretty soon. After that, we can let people we trust know."

"I hope I'm in that category."

Claire nodded. "Of course you are."

"How's Janie?"

Claire smiled. "She wants to be Jane now. For a couple weeks, she considered making it two syllables, soft J: Ja-né. But she got over that." They turned to look at the girl, who was now lying flat on her back, eyes closed, flowered shoes dancing to the music. "She's almost thirteen," Claire said. "That should be enough to tell you what we're going through."

"I remember being thirteen," Hannah said. "I don't know who suffered more—me or my mother."

"We have our moments." Claire paused, and Hannah could imagine the scenes: power struggles, resurgences of anger and mistrust. Janie had emotional ammunition that could take Claire down to bone and ash. "The counseling helps. Mrs. T. found somebody who can deal with our . . . situation. But I don't know how I'm going to repay you."

"You're not," Hannah said. "It's a gift to both of you." She didn't mention that she had started sessions, too, visiting a woman psychologist in her fifties who had managed to give Hannah whole nights of sleep.

"Well, thanks," Claire said. "I keep saying it. I don't think I can ever say it enough."

Hannah shook her head. "Forget it. How are you doing?" She hoped Claire would read the question's inflections.

She did. "Working step four, still. More than eight months sober. That's why I'm hooked on these." She flashed the cigarette pack. "Pretty soon, Janie and I are both going to quit."

Hannah counted back the weeks. "More than eight months? That's longer than Janie's been back with you."

"I called A.A. the day after you told me she was alive. People almost never get second chances. I decided not to blow it."

Hannah remembered her exasperation when Claire didn't instantly promise to stop drinking. She had judged Claire so harshly, out of her own neediness.

"Hannah?"

The voice came from behind her. Janie had taken off her earphones. She sat up, stubbed out the cigarette, and smiled. She wore braces that glinted in the sun. "Hey."

"Hey yourself," Hannah said. "You've grown."

She shrugged. "A little."

"She's playing basketball," Claire said. "And running track. That's another reason why the smoking has to stop."

"She's quite a runner, even with the cigarettes," Hannah said. Janie laughed.

"Your hair is a pretty color," Hannah said.

She touched her braid and nodded. "I'd like to dye it red, but Mom won't let me. Jared wouldn't either, so . . ." The slightest tremble crossed her lip.

Claire sat down at the table and took Janie's hand. "We're going to take him some flowers later, when we've moved and gotten settled, right?"

Janie nodded, and Hannah felt a lump in her throat. She hadn't gone to the boy's grave, either, although she and Bobby had paid for a plot and a burial.

Janie whispered in her mother's ear. Claire nodded, and Janie pulled out a lime-green nylon backpack. "I brought some things for you." She dug around inside with both hands, brought her hands out in fists, and then indicated that Hannah should pick one. Hannah touched the left fist, which opened to reveal the tiny atomizer of Chanel No. 5 that Janie had stolen from Hannah's purse. Janie opened her right hand. There was Bert.

"I'm sort of outgrowing him," she said. "I thought maybe you'd want him?"

Hannah nodded. She couldn't bring herself to hold Bert. Not yet. "I thought you liked the perfume."

Janie shrugged. "It's kind of old for me."

"Plus, the bottle's almost empty," Claire said drily.

Janie held Bert out. Hannah reached for him, bracing herself against the sadness that swept her. "Why don't I just act as caretaker? You might want him back."

"Maybe we'll come visit him." Janie said it not so much out of her own desire, Hannah thought, but as a way to soothe her.

"Okay," Hannah said. "But keep the perfume bottle. Refill it for the prom or something."

"Please!" She clicked her tongue. "The guys in my class are all geeks or jocks. I'm pretty sure I won't be there in some lacy Cinderella getup with one of those losers."

Hannah nodded. Boys and sex—how did Janie even begin to bring them into her life now? "Maybe they'll shape up by then."

Janie smiled. "I don't know. Maybe."

Claire cleared her throat. "I'm sorry, but I think we have to go."

"Write again," Hannah said. "I'll come wherever you are."

"Oh, it'll be just a couple of . . ." Janie stopped and clapped her hand over her mouth as Claire rolled her eyes. "Sorry. I forgot."

"It's okay," Claire said. "Just slow down and *think*."

"God," Janie said. "Like I don't do that all the time." She put out her hand to Hannah. It felt soft and slightly damp, from the sun or from nervousness, Hannah realized that she was a keeper of Janie's secrets now. She understood why this meeting might be hard for her.

"I'm really . . ." Janie shrugged, unable to give voice to whatever she really was. Happy? Relieved? Still grieving for Jared?

Hannah couldn't easily put her feelings into words, either. "I think good thoughts for you, Jane."

She smiled. "I think about you, too, Hannah."

Hannah watched as Janie and her mother crossed the parking lot. Janie caught Claire's hand and swung it, doing a little jig as she walked. She was probably pleading for some absolute

necessity, something that she'd simply die without: the latest
CD, a rayon dress in garish yellow, a perm, a sixty-nine
Volkswagen, a trip to Prague, or—barring that—free rein at
the mall for a couple of hours.

Hannah thought that anyone who saw the three of them
around the picnic table that morning might have thought it a
sweet but unremarkable scene. Here was a near-teenager whose
emotional tide had momentarily swept her close to her mother.
And the mother enjoyed the girl's warmth and effervescence.
She knew that tomorrow—maybe sooner—she would be left
in the wake, demonized for some unforgivable parental flaw.

An observant stranger would think that the other woman
didn't look like the girl or her mother. Probably not even
family. Maybe an honorary aunt, someone who could be a
sounding board for mother and daughter. The safety valve, the
fallout shelter, the mother confessor. Why did she seem sad?
Maybe because the child wasn't hers.

But even that sketch, shaded with its delicate hints of human
tension, didn't tell the story. Claire, Janie, and Hannah did not
form some perfectly warm and lovely feminine triad. They had
failed horribly, stumbled, deluded themselves, sinned, and been
sinned against. Each had died inside and tried in halting ways
to find a new life. Hannah knew she should cherish this
meeting, which was already on its way to memory. Its beauty
was fragile. It wouldn't last. It wouldn't be repeated.

Hannah knew that Janie was the most volatile of them. She
and Claire wanted to see her as the child she'd been. But that
wasn't possible. She couldn't be restored to the innocence she
had before her father and Hank Charles had violated her. She
couldn't unlive the time she'd spent in Jared's wonderland of
vengeance. Six years of a life couldn't be smoothed away,
talked out, or neatly erased. Her need to hurt those who hurt her
was a deep wound. It might bleed through again. It might never
heal. What would Claire do then?

Hannah could only hope that Janie would discover something Hannah already knew. Janie's soul was a pure core that
pain, chaos, and defilement could not touch. Hannah had a
glimpse of that unstained spirit when Janie refused to kill
Meister, when she said to Jared, who was ready to murder for
her, "Wait. I don't . . ."

Hannah didn't know how Janie meant to finish that: I don't

want you to kill for me. I don't know what to do. But it was always preceded by a command to wait. Hannah heard the words as a sign that Janie was in there, a whole person trying to find her way out of a broken life.

Jared thought victims could only reclaim wholeness through revenge. He believed he was honoring Janie by giving her name to a doctrine of retribution. But it was really Jared's Law that was being acted out, a tenet that washed the guilty in blood and explained away the occasional collateral damage among the innocent.

Janie seemed to know that revenge would only shatter what was left of her. Did her understanding go deeper? Did she know that killing was wrong? Hannah couldn't answer that. All she knew was that Janie had let her father have his life, even though he had never cared about hers—a pouring out of mercy, Hannah thought. That was the true expression of Janie's Law.

CARROLL LACHNIT

MURDER IN BRIEF   0-425-14790-8/$4.99

For rich, good-looking Bradley Cogburn, law school seemed to be a lark. Everything came easy to him—including his sparkling academic record. Even an accusation of plagiarism didn't faze him: he was sure he could prove his innocence.

But for ex-cop Hannah Barlow, law school was her last chance. As Bradley's moot-court partner, she was tainted by the same accusation—and unlike him, she didn't have family money to fall back on. Now Bradley Cogburn is dead, and Hannah has to act like a cop again. This time, it's her own life that's at stake...

A BLESSED DEATH   0-425-15347-9/$5.99

Lawyer Hannah Barlow's connection to the Church is strictly legal. But as she explores the strange disappearances—and confronts her own spiritual longings—she finds that crime, too, works in mysterious ways...

AKIN TO DEATH   0-425-16409-8/$5.99

Hannah Barlow's first case is to finalize an adoption. It's a no-brainer that is supposed to be a formality—until a man bursts into their office, claiming to be the baby's biological father. So Hannah delves into the mystery—and what she finds is an elaborate web of deceit...

Penguin Putnam Inc.
Online

Your Internet gateway to a virtual environment with hundreds of entertaining and enlightening books from Penguin Putnam Inc.

While you're there, get the latest buzz on the best authors and books around—

Tom Clancy, Patricia Cornwell, W.E.B. Griffin, Nora Roberts, William Gibson, Robin Cook, Brian Jacques, Catherine Coulter, Stephen King, Jacquelyn Mitchard, and many more!

Penguin Putnam Online is located at
http://www.penguinputnam.com

PENGUIN PUTNAM NEWS

Every month you'll get an inside look at our upcoming books and new features on our site. This is an ongoing effort to provide you with the most up-to-date information about our books and authors.

Subscribe to Penguin Putnam News at
http://www.penguinputnam.com/ClubPPI